The Death Maze

The Death Maze

By

Richard Parnes

Strategic Book Publishing and Rights Co.

Copyright © 2014 Richard Parnes. All rights reserved.

No part of this book may be reproduced or transmitted in any form or by any means, graphic, electronic, or mechanical, including photocopying, recording, taping, or by any information storage retrieval system, without the permission, in writing, of the publisher.

Strategic Book Publishing and Rights Co.
12620 FM 1960, Suite A4-507
Houston, TX 77065
www.sbpra.com

ISBN: 978-1-62857-511-8

Book I—The Death Maze

Dedication

This book is dedicated to my wife, Mila. Her love, devotion, and belief in my dreams kept me pointed in the right direction.

Prologue

There was a mist hanging in the room. It seemed to be standing, as if planted, without a trace of movement. If one were to try to touch it, it would recoil as if bending. Even though it would never allow this to occur, the mist did not have life.

There were no lights, yet there appeared to be an illumination, a sparkle that also hung without a beginning or an end. The light also seemed to bend in order to avoid any contact with the unknown. It too could recoil and also did not have life.

If this was the castle high above the cliffs, separated from an entire village, then this was the eeriness that attracted no one near its doors. If one were to say that it was the master and it controlled all that it inhabited, this statement would not be correct. It all came and went without a means and without an origin.

A strange, unaccounted wind arrived, blowing the mist toward one wall. It naturally bounced off the wall and then took up its original stance. It was a wind without a window, or some means of ventilation, to cause some change in the air, a mist without a sky to create it, and a sparkle without the serendipity of the origin: a gift.

This was the unknown, where no human had ever been.

Chapter 1

The sun was shining as bright as it could at one in the afternoon when they left Lake Havasu City, Arizona. It would only be a couple hours before Ed and Ruth Putnam would arrive at their new home and new life. They had started out in Miami, Florida, a little less than a week prior and were taking their time to reach their new home. Highway 95 was clear before the transition to I-40. I-40 was very smooth to the California border, with no signs of any hazards along the way. The gas tank was full and they knew they would not have to stop before they arrived in front of the home they had bought as an investment a couple years earlier and would use for their home-based retail business. The small U-Haul was evenly loaded and everything was set. Money was in the bank, the house was ready for them to move in, and their lives were destined for nothing but positive, uplifting changes.

Once they crossed into California and passed the border town of Needles, only twenty to thirty minutes passed before they saw the sign that said ARIONE NEXT RIGHT. Arione was perfectly situated just south of the Mojave National Preserve, with Laughlin, Nevada, to the northeast, Lake Havasu City, Arizona, to the east, and Palm Springs to the south. It had easy access to many places, and though it was out in nowhere-land, their practical and everyday needs could be met close by.

They saw two more signs before they exited the interstate and turned onto the main road leading to town. The first of the two signs was faded, and this made Ruth uncomfortable. She had remembered this sign as being small but vibrant and eye-opening. The second of the two signs was new and just said the name of the town, Arione, which was now only three miles away. The glare from the sun reflected off the windshield, and Ed lowered the visor to assist his vision. It really didn't help, as the brightness of the setting autumn sun stung his eyes even through his sunglasses. The road was a narrow two-lane stretch into Arione's town limits and was in desperate need of widening and new line painting.

In the distance, at the local Gas and Mini Mart, the engine of a huge eighteen-wheel gas tanker started. The driver revved the engine as he prepared to leave the station. He had filled the tanks and his next stop was the town of Vera, only a few miles down the interstate.

Won't take more than an hour, the driver thought. He couldn't wait to get home to his very horny girlfriend, who would do anything he wanted as long as he brought home enough bacon to keep her happy. "Oh, yeah," he called out. "Getting some more tonight!" He thought about calling her and telling her to get dinner ready. However, the radio was turned up high, and Brooks & Dunn's "Boot Scootin' Boogie" got him going as a karaoke-singing machine.

He began to pick up speed as he swerved on the two-lane road, totally ignoring the double yellow line. "Oh, heel toe do-si-do, come on baby let's go, boot scootin'," he blared out. He passed a NO PASSING sign, reached for the half-open can of beer in the console, and took a long drink. He wiped his mouth with his sleeve and put the can back in its rightful place. "Get down, turn around, go to town, boot scootin' boogie!" he bellowed as he looked at his watch one more time and hit the gas pedal, wanting to reach for another gulp.

The glare was still a problem for Ed, as he and Ruth were traveling in a southwest direction toward Arione. Their new home was only a few miles away by rural standards, and time was really of no concern out in the boondocks. They could see part of the interstate and a few cars in the distance but could barely see the road in front of them. *Slow down, Ed*, he thought to himself. *What's the rush?* He looked at his beautiful wife, smiled, and quickly brought his eyes back to the road.

It was too late. One quick look and a smile was all that was needed. The glare slid off the windshield and Ed saw that the large truck was out of control. He couldn't even steer out of the way. The truck's driver didn't even try to turn the wheel. Ruth let out a terrifying scream and grabbed hold of the door handle. "Ed!" she screamed.

Ed didn't even respond. His eyes bulged out of his head as Ruth pulled up on the door handle. Her door opened wide. Ed turned the car to the right to spare Ruth's side of the car from a direct collision. When the two vehicles did collide, the driver's side of the car took the worst of the impact. The door crushed into Ed as he bounced to the side and back toward the seat. His hands still firmly on the steering wheel, he jerked back again as the wheel broke from the dash and lodged into his skull. For Ed, death came quickly.

The truck continued transforming the car into an accordion. The car and U-Haul, now on their sides, quickly balanced on the wide-open passenger door and folded the door into three pieces. Ruth screamed again and hit her head on the dashboard before bouncing back against her seat. The car then rolled again, breaking the ball connection to the U-Haul. The driver of the truck grabbed his wheel and quickly turned to the right. The car rolled again, away from the truck, as the truck jackknifed and began to tip over. After one more roll, the car, with Ruth still in it, rested upside-down next to the U-Haul trailer.

The driver of the truck tried to undo his seat belt and open his door before the truck overturned. He was too slow. The beer had already clouded his brain. Brooks & Dunn were just finishing the song when the gas in the tank of the truck exploded and caught him as he tried to scream for help. Later, when they pulled his charred body out, his mouth was wide open. After the gas tank exploded, fumes from the fire began to burst toward the hundreds of gallons of gasoline spilling into the bed of the truck.

Then the silence of the late afternoon in the desert shattered.

Some residents in the town of Arione thought it was an earthquake. Others thought they'd gone deaf. Windows of a half-dozen homes cracked into pieces, and car alarms sang in unison. Dogs barked and howled because their ears were hurting from the noise. A man who owned a couple horses heard the back fence break and saw the horses run into the desert.

The burst of flames quickly engulfed the truck and billowed into the sky. With a soft wind blowing, the mushroom cloud, now gray and black with a devil's smile, eagerly swallowed the clean afternoon air. The entire northeast section of Arione grew uneasily dark. One resident later said that it jolted and scared him so badly he wet his pants and prayed it was not the end of time. A second swore he saw the desert split open, as if the San Andreas Fault had separated California from Arizona. A third said he thought he saw Satan take a huge bite out of God.

Chapter 2

He was unconscious for several hours. He tried to open his eyes, but they felt very heavy. After waiting a few moments, he tried again. Although his vision was slightly blurred, his eyes opened to narrow slits. He felt like he was being manipulated or commanded to open his eyes in an eloquent and slow fashion. He was the puppet. He was the pawn, and soon the game would begin.

Again, he waited. When the time was right, he would be able to open his eyes all the way. He tried to rise from the floor, but his hands sank into the tilelike material. He tried again, this time bringing his hands closer to his body. It worked. He was off his back and sitting up.

He was able to open his eyes fully. He didn't recognize his whereabouts. He still couldn't see clearly. He felt his vision was blurred and did not yet know that his eyesight was perfect.

The wind, which he hadn't noticed before, came again. Only this time, the mist did not bounce off the wall as it had before. It vanished before his eyes as if it had gone right up to the wall, held firm, and then moved beyond it. He saw the wall suck the mist into its mass.

Where was he? This awkward place was not of the earth he knew. The wind came again and this time he shivered. Soon another draft came and he felt beads of sweat on his brow. What next?

A strange word appeared out of nowhere. It materialized before his eyes, lingered for a few seconds, and then disappeared. It was a word he had never seen before. It consisted of just four letters: A P E P.

"What do you want?" he said in a loud tone.

"I . . . want . . . quiet!" the voice commanded. The room stood deathly quiet. "Later," the voice commanded again.

He turned around, thinking the sound had come from behind him, and was struck by an invisible object that threw him across the room and against the wall. He landed on the floor, sinking into the tile. He was out cold. However, the tiles soon rose, in automatic fashion, and he was level to the floor again. In his subconscious, he heard the word again: "*Later!*"

Chapter 3

It was a long drive from the busy, steaming city of Miami Beach, Florida, to the rural community of Arione, California. The difference in population was like night and day. Miami Beach was the mega metropolis of the southeast. It was a nonstop city of recklessness that had begun to grow up after the 1960s and the Cuban missile crisis. Originally known as the number one travel location for families escaping the brutal winters of the northeast and retirees wanting to spend their last years in the warm US south, Miami was now a hub for multiculturalism thanks to its "wet foot, dry foot" laws. Cubans who had escaped their beloved island by the thousands after Castro took control were welcomed once they stepped onto the dry sands of the Florida coast. The mayor of the city of Miami was bilingual and of Cuban descent. No longer a city that busted wide open in the winter months, it was now a year-round pleasure palace and a film and music mecca with many a sports team. So much could be done in a single day that the residents were calling it the "New York South." Others knew it as the "Salsa Capital of the United States."

Ed and Ruth had grown up in Miami and loved it. They met in high school and stayed in Miami for college. They appreciated its diverse menu of events, which could keep anyone filled with unending life almost twenty-four hours a day. However, it was not the place where they wanted to raise a family or spend the rest of their lives. Even as teenagers, they wanted to experience other places and learn how to slow down. They were always on the go in hustle-and-bustle mode and knew that there must be life beyond Miami's borders. Although many of their friends had recommended moving farther south to one of the Keys, Ed and Ruth wanted to experience the other side of the United States.

Ruth's life was the classic "ugly duckling turned into a swan" story. Shy and shapeless until puberty, she blossomed to possess the attributes every girl her age desired. Her aquiline nose was so perfect that everyone swore she'd had it fixed. Her long, blonde hair flowed and glistened even in the twilight. Her mixed olive and white skin—her father was third generation from Massachusetts and her mother from southern Italy—was soft, smooth, and clear. In fact, she'd never had a single blemish. Her mother was a dietician who kept her from too many sweets and taught her to constantly clean her skin due to the humidity of the Florida weather. Ruth was five-foot-seven and slender, with unbelievably full, firm breasts.

Her father was the typical protective parent who gave in to her wishes to date only because he remembered when he had met Ruth's mother—a story for another time—and because Ruth had the brains to outwit any male moron. She had common sense and was quick-witted enough to put down any crass remark uttered by the boys who ogled her. He also made sure she was a black belt in tae kwon do before he allowed her to date during her junior year in high school. She knew when to listen, understood the art of good speech, and had a photographic memory that would knock anyone off his or her feet. She was trilingual, knowing English, Italian, and Spanish.

Ruth had perfect white teeth from three years of wearing braces and brushed and flossed them daily. She was a true beauty. She captured the heart of just one man, although there could have been as many as she wanted. She was not a tease and never led boys on. She heard what people said about her from her close friends, but never let it get to her. Her life had meaning, spirituality, and a cause that made her reach for what she wanted instead of what others thought she should want. She wanted to be with one man, have a family, do constant volunteer work, and devote herself to a cause that would change the world. What that cause was, she did not yet know. But it was coming and she could feel it in the air. Her destiny was out there and she knew it was only a matter of time until she reached it. Ruth was patient and studious. Even when she met Ed at the end of her junior year in high school, she would not let herself get totally involved. True love would materialize when all the forces were perfectly aligned. By the time he asked her to the senior prom, she knew he was the one.

***

Ed was a middle-class dreamer with a talent for fixing almost anything. When the chain on his first bicycle broke at five years of age, he repaired it effortlessly in twenty minutes. His parents were amazed when he later was able to diagnose and repair a broken vacuum and stove at age seven. Any and all broken items were fixed and repaired in their true form. It seemed there was nothing he could not accomplish. He loved math because numbers came easy to him: All solutions had ones and zeros when broken down to the basics. When his father bought the family's first computer when Ed was only eight, he took it apart and put it back together within a couple days.

His wavy brown hair, though uncombed at times, gave him a boyish quality the girls enjoyed. His smile was genuine and the sparkle in his eye was honest. When he blushed because of a simple compliment, his charm appeared. He was tall, dark, and handsome, but also kind, considerate, and gentle. These were the qualities Ruth truly grew to appreciate and love. Ed was never gruff in his demeanor and could never go out of his way to hurt someone. However, he was firm in his convictions and did become an Eagle in the Boy Scouts. This was something he had wanted to do since he heard about scouting from a commercial on the television.

Although his father had never been a scout, he had enjoyed camping when he was a kid outside Boston and also in Maine. When Ed went to his father wanting to be a Boy Scout, his father took him to the local troop and signed him up. Fifteen years later Ed earned the Eagle Scout rank and joined a special group wanting to be leaders and continuing to serve as mentors for other boys. Scouting brought a desire to achieve and grow to be a better person, and Ed used these skills to become a better athlete and student. He may not have been a straight-A student, but he always tried to be the best he could. He settled for Bs and A minuses.

Ed's dreams were very humble compared to most young men in high school. He didn't want to be the big man on campus or the star of the football team. He was on the swim team and played tennis. He wanted out of the big city, to move to a place where he could afford to own a piece of America. He also wanted to be perceived as an asset in any place he settled. Ed did community service wherever he went and was always the first to volunteer. To be an owner of a business in a place where his services were needed on a daily basis would be enough. To expand this business to the Internet could mean access to the world in any remote place. With the right woman by his side, he could have it all.

***

Ed was six-foot-one: In Ruth's eyes, he was the perfect height for her. He felt great being next to her, and they complemented each other. They didn't need to be the center of attention in school, and so they kept to themselves whenever possible. He was there watching her tae kwon do classes, and she was there when he finished swimming practices or came home from scouting, waiting to hear what he had experienced. They studied together and learned to enjoy each other. He never pressured her for sex and was surprised when she made the first move by giving him his first kiss.

High school became community college and then the University of Miami. Ed studied business and marketing. Ruth received a full scholarship and majored in biology, but changed midway to sociology because of her love of humanity and devotion to others. There were, at times, the normal idiosyncrasies in dealing with other young women and men. However, nothing ever took them away from each other. At the beginning of their senior year in college, Ed proposed to Ruth in front of both sets of parents at the entrance of the Vizcaya Museum gardens. Her father, who had carried a bag thought to contain a picnic lunch, brought out four plastic glasses and a bottle of champagne. With the corkscrew stashed in his lapel pocket, he opened the bottle and they toasted to a long and happy life. One year later, it was in the gardens that they were married. Two years later, they announced that they had bought a home in the desert town of Arione, California.

Although not shocked at the announcement, both sets of parents were amazed that Ed and Ruth had decided this without consulting them. They were both the only child in their family. Both had been brought up to succeed and envision a world in which they could strive to make a difference. How could they change the world in the desert almost three thousand miles from home? Their friends were equally stunned. Why would they leave successful careers in a city they knew how to navigate and move to an area about which they knew very little? What had they been doing for the past two years? What was out in Arione, California? Who was out in Arione, California? And where the hell was Arione, California?

Chapter 4

The first person to reach the accident was Daniel Adams. The reason for this was fairly simple. He lived on the northeast side of Arione away from town not only because he preferred solitude while working, but because he had come to the area to escape the crowds and noise of a megalopolis, in his case New York City.

Upon hearing the crash and smelling the smoke, he rushed from his home, jumped into his Jeep, and sped toward the accident. When he saw the car, the U-Haul, and the tanker truck, he thought that no one could possibly still be alive. Then his eyes darted slightly away from the truck and he saw a woman slowly moving around to the driver's side of the car. Ruth was crying, stumbling, and trying to balance on one leg while holding her broken other leg and opening the door to get Ed out. Her face was bleeding from a broken nose. Her white blouse was bloody and ripped wide open, and a piece of glass stuck out of the lower right side of her stomach. Her jeans were torn on the side of her broken leg. She fell twice before he could reach her, and then fell into an unconscious state.

Dan rushed to her side, checked her pulse, gently picked her up, and laid her in the backseat of his Jeep. He quickly went back to the car to check on Ed, saw that he was dead, and ran to the side of the truck. He could barely make out a charred body and presumed it was dead before running back to the Jeep. Opening the rear door, he pulled out a blanket and wrapped Ruth so she would be warm. He pulled one of the seat belts around her so she wouldn't fall on the floor of the Jeep, making sure not to touch the piece of glass. He drove off toward I-40 to the west and to Vera, the next town. At the entrance to the interstate, he saw a police car driving in his direction, and he stopped and yelled to the deputy. "Hey, Bone! I've got a woman in my Jeep and I'm rushing her to the Vera hospital. Call it in."

Bone simply acknowledged Dan, said a quick "got it," and drove toward the accident. Another smaller explosion was then heard. "Be careful!" Dan yelled, and then got on the freeway for the five-minute drive to Vera. With no bumps and no traffic, Dan made it in three. At the hospital, there was a gurney, one nurse, and Dr. Shirley Anderson waiting to take Ruth.

"I got the call from Bone. Anyone else coming?" Shirley asked as they gingerly removed Ruth from the Jeep and put her on the gurney.

"She was the only one I saw alive, Doc," Dan answered.

"Let's get her into X-rays and prepare OR1, stat," Dr. Anderson said to the nurse as they pushed the gurney into the hospital, leaving Dan behind.

"Shirley!" Dan called out. "Do whatever is needed. I'll be back later." Dan got into his Jeep to drive back to Arione.

Shirley Anderson turned around. She knew there wasn't anything else to worry about. Whoever this woman was, she would not have to worry about anything ever again. Dr. Daniel Adams would see to that.

Chapter 5

Ed and Ruth were both twenty-six when they finally drove away from the noisy city of Miami to the home they had purchased a couple years earlier. When they returned to Miami from their honeymoon, they had hoped to leave the city in six to eight months. There was much to do to get ready for the move, and they had planned and perfected a schedule to save, save, and save more in order to make this change. Both had held secure jobs since graduating with their bachelor's degrees. Ruth finished her master's degree two years later while attending classes in the evening and working full time. Two years after that, they were in awe at the thought of having finally reached their goal.

They'd had enough of the bumper-to-bumper traffic jams during their commute to work each day. It only became worse with each passing year as the population of Miami exploded. The lines at the grocery store would bring out the lion in any lamb, and Ruth felt she was becoming someone she couldn't recognize. It took an hour to shop and at least half that time was spent waiting to check out.

The rude awakenings at six a.m. by the garbage collectors, or "sanitation engineers" as they liked to be called, had become such a nuisance that Ed had changed his work schedule the previous year. Ed would bet an entire year's salary that not one of these workers had obtained an engineering degree, much less a bachelor's degree. They didn't care how much noise they made. They were on a deadline, just like everyone else in the world today, and being late meant meeting the wrath of the boss without overtime pay. Everything was contracted out by the city for the lowest dollar figure. Was the city really saving money? Even the new trucks that were supposed to be quieter and more efficient were loud. What was worse was the fact that there were now three trucks: one for garbage, one for recycled plastics, and one for gardening debris. Nope, they didn't care about those who wanted to sleep until seven a.m. or later and didn't have to be at work until eight or nine in the morning. Their shifts began early and they got off early when the sun was still high in the sky and there was still life left in the day.

This was it! The bags were packed, the bills were paid, and a U-Haul trailer was filled. The forwarding address was left a few days earlier with the post office and the daily paper had been canceled. A Friday evening dinner with their parents and closest friends was their last get-together before what they hoped would be a life change. So long, Miami. It was all mapped out.

They had discovered the town of Arione, California, on their honeymoon. Having taken a couple weeks to relax and discover the southern United States, they drove from Miami north on I-95 to Tallahassee and met up with I-10 before heading west. Once they reached New Orleans, they stayed a couple days because they were fans of jazz music and wanted to see and hear some quality performances. Then they headed northeast to Nashville, Tennessee. Again they spent a couple days because they were both country music fans. They eventually acknowledged that they liked all music before leaving Nashville and taking I-40 west before detouring on Arizona highway 95 north to Las Vegas, Nevada. Again they stayed for a couple days and then went south to Lake Havasu City, Arizona.

In Lake Havasu City they discovered the original London Bridge. It had been, as the song goes, "falling down" in London, and so was brought over to this desert area, reconstructed stone by stone, and dedicated in 1971. It was erected across a narrow boat channel of Thompson Bay on the Arizona side of Lake Havasu.

Ruth and Ed made a special stop to see this attraction. They had never been to Europe and did not know if they would ever get there. This could fulfill an idea of what a special city looked like even though it was in the desert. It turned out to be a romantic day and night. They stayed in a small motel room with a view of the bridge, where they enjoyed a passionate and wild evening of lovemaking with the drapes open. The bridge was beautifully lit, and it felt like they were in another world.

When they left Lake Havasu the next morning, they were supposed to continue on I-40 to California highway 15 before heading to Los Angeles. But after passing Needles, California, and driving for what seemed like only twenty minutes, they saw a sign that said ARIONE, NEXT RIGHT. The next sign caught their eyes. It said, IN THE MIDDLE OF EVERYWHERE AND SURROUNDED BY A PEACEFUL QUIET. VISIT ARIONE AND EXPLORE.

It was as if everything stopped for both of them. Arione was being built north of three large hill areas. It was a town small enough to see the big picture. It was a town only beginning to grow. Though it was founded in the 1940s, vast amounts of land had been kept from development. In the main town of Arione was a central street appropriately called

Main Street. It was a quarter mile long and housed, at the south end, the Arione police station. This was a one-story building with an open area for the public, two offices, men's and ladies' bathrooms, and two holding cells in the back. At the north end of Main Street was the Arione Dune Motel, which had a dozen rooms for rent. Sandra and Buck Palmer, the owners, hoped to one day expand as the town grew; they also owned two acres adjacent to the motel. Between the police station and the motel were various businesses: a restaurant, a country emporium selling items like desert memorabilia and T-shirts printed with the names of local places, a gas station with two bays for automotive repairs, a small branch bank, and a local real estate office with pictures of every corner of Arione for sale or lease. There was a lot of activity, as most of the quarter mile of Main Street was already marked as sold and permitted for businesses. There were six other streets either completed or under construction, and signs advertised the names of the businesses coming to Arione.

In the real estate office was a map showing the town's housing growth. A small tract of land with thirty two-bedroom homes had already been built and sold in the southwest area of Arione. The southeast section had been bought by a developer and would soon see twenty-six three-bedroom homes. Between the southwest and southeast areas were two small eight-unit apartment houses. The northwest area of Arione was vacant. One tract of land on the northeast section was already fully fenced and boasted one large ranch home and a barn. The barn housed two horses. The fence extended fifty acres to the east and one acre to the west. The nearest building to this large parcel was the Arione Dune Motel, a fifteen-minute walk away. The land had been bought when Arione was just starting to blossom in the late 1980s. The owner wanted privacy and had guaranteed to keep the land, with the exception of his home and barn, in its original state. The owner was Daniel Adams.

Chapter 6

He opened his eyes and was able to see clearly this time. His head felt like it was coming off. He remembered being thrown across the room and into the wall as if he had no weight. Whoever or whatever had hit him didn't even have to exert that much energy.

He needed time to think about his whereabouts. He tried to remember how he got to this place. It was all a blur. *Okay,* he thought. *Get yourself up, but move slowly.*

He was able to stand. He moved slowly and meticulously, as if moving quickly would cause him to run into that fist, or whatever it was that hit him. He did not need to be knocked out again. He looked at his watch. It had stopped. The second hand was stuck on the number ten and the time was 9:32 p.m.

Lifting his head to look around, he surveyed the room. It was a large four-wall enclosure. *Wait!* he thought. *The room has five walls.* He saw another wall appear before him. Then the fifth wall disappeared and the room had four walls again. The mist that had disappeared into one of the walls came out again from a different wall. It crossed before his eyes and caused him to shiver. By the time the mist passed him, he was sweating again. Then the mist disappeared.

He looked up but saw only a black emptiness. He heard movement and saw the walls moving. No! They were manifesting into something else. Tiles were growing onto the walls, and one of the walls was changing from pure white to red brick. Then the wall changed quickly into a serpentine gold mesh. It was growing taller. Then the letter A formed in the middle of it.

Once it stopped, he heard something behind him. He turned and saw another wall begin to change. It mimicked the first wall exactly, only this time the letter that formed was a P. Turning to his right, he saw the third wall change and end with the letter E. Turning to his left, the fourth wall ended with the letter P.

APEP, he thought to himself, and then whispered the word aloud.

"Move forward," commanded a voice.

"What?" he heard himself say as he looked around the room.

"I said move forward," the voice commanded more loudly.

He took two steps forward. Then he saw something slither from the wall to his left and move to the wall to his right in a quick, jerking fashion. Whatever it was had a greenish-brown color that seemed to change. Or did it disappear? It looked opaque, not transparent, but then dematerialized. It would have collided with him had he not moved two steps forward.

"Now back," the voice said.

"What?" He moved instinctively backward just as the thing slithered right in front of him. This time it came from the right and moved to the left. Again, the same colors, and then gone.

"What do you want?" he yelled at the object.

"I . . . want . . . quiet," the voice said as the object jutted to his left and then to his right, boxing him into a corner. It was

The Death Maze

like he was being weaved into place. "Later," the voice said. He just stood there, trying to understand what was going on.

Every muscle in his body was tight. Suddenly, his body began to rise. Before he knew it, he was a foot off the floor. He could feel something boxing him in, but couldn't see it. It was invisible. Then he felt blood coming from his nose. It dripped slowly at first. When he felt blood come from his ears, his nose began to pour.

He opened his mouth to say something but couldn't make a sound. Soon blood came from his mouth. He couldn't stop it. He was sure that the voice telling him "later" would never come. This was it!

Then the object snapped! He shut his eyes in a reflex motion. *Like a whip*, he thought. Then it was gone. All of it was gone. He was not boxed in. He was not bleeding. His feet were planted on the floor.

"Later!" the voice said.

Chapter 7

Dr. Daniel Adams was a chemist who did not mince words, did not like crowds, and hated the establishment. He was a nonconformist who had no problems fighting the status quo and made it his business associating with those who did not lose. Thanks to a family fortune built on real estate and development and dating back to the early 1900s in New York, his wealth was valued at over a billion dollars, and so Dan had no qualms taking the course of action he had already mapped out in his mind. Whether it would take months or years, the woman he had brought into Vera Hospital today would be one hell of a rich woman by the time this nightmare was over. He knew that the road into Arione was only two lanes, and so did the oil tanker truck driver. He would not blame the small municipality of Arione; instead, he would go after the oil company.

He drove back to the site of the accident. He needed to see the wreckage again and confer with Deputy Bone and Chief Richard Dressler. When he got to the area of the accident, nothing had been moved. Bone was busy taking pictures of the scene. Chief Dressler was with the coroner's office representative of the city of Vera and two ambulance attendants. They were getting ready to move the body of Ed Putnam. When Chief Dressler saw Dan's car, he excused himself and walked over to him. Dan got out of his car and the two walked away from the accident.

Chief Dressler was a few inches taller than Dan Adams. He also had about thirty more pounds in his gut and more gray in his short, thick hair. The lines on his face suggested that Chief Dressler knew his business yet rarely let any of it out. He had known Dan Adams since the day he moved to Arione.

"I know what you're going to say, Dan," Chief Dressler said in an easy manner.

"Okay, Chief," Dan sighed, knowing what was next. "What am I going to say?"

"You're going to say that the two-lane road leading to Arione should have been widened ten years ago when Arione started to expand." Dan tried to say something but was interrupted. "You're going to say that that yahoo driver should have been fired by the oil company a long time ago after the second time he almost caused an accident a year ago." Dan tried again to say something but was interrupted a second time. "You're going to say that if we had kept Arione from expanding, this would never have happened."

Dan finally was able to respond. "If you know me that well, Chief, then why the hell wasn't any of this prevented?"

Chief Dressler waited for Dan's next statement, since he knew he wasn't done.

"That poor woman," Dan continued, "whoever she is, is now in surgery with no husband—I assume that's who he was—and knows no one. We don't know who she is, where she's from, and what she was doing in Arione!" Dan let out a huge sigh.

"Actually," Chief Dressler responded in an all-knowing manner, "I do know who she is—and who he is. They're Mr. and Mrs. Ed Putnam of Miami, Florida."

Dan looked surprised. "I haven't been back to Miami since I graduated with my PhD twenty-plus years ago."

"I knew they were coming and would be here today," Chief Dressler informed him. "I wanted them to meet you after they settled in. I knew you would be interested, since they were from Miami. They kept in touch with me after they purchased a home here in Arione."

Dan took a few steps away and then returned. "And why did they feel you needed to know their identities and arrival date?"

"Because," Chief Dressler continued, "after they purchased the home and inquired about businesses in Arione, they asked the development company about volunteer work and the best way to become a part of the community. The developer mentioned my name. We've been communicating ever since. They were well-liked and active in their community in Miami, Dan."

"Great!" Dan sighed again. He walked away again. He needed time to think.

Chief Dressler didn't follow him. He had known Dan Adams for almost fifteen years, and they had become good friends. While Chief Dressler was growing in the Vera-Arione Police Department, he made it a point to get to know the richest and most reclusive resident of either town. He knew Dan's mind was twisting and turning. He knew his friend would be contacting his lawyers this evening and that time and money was of no concern. Dan's lawyers lived and worked in Beverly Hills and New York. With the pictures of the accident Bone was taking, the background of the driver, the fact that there was a half-empty beer can in the cab of the truck, and the involvement of the renowned chemist Dan Adams, it was an open-and-shut case. Chief Dressler estimated two years maximum before the case was finally closed.

It actually didn't take that long. After eighteen months of discoveries, depositions, and preliminaries; meetings in offices in Beverly Hills, Miami, Arione, and Houston, where the oil company's United States media offices were situated; constant bantering and bickering over the phone and during video conferences; and one pissed-off judge growing more and more tired of the conglomerate's whimpering, smart-aleck attorneys, the case was settled without going to trial.

Dan was sure the case had been won right when his attorneys contacted the press and notified them of the accident and the particulars. He was especially pleased when the press mentioned why the driver was rushing and that he had been working extra hours to make ends meet. They compared his salary to that of the rise in oil profits; the unexplained shutdown of refineries, which caused additional increases in gas prices while the company's top brass made seven-figure salaries and seven-figure bonuses, was another eye-popping revelation. The public relations director's poor rebuttal and lame interview in front of news cameras did nothing to still a rising hatred of all oil companies and their inept attempts to prove they were going green. It was, frankly, a no-brainer and just reward.

Dan got what he wanted. He wanted justice. He wanted the knot in his stomach to finally disappear. He wanted the retribution to be harsh. He wanted this case to be watched and studied by those in the corporate world and the judicial system. Dan was tired of conglomerates hiring ill-equipped individuals who made a pittance compared to the CEOs and board members. If only they paid a better wage and trained their workers better. If only they made their employees feel like they were getting a fair share instead of constantly cutting corners in order to make the top wage earners richer. *If only*, Dan thought. He let his mind trail off before returning to his thought. *If only there were no if onlys.*

***

Ruth did not receive what she wanted or needed. After spending over a month in the hospital recuperating from two surgeries, one for the removal of the glass in her right side and one for a compound fracture in her right leg, she still did not have her husband and partner. A third surgery became necessary when it was discovered that her appendix had been perforated during the extraction of the glass. Ruth developed a high temperature that night and almost joined Ed, but she pulled through. Dr. Shirley Anderson was just relieved that she had remained on duty and was there to do the emergency surgery.

Ruth was the ICU's only patient that night. After six days, she was finally moved from intensive care and put into a private room. With daily visits from Dan Adams and Chief Dressler, Ruth began to understand why she and Ed had chosen Arione.

Both sets of parents flew out and stayed at the Arione Dune Motel. All costs were taken care of by Dan with no questions asked. Dan had already requested no arguments or reasons. Ed's parents stayed for one week before returning to Miami with Ed's body. They insisted that Ed be buried in the family plot with Ed's grandparents. Ruth promised she would return after the funeral when she was able to travel.

Her parents were with her every day and night for one more week until her father needed to return to Miami.

Her mother stayed an additional two weeks until Ruth requested that she leave to return to her father and let her get on with her new life. She assured her mother that this was still what she wanted. She promised she would return at some point, but could not bring herself to go back to Miami just yet. Ruth reiterated her desire to stay because of Ed. There were reasons she needed to be here. She just had to settle her mind before deciding whether Arione would be permanent.

After her mother left, Ruth became extremely lonely and depressed. Even though Dan still came by on a daily basis, she began having nightmares and flashbacks of the accident. Dr. Anderson knew that a therapist was the next step, and Ruth should have started seeing one sooner. With Ruth's parents spending so much time with her, Ruth had been unable to achieve final closure. She had never had time to seriously deal with the enormity of all that had occurred and what would come next.

After a little more than a month, Ruth was released from the hospital to Dan Adams. At his request, she agreed to see a therapist every day for at least two weeks. After four months of continued grief, frustration, anger, and remorse, she began discovering that life had reason. She began attending church in Vera every Sunday morning. Dan made sure he dropped her off and picked her up so she would always have someone there. She confided to her therapist that she didn't understand why Dan went out of his way for her, but was always glad he was there. Finally getting up the nerve to ask, she persuaded Dan to allow her to assist with his work. It was not only a means of paying him back, which she did not need to do or was ever asked to do, but also a way of allowing her to remain in his home.

The daily sessions eventually became once-a-week talks, and Ruth felt she was finally ready to let it go. It was at this time that the case was resolved and she knew she would not have to endure a long court trial. Dan took her out to dinner in Vera and presented her with a final letter of resolution and a check for twenty million dollars. Ruth didn't even look at the amount on the check, but began reading the resolution.

"All your medical and legal expenses up to this date have been paid in full," Dan explained. "I just want to ask you one thing." He looked into her eyes when she was finished reading.

She took his hand, squeezed it tightly, and then let it go. "I don't know what to say, Dan." She stared back at him and then realized he had wanted to ask a question. "I'm sorry. You wanted to ask me something."

"I just want to know if you would . . ." He paused briefly and then continued. "If you would continue to stay in the house with me. I'm not asking you to marry me or commit to me. But it would really mean so much if . . ."

Ruth interrupted Dan before he could finish. "Of course I'll stay with you." Dan let himself smile ever so slightly. "And it's not because of this check. I hope you don't think that this money will change me."

"I never thought you really cared about money," Dan explained. "I knew this was not all about money for you. Especially since you haven't even looked at the amount on the check."

"Thank you so much," she replied, knowing that these were not the words she really wanted to say.

There was so much going on inside her. He had made her feel like a complete human being again. He had taken care of everything for her without a thought of getting something in return. He never asked for anything, never lost his temper in front of her, and always remained very understanding during all of her moods, healing needs, and conversations. He was very much the gentleman throughout her ordeal.

"No! I need to thank you. I've come to actually understand a great deal more than I ever have in my entire adult life," Dan said.

"I'm not sure I know what you're trying to say," Ruth said softly. "I'm kind of lost."

Dan took a drink of coffee before continuing. He wanted to get the words right. "What I mean to say is that you have added something to my life that I haven't had in such a long time." He paused for an uncomfortably long time before continuing. "Look, I don't want to sound overemotional. But a year and a half ago, I reacted to a horrendous situation that left me angry and frustrated. I wanted to make sure that someone or some entity would pay dearly for the hurt caused. I reacted in my own style of blind rage."

"I never judged you for what you did, Dan," she said.

"Ruth, I'm not asking for an apology. In my own inept way, I'm trying to say thank you for allowing me to feel human again. It's been long overdue. I had been so closed up and dedicated to my work that I wouldn't let anyone get close. I'd been a loner for so long, and my work gave me a reason."

Ruth smiled. "That's not what I hear from Chief Dressler."

"I've known Chief Richard Dressler for a long time now. He's a close friend and actually the only one who really thinks he understands me."

"What about Dr. Shirley Anderson or Deputy Bone? What about the Palmers at the Arione Dune Motel? What about the few hundred other people who live here?"

"They're really just acquaintances, Ruth," he exclaimed. "People look at me and know I'm the man with the large ranch home in Arione. Then they discover I'm rich and reclusive and think I'm a curmudgeon." Dan paused before continuing. "I'm not! I just enjoy my space and feel I have earned what I have. I'm certainly not old and crusty. I hope I don't act that way. And I enjoy going to every town council meeting and putting in my two cents. Actually it's more like two dollars."

Ruth softly smiled. "I believe you are nothing like they say, Dan Adams. If I ever hear anyone calling you a curmudgeon behind your back or to my face, I'll let them know that they need to look it up in the dictionary and see the definition. And old is at least fifty. Right?" Ruth smiled again.

Dan looked at Ruth and she immediately puffed out. "I'm kidding." She stood up. "Let's go the large ranch house owned by the rich man!"

Dan also stood up. As they walked away from the table, Ruth blurted out one last comment. "Doesn't curmudgeondom start at age sixty?"

He looked at her. "You didn't even look at the check," he said.

Near the entrance, she opened her purse and pulled it out. After seeing the figure, she felt like she was going to scream.

"Quick," she said to Dan. "Open the door. I need fresh air."

Chapter 8

A room in the back of Dan's home was designated as his lab. It was the largest room in his home, more than three times the size of his huge master bedroom and twice that of the living room. The house was immense to begin with. At over four thousand square feet, Dan did have the largest home in Arione. It was very spacious, which would allow many people to congregate if needed, as Dan would often think. However, he rarely entertained and always was a loner. In short, he just really wanted a lot of room.

He spent most of his time in his lab. It was so precious to him that he rarely let anyone in. In fact, no one from Arione had ever been in his lab. When Ruth asked to begin assisting him, he was a bit apprehensive. He went over the pros and cons of someone actually being in the same room where he worked. He usually had tunnel vision while working during the day and concentrated to the point where he rarely heard any noises or noticed anyone around him.

***

It had been years since someone wanted to come into the room where he worked. The last time it had occurred was in New York. The young woman's name was Veronica. After over a year of working as his assistant, she finally asked to hear his voice, since she had no idea what it sounded like. She had seen him come and go, but now needed to know if he indeed spoke. Veronica got up from her chair at her work desk and proceeded to the lab door.

Veronica had been hired by a friend of Dr. Adams, who had warned her about his eccentricities. When she arrived in the morning, she would find a list of duties to complete that day. It usually included cleaning up, compiling notes from the previous day's work, managing the incoming and outgoing mail, arranging a schedule for visitors, doing some research, grocery shopping, and making sure she was always on call. The work was done out of his spacious and comfortable co-op on the Upper East Side, and the position was advantageous for any intern's resume.

Dan Adams never gave out his address. No visitors were allowed without an appointment, and no friends were permitted to show up just for the hell of it. Veronica actually enjoyed the work and the compensation she received. She was always paid promptly by the person who had hired her. She was also given a Christmas bonus, a yearly birthday card with a monetary gift—Dr. Adams never wanted to presume what his employee wanted—full health benefits, and three to five weeks of paid vacation. This varied depending upon Dr. Adams's schedule. If Dr. Adams needed to be out of town, he did not want anyone in the office. Since this was not the fault of Veronica, or anyone else employed by him, he felt that they should be paid. All vacations were to be taken at the same time he was out of town and this was nonnegotiable. An employee would need to ask the person doing the hiring for any additional time off. No one ever took extra time, for obvious reasons.

There was one stipulation, though. Whoever accepted the position could not discuss anything about the job or benefits with anyone. This position, Dr. Adams felt, was a unique opportunity. He was a very generous person and did not want anyone taking advantage of that generosity. Recommendations of a replacement, should the employee move on, were never accepted. The hiring individual had full backing of Dr. Adams. This was the reason that only three people had worked with him during the fifteen-year span before he decided to move to Arione.

Veronica came out of her thoughts and took the bold move of knocking on the lab door . . . twice. She felt perspiration on the palms of her hands. *Remember to wipe the doorknob*, she thought.

Dr. Adams answered, and she asked softly, with slight hesitation, "Excuse me, Dr. Adams. I just wanted to know if you had a voice."

"I beg your pardon?" Dr. Adams asked without getting upset.

Veronica almost laughed because she had thought that his voice would not fit his body. Dr. Adams was a handsome man, and she'd had this wild vision that his voice would be high-pitched and whiny. "I'm sorry," she said. "I've been here a little over a year and have never heard you speak."

"Oh?" he asked as his eyebrows stood up.

"Yes, sir!" was all she could think of as a response to his one-word question.

"I'm sorry for the lack of communication, young lady. I–" He hesitated and then continued. "I just assumed that if you were paid on time and were not mistreated, my voice, or lack thereof, would be of no concern. Again, I apologize."

"I hope I haven't caused you to be upset with me," she stated. "I enjoy the job. I hope this doesn't jeopardize my position."

"I'll tell you what," Dr. Adams said matter-of-factly as he looked into her eyes. "I won't say anything to the boss if you won't. Deal?" Dr. Adams held out his hand.

"Deal." She smiled as she shook his hand and watched him close the door. *Wipe the doorknob*, she said to herself.

***

Dan shook his head and brought himself back to reality. He had become comfortable with Ruth helping out. He was more than comfortable. He felt complete.

Dan was currently working on a new chemical reaction that would allow for the release of energy to maximize all forms of mechanized movement for public use. CHEMICAL REACTIONS THAT RELEASE ENERGY ARE ALSO KNOWN AS EXOTHERMIC REACTIONS, said a sign on a wall leading into the lab. This was very basic, and he needed to keep it plain and simple. He figured that if the next generation of energy, such as geothermic energy, biofuels, wind, and solar, could be expanded to produce further movement and greater output of movement without costing additional money, then people would be able to travel for pennies, instead of dollars, a day. His main focus of research was AGE, his acronym for alternative geothermic energy.

Geothermal energy is not new. Populations around the world have long been heating their homes and producing electricity by digging deep wells and pumping the heated underground water or steam to the surface. There are geothermal power plants of three basic types all over the world. The "dry steam plant" uses steam piped directly from a geothermal reservoir to turn the generator turbines. The "flash steam plant" takes high-pressure hot water from deep inside the earth and converts it to steam to drive generator turbines. Finally, the "binary power plant" transfers heat from geothermal hot water to another liquid. The heat causes the second liquid to turn to steam, which is then used to drive a generator turbine.

Dan Adams wanted to devise a way to use geothermal power in vehicles. The advantages of geothermal power were many, with the number one being the release of carbon dioxide at less than 1 percent. The main problem was how to incorporate geothermal power into a vehicle. Dan needed to devise an extra chemical reaction to allow for prolonged use and increased mileage without compromising safety. He was also trying to find the correct means to reuse the steam without allowing it to escape. In other words, he wanted it to be recycled, or reused, many times before being exhausted. Hence, the vehicular emission would be even less than the expected "less than 1 percent." Dan wanted virtually no carbon emissions.

It was for this reason that Dan Adams decided to move out of New York and into the desert. He had found the small town and land he wanted. He also knew that this area was ripe for the research he needed to complete his work.

Chapter 9

Dan had grown up in New York City and had attended the best private schools throughout childhood. Money was no object, and his family name shadowed him wherever he went. He was accepted early to NYU at the age of sixteen, graduated with his master's degree from Harvard at the age of nineteen, and received his PhD at the University of Miami at twenty-two. He was then offered jobs in every major city in the United States.

His parents wanted a politician. Dan wanted a lab, solitude, and peace. He returned to New York only because his parents wanted him to try business before politics. After three months of complete boredom and feeling as if his mind was about to explode, he went into his father's office, apologized for his misgivings, and left. He knew his sister would be perfect to fill the shoes he didn't want. She was about to graduate with a master's degree in business. His father would just have to admit that a female could run his huge corporation.

He did not go home, but crossed the George Washington Bridge in his own recently purchased and remodeled jet-black 1965 Mustang convertible. There was a single bag in the backseat. He picked up I-95 south to I-295, transitioned to NJ highway 30, and then cruised the freeway to Atlantic City.

The Death Maze

He took a room at Caesar's Hotel and Casino, went up to his room with his bag, put out the DO NOT DISTURB card, fell on the bed, and slept. Dan felt he needed it and wanted no conversation for as long as possible. He slept until three a.m., which gave him almost twelve hours of complete solitude. Upon awakening, he looked at his watch and smiled. He was away from his office. He no longer had an office. There were no sounds around him. He was just one relieved and disheveled PhD glad to be away for a while.

Walking into the bathroom, Dan looked into the mirror. He hadn't shaved since the day before he walked into his father's office. He had already known then that he would leave the family business. After taking off his shirt, he washed his face and brushed his teeth. He took his wallet out of his back pocket to check that the one and only credit card he had was nestled in its slot. It was gone, but he was not worried. He put his left hand in the front left pocket and found the card. He also pulled out four one-dollar bills and knew the card would get some use.

Dan was hungry. It was only three in the morning, and he didn't know if there was a restaurant open. He picked up the phone and called room service. After ordering a salad, medium-rare steak, vegetables, and a piece of blueberry pie, Dan turned on the television and proceeded to do something he rarely did. He watched a movie. He didn't care what the movie was. He opened the small, tactfully disguised refrigerator between the closet and dresser and took out a cold bottle of water. Inside of twenty minutes, he heard a knock at the door. He opened the door, tipped the guy the four singles from his pocket, and took the food. Once finished, Dan put the tray on a table and went back to sleep.

He awoke at eight a.m. Feeling much better, he showered, shaved, got dressed, and went down to try his luck at blackjack.

He had played cards only twice while at Harvard, where he learned poker from some buddies. After taking most of their money in about an hour, he was asked only once more to join in a game of blackjack, or 21, before being banned from the weekly game. Dan had a streak of luck that seemed to never end. The only thing he wasn't good at was maintaining relationships.

Dan entered the casino. It was only nine a.m. and in the middle of the week. Plenty of tables had only a few gamblers at each. He walked up to the cashier and dropped his credit card, asking for a hundred dollars. The cashier told him there was an ATM down the hallway.

"I don't like ATMs. Is it okay to get cash here?"

"No problem," the woman said, taking his card. Quickly accessing his card, she asked for ID and immediately gave him five twenty-dollar bills.

"Thank you," Dan said. He left the cashier after putting the cash and his credit card back in his front left pocket.

He walked around the casino once before sitting down. The large casino room was beautiful and decorated with scantily clad women dressed in Roman costumes serving drinks to those playing the games of chance. There were other men and women dressed in three-piece suits watching from the center area called "the pit." Dealers, also dressed in conservative clothing, called out chip colors and denominations of money exchanging hands. It was very exciting to those who enjoyed gambling. However, Dan felt bored. He figured he'd only be gambling for a few minutes.

The Death Maze

He found a blackjack table with only two people and sat down. A thin, middle-aged woman dressed in slacks and a tank top sat in the first position of seven chairs. On the opposite side in position number seven was a heavyset man shuffling two of his chips in his right hand.

"Morning," Dan said to the dealer as he sat down right in the middle and dropped all five bills in the betting circle in front of him.

"One hundred in," the dealer called out, handing Dan his chips: ten five-dollar red chips and two twenty-five-dollar green chips.

Dan took his chips and placed all of them in one column of the betting circle. The woman in position one quickly looked at Dan and turned back. She had one green chip in her betting circle and a stack of ten red chips and a stack of ten green chips next to the polished wooden edge of the gambling table. Dan quickly calculated that she had three hundred dollars in chips, not counting the one she was betting. The man on his left was betting only one hundred dollars in black chips and had two of them in his betting circle. Still playing with two chips in his right hand, he didn't even bother to look at Dan.

The dealer began distributing the cards, giving each player two faceup cards and giving herself one card faceup and one facedown. The dealer had a small mirror next to her position in order to see if she had a blackjack: an ace with either a picture card or a ten.

Dan's two cards showed a natural blackjack: an ace of spades and a king of hearts. The dealer gave him one and a half times his bet, and he now had $250 in the betting circle.

"Congratulations, sir," the dealer said.

"Thanks," Dan replied without smiling.

The woman looked at her two cards again, knowing that the dealer, who had a three of hearts as her up card, did not have blackjack. With an eight of spades and a three of clubs, the woman dropped a green chip next to her original bet. This was called doubling down, as she was hoping for a ten or picture card to give her twenty-one. The dealer dealt a card, turned down, to the woman. She looked at it and smiled, feeling good about the possibility of winning fifty dollars.

The man to Dan's left was next. He had a seven of hearts and a six of diamonds. He motioned right to left, indicating that he did not want another card. He was betting that the dealer's down card was a ten or a picture card for a total of thirteen. The dealer had to "hit" or take a card if her total was less than seventeen. He was hoping that with many more tens and picture cards than any other cards in the seven-deck shoe the dealer was using, she would deal herself a card with a ten value and go over twenty-one.

The dealer then flipped over her down card. It revealed a jack of hearts. Her total was thirteen, just as the man was hoping. Then the dealer had to draw a card for herself. She reached for the card shoe and drew an eight of spades. The dealer had twenty-one. The woman and the man lost.

"Damn!" the man exclaimed under his breath.

"Oh, crap," the woman said as the dealer picked up the cards from the table and took away their bets.

It was time to bet again. Dan placed the $250, now in two black chips and two green chips, in one stack. The woman put down another green twenty-five-dollar chip in her betting circle. The man again placed two black one-hundred-dollar chips in front of him. The dealer then reached for the shoe.

At the end of the second round, Dan had doubled his money to five hundred dollars and now had five black one-hundred-dollar chips. The woman had won her hand and the man had lost his. It was again time to place bets, and Dan again decided to bet everything he had. The woman looked at Dan.

"You must feel pretty lucky," she said while putting two green chips in her betting circle.

"I feel well rested and pretty good, thank you," Dan said as he turned and saw the man to his left put down four black chips.

The dealer then began pulling cards from the shoe. The woman's first card was a four of diamonds. Dan's first card was a queen of clubs. The man was dealt a seven of clubs. The dealer dealt her first card down. The second cards were exciting for all three bettors. The woman was dealt a seven of spades and now had two cards totaling eleven. Dan was dealt a queen of spades. The man was given a four of diamonds and also showed a total of eleven. The dealer's second card was a six of spades.

"Double down," the woman said as she dropped two green chips next to her bet. The dealer pulled a card from the shoe and dealt it facedown to the woman.

Dan was once told it was not smart to split a pair of tens or picture cards, which was an option if two of the same cards were dealt. A total of twenty was a good hand and could only be beaten by a natural twenty-one or the dealer dealing herself or himself twenty-one in a series of cards. A bettor could also beat himself or herself by splitting the cards and then having two hands totaling less than the original two cards. Dan stood "pat" and waved his hand, signaling that no cards were needed. The man doubled down and was given one card from the shoe. His bet for the hand was four black chips, and he put down another four black chips for a total of eight hundred dollars.

The dealer then turned over her down card and showed an ace of diamonds for a total of seven or seventeen. Depending on the hand, an ace could have a value of one or eleven. The dealer decided she would use the ace as a value of one. This way she could try to deal herself additional cards to reach twenty-one. She took one card from the shoe and dealt herself a jack of diamonds. In blackjack, the dealer must stand "pat" with seventeen.

"Yes!" the woman cried out. She had a total of nineteen. She was given one hundred dollars in four green chips.

"Congratulations," the dealer said as she looked at Dan's hand. "Five hundred out." She gave Dan five black chips as a man in a three-piece suit behind her acknowledged Dan with a nod. Dan now had one thousand dollars in front of him.

"Feels good, doesn't it?" the woman asked Dan.

"Yes, it does," Dan replied, not really feeling anything but trying to be polite.

"Eight hundred out," the dealer barked. The man in the three-piece suit behind her watched as she delivered one purple five-hundred-dollar chip and three black chips to his betting spot. There was now sixteen hundred dollars in front of the man. "Congratulations," the dealer said to him as he reached into his pocket and tossed a green chip to her as a tip. "Thank you, sir," the dealer said, tapping it on the table to let the casino know she had been given a tip.

The next round of bets was crucial for the dealer; with all three bettors at her table doing very well, she was being watched very carefully. No casino liked seeing everyone win and win big, even though big meant a lot more than what was being won at this table. However, it was only a morning shift and too early to see everyone doing well. The pit boss,

The Death Maze

the man in the three-piece suit, was now watching closely from the end of the table. He needed to make sure no one was cheating, not even the dealer, but also needed to appear cordial to the betting customers.

Dan placed all his chips in one stack and slid them into his betting circle. The woman put down two green chips, and the man to Dan's left put down four black chips. He had already placed the one purple chip in his pants pocket.

"Good luck," the dealer said as she reached for the card shoe. The woman was dealt a two of spades. Dan was dealt an ace of diamonds. The man was dealt a five of hearts. The dealer dealt her first card down. The second card quickly followed. The woman was dealt a four of diamonds for a total of six. Dan was dealt a ten of hearts for a natural blackjack. The man was dealt a six of clubs and now had a total of eleven. The dealer dealt herself a jack of hearts.

The dealer quickly checked her down card in the little mirror. She looked at Dan's hand and reached for three purple chips. She did not have blackjack. Dan had won fifteen hundred, for a total of twenty-five hundred dollars.

"Fifteen hundred out," the dealer said to the pit boss to her right. He only nodded as she continued to play the rest of the hand. "Congratulations, sir," the dealer said.

Dan watched the pit boss, whose face remained expressionless.

The woman motioned for another card, and then another. After looking at the second card, she stood pat.

The man put four additional black chips next to his original bet and was dealt one card down, doubling down on his eleven. He looked at the card and stood pat.

The dealer then turned her first card over and showed a queen of spades. She had a total of twenty. Both the woman

45

and man had nineteen. The pit boss showed a sliver of a grin.

"Damn," the woman said as the dealer pulled away her cards and fifty-dollar bet.

"Shit," the man said under his breath, as he had just lost eight hundred dollars. He stood up. "Thanks!" he said sarcastically as he turned and left the table while the dealer took away his cards and bet.

"Just you and me now," the woman to Dan's right said. "I'm Maggie," she said proudly.

He looked at her and she actually winked at him. Dan just smiled, placed his twenty-five hundred in his betting circle, and nodded to Maggie. "Just you and me," Dan echoed. He really didn't care, as his boredom was growing.

The dealer looked at the pit boss, who returned the look as if to say, "Keep dealing." Dan's bet was nowhere near the maximum allowed. She just kept going through the motions. Everyone knew that the cameras in the ceiling above them were recording every move.

Maggie placed one green chip in the betting circle, and the dealer began delivering the hand. She dealt Maggie a ten of hearts. Dan was given a three of diamonds. The dealer's card was dealt down. Maggie's second card was an ace of diamonds for blackjack, and she screamed for joy. Dan's second card was an eight of clubs for a total of eleven. The dealer dealt herself a six of clubs.

"Congratulations," the dealer said to Maggie, giving her one green chip, one red chip, two white one-dollar chips, and one fifty-cent coin for a total of $37.50 in winnings. She took away Maggie's cards and turned to Dan. "What would you like to do, sir?" she asked.

The Death Maze

Dan reached into his pocket and pulled out his credit card. "Access this, please," he said to the dealer.

The dealer reached for the card and gave it to the pit boss. He immediately took the card and went to his desk a few feet behind the dealer. He picked up his phone and waited. A minute later, he gave the card back to Dan and gave him a voucher to sign. Dan signed it, and the pit boss then deposited the voucher in the money slot to the right of the dealer, who placed five purple chips next to Dan's bet. His total bet was five thousand dollars.

Dan looked very calm. Maggie seemed nervous for him, her eyes wide open. The dealer just looked at Dan and dealt him one card down. "Good luck," she said. Dan didn't even look at the card just dealt to him.

The dealer then turned over her down card to reveal a seven of diamonds. She now had a total of thirteen. Reaching for the card shoe, she dealt herself a two of hearts. Then she dealt a second card showing an ace of diamonds. Her total was now sixteen. The dealer needed to continue, as the rules required her to stand pat on seventeen but continue with sixteen. She reached for the card shoe and pulled out a four of spades. Her total was twenty. The pit boss was pleased. So were the eyes of the cameras above.

"Oh my God," Maggie blurted out as she stared at the cards in front of the dealer. She looked back at Dan. "How come you didn't even look at your card?"

Dan looked at Maggie. "I'll let the dealer do that," he said nonchalantly.

The dealer reached for the card and turned it over, revealing a jack of spades. Dan had twenty-one. He had just won five thousand dollars.

"Oh yes!" Maggie screamed as she jumped from the table, turned around, and yelled again. "Yes!"

"Congratulations," the dealer said to Dan. She proceeded to dole out five thousand in chips. "Five thousand out," she barked, knowing the pit boss was right next to her.

The pit boss just acknowledged Dan. "Congratulations, sir," he said as he watched the dealer give the chips to Dan. "Are you staying with us at Caesar's, Mr. Adams?" he asked.

"I am," Dan replied as he stood up. "Cash me out, please," he said to the dealer. He would be walking away with ten thousand dollars on an original bet of one hundred.

"You can't stop now, sweetie," Maggie said to him. "You're on a roll."

"It's always good to know when to walk away, Maggie," Dan said as he turned to the dealer and tossed a purple five-hundred-dollar chip in her direction. "Thank you," he said to the dealer. "Have a good day." Dan picked up his $9,500 in remaining chips.

"Thank you, sir," the dealer replied enthusiastically. She banged the chip on the table and put it with her other tips. It was the first time she had ever received a five-hundred-dollar tip.

Dan walked over to the cashier and placed the chips on the counter.

"How would you like this, sir?" the cashier asked.

"Do you have any large envelopes?" Dan inquired.

"Yes, we do," she answered.

"I would like a total of three envelopes. Each is to contain three thousand dollars in one-hundred-dollar bills. The remainder is five hundred dollars. I would like that in four-hundred-dollar bills, four twenty-dollar bills, and two ten-dollar bills," Dan said matter-of-factly.

"Yes, sir," the cashier replied, preparing to give him the envelopes and five hundred dollars.

Dan took the envelopes and sealed each one. "May I have a pen, please?" he asked.

She handed him a pen, and Dan wrote something on each one. He handed the pen back to the cashier and thanked her. He then took the envelopes in his left hand and proceeded to walk out of the casino and toward the elevator. He had only gambled for about twenty minutes.

Entering the elevator, Dan pushed the button for his floor. He had decided to check out of the hotel and go back to New York. He had already planned to convert his co-op on the Upper East Side into a home and laboratory, and had mapped out his plan before leaving his father's office the previous evening. Five minutes later, he was in the lobby again. He settled his bill and walked up to the concierge.

"May I help you, sir?" she asked. Her nametag said she was Melissa from New York.

"I would like you to deliver these envelopes for me, please," Dan stated.

"No problem, sir," Melissa answered. "I get off at four."

Dan gave her the three envelopes and a one-hunred-dollar tip. "Please deliver these today and call me when you're done." Dan handed her a card. "Call me at the cell phone number on my card."

"Yes, sir, and thank you very much," Melissa replied. Dan walked away.

Melissa looked at the envelopes. The first was addressed to the Salvation Army, the second to the Atlantic City Covenant House, and the third to the Atlantic City Youth Advocate Program.

Melissa looked up to see where Dan had gone. He was already out the door and waiting for the valet to bring his car.

Chapter 10

Ruth had been with Dan for almost five years. In that time she had worked with him and learned what she thought was everything she could about this intelligent and reclusive man. There was just one thing missing. She knew what it was and decided that after her late afternoon walk around the grounds, which Dan had let her design, she would walk into the house, prepare a wonderful dinner for two, and discuss the possibility of being more than just a close friend.

Dan, as always, was working. AGE was his baby and he had written extensively on it. New technologies were always coming to fruition, and he often heard about others who were working on their version of a new type of fuel economy. He had been on this for a long time but knew his breakthrough would come soon.

He had built his own small version of a binary power plant on his property and was utilizing it for testing purposes. That had been his prime reason for picking Arione and the desert. He had done some research before driving out west and knew that the Mojave Desert was well known for geothermal activity.

***

What was not well known was an obscure article written in the early 1900s by a reporter for the small-town *Needles*

News. His name was Ben Stanton. The article was about a prospector named Stanley Moser. It told a story about a place in California not far from the main town of Needles. At that time, people were coming out and prospecting for silver between Barstow, California, and Nevada. Since Needles was east of Barstow, Stanley thought that maybe if he stayed east of Bartow but west of Needles, he would find his own mine, the place his dreams kept referring to, and strike it rich. There were too many looking around Barstow. He just had that feeling. He didn't know why, he just did. Usually his feelings were pretty correct. The dreams gave him further indication that he was looking for three hills.

Originally from Chicago and born around 1875, Stanley was a dreamer who loved the stories about cowboys and Indians, prospecting, and the "Wild West." The reason Stanton said Stanley's birth was "around 1875" was that Stanley could not recall the exact date of his birthday. When Stanley was a young boy, he had a small accident—he slipped and fell on his head. He was laid up for at least two weeks before he was allowed to get back to normal activities and chores. He developed a small lump on the top of his head during his two-week rest, but his hair covered it up.

Every night before he would go to sleep, Stanley would look at the sky and wish on the brightest star. Just before he closed his eyes, he would swear he heard a small, gentle voice tell him that he was a beautiful young boy and to follow his dreams. When his eyes did close, he dreamed of the open land, the three hills, and the glimmer of silver in the land a little more than a half mile in front of the hills. Just before he awoke, a gust of heat would rise from the ground. He didn't know what it meant. He just knew he had to get there.

He would then, unconsciously and gently, touch the lump and awaken.

Ben Stanton knew that Stanley found what he was looking for. What he didn't know was where Stanley had gone. He had informed Stanley that he would contact him as soon as the article was completed and in print. He found the wooden hut and canopy extension that extended from one of the three hills and that Stanley had built and used as his shelter. He found the opening in the hill that Stanley had made but hadn't dug deep into. He found the path that led about a half mile northeast of the hill to a flat area, with markers and a makeshift wooden cover where Stanley had dug a hole deep into the earth. He found the ladder that Stanley had used to climb down the hole. When he called out into the hole, he heard only his echo. It was too dangerous to climb down the ladder without a lamp.

Walking around the perimeter of the hole, making sure he didn't fall in, Ben saw a bush about twenty feet away. He walked over to the bush and saw a brown shoelace tied to it. He tried to grab the shoelace away from the bush, but couldn't. Then he noticed a black arrow drawn on the shoelace. The arrow was pointing down. Ben lifted a branch from the bush. Under the bush was another piece of a shoelace buried into the ground.

Ben knelt down and pulled at the shoelace. At first it was difficult because the ground was dry. With a little effort, the dirt began to pull away. At the other end of the shoelace was another shoelace. The two had been tied together. Ben pulled harder and then started digging with his hands in the dirt. After pulling out five handfuls of dirt, Ben saw a metal box.

He stood up and looked around. Then he called out for Stanley. He knew he wouldn't hear anything. Taking off his

The Death Maze

coat, he knelt down again and proceeded to dig until he was able to release the box from the dirt. It was heavier than it looked. It was a simple metal box about eight inches wide, six inches long, and four inches deep, with a handle on the top. There was a small latch on the front side. Ben lifted the latch.

What he saw inside amazed him. The box was filled with silver nuggets. They looked to have been cleaned and placed neatly into the box. They were beautiful to look at. But where was Stanley?

Ben closed the box and put it back into the dirt. He piled up the dirt as he had found it and even threw some sun-bleached dirt over the fresh brown to camouflage it. He stepped back from the bush; it appeared he had succeeded. He walked back to the hole and called out again, but there was no response.

Ben Stanton picked up his coat and took out his small notepad. He began writing down everything he had seen. He also, purposely, neglected to include finding the metal box. He knew that others at the office read his notes. By the time he got to his office, he would have already rewritten the notes so as to keep others from prying around Stanley's location. He would write a human-interest follow-up story and hope Stanley would show up.

Stanley never did.

***

By drilling into the ground to the geothermal zone, Dan was able to attach a pump to bring up hot water. He knew the hot water would be between 100–300 degrees Fahrenheit. The hot water then passed through a heat exchanger in conjunction with a second fluid. The second fluid, usually a hydrocarbon, would have a lower boiling point. The rising second fluid then vaporized, turning a turbine and driving the generator. It was then recycled through a condenser and sent back to the heat exchanger. It then returned to the reservoir, geothermal zone, or origin, emitting air and vapor water.

Dan was able to miniaturize the entire system into a prototype to allow for forward motion. He also built miniature vehicles equipped with three small turbines and one generator. Once pushed through the generator the first time, the fluid was recycled into the second turbine then the third turbine and back to the generator. This emitted heat energy through the generator. He just needed to make the energy release in a way that would push the vehicle forward and allow for longer life.

He installed a battery system for all the working parts like any vehicle. He added front and rear lights and an interior light. That was the easy part.

What he didn't have was the final molecular piece to allow the heat energy to be stored for a longer life. He tried mixing and matching different chemicals with the heat to produce a small reaction that could be contained within a separate system and increase the longevity of a tank from the source. That would then be funneled through the final turbine again to increase velocity and distance. This piece also needed to be easily refilled and cost-effective.

Dan felt he was close. Maybe he was too close at this point. He wanted to take a break. However, he knew it was a good time to keep working because Ruth had left to take her walk, which she took at the same time every afternoon. This was the perfect time to try some special experiments to increase the energy from the binary plant into the miniaturized

The Death Maze

vehicles. It was perfect in case something went wrong. He quickly double-checked his notes and then went out the back door of the lab to check on the main components of his binary plant.

Dan walked around the area where he had built the plant. Everything was under a tall enclosure and fenced in. A person would actually be able to see the plant if he or she walked up to the six-foot fence and looked over it. A binary plant was nothing new. He just wanted the privacy. He quickly checked all the parts to make sure nothing was leaking and everything was fitted properly. He did this because he knew it would calm his mind and let him think.

He checked the turbine. He checked the generator. He checked the condenser. He walked a few feet and checked the pump. Everything was in place. His mind was not calm. He kept walking in a circular fashion until he was ten yards behind his home. He picked up a small rock and tossed it. He heard it land, but not on dirt. It sounded as if it landed on wood. Dan walked to where he had tossed the rock and found not dirt, but a wooden cover. There was a small film of dirt over the cover. *Probably from the years being out in the desert*, he thought.

He tried to raise the cover but couldn't, and let it fall down into its place. He tried once more, but for some reason he couldn't lift it. He let it drop again and then felt the ground move. The shaking beneath his feet grew in intensity, and he tried to keep from falling. He tried to catch his balance but soon realized he would hit the ground. He saw a series of rocks fly upward and toward the front of the house. He put his hands out to try to avoid a hard impact.

He never felt the ground. He only saw the light. Then it closed around him.

Chapter 11

Ruth felt it also. However, she felt it inside of her. The shaking of the ground only occurred in the back of the house.

She was in the garden watching the sun go down. She was thinking how wonderful it would be to speak to Dan about wanting more. She was ready for a deep relationship and felt extremely amorous. She hadn't had this feeling since Ed. She knew she was ready and wanted to feel passion again. She wanted to feel a man on top of her and then inside of her.

She decided to walk into the house to start a beautiful dinner and speak to Dan. The sun was almost on the horizon. It would be a wonderful evening. What was even more important, she would be the initiator.

Then she felt dizzy. She felt nausea hit her stomach. She felt a rise in her throat. She felt a burning sensation. She felt her back quickly arch, which threw her head back and then forward. She let out a dry heave that immediately threw her back again before another dry heave. What stopped her in dead motion was the bright light.

She thought it was coming from the house. No. It was coming from the lab. No! It was coming from the back of the lab. She didn't know where it was coming from. The dizziness immediately left and she was able to right herself quickly. She was able to walk, and she picked up speed.

Then she felt the impact of the first rock. It hit her right on top of her head, and she immediately went down on her knees. Her body moved forward and then backward. The second rock connected between her eyes. She felt blood quickly ooze from the bridge of her nose before she fell backward.

A third rock missed her as her legs buckled forward and her head hit the grass. Before she lost consciousness, she saw the bright light spread upward. She'd swear that she then saw Dan's image rise above the house and disappear.

Chapter 12

Dan remembered hearing the word "later." Later for what? Later meaning the voice would get back to him? Later meaning he would die . . . later?

He really wanted to know where he was and whom he was dealing with. He tried to assess what he had so far encountered. There had been four walls, then five, then four again. Whatever or whoever or wherever he was could materialize things at will. It seemed to have total control of his whereabouts and could toss him around like a rubber ball. It could make him bleed.

Wait, Dan thought, *it had a name.* He remembered seeing the letters APEP. He remembered whispering them.

Dear God, he thought again, *how I wish I had my laptop.*

"God will not help you," a voice said.

"You can read my mind?" Dan asked.

"I can do everything," the voice explained. "And anything."

"How about informing me of where I am?" Dan asked. "Better yet, where are my shoes?" Dan looked down at his cold feet. This obviously would have some repercussion later on.

Dan waited. There was just silence. "What's the matter?"

He waited again. However, this time Dan decided to walk around the room. He wanted to try to understand where he

The Death Maze

was. He tried to touch the wall, but it just recoiled. When Dan pulled his hand back, the wall moved back into place. He tried again and received the same results.

Moving away from the wall, Dan walked 180 degrees to the other wall. As he approached, the wall changed from white to black, as if tiles were turning over. Then it changed once again to red. The final change Dan witnessed was the wall becoming white again, but with four tiles revealing red, shiny letters that read APEP.

"Apep," Dan called out. "You must like seeing your name." He moved backward. "You would have made a great graffiti vandal."

"Your sense of humor is lacking, Dan Adams," Apep announced.

"How do you know my name?" Dan asked.

"I told you before, Dan Adams," Apep reminded him. "I can do anything and I know everything."

"You must be God," Dan said sarcastically.

"I could have been," Apep informed him. "However, God was too forgiving."

"Too forgiving?" Dan repeated.

"You will see, Dan Adams. I enjoy too many other vices to be forgiving."

"I'm not sure I understand what you're trying to say to me," Dan said as he tried not to recoil from Apep's words.

"You do not need to understand. You will experience, and I will savor," Apep responded slowly. "I will let you start right now."

A large square object appeared from the blackness above. As it descended to Dan's level, it materialized into a screen.

Dan looked above the screen for wires or some lowering harness. Nothing was holding the screen up. Dan tried to walk around the screen, but it moved with him, mirroring his movements.

"I know you are a visual entity," Apep said. "You are from a world that seems to need its three-dimensional qualities. If you cannot feel it, see it, hear it, smell it, or touch it, then it becomes questionable. If one of your senses is lost, the other four take over for it. However, you still need these senses to regulate your three-dimensional objectives. Without any of these senses, could you exist? I think not," Apep explained.

"So what you are telling me, Apep, is that I'm human," Dan shot back. "I already contemplate and understand my world. Why haven't you explained to me where I am? Are you thinking my mind is not capable of understanding this?"

"You, Dan Adams," Apep replied, "would probably understand. I can read the electrical stimuli going through your brain and see that you are highly educated. So I will now explain where you are."

"I thank you," Dan responded in his sarcastic voice once again.

"You are in the sixth dimension," Apep explained. "You have traveled through a portal and disrupted this aura of life."

The voice stopped as Dan tried to understand. He had thought that there might be a sixth dimension. He had thought of the possibility of multiple dimensions. Three-dimensional space was normal. It represented everything on the earth plane. Man lived in a three-dimensional world consisting of height, width, and depth. The fourth dimension was designated as space in a three-dimensional world. In relativistic theories, time was the fourth dimension. The

The Death Maze

fifth dimension could be explained, in our language, as our system of objects, both animate and inanimate.

What was Apep defining as the sixth dimension? So far Dan had only heard the voice. He had not seen the person calling himself Apep. He had felt things within the room. He had seen objects as they were brought into the room. He could even react to fluctuations in temperature. He felt the cold. He perspired from the heat. He felt a slight fear as that thing slithered around him.

"Apep," Dan called out. "What are you saying?"

"I am saying that you have disrupted my dimension. You have contaminated it, and I want you destroyed," Apep stated in a matter-of-fact voice.

"There must be some reason you kept me alive this long," Dan retorted. "Otherwise you would have killed me from the beginning."

"As I said from the start, you will experience and I will savor. I will enjoy seeing you, Dan Adams, reach your end."

"What's the screen for?" Dan asked again.

"For you to see the beginning..." Apep paused briefly, "...of you end."

The screen began to change. Like a child playing with the remote control of a television, Dan heard clicking all around him. Different objects appeared on the screen. After a short while, the screen began to build a finite picture. There were two dots on the picture, one green and one blue. Dan soon realized he was looking at a puzzle.

"This is not a puzzle, Dan Adams," Apep informed him. "This is your death maze. Do not try to follow a path because this maze will change as you try to trace any course. The green dot is where you will begin." Apep began to laugh. He continued until it became painful for Dan to listen to it.

Dan had no idea why Apep was laughing. He didn't even think the statement was funny. It was, however, the first time that Apep did something besides talk.

"I'm laughing because you are standing on the green dot, Dan Adams," Apep said. Dan looked down and saw a fresh green dot under his feet. "The blue dot is your finish point. But I'm sure you will not reach it!" Apep continued. "In between are many choices you will have to make in order to save your life and return to your dimension. If you make five mistakes, Dan Adams, your life will end."

"When will I know that I've completed the maze?" Dan asked, afraid the maze would never end.

"When you see the blue dot," Apep replied. "There shall be no more questions because there are no more to ask. The obvious thing for you to do is to begin. Good-bye, Dan Adams."

The silence grew deafening. It was the kind of silence that could drive out the weaknesses of even the strongest of men. But Dan didn't need to be strong. He needed to be smart.

Apep was correct in that Dan was unable to follow any of the paths on the screen. Each time he tried to follow a path, the screen gradually changed. He just knew that he was at the beginning and the end was far off . . . if there was an end.

He was the pawn in some maniacal, twisted world called the sixth dimension. He did not know how he had disrupted, or even if he did disrupt, this world. All he wanted to do was return to his lab, his work, and the special woman he now had in his life.

"Oh, Dan," he thought. "What the hell have you gotten yourself into?"

His body jerked. It may have been slight, but he felt the quick movement. It was kind of like a shiver, but different. It was like a twinge that gnawed the back of his right shoulder

The Death Maze

blade. It happened again. His left hand reached over to the right shoulder and found the quick, jerky muscle spasm. It happened a third time. Dan knew this was not good.

The last time he experienced these spasms was in his office at his father's company. He knew he shouldn't have been there. However, he fought the spasms and stayed for a few months before realizing he wasn't right for the position. Once he left the office, the spasms stopped. It was his body's way of telling him that the uncomfortable could be altered by changing the situation. He did not know how to change his situation this time.

He began dissecting Apep's words. What did Apep mean by five mistakes? How would he know when a single mistake was made? What would he have to do to either decide correctly or make a mistake? What if he never made a mistake? How many decisions would he have to make before he completed the maze?

He stared at the screen, trying to take in an overall view of the maze. It appeared massive. It was obvious that he was being dealt with on a three-dimensional basis. Even though the place he was in had weird walls that bent, a screen that appeared without any means of suspension, and a green dot that materialized beneath his feet, it was all part of this world's reason to focus on his reality. He wouldn't be moving without the means of a floor. He needed to move by walking.

Now all he needed to do was figure out where to go from the green dot. He looked down again at the dot and saw a small red arrow appear. He was facing in the opposite direction of where the arrow was pointing. But how could he know if it was pointing in the right direction?

Dan looked at the screen again to see if the red arrow was part of the maze, but the screen was moving upward and disappearing at the same time. Within a few seconds, the screen was gone. The ceiling was still a black hole for all he knew. It looked like space.

Dan then turned around to obey the red arrow. He saw a door that had not been there a few moments ago. Then the words START HERE appeared on the door. Dan felt the spasm in his shoulder jerk him from his haze, and he slowly moved toward the door.

This is it, he thought. *This is the beginning of either the end or the start of my new life.*

He had never run away from a challenge and wasn't about to start now. He might even get lucky and beat Apep at his own game.

Before taking that one last, crucial step and reaching for the door, Dan turned around to look to see if maybe, just maybe, there was another way out. His eyes searched every inch of the room. The walls were blinding white and the ceiling was dark and unending. Knowing that he would not find anything, he reached for the door, but before he could touch the knob, the door began to open by itself. He took three slow, purposeful steps and stepped through. Then the door disappeared.

What was lying in front of him would cause many nightmares. He would recall many memories that he would wish had stayed in the deep recesses of his mind. His flaws would be brought forth. Before him was the death maze. He was going to make sure that his decisions, whatever they were, would result from careful, meticulous thinking.

Whatever he had done to this world or dimension, it certainly hadn't been voluntary or deliberate. If he did not complete the maze, he would request—no, demand—to know why he was to die. His death was not going to go unanswered in his three-dimensional mind.

Chapter 13

Ruth awoke in a daze. A bit of sunlight was sparkling through the window shade. Her head was bandaged from top to bottom. She felt a large piece of adhesive across the bridge of her nose. She was breathing on her own, but never would have known that she had been in the ICU for twenty-four hours.

Her throat felt raspy as she tried to swallow. "Water," Ruth mumbled.

"Hold on a second, Ruth," a voice said.

The person gently lifted Ruth's head and put a straw in her mouth. Ruth drank slowly, but only a few sips. It hurt to swallow, so she stopped drinking. The straw was removed from her mouth and Ruth's head was gently put back on the pillow. Her eyes closed again.

"Ruth?" the voice softly asked. Ruth opened her eyes a second time and tried to focus.

Ruth recognized the voice but couldn't remember the name at first. "Where am I?" she asked.

"You're in Vera Hospital, Ruth. Do you remember anything?"

Ruth stared at the woman in front of her. "How did I get here?" she asked in a slow whisper.

"Officer Bone found you outside the house, Ruth. He called the ambulance and they brought you here," the voice said.

"Shirley," Ruth said as her eyes focused.

"I'm glad you remember my name, Ruth. That's a good sign," said Dr. Shirley Anderson. "What happened, Ruth? Do you remember how this happened?"

"I need to see Dan," Ruth stated.

"Get a little more rest, Ruth. I'll be back in an hour," Shirley said and left the room.

Ruth tried to go back to sleep. She kept opening and closing her eyes. She realized her hospital bed had rails attached to the sides. She saw the television beyond the foot of the bed. She saw the bathroom to the left of the television and thought she'd like to use it. But trying to move caused her head to throb, so she decided to settle back down with her head firmly on the pillow.

She noticed the needle in her arm; it was an intravenous drip. She should have known not to try to move. Now her arm was uncomfortable and she didn't know if the needle had broken through the vein. She looked for the remote to call the nurse, but her eyes kept closing and then opening in an uncomfortable manner. She did not notice the light blinking from the alarm when she moved her arm. A nurse rushed in immediately to look at her arm, the needle, the intravenous drip, and the alarm. After making sure everything was in place, the nurse made a few comments, pushed a button that disengaged the blinking alarm light, and left the room.

Ruth was able to fall asleep this time. Only now she was having nightmares. The first came almost immediately, as her mind kept thinking of the worst. She saw Dan climb thirteen wooden steps. She saw a hideous, deformed, large man with a black hood over his head. Dan walked to the man, who offered a hood for Dan to put on. Dan refused. A noose dropped down, and the man put it around Dan's neck and tightened it.

There was something very strange about the man. The slits in his eyes were a muddy brick red. Ruth was sure that she saw a serpent's tongue slither from his mouth. His full-length robe concealed his steps. He appeared to slide toward Dan to put the noose around his neck.

Ruth tried to call out but couldn't. Her throat was dry, and all she could muster was a dry rasp. She closed her mouth and tried to reach out to Dan.

Then the man uttered a loud guffaw. A writhing hiss rang in Ruth's ears and she was now able to scream out, "No!"

The man slithered a few feet behind Dan to a lever. Ruth understood that the lever would open up the wooden flooring and drop Dan. Then Ruth saw four small letters on the collar of the man's robe. She didn't understand what they meant or stood for. As the man pulled the lever, Ruth yelled "Apep" and opened her eyes.

She saw the hospital room's white ceiling. She tried to slow her quick breaths. She brought her left hand to her face and felt sweat.

A dream, she thought. *A stupid nightmare.* She settled down. With effort, she turned her head to look at the small clock on the table to her right. She realized she had only fallen asleep for ten minutes.

Ruth calmed herself down and tried not to cry. Her eyes raced from side to side as she thought of Dan. The questions were normal and many. Where was he? What happened to him? How did he disappear? Was he safe? Why did this happen? Her eyes grew heavy and she fell asleep once again.

It wasn't long before the next nightmare began. She tried to move, but the needle in her arm informed her that she had to rest in place. "Settle down and take it," something was telling her.

She saw Dan being led to a gray wall by the large, deformed man, who was holding Dan's right arm and writhing forward. They stopped, and he again offered Dan a hood. Dan again declined, and the man slithered away.

Where did he go? she thought. She couldn't see that monster anymore. Instead she saw the wall, the gray brick wall, begin to change. One brick turned over and changed to red. Another brick then changed to black. Two bricks then moved and changed to yellow. Then they all moved as if someone were manipulating them to form a pattern. What was it? What did it remind her of? She could never do it. She could never solve it. The cube! It was a large Rubik's Cube! That was it!

Then it stopped, as all the colors now were one. Red. Blood red! Sickeningly and slowly, the bricks seemed to melt to the ground and disappear, only to reveal the same blood red in the next layer.

Dan didn't even notice the changes. He was just looking forward. His hands had been tied behind him and his feet were chained. He didn't even try to run. Instead he stood firm in the position he had been left in by that hideous monster. He was ready.

There were thirteen men in front of him, all of them smaller than the one who had escorted him. All were in robes and hoods, their identities hidden. All eyes were that sickening muddy red. The part of the face where the mouth would be stayed dark and hidden. The thirteen were standing straight and in one precise line. Ruth figured there were maybe six inches separating each . . . each . . . thing.

The Death Maze

They weren't men, Ruth surmised. They were ghastly thin but solid in stature. Their heads appeared large and oval. Ruth couldn't see legs.

She saw the leader, the large monster, raise his right arm to his chest. The thirteen stood at attention. Then something slid from the leader's mouth, and the thirteen lifted rifles that had not been there before.

Ruth tried to speak. Nothing came out.

The leader raised his other arm to the same level, and the thirteen separated what would have been their feet.

No shoes, Ruth thought as she moved in her sleep. "No shoes," she yelled as she found her voice.

That thing lifted both its arms above its head as the thirteen somehow cocked their rifles without moving.

"How? Wait. You can't," Ruth yelled.

The arms of the leader went down and the rifles were fired.

Only one of the guns had a bullet, but only one bullet was needed to enter Dan's heart. Dan dropped to his knees and fell to the ground.

"Noooooo!" Ruth screamed in her sleep. A nurse rushed in. She grabbed Ruth before she could rise from the bed and damage her arm with the intravenous needle. "Dan! No!" Ruth again yelled out.

Dr. Shirley Anderson was there a second later, helping the nurse on the other side of Ruth. "Ruth. RUTH!" Dr. Anderson yelled. "Wake up."

Ruth opened her eyes. She was dripping with sweat and crying hysterically.

Chapter 14

On the other side of the door was a hall filled with moving colors. It was like a kaleidoscope. Images were turning clockwise in one section, and other pictures and symbols were turning counterclockwise farther down.

Dan remembered playing with kaleidoscopes as a young boy. However, those kaleidoscopes had not been filled with deathly and depressing pictures. These were making him sick and dizzy. He quickly realized he had to move to the end of the corridor to continue the maze. That's where the first decision would be.

He quickly took in the dimensions of the hallway so he could remember its width and length. He closed his eyes and took one step before stopping, feeling as if he was going to vomit. His stomach had turned to jelly. He felt a bit of it come up and worked to keep it down. Opening his eyes, he tried to focus solely on the end point. The movement of images and colors was now faster and more terrifying.

Pictures of snakes and serpents were moving in opposite directions. In some pictures they were on land, choking their prey of precious air. In others they swam through the water only to coil around their victim. They fell from tree branches to land on top of unsuspecting soon-to-be meals. The fact that the predators were killing their victims was not making him sick. It was the way in which they were killing, salivating like maniacal, rabid animals, that was unappealing. Dan felt as if they were showing off for him. They all moved toward Dan as if they could see him. He instinctively threw up his arms to protect his face, though he knew that none of them would touch him. They slithered past him with guts hanging out of their mouths, and he imagined their drooling laughter. They looked human instead of reptilian.

It was all for show. All of it was meant to make him as sick as he could get. Apep wanted him to rush his thoughts and decisions when the time came.

Dan tried to concentrate and move past these images to the end of the corridor, but it seemed to be growing in length as he inched forward. Each time he tried to take a bigger step, he became a pawn again and lost his momentum. He stumbled but kept moving forward. Finally he reached the end. The hallway melted away, but Dan didn't notice.

His legs felt weak, and he decided to sit down on the floor and rest a few moments. Nausea again crept up his throat, but he fought it down once more. "This is not going to be as easy as I thought it would be," he mumbled under his breath. This was going to be a great task. It had been planned very carefully. It had been constructed to his every dislike and was able to read each and every one of his thoughts.

His deep brown eyes felt red as he brought his hands up to them and rubbed. Then he passed his hands over his dark brown and silver hair to wipe away the sweat. He wanted to sleep but felt dizzy each time he closed his eyes. He knew the feeling wouldn't last very long.

Water! That's what he could use. His mouth felt pasty and dry. When he tried to swallow, his stomach churned once more.

"Come on, Dan," he said to himself. "You've been through worse."

"Oh yeah? When?" he argued back.

"Give me time to think and I'll try to let you know," Dan replied.

But he couldn't think of any situation that was worse. He was in the beginning of what could be the last moments of his life. What could be worse than that? He wasn't a veteran. He'd never seen war. Instead, he had been able to go to school and impress all his teachers with his youthful looks and beyond average intelligence.

"Come on. THINK!" he said loudly.

Wait! This is exactly what Apep wanted. He wanted doubt and suspicion in his thoughts. He wanted to manipulate and control. He wanted Dan to miscalculate and misjudge each move.

Dan turned around and noticed it was all gone. The hallway. The pictures. The clockwise and counterclockwise rotations. The serpents and snakes. All of it was gone. It was just him sitting on the floor. The door he had gone through had also vanished.

He looked at the place where he thought the door had been. Suddenly there was another wall in front of him. When had it appeared? He looked up and saw nothing. The wall stood alone, without support. Maybe if he pushed the wall, it would topple away and Ruth would be on the other side of it. Another stupid thought. Where was he to go? The wall was just a wall, with no entrances or exits.

He turned around again and saw two doors right behind him. *Obvious*, he thought. *My first real decision.*

The Death Maze

"Fifty-fifty," he said out loud. "Not bad odds!"

But he was nervous. He could beat the odds at the blackjack table because he knew the cards. He could beat the odds playing his college friends at poker because he was able to read their faces. This was as bad as the true-false questions on his tests at school. They were simple questions, but designed to make a student think. *Never assume*, he thought.

A surprising thought did enter his mind. It suddenly felt ironic that he was recalling these thoughts from his past. First was the toy kaleidoscope. Then the dizziness from the rolling of the images. Now playing cards with his college friends. He wondered how many more times he would relive the past before his end was to come. Maybe he was already dead and he was on his way. He had heard that life flashes by in seconds.

He looked at the doors again and decided. "Right is right! Right?"

He opened the right door. Nothing happened. He moved forward ever so slowly and stuck his head through.

That brought another thought from the past. He used to perform the same motion when the door to his parent's room was closed. He would gently open the door and his mother would call out, "I see you, Danny boy." He would then run back to his own room and laugh and laugh. His mother would come into his room to make sure he was tucked into bed and to give him a big good-night kiss.

Dan didn't have his mother with him now, and there wasn't a bed to be seen on the other side of the door. Since nothing was moving or changing or fading from view, he decided his guess was correct.

Confronting him now was another corridor. Only this one was circular, and he was seeing it as if he were above it.

73

It was as though it was giving him a good look at it. Then it moved. Or did he move? He couldn't tell. However, he was now standing in front of the circular hallway.

This hallway was void of any colors or moveable effects. It was, however, smaller than he. Dan then realized he would have to crouch low to enter it.

Something's not right, he thought. His analytical mind was taking its cue and moving in all directions to assimilate his next moves. He didn't feel right getting down on all fours because this would make him more vulnerable to the sixth dimension and Apep's sick mind.

He looked for another way out, but now saw that everything around him was unusually black. *Again? When did this occur?* he thought. He realized that his mind needed work more quickly.

He couldn't see anything but the corridor now. He tried to go over it but was blocked by some sort of invisible barrier. *Oh, God,* his mind was telling him. *There's only the obvious.*

He knelt down before the corridor. He was still too tall. He conceded to his captor, crouched down on the floor, and then inched closer to the opening in the circular hallway. It lit up. He moved away from it and the lights went off.

He tried again and the lights came back on, but Dan did not know how. There were no lights. He didn't see any bulbs or small lamps. There was just nothing there.

"How the hell is the sixth dimension doing this?" Dan asked himself. He was really grateful for the light, since the rest of the area was pitch black.

He crept forward to get a decent view of the inside. It seemed endless. He decided to crawl forward. When his

The Death Maze

body was entirely in, he heard it. He reached back with his bare foot and felt that the entrance had closed shut. The only way out now was to move forward until he reached the other side . . . wherever that was.

Dan wanted to get angry and kick at the entrance, but knew it was fruitless. He was actually not that angry. He should have realized that this would happen. Getting angry would solve nothing.

If Apep, or whatever he was, was going to kill him, he was going to do it his way and without any errors in the maze. Dan was positive that the traps were failsafe. He knew this when he tried to push the wall.

As he moved forward, he soon noticed that a small area in front of him would light up at the same time that an equal amount of area behind him would darken. Reversing course was now impossible. As he crawled forward, some invisible block would set in behind him, not allowing him to reverse. This block he could not see or hear.

Dan was not one to get frustrated; he actually enjoyed challenges. *Okay, not this challenge*, he thought. However, if this had not been life and death, it would be worth it to figure out the intricacies of this dimension. It was total thought and manipulation of the thought. This was something he would try to remember as he continued to move through the circular . . . whatever it was.

Dan figured he was now moving at about ten feet per minute. He was purposely crawling at a slow pace. He was bobbing his head back and forth so as not to miss a single possible flaw or motion within his confines. He was able to look up and see an endless sky or high ceiling—he couldn't tell. Maybe it was just his imagination, and he was seeing something that couldn't be seen.

When he thought he had crawled about forty feet, he felt a change in temperature. He kept crawling, but soon began to touch the sides of the corridor. Placing his hands on his stomach, he turned onto his back and began to push himself forward with his feet. This immediately became a problem as the heat continued to rise. He managed to take off his lab jacket, place part of it over his feet, turn his body over, and pull himself forward with his hands. With his feet pointing upward, the lab jacket covered his feet and spread onto the floor of the tunnel. He pictured what an inchworm would look like at this moment.

It became harder to move as the heat grew in intensity. Dan was burning up. Sweat dripped from his forehead and evaporated once it touched the bottom of the hallway. He tried doubling the jacket. It seemed tolerable. He continued to inch along.

He saw his next decision about twenty feet away as the heat seemed to fade. Dan looked at his hands and saw a couple blisters. He felt others on his feet, but was glad things were returning to what could be considered normal. The corridor was showing three entrances.

"This is predictable," he said as the hallway began to get larger and he approached his next choice.

In the back of his mind, he kept to the conclusion that the sixth dimension was not the maze, but that the sixth dimension had developed the maze for his three-dimensional mentality. Dan really would have liked to understand more of the world of the sixth dimension. He was sure he would get the chance before the end.

However, he now had to make a choice. A wrong decision would bring his first mistake, but what would that mean? *What the hell*, he thought, and decided on the middle entrance.

The Death Maze

Dan crawled partway through the middle opening and quickly knew he was wrong. First there was a tremor and then a horrible quake. The doorway then threw him from side to side as it began to shrink in size.

Now he knew what an error would do. It was ingenious. If the maze shrunk it would eventually crush him, and his death would be as gruesome as the serpents tearing and ripping into the flesh of their prey.

Dan managed to grab both sides of the doorway and squeeze back through as the left entrance lit up. This was the correct choice. Or was it? If he had chosen the left entrance, would it have given him the same outcome? He didn't know. He just needed to move quickly.

Dan felt a sting on his left ankle; the middle opening was closing onto it. He pulled at his foot until he felt as if his toes would be cut off. He saw some blood. He screamed and pulled, tugged and angled. When his foot was fully free, he squeezed through the left opening, not knowing what was on the other side. All he knew was that the left opening was lit up and he was to follow the path.

Falling! He panicked. He was falling. The left entrance led to nothing but down. He wasn't moving at a fast speed, but he knew that at the end of the fall he would be hurt. It was too dark to see anything. All he felt was a wind brushing past him, slowing his fall slightly. *But where is the end?* he thought as he reached out to try and cushion the impact.

Before he made contact, his thoughts brought him to *Alice in Wonderland*. He loved that story. A pity there would be no rabbit to chase, no tea party. The Cheshire Cat would not be a continuous grinning pain in the behind. And most of all, there would be no fun when he awakened. There would only be more decisions to make.

He had now made his first mistake. Only four left before the final darkness of death. Dan's last words just before he hit the bottom echoed around the tunnel.

"Someone help me."

He fell unconscious. In his dreams he heard the laughing of a madman. He thought he felt the slithering tongue of a serpent. Apep was planning his next move. A move that would bring him closer to the end of his life.

Dan wanted Arione. Apep wanted justice—though what justice, Dan still didn't understand. The sixth dimension only had to wait until its victim opened his eyes. All the questions would eventually be answered. Time was on the side of the sixth dimension. It would make sure that its pawn had enough nutrition in order to stay alive to complete or not complete the maze. Apep already knew that outcome.

Chapter 15

Dr. Shirley Anderson knew there would be no way of calming Ruth down without a sedative. Ruth was talking so fast her words were garbled and did not make sense. Her sentences ran into each other and Shirley was only able to distinguish a few words, but the words that represented death were clear. She heard *noose*, *bullets*, and *blood*. Ruth was on the verge of a nervous breakdown. Then Ruth suddenly stopped her rage and was calm.

Shirley stared into Ruth's eyes and saw the final three words form in her mouth. They were simple and barely audible, but clear. "I love him," Ruth whispered.

Ruth closed her eyes and fell silent. Dr. Anderson stood straight and looked at the nurse who stood on the opposite side of the bed.

"I want you to check on her every twenty minutes," Shirley ordered the nurse. "Make sure she's comfortable and not writhing in the bed. Anything changes, page me." Shirley left the room.

Outside the hospital room, Chief Richard Dressler was waiting for Dr. Anderson. He had heard Ruth's rants and couldn't bring himself to question her. He was hoping that the good doctor could supply some answers.

"Is she going to be all right?" Chief Dressler asked.

"I'm sure with time and plenty of rest, she'll eventually pull through," Shirley informed him. "She's having terrible nightmares about death and different types of executions."

Chief Richard Dressler knew almost everyone in both Arione and Vera. The towns were considered sisters and only separated by a few miles. The chief was in charge of both of them, and everyone knew he cared for their neighbors.

The disappearance of Dan Adams was causing him to have one of the busiest days of his career. He had heard from almost everyone in Arione, which, thank God, was not as populated as Needles but still had a few hundred concerned neighbors. They all wanted to know how they could help and if there was any other cause for alarm. The chief knew this case was not going to be solved in a matter of a few hours or days. He still had many questions, and the answers were lying behind the door of the hospital room where he now stood.

His office had become cluttered with the ringing of phones. It seemed as if every resident had already stopped at the station by midday. Deputy Bone was trying to keep the office from reaching a boiling point and knew his boss would soon leave. He didn't realize that he already had left until he went into his office and saw the note: "Went to the hospital. You take over for now."

"Chief?" Dr. Anderson was asking.

Chief Dressler came out of his thoughts and saw Dr. Anderson. "Yeah," he muttered.

"Did you know that?" she asked.

"Know what?" Chief Dressler asked back.

"Did you know that Ruth loved him?" Shirley asked again.

"It was becoming obvious to me, Dr. Anderson," Chief Dressler said. "She's been with Dan Adams since she arrived in Arione. I haven't seen the two of them apart in awhile. I mean, she goes for groceries without him and he stops by the office without her to talk. But they always work together, and they're inseparable in the evening hours."

"Do you know their evening arrangements?" she asked, trying not to be too intrusive.

"To my knowledge, they were still in separate rooms. Dr. Adams was starting to think he wanted more from their relationship but didn't know how to approach it. It had been a long time for him," Chief Dressler explained.

Shirley Anderson nodded and said, "I believe she was on the verge of wanting more and was about to express it to him."

"Has she said anything to you?" he asked.

"Not yet," she admitted. "However, I've known her awhile now. When she lost her husband in the accident, I wasn't sure she would make it. Dr. Adams was there for her at each juncture. I'm not so sure now."

"What are you talking about? We don't know anything yet!" the chief stated harshly. "You can't rush to conclusions."

"I'm sorry, Chief. I'm only thinking of Ruth right now."

"When can I question her, Dr. Anderson?" he asked.

"Probably tomorrow, Chief." Dr. Anderson started to leave. "I'll make sure she's not disturbed."

"See you tomorrow!" the chief stated.

As he began to leave, Chief Dressler heard one last question from Shirley Anderson. "What was he working on?" she called out.

"Haven't got a clue," the chief replied, knowing that his answer was not the truth. "However, we're going to go into the home later and search. Maybe we can retrace what happened from his notes. We'll probably look for others who can explain what we're reading."

"I'd like to be a part of it. If that's all right with you," she stated before turning the corner of the hallway.

Chief Dressler nodded his head and turned to leave the hospital. When he was out in the sunshine, he thought again about finding others to go over Dan's notes. He knew there would be a mountain of documents and did not know what to expect once inside the house.

Besides, he thought, *who would I call? Where would I start?* Chief Dressler continued walking to his squad car and began formulating a plan. He knew of a couple hospitals that would probably be able to help. They were in the Los Angeles area and would need a few days before they could send someone to Arione. He was sure that once he mentioned Dan's name, someone would recognize it and want to drive out to help.

Driving back to Arione, he stopped in front of Dan's house, turned off the car, and got out. The house looked beautiful from the front. It didn't seem to be in distress from this angle.

He walked through the front garden area that Ruth had completed some time ago. The fenced enclosure contained a combination of desert plants and flowers and two stone benches. Drip tubing ran throughout the garden, distributing water in a focused manner and keeping the plants fresh and alive.

There was also a small area to the right with cacti of different sizes. They ranged from a few inches in height to as tall as five feet. It was a well-thought-out and smart representation of desert foliage.

To the left side was a small pond area somewhat secluded from the desert sun by bushes in full flower. Ruth asked Dan if she could put in a koi pond. Dan did not object, but first asked Ruth to look into the dangers of the excessive heat on the expensive fish. Ruth was in the process of finishing this project.

After looking at the garden, Chief Dressler walked down the center of the front lawn and walkway for about forty feet before coming to six steps that led to a front porch built of fine stones and wood. The porch covered the entire front area of the home. It was treated every couple years in order to repel water during the rainy season and simmering heat during the summer. The roof extended to cover the porch, making it perfect for sitting outside and relaxing after a full day.

Before climbing the steps, the chief noticed a few blood spots. This was where Ruth had been hit by the stones that flew from the back of the house. He didn't comprehend how far the stones had actually traveled before hitting Ruth. However, he did know that someone or something would have had to throw them quite a distance if coming from the back of the house. He looked to either side for specifics and perspectives, but couldn't reach any conclusions.

Beyond the front door, a circular entrance twenty-five feet in diameter with a wooden floor greeted the visitor. To the left was an extra-large living room with two matching sofas facing each other. Between the sofas was a large coffee table. On either side of the sofas were matching end tables. An armoire stood against one of the walls and a piano sat on the opposite side of the room. A stone fireplace adorned the last wall of this room. It was here that Dan and Ruth had spent a great deal of time enjoying each other's company before retiring for the night.

To the right of the entrance hallway was a smaller living room that Dan used as a second office. This was decorated with a smaller sofa, built-in bookcases, a few chairs, and an office desk with a laptop. A year after Ruth moved in, she asked if she could put her own laptop in this room. Again, Dan was very receptive and had no problems allowing Ruth to alter the room in any fashion she wanted. His real office was the lab.

Behind the large living room area was a formal dining room. There were enough seats for eight when the center section to the dining table was in place. As such, it was enough for four, and the other chairs had neatly been placed around the room.

Toward the back of the house was a large kitchen, a breakfast area with many windows, and a back porch addition. Dan hadn't had many of the smaller appliances prior to Ruth arriving. Once she moved in, the kitchen grew in size and now had a large center island for cooking as well as new granite counters, a new refrigerator with a sub-freezer, and a matching dishwasher, sink, double-broiler stove, and microwave. Ruth had even added a pantry area for more spices and a canned cornucopia of vegetables and foods that Dan had never utilized in his small repertoire of cooking.

It was an unbelievable change for Dan Adams to have Ruth as a roommate, and Dan relished her expertise in cooking. She loved experimenting with new dishes. She didn't believe that a person should eat the same meal more than once a week. Ruth was very comfortable cooking for two, and there were never enough leftovers for a snack, much less a second meal.

As one entered the kitchen from the living room and turned to the left, he or she was confronted with the large section of the house devoted to Dan's lab. A small three-step hall area led to the door. To the right of the hall area was the laundry room. However, the door to the lab was what the chief was concerned with right now.

The lab door was ajar. Chief Dressler knew this was wrong. It was never left open. Whenever he was invited into the home, the door was closed. Rule number one in the house was to keep the door to the lab closed. What went on in this room was only for those who needed to know. At this point, Chief Dressler couldn't think of anyone who needed to know except him.

He felt the hair on his arms begin to rise. He moved his right hand to the holster of his gun, unbuttoned it, and grabbed the steel weapon. Bringing the gun to his side, he slowly moved toward the door and gently pushed. It opened fully to reveal the large room inside.

Chief Dressler was nervous. Every other time he had been in this house, he had walked to the kitchen with its owner, pulled a couple beers from the refrigerator, and sat down as the two conversed about nothing special and everything trivial. It was their bullshit hour, and he knew Dan's moods and vice versa.

Now was not the time to bullshit. He knew that a piece of the house had been invaded and violated. He did not know what to expect; all he knew was that he didn't want to be another victim. The goose bumps on his arms rose higher as he inched toward the open door. He moved to the right of the doorway to look inside. He could smell something burning. He quickly turned to the left side of the door frame, but couldn't see well since the door was blocking whatever was behind it.

Lifting the gun from his side, he took one step into the room to look behind the door. Still nothing. He noticed the smell was more pungent now. He looked up and saw a gaping hole that went through the ceiling and the roof. He was able to see the stars above. *What the hell?* he thought. *When did this happen?*

He felt a shiver go down his spine as he stepped fully into the room. He looked around and saw Dan's notes on the floor. He eyed the miniature vehicle on the floor as well. The smell, he determined, was coming from outside and traveling into the lab. He stepped farther into the room and couldn't believe the mess. The Dr. Dan Adams he knew would never tolerate the lab looking like this!

A hand tapped his shoulder and Chief Dressler almost jumped out of his uniform.

"What are you looking at, Chief?"

Chief Dressler quickly turned, having recognized the voice. "Bone! Don't ever do that again, you understand?" Chief Dressler almost yelled, but somehow managed to contain his agitated state. It was, however, pleasing to see his smiling deputy. "I almost shit in my pants!" he said as he replaced his gun in the holster.

"Sorry, boss," Bone apologized, wanting to laugh. "I saw your car out front and walked in. Thought you might need some help."

"When did this happen, Bone? You didn't say there was a huge mess or a hole in the ceiling!"

"I haven't been in the house, Chief, I swear!" Bone said with great conviction. "I just saw Ruth Putnam on the ground outside, picked her up, and took her to the hospital like you told me to after I called you."

"I know that, Bone. I'm sorry. I'm just thinking out loud," Chief Dressler tried to explain. "Do you know of anyone who would be in the house?" he asked directly.

"No, sir," Bone stated as fact. "Although I did notice a smell as I entered. It wasn't there when I took Mrs. Putnam to the hospital."

"I smelled it also," Chief Dressler acknowledged.

Chief Dressler walked a few steps farther into the lab and saw a miniature version of the binary plant against one wall. He knew what this was because Dan had informed him of his plans. Dan knew he would need a permit to build the real thing in his backyard. Chief Dressler did not know the actual reason for the plant and thus was surprised to see a small car on the floor.

He pulled a pair of plastic gloves from his right pants pocket and put them on. Then he gently picked up the car by its sides and looked at it. He made a mental note to do some research about binary plants when he returned to his office. He sniffed the car. He could smell the same pungent odor on it.

"Smell this," he said to Bone.

Bone walked close to the chief and smelled the toy car. "That's what I smelled when I came into the room," Bone insisted. "What do you think it means, Chief?"

"I'm not sure, Bone, but I have some research I need to do," Chief Dressler commented. "This smell seems to be burned rubber with something else. Don't you think so?"

"I'm not sure, Chief," Bone replied. He turned his head farther toward the back of the room and saw a pair of shoes.

Bone began walking before Chief Dressler warned him not to touch anything. Bone was ready, and pulled out a pair of plastic gloves in anticipation of the chief's rebuke. "I got gloves, Chief," Bone said. He put on the gloves and stopped before the pair of shoes. They had the same smell. He leaned down and tried to pick them up but couldn't.

"Hey, Chief?" Bone asked. His tone also said *come here*.

Chief Dressler walked to the shoes and stared. He couldn't believe what he was seeing. They appeared to be embedded in the floor.

It was too ominous for him. Chief Dressler turned and looked over the entire room. There was so much to go over, as everything now looked out of place. He took out a small pad of paper and pen from his breast pocket and began writing:

Lab door open
Hole in ceiling
Burning smell with other odor
Small car
Shoes burned into the floor
Lab a mess
No blood
No broken glass

What else? he thought. He was missing something else. He looked up and saw it. The back door!

"Bone," he called out.

"Yes, sir," Bone answered.

"Check to see if the back door is locked," he ordered.

Bone walked to the back door and pushed. It wasn't locked. It had been left slightly open.

"Chief?" Bone called out.

They exited the lab and immediately heard a hum. They saw the large binary plant and couldn't believe what they were looking at. Then the hum stopped, and a whoosh of heat blew from a gasket to the pump. They were both startled from the sound and jumped backward, not knowing if it would blow up.

Then they saw the footprints.

Chapter 16

Wallace Johnson Jr. was his real name, and he had a good reputation as being an honest cop. He was from an unincorporated town west of Los Angeles called Palms and had been brought up by his mother, Olivia. They lived together in a two-bedroom apartment. Wallace was named after his father, a police officer in the LAPD who was killed in a drive-by shooting that left one officer and two crooks dead, two others prosecuted for grand theft, and his father's partner in a wheelchair paralyzed from the waist down. This all happened when he was just three years old. The papers covered the story in full, so Wallace Johnson Jr. knew the heroics of his father. He always kept a picture of his dad in his wallet.

WJ, as he liked to be called because he hated the name Wallace and even more the nickname of Wally, was a good student. He enjoyed reading everything he could get his hands on. After he discovered the library at age seven, he spent most of his free time reading books beyond his academic years. It didn't matter what books they were. He read fiction, nonfiction, sports, medicine, and law.

Then he found the encyclopedia. This was his heaven, and he learned and remembered as much as he could. It didn't matter which volume, which city, or which era. This group of books opened his eyes to the past and present and kept him alive with every subject imaginable. He finished the entire encyclopedia inside of one year.

Wallace Johnson was, however, an even greater son. WJ would go out of his way to help his mother, who was a nurse working twelve-hour days. He would cook and clean the apartment for her so she wouldn't have to worry when she got home tired. There was always something ready to be eaten and clean sheets on the bed for a good night's rest. He even did the laundry once a week and ironed wrinkled blouses and shirts.

Sports were also a part of his routine. He learned to swim and play baseball and basketball. The swimming was easy because there was a pool outside the three-story apartment complex where he and his mother lived. The neighbors knew who he and his mother were, and they acted as surrogate parents when his mother was working.

WJ felt he had a great upbringing despite losing his father. He felt lucky to have so many watching over him and knew to stay away from the vices of drugs, gangs, and liquor. He had other things in mind for his career. He knew it at age twelve when he saw his first rerun of *Dragnet*. Although television was not a crutch for him, he saved time for this one show at least twice a week.

"This is the city, Los Angeles, California. I work here. I carry a badge." That was how Captain Joe Friday began each episode. WJ wanted this more than anything else in the world.

He received his badge when he was twenty-two, having applied to the LAPD just before he turned twenty-one. He learned the rules and regulations quickly and never sacrificed his morals for the quick turn of cash through the sordid streets of Los Angeles. The City of Angels did indeed have

The Death Maze

its underground network of "look the other way" officials. There were those who made thousands in unaccounted cash by making their turf free from the rigors of routine roundups and searches.

Unfortunately, WJ ran into the wrong official too soon in his career. He witnessed an exchange one night while on patrol: A large envelope went into the hands and then pockets of one high-ranking officer and one politician, courtesy of a group he had been watching for some time. When the politician caught sight of WJ, the officer tracked him down and gave him one warning. WJ would either look the other way and never mention it, or end up like his father. It seemed someone did his homework on the history of Wallace Johnson.

At the same time, Richard Dressler was in Los Angeles looking for someone to take back with him to Arione. Dressler needed a deputy for his small force because Arione and Vera were growing communities and he had just fired a cop for taking bribes from motorists speeding on the highway. The deputy would stop cars and settle for a couple twenties instead of giving the motorist a ticket.

Dressler hated a crooked cop. When he found out why revenue was down and who was on the take, he almost killed the son of a bitch. There was nothing worse than a dishonest cop. Chief Richard Dressler made sure that cop would never receive another job in law enforcement. He also kept him in the Arione jail for thirty days before letting him leave town with just his belongings and enough money to get a couple nights in a cheap motel. The last he heard, the bastard was waiting tables in a dive in Phoenix.

At the same time Dressler was talking to an officer friend in Los Angeles, WJ was just getting off his shift. WJ was in a small cloud of confusion over his recent incident and wasn't looking where he was going. He bumped into Dressler, excused himself, and kept walking. Dressler finished his conversation with his friend and followed the tall, thin young officer.

"Hey, Officer," Dressler called outside the station.

WJ knew it was him the large man was calling to, and he turned around. Dressler was not wearing his uniform, so WJ didn't know that the man was a fellow officer of the law.

"Can I help you?" WJ asked.

"Actually, you can," Dressler answered as he walked up to WJ. "Officer Johnson," Dressler said as he read the nametag on WJ's uniform.

"Do I know you?" WJ asked.

"Not yet," Dressler acknowledged. "But you soon will."

"What's that supposed to mean?"

"Hey, look. I just want to talk to you for a few minutes. Are you off your shift?" Dressler asked, already knowing that WJ was. "Let me buy you a cup of coffee so we can speak."

"Why?" WJ was getting a bit antsy at the forwardness of this man. He had already sized him up and knew he was not a threat. He also knew that Dressler was told something back at the station. "What do you want?"

"Why don't you let me buy you a cup of coffee, and maybe a burger and fries so you can add some pounds to your thin, bony frame, and I'll explain it to you?" Dressler answered plainly and in his usual up-front manner.

WJ was used to people making fun of his thin frame. However, that was from other officers and friends. He had never heard it from a stranger. But he somehow liked this man and knew something was up. Something good was about to happen. He enjoyed the mystery.

"What the hell. I was going to go get a bite to eat anyway. Might as well get it for free."

"I like a man who enjoys a free meal," Dressler retorted. "Now just lead me to a good place where the food is American and our conversation is private. I believe you and I are going to be friends, Officer Johnson. I'll drive."

They walked to Dressler's car in silence. Seeing it was a surprise for WJ. It was a typical police sedan without all the extras that the Los Angeles Police Department had on its cars. On both sides of the doors was the insignia of the Arione Police Department and the words "To Protect and to Serve."

"Same slogan, but different PD," WJ said.

"Listen, Bony," Dressler called at him. "All cops protect and serve. No one owns the saying. Chief Richard Dressler," he introduced himself as he got into his car.

"Bony?" WJ interrupted while opening the passenger door.

"Okay. How about Bone?" Dressler smirked. "It fits."

"Yeah, whatever!" WJ muttered. He got into the car.

They drove to a restaurant just west of downtown on Wilshire Boulevard. It was exactly what Dressler wanted. A place with no ambience and good food, and the letter A in the window for cleanliness was satisfactory.

"You're honest, kid," Dressler stated as they sat down. "That's what I need."

"That's what the sergeant said at the station?" WJ asked.

"Look, Bone. They all like you," Dressler continued. "I got good words from many who think you're smart, on the ball, and care a great deal."

WJ listened as Dressler explained who he was, where Arione was situated, and what he wanted from him.

"I don't know, Chief," WJ answered.

"Look. It's not like you're going to another state or country. It's beautiful and not far from the state border. It's clean and the place is growing. I can't stand a crooked cop, and I need someone I can mold into an officer capable of running the place one day," Dressler said.

"I was hoping to be a big man in the LAPD one day," WJ explained. "My father was a great cop. I owe it to him."

"You owe it to yourself not to get screwed up by a bunch of crooked politicians and cops who can't see that an honest life is better than even one day in jail," Dressler lectured. "I'm sure your father would want you to build your own legacy. It doesn't have to be in a big-city department. And I need to build two towns." Dressler looked at WJ and knew he was getting to him. "Look, even though the pay is not exactly the same as the LAPD, it is good. Life out there is good. The people grow on you because they sincerely care about their communities."

WJ looked at Chief Dressler and understood what he was talking about. There was more to California than Los Angeles. He knew his mother would want to retire soon, anyway. She was the reason he had never been out of Los Angeles.

"Look, Bone," Dressler said. "I'll make it a six-month sabbatical. If you don't like it, you can always come back and get your job back at the LAPD."

That was the kicker for WJ. He could try it, and if it didn't work out, he'd return. His mother could visit anytime, since it was only a few hours from home. Besides, the air would be good there.

"Okay, Chief," WJ said. "You sold me. Just keep it to WJ."

The Death Maze

"No problem, Bone," Dressler said as the food was served.

They made small talk for the rest of the meal. Afterward, Chief Dressler drove WJ back to the station.

"I'll wait to hear from you."

"Thanks again," WJ said as he closed the door.

It wasn't long before WJ arrived in Arione and adjusted to the friendly atmosphere. He enjoyed living in the small community. Dressler had a two-room apartment waiting for him when he arrived. Inside the apartment were a couple uniforms and a note. "Welcome to Arione, Bone. Not sure if these will fit. If not, don't worry. I'll exchange them. Come down to the station in the morning."

A special woman entered his life a couple weeks later, and Bone soon became a fixture in town in his new role. Things were moving in a positive and upward motion, and Bone knew that his future was in Arione and Vera. The six-month sabbatical came and went in no time.

Dressler knew he had the right guy. Bone was young and had a quick mind. He learned new procedures rapidly and understood the mentality of the small-town cop. People liked him also. They trusted him and knew that with this young man, the next generation of police officers would keep the town as safe as Chief Dressler was currently keeping it.

****

They had recovered from the shock of footprints and felt more at ease. The normal questions came from both of them. "What do you think happened, Chief?" Bone asked.

"Damned if I know, Bone," Dressler replied. "We have the shoes inside and the footprints outside. I don't even know how that works." Dressler walked around the shoes and back to the door entrance. He then walked back to Bone. "I want a team out here as soon as possible to retrace Dr. Adams's notes. Maybe we can find out where he is and what the hell happened."

"I'll get started right away, Chief," Bone said, walking to the door.

"Call UCLA or Cedars-Sinai," Dressler ordered. "Maybe they have someone who knew Dr. Adams and what he was working on."

"I'm on my way," Bone said and left.

Chief Dressler heard the motor of Bone's car start and then fade away. He took one last look at the house from the backyard and then walked to the door and closed it so no one could enter the home from this entrance.

Both he and Bone had totally missed seeing the wood in the grassy area. As Dan Adams walked by the wood, prior to disappearing, moss had suddenly appeared over it, camouflaging it. Right now, it only slightly looked out of place. It was waiting.

Chief Dressler walked through the lab once more and studied the shoes. He stared at the ceiling and the hole. He paced through the rest of the house, making sure the doors were shut and the windows secure. Arione was a town of curious residents who were always concerned for their neighbors. They were good people but could be a bit nosy.

Chief Dressler walked to his car and started the engine. His main concern was getting back to the office and finding out if Bone had called the hospitals.

"What a lousy day," he mumbled, driving off.

By the time he got back to the station and opened the door, Bone had completed his calls to UCLA and Cedars-Sinai. He informed Dressler that two chemists familiar with

Dan Adams's work had volunteered to drive out to Arione in a couple days and look over any notes that may indicate where Dan Adams had gone.

"Did you get their names?" Dressler asked.

"Sure did. The first is a Dr. Theodore Ryan. The second is Dr. Allyson Rayburn. Both are with the UCLA Department of Chemistry." Bone spoke with pride, having known that his boss would have only one question when he returned.

"Good. Maybe we'll get a break soon," Dressler replied. He then saw two women waiting for him in his office. *Why me?* he mouthed to his deputy as he trudged toward his office.

Bone laughed as he saw the two women begin to blabber away once the chief entered. He thought of how his boss was a good man and remembered how grateful he was for coming to Arione.

Chapter 17

The next day Ruth was sitting in Dr. Shirley Anderson's office when Chief Dressler arrived. When he opened the door, he was amazed to see that most of the black and blue marks were gone from her face, and just a couple scratches remained. But Ruth did look pale, and her appearance was almost deathlike. Dressler sat in the chair next to Ruth and looked at her.

"Hello, Ruth," Chief Dressler said. "How do you feel?"

"Hello, Chief Dressler. How do you think I should feel?" Ruth said in a monotone.

"I'm glad your bruises are almost gone," he said. Her eyes batted as though she could hardly keep them open. "Ruth," he continued, leaning in a bit closer. "Do you remember anything about the other night?"

"Do you know what happened to Dan?" she asked while staring into his eyes.

"That's all she's been saying," Shirley Anderson stated. "She seems fine and then gives a blank look. Then she asks for Dan."

Ruth just sat still, waiting for an answer from Chief Dressler. He looked at Shirley, who looked at him, and then they moved their eyes to Ruth.

"Dan?" Ruth called out as a few tears rolled down her face. "Do you know where Dan is, Chief? You've got to help him!"

"Calm down, Ruth," Shirley said as she put her hand on Ruth's.

"Ruth," Chief Dressler said, "we're looking for him. We'll find him."

"I'll take you back to your room now, Ruth," Shirley said as she helped Ruth stand. She left to find a nurse to take her.

Chief Dressler was now standing also. He didn't understand what was going on. He had so many questions. When Ruth left the room and Shirley Anderson returned, he pounced.

"What was that? Where did the bruises go? She looked like hell yesterday. Does a person heal that fast?"

"Now you need to calm down, Chief," Shirley demanded. "I'm trying to absorb it all myself."

"But how did she heal so fast? Yesterday it looked as if her face was bashed in!"

"I've never seen anyone heal that fast, Chief," Shirley said. "It's almost like a miracle. Except that she's tired, has a fever, and is disoriented." She paused and thought. "Do you have any news on Dan Adams?"

"Bone and I were at the house," he explained as he sat down in the chair that Ruth had occupied. "We inspected the entire area and found some unusual aspects of the lab and backyard."

"What do mean by unusual, Chief?"

"The main concern was a pair of shoes inside the lab and footprints outside the lab in the back," he explained.

"Would that have been unusual for Dan Adams?" Shirley asked.

"Don't you think it's a large concern to see a pair of footprints in one area and the shoes in another without a trace of other footprints in between?"

"Only if Dan always wore shoes outside and never walked barefoot!" she answered.

"That's exactly what I'm trying to explain, Dr. Anderson. I've never seen Dan Adams without his shoes while walking outside his home. In fact, he always wore shoes inside the home as well."

"Come on, Chief."

"I've been at his home numerous times over the years. I've never seen him without something—slippers, shoes, sneakers, whatever—on his feet."

"Okay," Shirley admitted. "Dan Adams always wore something on his feet. What else?"

"There was a hole in the ceiling of his lab. I'm sure it wasn't there when he first disappeared."

"Maybe Ruth can explain it," Shirley said as she rose from her chair and looked out her window. She saw a patient cross the street from the hospital parking lot to a gas station. She immediately ran to her door, opened it, and called for a nurse.

Chief Dressler stood up. "What the matter?" he asked as Dr. Anderson rushed out of the room. "Dr. Anderson," he yelled. "What's wrong?"

Chief Dressler rushed to catch up. He passed Ruth's room and noticed she was not there. He saw Shirley and the nurse running down the hallway.

"Didn't you escort her to her room?" Shirley asked the nurse as she ran.

"I did, Dr. Anderson," the nurse explained. Shirley brushed by her, running down the hall to the stairs.

Chief Dressler followed the doctor down the stairs and through the lobby. He saw her run across the parking lot and look toward the freeway. A car revved forward, as if it had just picked up a passenger.

"Oh my God! Ruth!" she screamed as Chief Dressler caught up with her.

"Where is she?"

"I think she was just picked up at the gas station across the street. The car just entered the freeway going east toward Arione," she explained while breathing heavily.

"I'll get my car."

Chief Dressler ran back through the parking lot and got into his patrol car. He quickly started it and picked up Dr. Anderson.

"Whoever picked up Ruth doesn't know she's sick," she stated.

Chief Dressler grabbed his receiver, pushed a button, and spoke. "Bone. Come in, Bone." Chief Dressler waited only a couple seconds before getting angry. "DAMN IT, BONE. ANSWER THE FUCKIN' RADIO!"

Dr. Anderson gave Chief Dressler a shocked look. He returned the look, shrugged his shoulders, and apologized.

"Bone here, Chief. What's up?"

"Where are you?"

"At the office, Chief," Bone explained.

"Well, get over to the Adams house and wait for me there. And watch out for Ruth Putnam."

"Isn't she at the hospital, Chief?"

"She just walked out of the hospital and was picked up at the gas station across the street."

"What do I do once she shows up?" Bone asked.

Shirley Anderson grabbed the receiver from Chief Dressler. "Just watch for her, Officer Bone, and don't touch her."

"Yes, ma'am," Bone said. He cut off the conversation.

Before leaving the hospital, Ruth quickly took off her hospital gown and put on her clothes without any undergarments or shoes. She was sweating as she raced out of her room. She wanted to get home as fast as she could and search for Dan.

Now in the car, Ruth looked at the man who picked her up as they entered the freeway. He looked about twenty-two and resembled her dead husband. He had wavy brown hair and dark brown eyes and wore thin wire glasses. Her eyes were slightly glazed and her head was spinning.

He glanced at Ruth and saw the perspiration on her face. "Lady, are you all right?" he asked.

Ruth's head bobbed. She wiped the sweat from her face with the palms of her hands and then wiped her palms on her pants. She was hot and becoming delirious.

"Take me home, Ed," Ruth said softly.

"What?" the man asked. He didn't think he had heard her correctly.

"I said take me home, Ed. I want to go to bed."

"Lady, I'm not Ed. But I will take you home. Where do you live?" he asked as he saw the sweat beading on her face.

"Come on, Ed. Stop playing games." Ruth wiped her face again and moved closer to the driver. "We can have fun tonight, Ed. Just like the night before we arrived in Arione," she said softly. The sweat on her blouse outlined her firm breasts. She nudged her body against the driver.

Ruth started taking off her blouse. The man quickly pulled her blouse down below her breasts with his right hand. He felt her nipple and the sweat that had seeped through. He knew that the woman was sick, but he couldn't make a U-turn to go back to the hospital. He decided to speed up a bit and drive to the next exit.

Ruth didn't give up. She quickly took the man's hand away and removed her blouse. Her breasts were firm and her nipples hard. She grabbed the man's right hand and tried to place it again on her breasts.

The Death Maze

He was becoming upset, knowing that she was sick and he needed to be gentle. His thoughts were rambling. She was a beautiful woman and he hadn't had some for a while. Her perspiration gave her breasts a glow. For just a split second, he thought of sucking them.

He felt himself getting hard and he rushed back to reality. He pulled his right hand from her grasp and tried to keep his mind on the road. Quickly looking for her blouse, he reached across and handed it to Ruth before bringing his eyes back to the road.

"Lady, please put your top back on."

"Come on, Ed. Touch me," Ruth pleaded as she grabbed his hand again and wiped it across her breasts.

He became hard again and tried not to think of how good her breasts felt. She was ill and needed help. She obviously didn't know what she was doing. Taking his hand away once again, the car swerved and he corrected it.

Ruth turned to him and began kissing him. He tried to pull away, pleading with her to sit down and be calm. Those really weren't the right words, because she immediately pulled away and grabbed at his groin. She felt the hardness of his crotch and continued to rub.

"Isn't this nice, Ed?" she asked as he tried to remove her hands.

He became angry because he could not control the car and yelled, "Look, lady! I'm not Ed!"

The swerving became worse as Ruth began to fight him. She couldn't believe that Ed was turning her down; he had never let her down at any moment in their relationship. And, she was horny.

"Lady, you're sick," he yelled. "You need some help." He shoved Ruth to the other side of the car.

Ruth retaliated immediately. Taking him totally by surprise, she pounced on him and both of his hands left the wheel. She was now one pissed, sick, scorned woman.

The car was now out of control. It swerved from one side of the freeway to the other while the man tried to get Ruth off him. When Ruth dug her nails into his hands, the car almost hit a sign. Blood began to drip from his left hand.

In the distance, another car was coming toward them, and its driver began to see that something was wrong. He had been driving all day and was tired. At first he thought that the sun was playing tricks on his eyes, but then he realized that within five hundred feet there would be a serious problem.

Ruth was all over the man, screaming at him for the rejection. Her mind was lost from the illness. Still thinking that Ed would never have turned her down, she was playing the bitch to the nth degree.

The man kept trying to gain control of the car. It was no use. Ruth climbed on him and slapped at his face. He grabbed Ruth with both his hands and threw her into the passenger seat. When he reached back for the wheel, they both saw the car approaching.

Ruth suddenly remembered the accident on the day they arrived in Arione. She screamed and tried to grab the steering wheel. Apologies flew from her mouth as she turned the wheel sharply to the right.

They missed the oncoming car, but when the man tried to turn the car to the left, they began to roll. The car turned upside down and tumbled twice. It stopped upside down, with no movement from either passenger. This was now the third tragedy in her life.

The man driving the other car quickly stopped his vehicle and got out. He ran to the battered mess that he had just avoided. Little did he know that his turn was coming. He should have just kept in his car and driven to his destination. But that wasn't in his nature. It wasn't like him to keep on moving. Not only would it have bothered him, he would have received a verbal lashing from his boss for not stopping. It was his job to see what had happened, why it had happened, who it had happened to, and where it had occurred. He never even thought about leaving this scene. How he would regret it later on.

Chapter 18

When Dan became conscious, he was standing erect. He remembered having fallen headfirst. He remembered feeling pain on his hands and chest when he tried to break his fall. There should be broken bones and bruises all over his body.

Where was he? How did his body heal? When did he heal? What the hell was going on? All of these questions had no answers, but he kept searching for them. He couldn't figure it out.

Dan didn't realize it, but there were more laughs and enjoyment at his expense in store for him in the sixth dimension. Apep didn't want a mutilated and broken victim who couldn't try to complete the maze. That was no fun! Where would the challenge be if his pawn couldn't surrender himself to the knowledge that he, Apep, Lord of the Sixth Dimension, wanted to see this subpar third-dimensional species try and fail over and over?

The mind was only superior if one utilized it to its full extent. Oh, yes! Apep was salivating from his thoughts. *This mere human will continue to give me my entertainment. He will not crack and will not break. Whenever he becomes injured, he will heal right away. Let him continue to wonder. Let him over evaluate each situation. There is nothing he will not contemplate to its fullest extent. He will not get it. The mind, baby, the mind.*

The Death Maze

Dan did know certain things. He knew Apep was watching. He knew he was being played with. He knew he wouldn't be able to get out of this world at this moment. He knew he would have to continue with the maze.

He lifted his head and turned it back and forth, hoping his neck wouldn't feel as stiff as it should. It wasn't, and he was thankful for that. He bent down to the floor and felt the knot in his back loosen.

When he rose from his bend, he saw two entrances. They hadn't been there a second ago. But this was the sixth dimension. Anything could be manipulated at any time. It was up to him to just play along until his death was deemed final.

He began studying the two entrances. He couldn't make up his mind about which to pass through. He thought back. His first choice, the right door, had been correct. That was one in his favor. His second choice, the center door, had not been correct. The score was one for him and one for the sixth dimension. But who was keeping score, really? Did it even make a difference?

Dan thought hard. He was beginning to understand that his choices really didn't make a difference. It wasn't that it was a fifty-fifty or one-in-three decision. The dimension was playing. It was enjoying his suffering. It grew on his suffering. No matter how hard he concentrated on a decision, it didn't make a difference. The dimension was the controller and he the controlled. No matter which entrance he chose, he was automatically the loser.

That was how he would continue on in this world. He would try to condition his mind so that he wouldn't care what the outcome would be. Dan knew he would ultimately lose. If he moved forward without a care, maybe the size of the dimension would shrink. If he stopped giving a damn, stopped thinking and analyzing, maybe this sixth dimension or world or whatever the hell it was would begin to grow back to its normal size.

He allowed his eyes to concentrate less on the two entrances as he approached them. He would just go through one of them without a thought.

Just do it, he thought. And then he heard it: a low hum. It tickled his right ear as he moved closer to the right entrance.

Then he heard it from behind him. He turned his head slowly and saw his home, with the neighbors standing around the front yard. It felt as if he was standing there too, that he could reach out and touch his home. Dan stopped thinking about the two entrances and began to move away from them.

"Hey," he shouted. "I'm over here."

Dan took a few steps toward his home. He took only three steps before he bumped into an invisible wall. He reached out and felt the wall. It extended the entire length and height of the room.

It couldn't be. It was so clear. It seemed as if he could actually speak to his neighbors. Up until that point, there had been some form or structural change in the makeup of a room when a barrier appeared. To be able to see straight through the barrier without anything else being altered made Dan irritated. It was like going to the zoo, with a thick glass partition keeping him from touching the animals. That's how he felt.

Then something did change, Dan was sure. As crystal clear as the image had been just a second ago, the image became even clearer. Like watching a regular digital television channel on a regular television set and then watching an

The Death Maze

HDTV. There were more pixels, more definition. Only he did not know exactly what had changed.

Dan moved slowly toward one of his neighbors. His movement was painstakingly structured so he would not bump into the wall. After three tiny steps, he remembered that he had bumped into the wall two steps ago. *What the hell is happening?* he thought. He was now beyond the wall and closer to another human than he had previously been.

He reached out to Buck Palmer from the Arione Motel. He was closest to Dan. The length of his reach actually went beyond Buck. No. It went through Buck. He saw his hand on the opposite side of Buck's right shoulder.

Dan retracted his arm. He couldn't believe what he was doing. He tried again, and this time his hand went through Buck's stomach. Dan recoiled in disgust and then thrust his arms out to try and shake Buck. He lost his footing and fell forward, and his entire body merged with Buck's and then moved beyond it.

Dan caught himself before falling to the ground, or what he thought would be the ground. He looked back at Buck as he heard him ask his wife where she thought Dan had disappeared to.

"Buck," Dan yelled. "I'm here! I'm in front of you!"

Nothing. Not even a wink of an eye. Buck just looked at his wife and said they needed to get back to the motel. Dan heard him say that two chemists from UCLA were staying at the motel and they needed to get the place cleaner than it already was.

"What are you talking about?" he hollered after them.

Then he sensed a change again, and his eyes quickly shifted around a room. He was in the police station. He saw Chief Dressler and Officer Bone. The chief was walking around the front while Officer Bone spoke on the phone.

"Chief! Oh, please, Richard. Can't you hear me?" Dan cried out, his frustration mounting. He jumped up and hit his head on the top of the area he was in, forgetting totally that the maze had shrunk when he made his first mistake. Dan was about five-ten, and the height of the maze was now only about six feet.

Then Dan saw something he had not seen before. He saw Chief Dressler stand and walk right toward him. The chief looked directly at him. He smiled. He laughed.

Bone then got up from his chair and stood next to his boss. He looked at the chief and then turned to face Dan and smiled. Then he laughed.

"What are you doing? What's going on?" Dan asked. He looked back behind him, but didn't see anything except the two entrances. He looked back at the two and grew upset. "What are you laughing at?" he screamed as they both walked right through Dan.

Dan turned his head and saw both of them walk out of the police station and disappear.

It was weird. It was depressing. It was a total mockery of his situation. Dan began to realize that this dimension overlooked, or overlapped, his world. He sat down and put his face in his hands and wiped some sweat off it.

He tried to calm down. He tried to get comfortable in his prison. He needed to bring himself back to his reality and push everything else out of his mind. He looked up and saw the empty police station and felt a change again.

This time his eyes immediately focused on the figure in the room. She was sleeping in the bed and having nightmares. Her face and hands were bandaged. The intravenous drip in her arm was steady and keeping her sedated. The pulse and heart monitor showed a continuous output of numbers and beeped at intervals.

"Ruth," Dan whispered. "Ruth, can you hear me?" Suddenly, another change occurred. He reached out his arm and felt the invisible wall. There were fewer pixels.

Ruth then started to talk. If anyone had been in the room with her, they would have thought she was crazy. She mumbled and then spoke clearly and then returned to incoherent gibberish.

"Dan, the wall isn't safe. Be secure. Don't stand," Ruth said, crying now. "You'll hit the ceiling. Ed wasn't in the car. I did it again." Ruth calmed down and stopped for a few moments before speaking again. "I hurt someone else. Why me? Oh God, why me?" Ruth fell asleep again.

Dan felt tears load up in his eyes. The first one fell, hitting his right cheek. He tried to think of what he had done to cause this to happen. He was happy with Ruth. His life was moving forward. They were so close that he was ready to take a step that he had never before contemplated. He knew Ruth was the one he could spend the rest of his life with. Why had this occurred?

"Dan," Ruth yelled, startling him. "Don't go through the door!"

"Ruth," Dan responded quickly, totally forgetting he couldn't be heard. "Wake up. Talk to me."

He threw his fists at the wall. He repeated his outburst and stood up. "Damn you!" he yelled at the sixth dimension. He began pounding his body against the wall. It felt good, and he did it again and again. His fit became a tantrum and he seriously tried to break the wall.

On the next thrust of his body, he fell forward through what was supposed to be the wall. Dan got up and went berserk. He began kicking at what was supposed to be the wall and throwing his body in all directions. He lunged from one side to the next. It didn't matter that he wasn't hitting anything. He wanted revenge.

Bouncing like a ball from side to side, Dan began to scream. He cursed at the sixth dimension and then at Apep. He made a 180-degree turn and kicked at the two entrances. Not realizing it, he went through the right entrance.

It was immediate. A tremor started and the room began to shake. Dan fell to the ground and tried to stand and get back through the entrance. He saw the maze begin to shrink and the ceiling begin to drop.

Reaching out and placing his hands on the floor, he steadied himself and willed his mind to calm down. He rose to his knees and crawled. As he tried to hurl himself through the entrance, he felt his left foot catch. Looking back, he saw the entrance break up and crumble as he kicked out his left leg and freed it of whatever was holding him back. He didn't realize this was an anomaly. Maybe he would think about it later.

Trying to stand once more, he saw the invisible wall begin to break. The image of Ruth crumbled. The pieces fell to a nothingness, disappearing before they hit the floor.

Looking up, he saw the left entrance begin to crumble as well. "WAIT!" Dan yelled, positioning his feet. The height of the ceiling was now about five feet, and he needed to bend his legs to stand. He lunged for the left entrance and cleared it before falling to the floor again. He looked back and saw the destruction of the entrance.

He was tired. Sweat poured from his face. Dan had done it again. He had let the sixth dimension get the better of his frustrations. He needed to stay calm. He shouldn't have displayed his emotions. He knew Apep thrived on his mistakes.

He sat down on the floor, knowing the height of this new room was about five feet. He had made another mistake and was now up to two. He didn't know where he was walking, jumping, thrusting out, crawling, and hurling himself. What he did know was that he was doing it and getting closer to his death.

Chapter 19

Apep was laughing hysterically, even though he was not allowing Dan to hear it just yet. He was amused and entertained beyond his original expectations. This man, Dr. Dan Adams, was superior in intellectual capacity but still couldn't figure it out. Apep was truly amazed he had gotten this far.

It had been a long time since he was able to feel such pleasure. The last time was Stanley Moser. He remembered the poor, simpleminded miner. It had been easier for Apep at that time, but disappointing. Stanley had given up after a couple attempts because he knew there was no way out. While waiting to die, Stanley stopped all movement and attempts to discern the maze. He hated games anyway and understood his demise was only a matter of time. He accepted it, believing it was the decision of a higher being. Apep decided to accelerate the process and let Stanley meet his fate.

Things had become so boring for Apep. He had originally arrived in the sixth dimension after his transformation from Earth's three-dimensional surface around 723 BC. Apep had lived in ancient Egypt. He had been the mystic leader to the king before Egypt was invaded by Nubia, its sister civilization to the south.

The Nubians had built a civilization to model that of Egypt. Having previously been invaded by Egypt, the Nubians

The Death Maze

had learned from their mistakes and eventually retaliated after Egypt experienced three hundred years of turmoil and political chaos. It was in 728 BC that Nubia saw its causes triumph and succeeded in the overthrow of Egypt. They then maintained Egyptian values and culture with a high degree of conservatism.

Apep was never able to adapt to the Nubians. He thought their hierarchy was incapable of understanding his mysticism and saw that they would eventually mark him an outcast. He needed to prepare for his departure. He was ready to accept his fate and was preparing for their judgment by making sure he outsmarted the Nubian king.

Apep had long ago studied and even worshipped the serpent. He kept many asps and snakes and used them to stockpile the poisons they could deliver with each treacherous bite. He thought that if he could become immune to the toxins in the venom, he could become a god.

At first there were trials. After working for years learning to handle the snakes, Apep began extracting the venom into small clay jars. He would take tiny, minute samples of the venom and ingest it with water. At first this would cause fever and chills mixed with violent stomach cramps. However, it was nothing that Apep wasn't willing to experience in order to meet his goal.

As soon as he was able to build a resistance toward the small amounts, he began taking larger portions of venom. Apep was drinking cupfuls within one year's time. His fits and bouts of high fever and chills grew shorter. The venom blended with the acids in his stomach and the stomach seizures subsided. His goal was to eventually make one of the asps bite him to see if he could handle the venom's immediate delivery to his system.

After two years of full experimentation, Apep was ready. With him were seven followers also ready to meet their fate in the new Nubian Egypt. These were individuals Apep easily controlled through his magic. These followers were relative idiots who idolized anything that would provide a better way of life. Before Apep found them, they didn't work, they begged for each day's meals, and they stole from anyone they could.

Now they were all living in the compound Apep called his home. Each had his own reason to succeed. They had been nothing during their time in Egypt. They all thought they would be put into slavery now that Nubia ruled. When Apep found them, they didn't question his motives, but only followed to what they thought would be a better life. How sorry they all eventually became when they realized where they were being led.

They surrounded a six-feet-deep by four-feet-wide hole that Apep had prepared for the final experiment. In a room lit only by a few candles, Apep sat in the middle of the hole with his legs folded. He was naked except for a loincloth around his waist. He had already put himself in a mystical state of meditation. His mind was nowhere near his body.

The large black asp was brought to Apep in a canvas sack. It was lowered into the hole by a thin rope. One of the disciples pulled the rope to open the sack.

At first there was little movement. Then the seven, looking down upon Apep and the sack, noticed movement from within the asp's enclosure. The head appeared. Apep didn't even notice. His body didn't flinch. He was actually watching the scene from about a mile above his seven followers. This was something the seven knew would occur.

The Death Maze

One looked up to see if he could spot Apep's image. Yeah, right!

The asp moved to reveal six inches of its body. Apep sat motionless. Then the asp moved again to show its full fifteen inches. Its movement seemed majestic. It stood upright, with ten inches of length facing Apep and five inches still on the ground.

It saw the motionless man before it. The large eyes glared, barely blinking, as it cautiously stopped to survey if it was in danger. It glided effortlessly to within a few inches of Apep's body. Not knowing what danger the asp was in or if the man would even move, the snake hissed. It became eager and ready to lunge toward the man's chest.

Then the image above the seven moved swiftly to its body. With a surprising spring and snap, Apep seized the asp with his right hand just below its head. The seven men jumped. The asp's mouth was brought to the space between his left thumb and forefinger. The snake clamped down and retracted, and Apep felt the venom enter his body.

Without a worry in the world, Apep stood and put the snake back into the sack. He snapped the fingers of his right hand as the rope was dropped from above. Apep tied the sack so the snake would not escape and sat back down away from the sack. He then meditated and left his body once again.

The entire episode had lasted only a few moments. Suddenly, Apep's body convulsed and shook. The seven watched; their leader appeared helpless and dying. They stood in awe when the body stopped moving altogether.

"Do we go into the hole and get the body?" one of them asked.

"We were ordered to leave the body," a second said.

"What about just getting the sack and removing it from the hole?" a third asked.

"Apep says to stay, watch, and do nothing," the fourth said.

"How long do we watch?" the first asked.

"As long as it takes," the fifth answered.

They stood and waited. After what felt like an eternity, they saw movement. The image above them had reentered the body. Another few minutes passed before Apep stood and greeted his followers. They bowed before their master.

"Come," Apep ordered. "We will prepare for the exit from Nubia. All of you must complete the same ordeal I have just exhibited. We will leave within one year."

They all stood up and just looked at each other. They had not known that what they had just witnessed was to be repeated by them. A couple of them began having second thoughts.

Chapter 20

*H*ome, he thought. What a lovely word. Had he taken advantage of where he lived? Did he treat others like he would want to be treated? Had he been unkind to anyone? Didn't he really live the way he felt he should without hurting others? Wasn't that right?

Dan tried to think rationally. He knew he needed to keep his emotions intact. The world he was now occupying could read everything about him. This was its *coup de grace!* Apep knew his suffering would be the end, and he lavished in knowing it.

What a great game he is playing, he thought sarcastically. Only this game was not a win-lose board novelty. It was life and death. And Dan didn't know what he had done to deserve this finality. How many more decisions would he have to make? Where would the end to the maze lead? He had now made two mistakes and the maze was currently only five feet tall.

Five! That was it! He remembered now. His question was answered by the relaxation of his mind and body. He savored the rest as he looked about the room he now inhabited. It was once more an empty space. Square in shape, it possessed four white walls. Four redundant, ridiculous, clean white walls with a ceiling above.

This was nothing new. Dan scanned the room over and over, knowing something would materialize that he hadn't seen at first. He just didn't know when it would arrive.

Soon, he thought. He knew it would be soon.

He heard a grumbling sound and looked around the room again. A few moments passed. Then he heard it again and looked down. He realized exactly what it was and felt relieved that it wasn't the sixth dimension.

He hadn't eaten a thing since he arrived in this hellhole. When was that? How many hours had he been incarcerated in this life-ending game?

"Hey!" he called out. "Apep!" Dan yelled a bit louder.

Dan waited for some response but received none. Looking once again around the room, he saw a tray in one corner. Dan stood, making sure not to hit his head, and walked hunched over to the tray.

When he reached the tray, there was nothing on it. Within the time it takes to blink, a large plate appeared. Soon a club sandwich materialized.

He sat down on the floor. A large glass appeared, but it was empty. As he looked into it, it filled up with a clear liquid. When the liquid reached the top of the glass, Dan stuck his finger into it. He lifted his finger to his mouth and tasted the liquid.

Simple water, he thought. *What else could it be?*

This place wasn't going to poison him. Not yet. It needed him. It needed the continued entertainment of this simpleminded, three-dimensional human being. Although Dan had never thought of himself as simple. He brought himself back to the present and saw a piece of berry pie on a plate next to the club sandwich.

Oh, yes. Now he understood fully. There was no reason to poison him. That wasn't in the rules of the game. A one-way contract had been made, and he had not yet completed his five *faux pas*. Apep wasn't finished with him yet. He needed to keep him replenished so he could continue with his demise.

In other words, if Dan needed to eat, there would be food. If he was thirsty, there would be drink. If he needed to relieve himself, would a toilet appear? What about sex? What if he wanted a passionate and intimate physical encounter?

"Nope!" Dan mumbled out loud. "Not part of the maze." That was not required to keep one alive and thus not needed to sustain the balance of his journey. Besides, the last thing Dan needed was to be the subject of someone or something else's voyeurism.

Dan looked at the meal before him and decided to eat. He would enjoy and savor the meal. He picked up a section of the sandwich and took a bite.

He chewed slowly and purposefully, relishing each morsel. He tried to think of two things at once. If Apep could read his mind, he wanted to split his thoughts between the food and his next move. Dan sank his teeth into the sandwich, swallowed, and took a drink of water while moving his eyes in the area he could see.

Another bite and more chewing. He closed his eyes for a moment, opened them, and searched from left to right while thinking over his previous moves. Taking another drink of water, he slowly swallowed the liquid, letting the coolness fall down his throat.

After the sandwich was finished, he picked up the piece of pie and took a bite. Then more water and another bite of pie. He picked up the water glass once more and noticed it was again filled to the top. He almost spilled some, not realizing that as long as he needed to drink, the glass would be filled. It was calculating and smart. Dan continued to feel off balance no matter how hard he tried to outsmart Apep.

When he had finished eating, Dan looked to the ceiling and sighed. Although his stomach was relieved, his mind was not. He couldn't think of one thing he had done to put himself in this situation. What wrong could he possibly have committed to put himself in this dreadful world? Why would he be chosen to be sacrificed? One thing was sure. Before he was to die, he was going to demand that answers be given to him. Although Apep was no moral entity, he surely could supply some answers.

Dan lifted his eyes once more and saw blurred images coming into view. They became sharp and defined, and he saw that they were two large screens with a button in front of each. They seemed solid in mass.

He crawled closer to the left one and tried to touch it. Just as his finger was about to come in contact with the screen, it bent to avoid him. Doing this a second time only gave him the same outcome.

He remembered the first room he was in. The walls. They also contracted. He didn't understand then and he certainly didn't comprehend now why he could not touch these items.

"Why are you doing this to me?" he yelled. There was no response. "APEP!" Dan screamed. "Why don't you show yourself and confront me face to face? What kind of man are you?" *Probably not a man*, he thought.

Dan looked behind the screens. There were no wires or input cords.

He quickly reached out his arm to touch the back of one of the screens. His hand went through it. He retracted his hand, wondering why it had not bent this time. He knew it was just another avenue of the maze. It continued to puzzle him and put him off guard.

Dan then realized that he could probably die and be brought back to life. He was sure he was the new toy for this

The Death Maze

world. Why not just continue to be the entertainment for as long as they wanted?

He pictured himself with marionette strings attached to his head, arms, and legs. The strings dangled from unmentionable heights with no view of who controlled them. When they needed him to move to the left, the strings were adjusted and he did their bidding. Wasn't that his life at this moment?

No, he thought again. *Because if they controlled all my movements, it wouldn't be any fun.* Apep wanted the advantage, but also required some aspect of choice. Even though it all played toward the same morbid outcome, Apep wanted to add a little "free will" to the mixture.

Life did not exist here as it did on Earth. Dan surmised that maybe he was even on another planet.

No. Not another planet, but another dimension.

The hair on the back of Dan's neck began to stand up. He felt that something was about to change. He heard a low, growing hum.

Another vision of my home about to materialize? he asked himself.

No! It sounded like a fly was in the room. His eyes moved back and forth, searching for it. Actually, he was hoping it was a fly. That would give him a sign that maybe he could get out of the maze. If a fly could get in, he could certainly get out.

As his eyes searched each stitch of the room, Dan couldn't find even the smallest hint of abnormality. He hoped that maybe there was something that would allow the tiniest of insects to invade the dimension.

Then the hum stopped. Dan stopped his movements also, with the exception of his roaming eyes. The only noise he now heard was the pounding of his heart.

The hum returned. Only now it seemed as if it were moving around him. Dan kept still and waited. His ego was thinking *please be a fly*, while his alter ego was thinking *what game are they playing now?*

Dan threw out his hands and clapped them together just in front of his nose. The noise ceased immediately. Dan kept still for an extra moment and then slowly opened his hands.

Fly? he thought, his eyebrows raised. *No fly*, he concluded when he was able to see nothing inside his palms.

Then the hum continued, growing in pitch. Dan looked at both screens and thought the hum might be originating from one or both of them. With his knees firmly on the floor, Dan closed in on the screens. As his face was about to touch the right screen, he heard the hum coming from behind him.

It grew again in loudness and pitch. The hum continued to grow until Dan had to put his hands over his ears to save himself from the uncomfortable, annoying sound. It felt as if it were moving beyond his hands and into his ears, where it began pounding and vibrating.

Unable to take the pain any longer, Dan let out a scream, hoping it would stop.

"Apep! Damn you!" He fell backward and writhed. He tried bending the outer portion of his ear over the auditory canal in the hope that it would muffle the sound. The pain was excruciating, and he was sure his eardrums would break.

"YOU COWARDLY BASTARD!" He just knew the bleeding would start at any moment.

Again the noise grew, and he screamed out one more time. The knife was cutting a thin line in his head. Dan thought he would black out.

The Death Maze

It stopped, and Dan fell forward. He didn't move.

The noise was gone and his face was literally on the floor. Sweat covered his upper torso. The plate and glass had disappeared from the room, but the screens were in the exact same position.

Dan didn't know what to think. The room was absolutely silent. He sat up and felt the sweat dripping from his face. He wanted to scream once more, but wasn't sure there would be noise. He opened his mouth. Nothing came out.

DAMN YOU were the words he wanted to form, but there was no sound.

"DAMN YOU, APEP," he finally screamed. Under his breath, Dan said, "You son of a bitch," and heard every word. He coughed and heard that noise as well.

He took his lab coat sleeve and wiped the sweat from his face. He had relaxed enough to release all his tensions.

Looking around the room once more, he remembered that he was in this small white area and there were two screens with a button before each.

Prior to deciding which button to press, he looked around the room for what he felt was the umpteenth time, hoping there was some opening for him to crawl through. The screens could be a trick. They could be a diversion just like the hum. He needed to think.

"Come on, Dan," he said in a low voice, relieved that he could hear himself speak. "Get a hold of yourself."

He was sure this was his next choice. He knew the room was free of anything else. "Please. Dear God, help me," Dan muttered, looking at the screens.

At that moment, the word NO appeared on the left screen and the word WAY appeared on the right.

"What's that supposed to mean?" Dan called out.

125

No response. Nothing else on the screens and nothing in the air.

The words disappeared from the screens, and Dan realized he had said something that caused a ripple within the maze. It was the first time he had gotten a response.

"What's the matter, Apep? Don't believe in God?" Dan called out, waiting for another response.

CHOOSE, the left screen ordered. CHOOSE, the right screen mimicked. CHOOSE, CHOOSE, CHOOSE, CHOOSE. Back and forth the screens blinked as the words grew to cover both screens.

Dan began to laugh, knowing he had hit a vein. He laughed harder and more loudly. He could hear a thud with each blinking of the word CHOOSE.

His taunts had finally caused a reaction within the sixth dimension, which warranted some feeling of success. Dan was about to speak again when he felt a small tremor. The room then began to shake harder.

"Wait!" Dan said. "I haven't chosen."

The screens were still blinking when Dan rushed to them and pressed the right button. The room stopped shaking and became silent again. However, nothing else happened.

Dan quickly looked around the room, thinking there might now be an entrance for him to move through. He pressed the right button once more and knew it was a mistake. His newfound hope faltered as the tremors started again, more violently this time.

He felt he had been deceived. He knew the rules had changed. He understood what the consequences would be of taking on the ire of the sixth dimension and Apep. He had pressed the right button knowing it was the correct choice.

The Death Maze

The room now started to shrink, and Dan knew he had to press the left button in order to move forward in the maze. He also knew that there was now no way out. He had no choice but to resign himself to his death and continue to play. His choices would no longer mean a thing. And he didn't care.

The left screen shook violently before revealing an opening in the middle. Dan lifted himself to the opening and crawled through. He didn't rush and didn't care if a part of his body got caught. If something broke, he knew Apep would fix it.

Before his body was completely through the hole, the room reduced itself to only four feet in height. This was the new norm. Dan had now made three mistakes, but he brushed this thought aside. He knew that he would play this to the end. He could still respect himself for finishing.

Chapter 21

During the period of adjustment after Nubia took over the Egyptian lands, anything and everything that had a correlation to "bad times" was blamed on the serpent. It was the serpent that caused earthquakes, because it was able to slither into the cracks and crevices of the land and move throughout the underground. It was the serpent that caused droughts, since it moved about the fields and disturbed the nutrients in the land. It was even the serpent that caused eclipses, although no one was ever able to explain the reasons why. It was just because, and it was because of the serpents.

Anything evil that occurred was blamed on "their" Apep, the god of evil. That was why Apep took his name and allowed the mystical rumors about him to continue after the Nubians conquered Egypt. If he was to lift himself into the upper echelons of the Nubian royalty, he felt he needed to be intimidating and feared. If he wanted to be respected within his current surroundings, he would let their fears surround the mysteries of his existence and exacerbate the rumors.

Wherever Apep walked, his seven followers increased their intimidations. In an area where many would congregate, a path would always open when Apep showed up. His mere appearance caused children to cower behind their parents.

The Death Maze

Women covered their eyes in the hope that he would not look in their direction. Shop owners prayed that Apep would not covet their businesses and cause others to stay away.

The small entourage of seven learned quickly that their master could cause the strong to become weak. On one occasion, Apep was walking through an emporium of open vendors when he came upon two large guards who had been following him. Apep was wearing his traditional black robe and hood with a beige front and black spots. He had made a slight gesture to a woman whose covered face inspired him. Fearing for her well-being, she ran off as the guards moved in to block him.

"You are to leave the premises, Apep," the first guard ordered.

"And what was my crime?" Apep asked.

"Your presence causes fear," the first guard explained.

"Assault on that woman could be construed as the crime," the second guard announced.

"I did nothing of the kind," Apep replied.

"I am witness to the lifting of your fist toward a citizen of Nubia," the second guard continued.

The seven followers soon surrounded the two guards. Apep lifted his covered right arm, which caused the seven to hold their places. He was in control.

The second guard watched the seven as the first took a step closer to Apep. He was feeling extremely powerful at the moment and wanted the chance to drive his sword through Apep's stomach. As the guard's right arm crossed his chest and reached for his sword, Apep moved forward and stood face to face with him.

"Feeling a bit of excess masculinity, my dear fellow?" Apep whispered as he withdrew the hood from his head. He revealed a completely bald head covered in blackened scales with a few beige spots over the black, making him look like the evil serpent himself.

The crowd gasped and stepped away from this madman. They did not want to be any closer than they needed in case something drastic happened.

"I suggest you look into my eyes and see how your feeble display may play out should you indeed lay a hand on me," Apep continued.

The guard, feeling even stronger, did look into his eyes. They were a bright, piercing red. Deep within the dark pupils, the guard saw an image of himself burning, his face melting away.

He then saw Apep's tongue slither from his mouth. It was long, thin, and split down the middle in the shape of an open V. The tip shook at the guard and then recoiled back into Apep's mouth.

The guard realized that he had just relieved himself. He looked down and saw the dripping of urine. The small puddle around his feet caused him to shudder further, and then he stiffened and felt frozen from fright. Apep stepped closer to the guard.

"I suggest you be the one to depart this emporium and allow me to continue on with my business," Apep ordered in a soft, malicious tone.

Hearing only the word *depart*, the guard slowly looked to his partner. Without saying a word, he began walking hesitantly and then ran out of the area. His partner followed before the seven took it upon themselves to do as Apep ordered. There were loud laughs and grunts from the seven. There was only silence from the people in the crowd as they tried to go back to their work and avoid the unwanted.

The Death Maze

It wasn't the first time this had occurred. However, it was the premiere of the new Apep and followers. They had been working diligently to become what their master ordered. The sickness and pain had long been overcome. The deathlike feelings had dissipated into the aura of the invincible. All seven were fully ready to give their souls to the one all hated and despised. The power of Apep could, in due time, be transferred to any one of them. And all seven were maligned enough to believe that their evil would live forever.

Apep was even working on completing his transformation from God of Evil to God of All. Had he taken off his robe in the emporium, he would have revealed black scales tattooed over his entire back, cream scales with black spots tattooed over his chest and belly, and fingernails and toenails painted black. Had he opened his mouth, he would have revealed two sharp incisors that injected poison upon contact.

Apep had no other goal than to be fully transformed into a venomous serpent that Nubians would one day bow down to. He felt it was only a matter of time before the populace came to him to solve all their problems. Look at how they had parted when he arrived in the courtyards.

His notoriety was, however, becoming more than worrisome to the Nubian hierarchy. While the main population was afraid of him, the royalty knew better. They knew his background. They understood his evil mind and what he had set out to conquer. After one too many incidents with the peaceful Nubian populace, they knew Apep had to be destroyed. If he were allowed to continue, it could be the end of Nubia, since he was threatening the strength of the royal family. Over many late evenings, a plan was finally set in stone. It was decisive and to be implemented in three stages.

The first stage involved the deepest dungeon in the Nubian jail. A large hole would be dug of more than twenty feet in depth and ten feet in diameter. In one section approximately five feet from the top, there would be a wooden enclosure. Within the enclosure would be placed the deadliest of creatures, including scorpions and cobras.

Above would be an area for the Nubian guards to view the enclosure and to open it from the bottom sections. This would be completed with long poles hooked to two bottom pulleys at the five-foot level. The poles would only need to be pushed or pulled from one side to the other. The enclosure would also need to be hidden at first. This way, Apep and his followers would not know of the outcome until the wooden apparatus was in place.

The second stage involved the capture of Apep and his tribe. This was to be completed within one day after the enclosure was tested and ready. Fifty of the most loyal, trusted, and strongest soldiers of the Nubian army would surround Apep's complex. They would be in groups of five with one final group of fifteen. Each group of five would be enough to take on one of the seven followers. It was thought that fifteen men would be enough to capture Apep, since no one had ever really seen him in battle. The soldiers would wear thick leather arm coverings in case anyone decided to try to bite. Also required was the standard armor.

Once they were captured, stage three would be their elimination. Each captive would be either lowered or dropped into the twenty-foot hole. No one seemed to care. If anyone caused delays or problems, dropping them into the hole, via a brief pushing, would be the preferred beginning of the end. They were misanthropes as far as the Nubian

The Death Maze

hierarchy was concerned. They needed to rid their peaceful society of these outcasts.

After these notorious eight men were in the hole, the wooden enclosure would be pulled across the opening. After a few moments the poles would be in place and the scorpions, cobras, and other deadly creatures would be dropped on top of the men. How long would it be before they all died? No one knew. And no one thought twice about it.

Stage one took the better part of two full days to complete. Many prisoners were used to dig the hole so none of them could later talk about what they had dug. They used large wooden ladders to bring up excess dirt, which was scattered in another section of the prison.

In another area of the prison, other inmates were selected to build the large wooden enclosure. This would be ten feet in diameter and two feet in height. The men chosen to put the enclosure into place needed to be strong and resilient, as the enclosure would eventually need to be turned 180 degrees.

The second stage took seven lunar days to put together. The guards were selected for their strength and quickness as well as their ability to resist intimidation. They were told that failure was not an option, and a month of extra wages would be given for total success.

Stage two began well after the sun went down. The fifty guards surrounded Apep's small complex without being noticed. Since no one ever showed up at his door without prior arrangements, Apep did not expect to receive such company.

The soldiers scaled the walls in groups of five. The last fifteen, also in groups of five, entered only after they had confirmation that the other thirty-five men had been successful. For extra security purposes, twenty other men had been chosen to wait around the complex in case anyone escaped.

Once inside, the thirty-five men found all seven of Apep's entourage. Their hands were tied, their mouths were secured shut, and their heads were covered with hoods so they would not know where they were to be led. The operation went without a flaw.

Now the final fifteen needed to locate Apep. He slept in an area away from the others. Although it wasn't hard to find this area, the first two guards who entered were confronted with four large snakes. This was Apep's way of saying that in order for him to be captured, many had to die.

The snakes were no match for these men, who had no fear. With swords drawn and ready, additional guards entered the room and hacked the snakes into many pieces.

After walking through the foyer of Apep's sleeping area and reaching the curtain to his room, the guards confronted the mystical sorcerer. He stood erect, his body fully tattooed. It was like seeing a six-foot-tall viper. Every inch of his body had the look of death. He seemed to be ready and wanting to strike, having just witnessed the death of his four slithering pets.

"You require that many to take me into your hands?" he asked.

The first guard only nodded. "More are ready to assist should you fail to come with us."

"I congratulate you for your fine work," Apep said and walked toward the first guard.

With his sword stretched out, the second guard stopped Apep from continuing. "You are to refrain from further approach, Apep," he ordered. "You will hold out your hands."

The Death Maze

"As you wish," Apep responded. He brought his hands in front of his body.

The five guards surrounded Apep as an additional five entered. It was easy to see that Apep would not strike out or try to talk his way out of their intended goal. He was blindfolded and gagged, the sharp incisors in his mouth rendered useless. They put a hood over his head and led him out the door.

Stage two was successfully completed well before the next sun rose in the sky. No one would know of the capture of this hideous monstrosity until the morning, and by then it would all be over. Not an innocent soul would ever have to fear this man-thing again.

The eight were brought to the prison area, where they were led deep into the structure and down into its caverns. One by one, their hoods were removed and their hands untied. Their mouths were kept covered for obvious reasons, and they were ordered not to use their own freed hands to remove the gags.

They were lowered to the bottom of the pit. After all eight were within their confines, they were permitted to remove the gags. They looked up and wondered what their fate would be. They watched as the large wooden enclosure was secured fifteen feet above them. They saw the poles inserted into the sides and the enclosure rotate 180 degrees. They saw the many guards watching over them.

"Now that you have us," Apep said in a low, commanding voice, "what do you intend to do next?"

The main guard spoke. "We are to now wait for the morning, Apep. As of this moment, the Nubian king is being notified of your capture."

"And what will occur in the morning?" Apep asked, almost knowing what the answer would be.

135

"Your death sentence will be carried out," the guard informed him.

"And what are our crimes?" he dutifully asked, assured that the other seven were scared to death and did not understand the scope of their crimes.

"Your group, ordered by you, has intimidated the population of the kingdom of Nubia. You have instigated unprovoked acts on the female gender. You lead your group to steal for their existence. For this, all of you will face your death."

All seven looked at Apep as if he were now the devil incarnate. Although they followed him, they were really the lowest forms of intellect in all of Nubia. How could they not know what they were doing? How did they let this creature wrap himself into their lives? They had let Apep manipulate every second of every day since he supposedly rescued them from the streets.

They looked at each other to see what they had become. They truly were hideous figures.

"Do I not get my due process? My chance to rebut these charges?" Apep almost yelled.

"It has been decreed. You have been sentenced," the guard declared before walking away.

All but four guards left when the final words were spoken. Only a few more hours before daylight, and the world would be rid of eight pieces of scum.

At the bottom of the hole, Apep was the only one still standing. The others had grown tired and sat down on the cold ground. He looked up at the enclosure and saw the different openings that revealed the top of the hole. He could see the four guards watching over them.

"I don't suppose any of you realize the advantage you have right now," Apep said in a low voice to his motley group.

One of them immediately looked up at Apep. "I'm not sure I understand what you mean, Master."

Apep moved closer to the group. He now had their attention. "No matter what they intend to do to us, we are the ones with the upper hand."

"How is that, Master?" a second whispered.

"Look at where we are," Apep instructed.

They all looked up to the opening of the hole after Apep's remark.

"Don't you realize that what I've been teaching you now has validity? We are in a position of impending immortality." Apep's eyes grew with his enthusiasm. "We can cross into a new world and live forever without cause or effect. We will be able to move into any realm without thought or reason. By using our minds, we will be able to conquer any circumstance. We may not be in this world, but we will be of this world. We will exist without the knowledge of this world."

They didn't understand, but they saw his emotion and felt good again. Maybe this was what they had been preparing for all along. No longer would they be perceived as the lowest of human forms. Now they needed to know more.

"Apep, my master," a third follower said. "Tell us what we need to do before they come back."

"Oh yes, Master," a fourth chimed in. "Prepare us for immortality."

He knew he had them once more. They had shifted in their places to listen intensely to every word he was about to utter. Each morsel of speech would be a full meal as the words fell into place.

Apep instructed them for the next hour. The guards looked down into the hole and saw the group in conversation, but dismissed it simply as last-minute prayers. They went back to their idle gossip and boredom.

***

Sunlight appeared in the city of Nubia, but no one in the prisons knew this except for the many guards who now entered the prison area housing Apep and his men. The fifty guards surrounded the pit. The Nubian royalty had issued its final proclamation: Apep and his men were to be executed immediately.

The guards looked into the pit and called out for Apep. Two guards stood at each pole, ready to open the enclosure doors.

"Do you have anything you wish to say, Apep?" the lead guard asked.

Apep looked up and shook his head. The others didn't move. They were sitting and meditating. Their bodies were in the pit, but their minds were floating above it. All were actually looking down at the guards looking down at the prisoners.

"We are ready," Apep commanded. He immediately went back into his meditative state.

A Nubian prince entered the prison to be the witness for his family and country. He gave the orders. The guards manning the poles pulled them to open the enclosures.

Hundreds of deadly scorpions, asps, vipers, and spiders dropped onto Apep and his men. In no time, all the guards could see were crawling and slithering objects. Some of the snakes struck at the scorpions. Some of the scorpions tried to grab the spiders. The guards were surprised that not one scream or yell could be heard.

The Death Maze

A loud boom then shook the deep hole. Some of the guards ran, thinking the prison would collapse.

"HALT!" the lead guard ordered.

The men stopped in their places and returned to the hole. When they looked into the pit, it was empty. There was no sign that anything had even been in the hole. The enclosure was also gone.

"What do you think has happened?" the Nubian prince asked.

"I am not sure, Your Highness," the lead guard replied.

"And what do I tell my father, the king?"

"Tell him that they have been extinguished and are no longer able to intimidate the Nubian people."

The Nubian prince left the prison escorted by a guard for his safety. The lead guard grew nervous. He knew that Apep and his men were gone. He was able to conclude that they would never harm anyone in their city ever again. What bothered him most was the hole. It was cursed and needed to go away.

"I want every able prisoner to immediately fill up this hole. I want it so that no one will ever know a hole was here."

Chapter 22

Chief Dressler and Dr. Shirley Anderson were speeding north on I-40 toward Arione when they saw the overturned car. They couldn't believe it. How many times would this have to occur in order for it to stop? Ruth had experienced more than her fair share of accidents and bad luck.

A man was trying to wave down passing vehicles, but it seemed that no one wanted to involve themselves with an accident. The many vehicles that had slowed only did so to get a good look. They were the normal "lookey-loos" of a society that prided itself on reality TV and as much gore and hype as it could get. No one wanted to get their hands dirty and have their lives interrupted with inquiries from officials. Society had really become pitiful in the twenty-first century. A car slowed and the man tried to run up to it and plead for help, but the car sped away.

"Ass," the man yelled.

Then he saw the police vehicle with its flashing lights approach. Dressler slowed his car, and the man ran back to the wreck to try to help its two victims. Dr. Anderson quickly got out of the car while Dressler radioed for an ambulance. It was only a minute before Dressler exited the car and ran to help.

"Help me get her out of the car," Dr. Anderson ordered the stranger.

"What about the man?"

"One at a time, okay?" Shirley told him. "Besides, here comes the chief. He'll start on the man. Be careful with her arms."

They moved Ruth as gently as possible while extricating her from the car through the passenger door. They then carried her behind the police vehicle and to safety in case the wrecked car blew up.

Dressler was working on the man when he saw the first of the flames. He was having trouble because the man was wrapped around the seat belt and wedged in by the air bag. He ran around the passenger side and got into the car. He took out his pocket knife and punctured a hole in the airbag. Then, shoving the man against the driver's door, he pushed down on the seat belt buckle and loosened it. Running back to the driver's side, he was now able to open the car door, get his arms around the man's torso, and drag him out of the car.

The Good Samaritan ran to help Chief Dressler pick up the unconscious, injured man and carry him away from the wreck. As they set him down next to Ruth, they heard a spark snap and the car explode. They were all lucky to be behind the police vehicle. Dressler and the stranger stood up to look at the burning car.

Leaning back down, Dressler looked at Shirley Anderson. "Too many close calls as far as I'm concerned, Doc."

"At least they're safe, Chief," Shirley said.

"Not many people willing to help out," the chief said to the mystery man. "Thank you. Name's Dressler."

"Well, I guess I'm not like many people, Chief. William Barrish!"

"How's Ruth, Doc? She going to make it?" Dressler asked.

"She's not hurt that badly, Chief. The only reason she escaped further harm is because she's so groggy and loaded down with pills. Her body was totally limber at the time of the accident in spite of the fact that she knew it was happening."

"What about this poor man?" Dressler asked.

"I'm afraid he's not doing well. He's unconscious and bleeding from the mouth and ears. I need that ambulance here right now. Not sure how much internal bleeding he has."

At that moment they heard the siren of the ambulance in the distance. Chief Dressler opened the trunk of his car and brought out three emergency orange cones and two orange flags. He placed the cones five, fifteen, and twenty-five feet behind his car and used the flags to wave the passing vehicles.

William Barrish walked up to Chief Dressler. He was curious and needed some answers. He should have kept his mouth shut.

"What happened in the first place, Chief?"

"The lady walked out of the hospital without being released by her doctor and was picked up at the gas station across the street. Poor jerk must have been crazy to give her a ride. He should have known she was sick since she was sweating so badly."

"I guess he wasn't that observant. How did she get out of the hospital without a release? She just walked out?"

It was one question too many for Dressler. He became uneasy. "Who did you say you were?"

"William Barrish, Chief. I'm a reporter with the *Los Angeles News*." Barrish reached in his pocket and pulled out a business card.

Dressler looked at the card and mumbled the name to himself. He didn't have all the information he wanted right now and certainly didn't need this in the paper. Ruth skipping out of the hospital could lead to questions about Dan. As far as Chief Dressler was concerned, that was not going to happen.

"Look, Mr. Barrish. I don't want this in the paper just yet and would prefer if you could hold the story until I get more answers and then give those answers to you."

"I don't understand, Chief. This is news. No matter how small the story, it still presents itself to be written and told."

"You have to have answers before it can be told, Mr. Barrish. I would consider it professional courtesy to refrain until your questions can be answered. Understand?" Dressler was getting riled up and didn't need to show his full anger to this man just yet.

Shirley wanted to interrupt and shut Dressler up, but she was more concerned about keeping Ruth and the unidentified man warm. She had already taken off her hospital jacket and put it over Ruth. She needed another covering. She rushed to the back of the police vehicle and searched for a blanket.

The ambulance stopped. Two attendants got out and unloaded stretchers. They loaded Ruth and the man into the ambulance. Without a minute to lose, Shirley climbed into the back of the ambulance. Before she closed the door, she hollered back at William Barrish and thanked him for helping.

"No problem," he answered. He made a mental note to get in touch with her later on.

The ambulance was gone within five minutes of arriving and headed back to the hospital. Just Chief Dressler and William Barrish remained. Chief Dressler felt he needed to be a bit cooler in the head and not show his anger. It had never entered his mind that something or someone might interfere with him dealing with his towns. He needed to make sure that did not happen; he felt his veracity should never be questioned.

Barrish, on the other hand, knew to keep quiet. What he thought was just a routine traffic accident had all of a sudden blossomed into something he did not understand yet. He felt Chief Dressler's personality had all of sudden changed when he asked his questions. He thought they were routine questions. He hadn't delved into any private matters because his was actually the second car involved. Chief Dressler hadn't even asked how he had become a part of this yet. William Barrish knew that would eventually be brought out into the open. He needed to keep his mind alert and be ready for anything out of the ordinary. He was still a few hours away from his home turf. Playing it safe would be his motto until he had more information. And he also knew that if he played his cards correctly, he'd get the entire story from either Chief Dressler or Dr. Shirley Anderson.

"Did you happen to see how the accident occurred, Mr. Barrish?" Dressler asked as he approached the reporter.

Think quickly, Will, Barrish said to himself. *Don't lie, and don't make him think you're hiding something.*

"I'll be honest with you, Chief," William said, knowing other questions would come. "My car was traveling in the opposite direction when I saw the oncoming car swerving on the highway. I had to avoid a collision."

"How fast were you driving?"

"Just the speed limit, Chief."

Something was not right, at least to Chief Richard Dressler and his instincts. He knew the reporter's story of how he became a part of the wreck was true. Whoever picked up Ruth was just a poor son of a bitch who was at the wrong place at the wrong time. But Barrish was stalling for time. The chief had a feeling this LA reporter could outsmart a "small-time cop," which he was not. And he felt Mr. Barrish could eke out a bigger story from someone not as seasoned as he. It was the bigger story that worried the chief. He needed to keep Barrish off guard.

"I'd like for you to follow me back to town, Mr. Barrish. Please get back into your car and follow me."

"And the reasons for me being asked to do this, Chief?"

"I'd like you to fill out a report. I have an overturned car over there that has obviously exploded. You are my eyewitness. A report is routine. Any other questions, Mr. Barrish?"

"None, Chief. Lead the way."

Chief Dressler got into his squad car and picked up the radio. After getting a hold of Bone, he ordered him to get a tow truck and have the car taken off the highway right away. Bone would need to be with the truck to keep traffic moving. He also wanted Bone to contact the CHP to assist. He would keep traffic moving until Bone arrived. He got out of his car and walked to the cones; he would adjust their position now that he was moving his car. He set them toward the side since the overturned car was off the highway. He knew Bone would pick them up after the accident was cleared.

William Barrish entered his car and waited. He had already decided he would stay in town and find out everything that the chief was hiding. He pulled out a map and looked at his whereabouts. He was near two small towns, Arione and Vera, which were both nestled west of Needles. Now he had to find a motel and call his boss. However, he did not want Chief Dressler to see him on his cell phone.

William Barrish put the key in the ignition and turned over the motor. Purposefully keeping the car in park and idling, he turned on the car radio and rolled down the window while waiting for the chief to move his vehicle. He figured Chief Dressler would see him, and that listening to the radio would calm the chief into thinking he had other ideas.

William Barrish then took his cell phone from the seat of his car and dialed his own number. Looking toward Chief Dressler, he answered the vibrating phone and then left the following message:

"Driving west on I-40, avoided accident between Arione and Vera, California. Two injured and taken to the hospital. Car exploded. Need to find out names. Assisted the police. Chief's name is Dressler. A doctor's name is Anderson. Told to keep my mouth shut by the doctor. Don't know why! I'm instructed to follow the police to fill out a report. Waiting to do so. What I know is that the woman in the accident exited the hospital without being released. What I don't know is why, and why Dressler and Anderson are hush-hush about this woman. Out."

William then closed his cell phone and waited for the chief. Soon, two CHP motorcycles, another police car from Arione, and a tow truck with a long bed arrived. He saw the chief talk to the officer in the car and then walk to his vehicle. The other officer got out of his car and spoke to the CHP cops while the tow truck driver worked to get the car on the long bed.

When Chief Dressler got into his patrol car, William Barrish put his car in drive and followed him. He figured it would only take a few minutes to get to the station and file a report. He would then find a place to stay for a day or so. He was wrong.

Chapter 23

Bone waited with the two CHP officers as the tow truck operator lifted the mashed vehicle onto the long bed. The two officers were directing traffic to keep it moving even though there wasn't an excess amount of traffic. It took a little over an hour for the truck operator to clean up the mess and sweep the highway before leaving.

Bone had already taken plenty of pictures as directed by Chief Dressler. He thanked the CHP officers. Chief Dressler always kept the highway between Arione and Vera clean, and they always appreciated any help from the local jurisdiction.

However, Bone needed to get back to the Adams house. He was expecting the two chemists from UCLA and didn't want to miss them. Driving quickly but safely, he arrived at the house within a few minutes. It was perfect timing, because as he got out of his patrol car, a second car approached. A man and woman got out of the car and stretched.

"Long drive?" Bone asked.

"Not too bad," the man said. "I'm Dr. Theodore Ryan."

Bone reached out to shake his hand. "I'm Officer Johnson. You can call me Bone. Everyone does."

"Bone?" the woman asked, getting out of the car. "You must have always been thin!" She chuckled. "I'm Dr. Allyson Rayburn."

Dr. Theodore Ryan was six feet tall and balding, and carried a few extra pounds. Although not too enthused about coming out to Arione, he did it for Allyson. He had worked with her for ten years. Even though he was married with three kids, he was waiting for any chance he could to get extra time with Allyson.

Allyson Rayburn was a beautiful, voluptuous redhead, slender and definitely one to do all the right things to keep her shape. She never allowed business to interfere with her private life, and never got involved with others at work. Dr. Theodore Ryan didn't have a chance. She knew her coworker was married and wouldn't even think about being the other woman. She had her share of dates, but always knew there was only one person who could take her breath away.

"Pleased to meet both of you," Bone answered. "And yes, I've always been thin. Chief Dressler gave me the nickname and it kind of stuck."

"Is the chief in the house?" Dr. Ryan asked.

"No, sir. But I'll call him on the radio right now. He's expecting to hear from me as soon as you arrive."

"Thank you, Officer Bone," Dr. Rayburn said.

Bone walked back to his car and picked up the radio.

"Hey, Chief?"

"Yeah, Bone. What is it?"

"Doctors Ryan and Rayburn have arrived."

"Take them to the motel and get a couple rooms. I know the Palmers are expecting them. Show them where the restaurant is and inform them that I'll speak with them tomorrow morning over breakfast around eight."

"What about the house?"

"They're probably tired, Bone. Check to make sure the house is secured and take the rest of the day off."

"You sure, Chief?"

"I'm sure, Bone. I'm at the station and all is okay here. See you tomorrow morning as well. Out."

Bone walked over to Drs. Ryan and Rayburn. He explained that the chief was busy and asked them to meet him tomorrow morning over breakfast. He said he would show them to the motel and restaurant and asked if it was okay to start tomorrow around eight.

With no objections to the schedule, Drs. Ryan and Rayburn got back into their car and followed Bone to the motel. Their rooms were waiting for them when they arrived, and they checked in. Bone showed them where the restaurant was and also the bar, in case they needed something a bit stiffer than iced tea.

This was the preference for Dr. Theodore Ryan, since he knew nothing was going to happen with Allyson. The conversation in the car, dominated by Allyson, had set the rules before arriving. They were there to work. That was it! No hand holding. No petting. No attempts at any kissing. This was business as usual.

Dr. Allyson Rayburn opened the door to her room and put her bag on the bed. She looked around the room, went into the bathroom, and eyed the shower. Walking out of the bathroom, she drew the curtains and unbuttoned her blouse. After throwing the blouse on the bed, she undid the clasp to her skirt, undid the zipper, and let the skirt drop to the floor. Walking back into the bathroom, she closed the door and started the shower. After unhooking her lace bra and dropping her matching panties to the floor, she entered the shower and adjusted the hot and cold levers.

She couldn't believe she was finally in Arione. This was the hometown of Dr. Daniel Jeremiah Adams. Just being in the same town as him made her hot. Allyson Rayburn had thought about Dan for many years. She would always become withdrawn and unhappy when she reminisced about her past life. She had many times regretted never calling him after the death that drove them apart. No one had touched her life like Dan.

To this day, she had never felt as beautiful as she did when she was with him. Others came into her life after Dan. However, Allyson never let go. She was polite and giving. She was extremely generous as a lover to those who wanted her. But no one, not even the affair that touched her life after she left Dan, was able to make her forget. She would have traveled the world, achieved her dream of becoming a top-notch lawyer, or even married a king if only she could get him out of her head. It wasn't meant to be.

Law faded from her world while seeing her mother die. Allyson knew there was more to life than courtroom dramas and rich clients waiting to take over the next downtrodden company needing a merger. After watching her mother writhe in pain, money and power were no longer her realities. The nightmares ended after she chose to do something benevolent as a career.

She became drawn to the same occupation Dan had. He wanted to make a difference. How wonderful it would have been to be reunited with the only man she had ever told she loved. In a strange sense, she hoped that the call that drew her to Arione would be the reason for her to stay permanently.

Tomorrow would be one of the most important days of her life. She wanted to look magnificent and refreshed. She wanted to feel more alive than she had in the last twenty years. After taking a long shower, she changed into jeans and a long-sleeve blouse. She rolled up the sleeves to her

The Death Maze

blouse and stepped out of her motel room to get a bite to eat. Tomorrow was her only thought. Tomorrow would be the beginning of the rest of her life.

***

Bone walked over to the bar after showing Drs. Ryan and Rayburn to the motel. This was the first time since he set foot in Arione—how many years ago?—that Chief Dressler gave him the afternoon off. He knew something was off-kilter when he saw that young man in the car. The chief had told him little. But he did know that the man would follow the chief back to the station.

Bone wanted to celebrate having the afternoon off with a few cold brews. His throat was hot and dry from helping to clear up the accident. After opening the door to the bar, he walked up to the bartender and ordered a beer. Bone saw Dr. Ryan and waved.

"How are things going, Bone?" the bartender asked. He knew everyone in town, and Bone came in regularly when his shift ended. Seeing Bone a few hours earlier than normal brought nothing but questions. He brought Bone his beer.

"Well, Lou," Bone replied. "Things couldn't be any better than they are right now."

"Does the chief know you're in here at this time of day?"

"He gave me the rest of the day off. I'm sure he'll fill me in tomorrow."

"Chief must be crazy," Lou stated, not meaning a word of what he said. "Any news about Dan Adams yet?"

"None yet. But we have company who just arrived in town who'll be helping tomorrow. Dr. Ryan is at the other end of the bar."

Lou looked at his customer. Dr. Ryan was drinking a scotch and water. Lou waved.

"Welcome, Dr. Ryan. I apologize for not introducing myself sooner," Lou stated.

"No problem, Lou. I'm just here to help." Dr. Ryan went back to his drink.

Bone took a long gulp from his glass of beer, downing almost half. He looked around the bar and brought himself back to his drink. Before taking his next gulp, he needed to ask Lou another question.

"Arlene show up yet?"

"You probably didn't look at your watch, Bone," Lou said. "You know Arlene doesn't get off until four."

"I didn't take a good look, Lou. I just needed a beer," Bone stated as he looked at his watch. It showed 3:45. "Hell, I got fifteen minutes, Lou. If I finish this beer, make sure another one replaces it!"

"Arlene will kill me if you're drunk by the time she gets here, Bone."

"No she won't. And she knows a couple beers aren't going to get me drunk."

Dr. Ryan was listening to the conversation and chuckling under his breath. He wished his life were as simple as this. He had spent so many hours in the lab with Allyson that he was sure his wife thought something was going on. He had no idea that Allyson and his wife were friends and that Allyson kept her up-to-date on all the gossip.

"Think you'll find anything, Dr. Ryan?" Bone asked.

"I believe I'll know once I get a look at the notes, Officer Bone."

"Well, the chief and I have been in the house and can't seem to put the clues together."

"I'm not sure you or the chief know what clues to really look for. Maybe you're looking for the usual instead of the unusual," Dr. Ryan replied.

"I never thought about it in that manner, sir," Bone said as he thought about Dr. Ryan's statement.

Just then, the door to the bar opened and a woman walked in. She had a pretty face, not beautiful, and was of medium height with dark hair and large, firm boobs. She had on a waitress outfit and looked tired. She looked straight at Bone and walked up to him.

"What the hell are you doing in the bar at this time of day, Wallace Johnson?" she said, not sounding angry but definitely concerned.

Bone was a breast man and definitely proud of his woman. He was led by the daily prospect of her wonderful assets. She also kept him in tow and knew all his weaknesses.

"Hi, Arlene," Bone said. "Chief gave me the rest of the day off."

Arlene was as surprised as Bone knew she would be. "What did he do that for? And how many beers have you had?" Arlene gave him a peck on the lips.

"This is my first beer. Ask Lou."

Arlene gave Lou a suspicious look.

"It's true, Arlene," Lou admitted. "He just started. Hell, ask that guy down at the other end of the bar."

Arlene looked at Dr. Ryan, who only nodded in the affirmative. He wasn't about to get anyone into trouble, not knowing Arlene and being the new guy in the bar.

"Well then, don't just stand there with your mouth open and catching flies, Lou," Arlene said. "Pour me a beer. I can't let my man drink all by himself. Just remember the limit."

By the time Arlene and Bone exited the bar, it was seven o'clock. Arlene had only had two beers. That was always her limit, as she was able to make it last through her shift. Bone, on the other hand, was sloshed. Although Arlene was not happy and would definitely let Bone know when he sobered up, she wasn't too concerned.

Chief Dressler hated it when Bone got drunk. At first he blamed himself for not giving Bone enough to do. When he first arrived, Bone was the model cop. He still was. However, the drinking became a problem. Dressler gave him one warning and only one warning. He told Bone that he was never to come to work hung over or else he would be out and back in Los Angeles.

Bone had kept that promise. He hadn't even started drinking until about a year after he arrived in Arione and made many friends. He found it easier to join the crowd than keep the booze at a safe distance. He was young, affable, and still very impressionable.

Arlene was up to the task of keeping him sober. When they met, she thought he got drunk only occasionally. Being the hard woman she was, she laid her laws down on the table early. If he wanted her, and he always did, he would consume as little alcohol as possible. She wanted a future and a man with a steady job. She rarely let him get into the intoxication zone. As a matter of fact, it had been a while since he had gotten drunk.

Bone hung on to Arlene as they walked to their two-bedroom apartment. Arlene was hot and horny but knew damn well that Bone needed food. She decided to take him home and make him a good meal with plenty of coffee before getting him into bed. He would either fall asleep on her or make a path to the bathroom to barf up his beer. If she didn't succeed, his head would probably roll on the floor when he woke the next morning.

"It's just a good thing that the chief isn't here to see you, Bone. You know how he hates his guys getting drunk," Arlene whispered in his ear.

"Thanks, baby. I know you'll take care of me," Bone stated as a reflex admission of guilt.

When they arrived at their apartment, Arlene dragged Bone to the kitchen and sat him down in one of the chairs. The cool air from the walk had made him feel better. Arlene took a pot from the cupboard and carefully laid it next to Bone's right shoe.

"What's that for?" he asked.

"Bone! I just know if you need to bring it all out, you'll do it in the pot and not on our floor."

"You know I will, Arlene," he admitted.

She looked him straight in the face while he lowered his head to the table. "Yes, Bone, I know damn well you will."

He just smiled as he rested.

Arlene went to the refrigerator and opened it up. She took out a thawed chicken, seasoned it, and threw it into the oven. She took the can of coffee from the cupboard and measured it so it would be strong. She put enough water in the coffee pot for four cups and poured it into the automatic coffee reservoir. Then she pushed the start button.

A few minutes later, she heard Bone let go of the beer and hit the pot just as she had planned. Five minutes after that, she put a hot cup of coffee in front of him.

"Drink," she ordered.

"Oh, the pain."

"Just drink the coffee, Bone."

"Give me a shot of beer, Arlene. That'll take away the hangover."

"Bone, I never believed that hair-of-the-dog thing."

She went to the refrigerator, reached for a can of beer, and opened it. Grabbing a glass from a different cupboard, she poured a couple swigs and gave it to Bone. He promptly swallowed the contents.

"I can actually feel the pain leaving my head."

"Whatever," she said, picking up the pot with the vomit in it and dumping it in the sink. She then washed the pot. "Want some food?"

"You know I do, babe," he said as his eyes lit up.

"I'm talking about the chicken in the oven, Bone."

"I know, Arlene. I'm just having fun." He stared at her for a few moments. "You're a good woman, Arlene. You know that?"

"I'm glad you noticed." Arlene then changed her tone and became softer. "Bone? Baby?"

"Yeah?"

"Do you think we'll ever get married?"

"Sure we will. Why do you have to ask?"

"Because you keep promising me that we will but you haven't asked! I get the feeling that you like this arrangement."

Bone was able to stand without wobbling and walk to her. He placed his hands over her shoulders.

"I'll tell you what. When the Adams case is closed, I promise to marry you."

Arlene smiled, gave him a kiss, and went back to cooking the chicken. When they sat down to eat, it was just as perfect as she knew it would be. And it wasn't just the chicken.

After dinner, they went to their bedroom and made love. The evening turned out exactly as she'd hoped. Just

The Death Maze

prior to falling asleep, Bone promised to cut back on the drinking even more than he already had. He again told her that she was the woman for him. She fell asleep beaming and dreaming that her life as Mrs. Wallace Johnson would soon begin.

It wouldn't happen as soon as she had hoped.

Chapter 24

Chief Dressler was still fuming inside when he arrived at his office the morning after taking William Barrish's report. Before going to bed, he realized it was a good move to never have married. He'd had many chances when he was younger, but he was married to his work. After leaving Los Angeles a long time ago, more years than he cared to remember, all he wanted to do was build two crime-free towns and keep the peace.

He had completed this goal a long time ago. His relationships with the Needles Police Department and the California Highway Patrol were impeccable. No one ever had to worry about Arione or Vera. There were no murders, drugs, or assaults, and there was no small-time theft to speak of. The only time someone had actually tagged a building—the Arione Motel on a winter night when the bar closed early—that person regretted ever hearing the name Arione. His fine was stiff, given by a municipal judge, and his week in Dressler's jail included hard work cleaning up the town and the highway. He never returned.

Now this incident was causing him headaches and stomach pains. He knew he had an ulcer. The two other deputies watching over Vera were not as adept as Bone at following orders and anticipating the work schedule Dressler wanted to keep. Bone was a good find and would

The Death Maze

easily be able to take over when he decided to retire. That wouldn't be for awhile, though, as far as he was concerned.

This William Barrish character was enough to make him lose it. The report showed that Barrish had indeed swerved to avoid the accident. He did try to help by first attempting to flag down cars to assist. He did help by carrying Ruth and Lawrence Welles, the man who picked up Ruth. He did follow instructions without questions.

But that was what was causing him the headaches and stomach pains. He was too cooperative. He didn't show any objections to any of Dressler's instructions. He volunteered to get a room at the Arione motel and said he would stay a couple days. Why did he do that? Dressler didn't ask him to. Why did he want to stay out in the boondocks? Didn't he need to get back to Los Angeles? Something was not right. Something stunk and Dressler smelled it last night when he went to sleep, that morning when he took a shower, and even now when he was back in his office.

It was almost eight o'clock. He knew he needed to meet Drs. Ryan and Rayburn at the restaurant for breakfast. He picked himself up and exited the station just as Bone showed up.

"You going to meet the two doctors for breakfast, Chief?"

"Nope! *We're* going to meet the two doctors at the restaurant for breakfast. I want you there as well."

"No problem, Chief. I'm always there for you."

"You know something, Bone? I know you are!" he said. He slapped a hand on his back and the two proceeded to walk.

When they entered the restaurant, it was full. Somehow, some way, something was going on, and the place was packed with about fifteen women. When Chief Dressler and Bone walked in, the women all shifted in their seats and stared at them. Dressler looked at Bone and Bone at Dressler.

"Outside. Now!" Dressler ordered Bone in a hushed voice. "Be right back, ladies."

After they closed the door, Dressler stared at Bone.

"What?" Bone looked befuddled. Dressler just stared. "Chief, I didn't say a thing to anybody. I swear!"

"What the hell is going on, Bone? It looks as if they knew we would be here!"

"Maybe they're all hungry, Chief."

"Hungry my derriere! All of those women have already eaten their breakfast with their husbands, sent them off to work, and came here."

"How can you tell that, Chief?" Bone seriously wanted to know.

"Did you see one plate on any of the tables?"

Bone needed to think. He didn't know how his boss came to such a conclusion so fast. He quickly put his nose up to the glass in the restaurant window and saw that the ladies were all staring at them. There were only coffee cups on the tables. He went back to Dressler.

"That's pretty good, Chief. I will try to be more observant next time."

"Forget next time, Bone. I need you to think. Did you say anything to Arlene?"

"Chief, I swear again. I said nothing to Arlene. As a matter of fact, she sobered me up last night, made me a good supper, and then made love to me."

"I do not need to know your intimate details. I just want to know what the hell is going on! And we'll talk about the sobering up later on."

"Chief. Why don't we ask the women?"

They opened the door and walked back into the restaurant. The women were still staring at them. Chief Dressler walked up to the counter with Bone in tow. Charlie Stinson was the owner and chef. He had one waitress, Sue, and one young man, Rand, who washed the dishes and bussed the tables when Sue needed help and cleaned up the place before closing time. Rand was standing next to Sue at the counter.

"Want to tell me what's going on, Chief?" Charlie asked as he walked up to Dressler and Bone. Charlie folded his hands over his stomach and looked around. "Nobody is eating. They're all just drinking coffee. I do not make money on coffee alone."

Just then, Dr. Theodore Ryan and Dr. Allyson Rayburn opened the door. Everyone turned their heads to look at the out-of-towners. Everyone except Chief Dressler and Bone. They looked at each other.

Chief Dressler took charge, as usual, and asked two of the ladies in a corner booth that was able to seat four to kindly move. They just acknowledged Dressler and moved to another table. Dressler motioned for the two doctors to sit at the booth and said they would be right with them.

"Ladies," Chief Dressler said. "There's nothing to know just now."

A bright-eyed woman with a smile that never seemed to leave her face stood up. She was Cynthia Hernandez, a woman whose husband had a landscaping business in Needles, and was obviously the spokesperson.

"Chief Dressler," Cynthia began. "We just want to know what happened to Dr. Adams."

"Mrs. Hernandez," Chief Dressler began, hoping he didn't sound condescending, but polite. "When we have some concrete information, I will be very happy to inform all of you. Right now we're still investigating and trying to learn all the particulars."

"We just want to know if we're safe," Cynthia stated.

"Do you feel as if you're not safe?" Dressler asked.

"I feel that if we had more information, we would all relax more."

"Well, I want you all to know that you can go back to your homes, and your lives, and go on without a care. The town is safe and secure. Officer Bone and I have everything in order."

The women looked at their chief of police, knowing that he would explain once he had any information. Chief Dressler was pretty good about keeping an open-door policy. As if they were taking a cue from a director in a movie, they all stood up.

"Please allow me to purchase your coffee," Chief Dressler said. "I hope you all have a good day."

"You're buying the coffee, Chief?" Charlie Stinson asked. It wasn't as if he was bewildered by the comment. He just hadn't seen it in a while.

"And I'm buying breakfast for four, Charlie. Sue!" Dressler looked at her. "Please bring three menus to the booth. I want coffee, scrambled eggs, sausages, toast, and a large glass of ice water."

"Right away, Chief," Sue replied, moving quickly.

Charlie Stinson looked at Rand and motioned for him to get back in the kitchen.

All the women began exiting the restaurant. In no time, the place was empty except for Drs. Ryan and Rayburn and Bone.

Chief Dressler followed them outside and motioned to Cynthia.

The Death Maze

"Excuse me, Mrs. Hernandez?" he asked.

Cynthia Hernandez turned around and walked up to Chief Dressler. "Yes, Chief?"

All the other women stopped in their tracks and turned their attention to Chief Dressler.

"How did all of you know about this?"

"Sandra Palmer informed me. Yesterday she called me from the motel and said there were two doctors in from Los Angeles."

"Sandra Palmer. Thank you, Cynthia," the chief said and walked back into the restaurant. Sitting down next to Bone, he informed them that the good proprietor of the motel was the town gossip.

"Interesting," Dr. Rayburn stated after the chief sat down.

"No one knows what's going on?" Dr. Ryan asked.

"Not really," Bone said.

"Nice to meet both of you," Dressler said. "We're kind of in limbo here."

They just looked at him.

"Small town, you know. Bone and I have to make sure the town goes on without everyone knowing everybody else's business."

"Chief likes to make sure this is not Mayberry," Bone chimed in.

"Mayberry!" Dr. Ryan retorted. "I haven't heard that one in years."

Sue came up to the table with four cups in hand and asked if they all wanted coffee. She set them down and began pouring. After they placed their orders, Dressler started talking.

"Did Bone take you into the house yesterday?"

"Not yet, Chief," Dr. Ryan admitted.

"Remember I spoke with you after they arrived, Chief," Bone reminded him.

"Yeah. Now I remember," Dressler said, nodding. "My mind has been going in too many directions lately."

"Understandable, Chief," Dr. Rayburn said. "Though the request for assistance is not out of the ordinary, the reason is."

"Well, I would appreciate it if you would go over to the house after breakfast and see what you can find."

"No problem," Dr. Ryan said. "Do you know what he was working on?"

"Dan Adams and I have been close friends for many years now," the chief explained. "He confided in me about a lot of things. He is also very civic-minded and a great asset to the town. Many people only know him as a wealthy advocate of Arione and Vera. He keeps his business mainly to himself."

"But did he ever confide to you about his most recent business?" Dr. Ryan asked.

"The only thing I knew was something he called AGE."

"AGE?" Dr. Rayburn asked. "That's alternative geothermal energy!"

"You know of it?" Dressler asked.

"Dr. Adams and I knew each other in college, Chief. We talked about it thirty years ago. I didn't even know if it was possible, but Dan always did."

"How close were you and Dan?" Bone interrupted with a small emphasis on *Dan*.

"It was another time and another life, Officer Bone," Dr. Rayburn assured all three gentlemen. Boy was this a lie; she hoped it didn't show on her face.

"Okay," Dressler said just as Sue brought all the meals to the table and set them down.

The Death Maze

As they began to eat, the doctors assured Bone and Dressler that they would keep them up to date on any and all discoveries. It was important to find Dan Adams, whether dead or alive, and figure out how his disappearance occurred.

As they finished their meals, Chief Dressler took the bill up to Sue at the cash register and handed her the money for four meals and nineteen cups of coffee.

"It's all yours, Sue," Dressler said before turning back toward the booth.

It was then that William Barrish opened the door, walked up to Sue, and ordered a cup of coffee to go. When he exited the restaurant with his coffee in hand, Chief Dressler excused himself.

"I'll see both of you later," he said to Drs. Ryan and Rayburn. "Bone, keep an eye out for a while."

"Sure, Chief," Bone said as Dressler went out the door.

He saw William Barrish driving out of town and decided to follow him. That smell was still in his nostrils and he had a feeling his next stop would be the hospital.

He got into his patrol car and headed west on I-40. He saw Barrish's car in the distance and kept his speed at a minimum. When the car exited toward the town of Vera, Dressler knew his instincts were correct. The one thing he did not want was for Barrish to question Ruth.

Barrish drove to the hospital and parked in the lot. Seeing Barrish enter the hospital only elevated Dressler's concerns, and he quickly parked, got out, and ran through the lobby.

"Barrish," Dressler called out.

William Barrish didn't stop to turn around. Instead, he entered the elevator and pushed a button. The elevator doors closed before Dressler was able to follow him in. He saw that the elevator stopped on the floor of Ruth's room.

After waiting for the second elevator to open, which didn't take long, Dressler entered and pushed the button. A few moments later, he got out of the elevator and rushed down the hallway. He saw Barrish opening the door to Ruth's room.

"Mr. Barrish," Chief Dressler called out.

William Barrish let the door close before acknowledging him. "Hey, Chief. What's up?" Barrish asked as if nothing was going on.

"Certainly not you," Dressler stated.

"I'm not sure I understand."

"I mean you are not to question Ruth Putnam," Dressler ordered.

"And why is that, Chief?" Barrish almost demanded.

"Because I said so," Dressler ordered. "She's been involved in an accident and has not yet been questioned."

"It was an accident, Chief Dressler. Not a murder."

"Questioning her before I get her statement will not be allowed, Mr. Barrish," Dressler ordered again.

"What are you hiding, Chief?" Barrish asked, his voice rising a bit.

"How about you and me step outside the hospital, Mr. Barrish," Chief Dressler ordered in an even louder voice.

The argument continued to grow, and soon a few nurses turned their heads. Dr. Shirley Anderson overheard them while walking down an adjacent corridor and couldn't believe the volume coming out of the two men. She rushed over and began putting in her two cents.

"If you two do not lower your voices, I'll ask you both to leave," she demanded.

They just looked at her while thinking about continuing.

"Now if you boys—" She stressed the word *boys*. "—have forgotten, this is a hospital and not a bar. Take it out of here immediately, Chief."

Shirley entered Ruth's room. She wanted to check up on her patient, who had only suffered a few cuts and bruises, and find out what she remembered. There was just too much drama going on in Ruth's life, and she hoped that the accident hadn't registered in her mind.

Lawrence Welles, the driver, was in poor condition. His injuries were a lot worse. He was in a coma when he was brought in, and he had not yet regained consciousness. His vitals were poor, and Shirley didn't think he would make it through the afternoon. The next of kin would have to be contacted, and Chief Dressler would need to know as well.

Dressler's an idiot, she thought as she checked on Ruth. There was no excuse for his behavior. This complete, complex, irrational mess was news. The public had a right to know what went on in this crummy world. Trying to keep the accident out of the paper would only open up the eyesore that hid in the depths of the town. Barrish would easily discover the secret.

It was easy to see that the chief's personality had changed. Normally a rational individual, Chief Dressler had let the wrong person get under his skin. She should have told him to let William Barrish report the accident. He would enter it into the world of the print media and it would die within a couple days. Nothing would be said of the disappearance of Dan Adams, and the investigation would continue unabated.

Shirley Anderson dismissed these thoughts from her mind and continued to examine Ruth, who was sleeping as if she had never left the hospital.

Chief Dressler and William Barrish had taken the conversation just down the hallway and into a waiting room. The volume was lower, but the intensity was just as high.

"So what you're telling me, Chief, is that you're not permitting me to do my job!"

"For the time being, Mr. Barrish, the answer is yes. I reserve the right to have you refrain from questioning Ruth Putnam until I investigate the accident fully."

"You know you're breaching my rights to the first amendment," Barrish stated, hoping that Dressler would not know what the first amendment was.

"The first amendment does not state that an officer of the law can inhibit your work while the investigation of an accident is continuing. In fact, you are breaking the law if you, in fact, do interfere with the investigation," Chief Dressler explained. "Should I cite you for that?"

Barrish thought for a few moments. This cop was not as much of a hick as he thought. If he tried to press the issue, he knew Dressler would have the right to arrest him. But for how long?

William Barrish's boss had told him about run-ins with the law. He said there would probably be many. It was best to pick the right fight, the just fight, and not put himself into a situation he may not be able to get out of.

This was the right fight, he continued to reason. Only now it was becoming larger. What was Dressler hiding? Who could he speak with? There had to be someone. Maybe Dr. Anderson. She had told Dressler to button it up. Maybe she was the next person to speak with. Maybe she could enlighten him.

Dressler wondered what Barrish was thinking. He was proud that he knew the law and the rights. He had been a cop for a long time and had heard every excuse in the book.

He had the right to do his work and investigate. He would wait for Ruth to get better before questioning her.

"Look," Barrish said, breaking the silence. "My boss will want to know where I am. Mind if I call him?"

"Nothing against the law in that," Dressler told him.

He thought it was a trick. That stink entered his nostrils again. Dressler suspected that Barrish was looking for any avenue to get away so he could snoop around. He knew this guy would do anything to get the story. Even if it meant hurting others or stepping on their personal rights, the story was the paycheck. However, it was a reasonable request. That damn smell permeated his entire body now.

"As long as you inform him where you are and that you are working on a story, I have no problems," Dressler said.

Barrish left the room to find a phone just as Shirley Anderson walked past the waiting room. Barrish looked at her as they passed each other. Dressler saw the anguish on her face and knew something had happened. She saw the chief and approached.

"What the matter?" Dressler asked her.

"I've got some bad news, Chief."

"Ruth okay?"

"Ruth's fine. In fact, I'm not sure she's even going to remember the last twenty-four hours."

"Then what's wrong?" he asked.

"You're not going to be able to question Lawrence Welles. I've just been informed he passed away."

Chief Dressler looked down at the floor. The day seemed to be going in the wrong direction. He needed to get a firm grasp on the situation and put it to bed. William Barrish was not letting him do his job. Once he had this information, who knew what would come out?

"Chief," Shirley said. "Let him have the accident. Once he gets the accident, he'll go home."

"I'm not so sure. There's too much coincidence around it," Dressler explained. "That's why I've been so adamant."

"What are you talking about?"

"One wrong question, one wrong answer, and the entire cat is let out of the bag. Ruth is not coherent enough to give him the answers that I want."

"Ruth is not even awake!" Shirley informed him.

"Once she is, she'll leak it out. You know how Dan valued his privacy."

Shirley couldn't argue that point. Dan Adams kept everything out of the news until he decided it was worthwhile to let the news in. He taught Chief Dressler the value of using the media for his own purposes. This was why he had remained so successful.

***

Meanwhile, Barrish took advantage of his newfound freedom and quickly located a private area where he could use his cell phone. He knew he had only a few moments and hoped that Dr. Anderson would keep Dressler busy until he completed his conversation.

He opened his cell phone, saw that he had reception, and quickly pressed the contacts button. Pushing the letters G and R brought up Robert Graves. He pushed the call button.

"Barrish," Robert Graves answered. "What's up?"

"I don't know, sir. Something's weird out in the boondocks."

"What do you mean weird?" his boss asked. "I thought you were supposed to be back at the office today."

"I was, sir. I ran into some trouble outside a small town called Arione," Barrish explained.

"And where is Arione?" Robert Graves asked.

"Near a town called Vera," Barrish continued.

***

Dressler was finished speaking with Shirley Anderson. The smell was again in his nostrils and he wished he had not let Barrish out of his sight. His instincts told him more trouble was on the way. He knew Barrish was the reason.

He asked Shirley to get him the information of Lawrence Welles's next of kin and said he would have Bone contact them. He also wanted someone from the hospital to be ready to speak to his family. They would want plenty of answers. He now needed to locate William Barrish.

"Okay, Will. Where is Vera?" his boss asked.

"About twenty minutes west of Needles on I-40. There was an accident, and the police don't want me snooping around."

"What do you know?"

Robert Graves was an old newsman from before the Internet world. He loved snooping around and smelling for a real story. When William Barrish sent his resume to him just out of college, he knew this young kid had what it took to become the next Robert Graves.

He hated the new round of television personalities who just read the teleprompter instead of doing real investigations. The true newsmen and women weren't the beautiful airheads the networks wanted for ratings. Those were the ones with the Botox treatments, boob jobs, liposuction, hair transplants, and big salaries they didn't deserve. Robert Graves longed for the good old days when true journalism breathed from the reporter's pores.

"I know there's something going on that no one wants to tell me, Mr. Graves," Barrish explained. "There are too many people keeping quiet and one doctor telling me to button up."

Alex Miller knocked on the door to Robert Graves's office. He was the star reporter for the *Lost Angeles News*. Of medium height and build, Alex had his share of rough encounters and always got his story. He had a few scars—one small one on his cheek and one larger one on his chest—that showed he deserved the award for journalism he received while covering the first Gulf War.

Robert Graves waved his star reporter into his office.

"Look, Will," Graves said, "keep it under wraps and I'll have Alex out there to help."

"Help where?" Alex asked.

"I can handle it, sir," Barrish exclaimed. Suddenly he felt a fist hit his head from behind. He dropped the cell phone.

"Will?" Graves said. "Will!"

"What's the matter, Bob?" Alex asked.

"I need you to go to Arione, California. Will is in trouble."

"And where is Arione, California?" Alex asked.

"It's west of Needles off I-40."

"That's only a couple hours, Bob. I'll pack and leave right away."

"Just be careful, Alex," Graves warned. "Sounds like one of those hick towns where the head cop is also the local judge."

"I'll use my old lawyer trick. Should do fine if that's truly the case." Alex started for the door.

"Call me with an update the minute you get there," Graves said as Alex left the room. "God, I hope that kid is safe," he said to himself.

***

Barrish wasn't! Dressler was all over him.

"So you don't know anything?" Dressler said as he pushed Barrish at the wall.

Barrish bounced against the wall and knocked over the magazines sitting on top of an end table. He was on his feet but wobbly.

"I want answers, Mr. Barrish. And I want them now!"

Again Dressler came at Barrish, and Barrish did something he never would have contemplated doing. He kneed Chief Dressler in the groin as a reflex, thinking Dressler was going to hit him. Although it wasn't smart on Barrish's part, it did give him some satisfaction.

Chief Dressler doubled over, grabbed his nuts, and screamed. He knew he was wrong for pushing Barrish, but now he had a good excuse to retaliate.

It was only a few seconds before Chief Dressler was able to stand, push Barrish against the same wall, and throw a hard right fist to his left cheek.

William Barrish wasn't thin, but he wasn't hefty either. His body ricocheted off the wall and fell on top of the end table. It was the first time anyone had ever hit him in the face, and it definitely hurt. The table crumbled and he fell to the floor.

When Dressler went to pick up the injured reporter, Barrish kicked him in the stomach. Again, it was just a reflex, but it did give Barrish a little satisfaction even though he knew he would be in even bigger trouble with this cop.

Chief Dressler wanted this over. He backed up a few steps before rebounding. He was faster than Barrish would have thought. With one quick look and one large left fist, Dressler connected with Barrish's jaw and heard it break.

Barrish flew backward and fell on the floor. Blood oozed from his nose and lips. He was out. Still slumped over from the kick to his balls, Chief Dressler went over to Barrish and checked to see if he was breathing. He was. Dressler tried to stand up straight.

Dr. Shirley Anderson and two nurses had come running down the hallway just after the commotion began. As they arrived, they witnessed William Barrish falling to the floor just after Dressler's jaw-breaking punch. Although the fight had taken no more than one minute, it was enough to arouse her temper to full steam. Before she ripped into Chief Dressler, she instructed the nurses to get a stretcher and take the fallen reporter into the X-ray room. She wanted a complete set.

"His jaw," Dressler said. "His jaw is broken. X-ray the jaw."

After Barrish was taken away, Shirley let it all out.

"You're CRAZY! Not only that, but you're a lunatic. An animal who ought to be caged. You could have killed him."

"I warned him, Shirley. You heard me say it." Dressler was trying and failing in his excuses.

"I don't care, Chief. What you want or say has nothing to do with what will eventually happen in the papers." Shirley came closer to Dressler so she could get into his face. "It's going to happen now, Chief. Because who knows who he

The Death Maze

called? Someone is going to come out here. You've blown this entire mess out of proportion."

"Listen, Shirley," Dressler said before he was cut off.

"I will not listen to you, Chief. I want no more outbursts or I'll . . . I'll . . ." She saw him grab his crotch and bend over. "I'll make sure you'll never recover from another blow to your precious masculinity. You understand me, Chief?"

"All too clearly. However . . ." Dressler stopped before he said the next word.

He looked at Shirley and saw her eyes riveted on him. He noticed the redness in her face and was sure that uttering just one vowel would set her off again and make him into a eunuch.

It wouldn't do any good. He remained silent, having already accomplished what he had set out to do. Barrish was out of the way and well deserving of his downfall. Dressler's precious ego was fulfilled and he had a little time to think of how to remedy the overblown situation.

Shirley Anderson's eyes were still glued to Dressler's. She wanted Dressler to understand and register her anger. *Just please,* she thought, *please let him open up his maniacal, egotistical mouth.* God, did she want to be told off. One kick in the groin by *this* doctor would be the end, because she knew how to make it last a lifetime.

Unfortunately, Dressler was calming down. His eyes were no longer red and angry. The lines on his forehead were gone, and his left hand was now unclenched. It was red, purple, black, and blue in color. She knew he wouldn't say one thing in defense of his act. Her knee was still only a few inches away from his family jewels.

"How about fixing my hand?" Dressler asked in a low voice. "I believe it's broken."

After taking a few moments to release her stare and bring down her guard, Shirley was able to speak again.

"I'm not surprised, after that last punch. Maybe we should X-ray your head while we have you in the examining room. It, too, might be broken."

She took a deep breath and dropped her eyes to his hand once again. She gently touched it and he winced at the pain.

"What about your balls?" Shirley decided to ask.

"Forget about them, Doc. They'll live."

"Too bad," Shirley sarcastically responded as she led him out of the room.

Chapter 25

With the ceiling only four feet high now, Dan was moving forward either crouching on the floor or kneeling. For now, he was crouching. And it was beginning to hurt his back. After the third mistake, he had traversed down a small and meandering hallwaylike area. It seemed to have no beginning or end, and Dan felt as if it were being created as he walked—or, more accurately, crouched.

He dropped to his knees.

His legs were tiring too easily. It felt as if he had only traveled, if that was the correct terminology, maybe ten yards. Why that term? Why not thirty-six feet? Why not . . . wait! What was he thinking?

Was it he who was thinking? Or was someone or something doing the thinking in his mind? Could they get into his mind?

Stop it, stop it, STOP IT! he thought. *I am in control of my mind. I am master of myself.*

Dan halted in his tracks. He needed to think and recall where he had heard that before. It was something he had studied. It was from the teachings of who?

"Agasha," he said out loud. "That's it!" He smiled as he took a few steps on his knees. "I am master of myself. I am all powerful. And nothing can come to me of an inferior nature. I am peace. I am power. I am all there is."

Those were the words of an ancient teacher of five thousand years ago. This ancient teacher-master lived before Christ, before the beginning of the Jews, during a period of peace in ancient Egypt. Agasha was one of many master teachers. Thousands came to discover and learn these teachings. They wanted to learn karma and reincarnation and what it meant to live in a godly manner.

No! He was not from Egypt. He was from a place that would eventually become Egypt. He couldn't remember the name.

"Think," he said. These were the first thoughts that had made him feel good.

He couldn't remember. He felt that something, or someone, was blocking his mind.

As if on cue, the area in the distance widened into a room. He moved toward it while putting these thoughts of Agasha in the back of his mind. He made a mental note that those thoughts would be needed later, although he did not know when later would be.

Coming into the room, he smiled. It was different. It was happy. It was not a hospital room, but a nursery. There was a crib and a bassinet, and the walls were pale yellow, blue, and light green. There was a window with drapes matching the colors of the walls.

It brought Dan back to the days of his early childhood. His room always had a light, breezy feeling, and the air was clean and pure.

Dan knew this was the nursery in the summer house, not the home in the city. These breezes came from the open window through which he could see the Atlantic Ocean. Even now, it appeared that a breeze was coming through the window. The air was not stale as it had been in the rest of

The Death Maze

the maze. This air was fresher. Maybe it was the air that had made him recall his earlier years.

Putting his past aside for just a few moments, Dan turned his head in every direction to look for his next decision. He couldn't find it. That was becoming typical of the sixth dimension. The longer he spent in the maze, the more difficult it became to find the exit and be free from it.

He had made three mistakes and did not want to make a fourth. He felt he couldn't afford it. Slowly but surely, his time was running out. He knew it was because of him that time felt deficient, so he purposely tried to slow down. He needed whatever extra seconds or minutes he could receive.

Death was in the back of his mind. Since it was not the subject he preferred to keep there, he now wanted to hold on to it. The sixth dimension was not some level of intellectual superiority. At least not to Dan Adams. Apep was making it into a physical and mental hell. His decisions needed to be augmented by the fact that his whereabouts capped the realizations of his choices.

"Where is it?" he muttered softly to himself, wanting to get on with the drama. "Master of myself," he continued, and took the extra denominations of time.

He looked straight ahead. *The window?* he thought. He approached it and saw a slight reflection of himself and the room's brightness.

No. Too easy, he surmised.

He kneeled over to the crib. The pain in his knees was becoming unbearable again, and he wished he had not made that third mistake. He could be enjoying that extra foot of height and standing at this very moment.

Stop thinking of the past, his mind said. "Master of myself," he said again out loud.

Dan looked into the crib and saw a doll lying on its stomach. He reached to pick it up. It wouldn't budge. He tried a second time by putting the fingers of his right hand firmly under the doll's stomach and placing his left hand over the back of the doll.

As he mentally prepared to pull upward more strongly, he counted to three and lifted the doll lightly before reaching number three. Dan figured Apep was going to do something to cause him to fall backward. He purposely willed himself to proceed in a fashion he never would have originally done and thought he had beaten Apep at this one game at least. Dan did not want to be the brunt of another joke of this horrible creature.

"How strange you are, Dan Adams," Apep boomed.

"Not strange, Apep," Dan responded. "This place is strange. Your sense of humor is strange. Your reality and vision of it are strange."

"I will take that as a compliment."

"Now that also is strange, Apep."

"How so, Dan Adams?"

"I did not mean for it to be taken as a compliment."

"I will take it as a compliment anyway," Apep said in a condescending voice. "Have you been enjoying your journey through the maze?"

Dan couldn't believe his ears. This arrogance from a monster who would decide the outcome of the rest of his existence! He wanted to know what he had really done to be brought into this world. He wanted to know which choices he had been given.

That was it!

"Apep," Dan said. "Have you ever heard of free will?"

"But of course!" Apep said in a matter-of-fact tone. "It was not first introduced in your world."

"It may have been introduced in your world."

"Long before that."

"What do you mean?" Dan asked.

"I mean that I had heard of free will and its ramifications, faults, and other causes during my time and before my time."

"I want to know what I did to get here," Dan demanded. "What did my experiments have to do with getting into this miserable place?"

"Know that it was not your experiments that caused you to be here," Apep said, almost laughing.

"What's so funny?" Dan asked.

"The others who preceded you did not think like this. Your intellect thinks you caused this to happen. I know otherwise."

"What others?"

"Soon, Dan Adams. Soon."

"Apep! What does that mean?" Dan demanded.

No answer.

"APEP!" Dan yelled as he lifted the doll above his head.

It didn't go too high. The back of Dan's hand hit the ceiling of the enclosure. That's what he felt he was in at this point. In his mind, it was no longer a room, but a small box.

Dan brought the doll down to eye level and looked at it. He was amazed at the similarity between this one and the one he had had as a small child. He stared carefully at the features and noticed a small tear on the upper left arm.

"Couldn't be," Dan whispered.

Dan's doll had also had a small tear on its upper left arm.

He then lifted his head to look at the enclosure. This room was identical to his childhood room. The measurements were the same with the exception of the height. Even the breeze from the window appeared the same. It was unbelievably uncanny.

Dan looked into the crib again and saw a small boy playing and laughing. He obviously enjoyed the make-believe utopia he had created with the stuffed Raggedy Andy doll in his right hand.

What the . . . ? Dan thought. *Where did this boy come from?*

Dan then saw a small airplane mobile with five planes hanging above the crib. It was suspended without wires. The boy tried grabbing the mobile and laughed as it went around in circles and then reversed directions as if it were unwinding.

Dan tried to touch the mobile. The boy swatted at the planes, barely missing Dan's hand. The boy continued to laugh. He even made engine noises as if the planes were buzzing past.

The boy brought the Raggedy Andy doll to his face.

"See?" he asked the doll, turning its face toward the planes.

The boy waited for an answer.

It was too surreal for Dan. In this world, he even expected the doll to answer the boy. He was not ready for the actual outcome.

"SEE?" the boy asked in a louder voice. "Andy! You SEE?" the boy shouted, becoming totally disturbed and impatient with his doll.

The boy grabbed the doll by the neck. He began to stare into the eyes and make faces.

The doll didn't laugh. It didn't change its perception of the world. It just kept the same grin the manufacturers had given it. It didn't seem to be bothered by the boy's reaction to it.

The Death Maze

The boy then looked at the doll with hateful eyes and threw it against the crib in disgust. He reached for it a second time and threw the doll behind him, against the other end of the crib.

Looking back at the mobile, the boy grabbed at one of the toy planes and ripped it away from the other planes. He kept grabbing until all five planes were torn away. He shoved each plane into the face of the Raggedy Andy doll and then threw them out of the crib.

"See, see, see," the boy yelled as he started to cry.

The helpless doll just remained in the crib. The grin stayed firm as the boy's rage escalated.

Dan was utterly shocked to see this and tried to comfort the boy. He attempted to touch the boy's head, but his hand passed through it. Dan tried to touch his shoulder, but again, his hand passed through.

The boy then closed in on the doll, choking it with one hand while hitting it with the other.

Over and over, again and again, the boy ripped at the doll. He was completely out of control. The doll flew against one side of the crib, and then he picked it up and tossed it to the other side.

Finally, with a strength Dan would never have expected, the boy ripped at both arms and tore them apart. He threw all the pieces out of the crib and sobbed uncontrollably.

No one entered the nursery, and the cries went unheard. Raggedy Andy was now in pieces and away from the boy's grasp. He was free from the tirade. The black buttons of the eyes just stared into space.

The tantrums continued. The boy stood up and shook the crib, rocking it back and forth. One corner lifted off the floor. Another corner followed as the rocking grew wilder.

On the fourth cycle of rocking, the crib teetered to the side and then toppled over.

Dan was shocked at the dramatic course of events he had just witnessed. The crib was in pieces. Raggedy Andy was torn apart. The mobile planes were ripped to shreds. The boy was . . . the boy was . . . wait!

Where was the boy?

He felt sweat dripping from his forehead and the back of his neck. The perspiration began to flow steadily. Dan was on the floor in the middle of the broken crib, searching for someone who was not even there.

But it had felt so real. He had seen the events unfold with twenty-twenty vision. He was sure he had seen it all. The doll was even in the middle of the debris that surrounded him.

The doll! That stinking Raggedy Andy doll. He hated that doll back then and he despised it now. Dan reached to pick up the doll. He looked into the face and saw himself.

"What?" Dan murmured out loud. "What the hell is this?"

Apep had changed the face to that of Dan Adams.

"What kind of crap is this? You're a sick son of a bitch, Apep. You know that? YOU ARE A PIECE OF SHIT!"

Dan grabbed what was left of the doll and began tearing it to pieces. It was sheer, volatile hate. It was worse than the little boy ripping the arms. It was blind rage. He then picked up pieces of the crib and flung them in all directions.

Next he went for the bassinet. Even though he was on his knees, Dan's anger seemed to make him superhuman. He picked up the bassinet as if it were paper and slammed it to the floor. It broke, and he lifted it again and brought it down to the floor a second time. The third time, the pieces were smaller. It got even smaller, until there was nothing in his left hand and a stick in his right.

What was at first a nice memory from his childhood had been soiled and distorted by Apep. Dan wanted to know why. His anger began to subside and grow into frustration. His stomach grew tense and he screamed.

"Why? Damn you, why? All because I invaded your world?" Dan yelled.

He lifted himself into a crouching position and threw himself against the wall. He wanted to break every bone in his body. He wanted the pain that would come with each crack and fracture. He wanted out. Out of this world and this crummy existence and into one of love and kindness and consideration and . . .

"Master of myself," he repeated, having remembered these words from before. He picked himself up and slammed himself against another wall.

After dropping to the floor, he slowly lifted himself up again into a crouching position and ran to the window. In his anger he jumped through the window and disappeared. There was no glass to break. There were no slivers to lodge into his skin. It was all a ruse. Even though he had seen his reflection a few minutes ago, it was now gone.

Totally forgetting that there could be another way out, he waited for the quake. If the space he now consumed shook, he would be unable to retract and reverse directions. He kept falling and screamed.

Death was surely imminent. When he came to the end, he would welcome it. He would rejoice. He would say his hallelujahs and hope that he was at the end of his misery.

But there was no quake!

Chapter 26

Apep and his seven followers did disappear. They were gone before the snakes, scorpions, spiders, vipers, and all the other crawling monstrosities of the regular world were dropped on them.

In fact, they were ready for it. Deep in meditation and far away from it all, the creatures were eliminated during the transfer and sent to their own deaths. As far as Apep knew, they were all part of their own reeducation in the afterlife. However, Apep was by himself.

He had succeeded. Only he did not know where his success had brought him. Apep had thought he would go to a different plane in the post-life experience. His egocentric mind, full of ever-expanding, overblown realities in one world, did not match the world he was now a part of.

He needed to become its God. He wanted to be superior and king of the world. His years of studies in Egypt and then Nubia were to bring him to a new level. His mind was ready to lift itself beyond that of mortals and into the realm of Supreme Being. However, being a supreme being meant controlling all.

He thought there would be riches beyond what the normal mind could ever conceive. These riches would not be gold or silver or anything that extreme taxation would usually bring to a king or empire. These were the riches of total control of the universe. After all, what would gold or silver be worth to one who could control all of mankind forever?

Yes, Apep thought he had it all.

But who was with him? Who would be there for him to act as the supreme being of all? Where were the seven? What had he truly committed himself to be? And for how long?

Trying to concentrate and allow his mind to become at ease, Apep soon found himself looking down on his mortal self. He was lifting his subconscious above that which was in order for him to see what could be or what should be. As far as he was concerned, he wanted control to begin now and forever. He needed his mind to search for all things answerable to only him.

What he found, after much meditation, astral projection, and inner realization, was that he was not where he should have been. In fact, he was alone. The others were gone. They were dead and beyond his control. They answered only in the afterlife to God Almighty.

They had become victims of his inner wickedness and arrogance to the point that they could not be held responsible for their own lives in the mortal world. As is normal with any life on the Earth plane, time had ended in its current incarnation and was, in fact, being reeducated for the next incarnation whenever the soul was deemed ready.

This was something familiar to Apep. He had felt that his own mortal life on Earth had existed many times in the past in different incarnations. As he was to explain it, life is everlasting and humans are always in search of becoming the best they can be.

The best at what, Apep never understood. For him, it was being the best villain or the best sorcerer or evil madman.

It was trying to enhance himself at the expense of others. It should have always been for the bettering of mankind.

When Apep took the other seven souls into his tutelage, he became responsible for them even though they all had free will. These seven had not been given the rudimentary understandings in the early part of their lives. These seven had been discarded and had learned to fend for themselves without understanding that what they were doing was wrong.

When Apep found them, their young minds were able to be totally influenced by a teacher. He was the teacher. By educating them to be something other than the best they could be and in the atmosphere of only evil, Apep was in fact manipulating them for the betterment of Apep and not for society as a whole.

Apep knew right from wrong. He learned to twist and form this when he was in the employment of the hierarchy of Egypt. Knowing that his world was to change dramatically and that Nubia was to take over, Apep became something worse. And he needed others to carry out his evil. His decadence in depravity enhanced only the ugliness in the outside world. He had gone far beyond the normal reality of the everyday world.

Now he was in the sixth dimension with nothing but his body and mind to control. It was Apep, the hideous man-serpent he had become, who would be held responsible to rise to the upper level or fold to the depths of the abyss.

And Apep liked the depths of the abyss. He only wanted control and liked the idea of forever manipulating the world into the form he saw fit. Apep truly worshipped the evils of the universe.

But control what? he thought. *What can I control if not the people and the world of which I was a part?*

It would take time, but Apep knew the answer would eventually come. He knew how to dwell in eternal darkness. His need to devour the brightness of his or any world was the ultimate of his being. He felt he had completed his goal before. It would only be a matter of time before he would be successful again.

He closed his eyes from the world he was now a part of and went back to meditation. At this he was a master. Only a few seconds would pass before he would rise once again to the level above his mortal body. This was his utopia, because he did not long to keep his body. He could exist beyond the limitations of walking, talking, eating, and breathing. He could intermingle within each molecule of this world's id without mortality.

As time would not pass too quickly, Apep stayed in the meditative state. The pieces were coming together. He sensed, over a long period of time, the deterioration of his mortal self. It became dry. It shrank in size. The clothes dropped. The moisture evaporated. It then fell to the ground, where it remained.

Apep's laughter was deafening as he created a wind to blow away what was left on the ground. While watching it disappear from sight, a bolt of lightning struck and ignited the remnants in the distance.

With nothing left of his mortal being, Apep was ready.

Chapter 27

There was no excuse for Dan's rage. He had long ago known that his fits as a child were the direct result of feeling little love from his father, though his mother more than made up for his need for affection.

Growing up as the only son in a wealthy family, his curiosity about science and the unexplained far outstripped his father's yearning for an heir to manage the fortune. Dan accepted his father as he was. He knew his sister would take over. When he left the business and told his father he was through, he knew his father's love, in the capacity he had always shown, would not diminish. His father would simply have to accept him as he was.

Knowing that he had conquered those insecurities far too many years ago, he continued to be amazed that the sixth dimension was able to reignite so much of what he believed were distant memories. Frustration, disappointment, bitterness, and loneliness had all been part of that child. They were not part of Dan Adams, the adult. Jumping through the window was the result of how he had felt in his childhood. He should have known that.

Now he was falling. However, he was also remembering. A lot.

He had put these memories in the recesses of his mind long ago. He didn't understand why they were being brought to the surface now. He was sure it would all end at the point when he ceased to fall.

He was a scientist. He relished in the unknown becoming known, his testing revealing answers. Dan felt he was entitled to the explorations of unknown chemicals and mixtures because they would eventually be used for the betterment of mankind. This was his calling.

Now he was being ostracized, banished, and expelled from his principles and education. These were not the ingredients for his success. This world was setting off too many alarms in his mind right now and he needed to get control of it.

But he was falling. When he saw lights come into view in the distance, he prepared for the end. He couldn't determine how fast he was falling. Dan perceived the end to be near and just hoped it would be decisive and swift.

His mind grew hazy as he passed through a dense cloud. He saw a quick flash of lightning. He heard a grumble of thunder. Closing his eyelids, he flashed back to his days at college.

***

These were golden years of bliss. He loved being in class. He luxuriated for many hours in the laboratories and libraries. His studies took him far from his home in New York to the suburbs of Coral Gables, Florida.

Then there was Allyson Rayburn.

Her long, rust-red hair flowed. Her green eyes sparkled. Her slender body and large, voluptuous breasts caught every breath of fresh air he could inhale. She was his.

When their bodies touched, it was as if the heavens called out for them to be one and forever eternal. This was the life he should have had. They were the envy of the entire department of chemistry.

They walked to each other's classes together. They ate their meals together. They studied together. They never tired of each other's company as they discovered every morsel of their being, both past and present. They longed for nothing but the future together.

Why had they parted?

Dan had bumped into Allyson while coming out of a biology class. He had stayed after class to talk a bit with his professor before realizing that he would be late for his next class. While he rushed out, the two collided. They both dropped their books, and Dan held on to Allyson, keeping her from falling to the floor.

"I'm really sorry," he said as he stared into her face.

Her eyes caught his and she blushed. "No, it's my fault," she admitted. "I should have looked where I was going."

"I shouldn't be racing from one class to another."

"Class that bad?" She smiled.

"No. That's not what I meant," he responded while picking up her books. "I just didn't want to be late going from one class to the next." He was still staring at her. "However, I'm glad . . ."

"That we bumped into each other?" Allyson said, completing his sentence.

Dan stared into her eyes. "Yes."

"Well, apologies accepted," Allyson stated, her books now in her arms. "Thank you for helping me."

"I'm Dan."

"Allyson Rayburn," she said as she reached out to shake his hand.

Dan took her hand into his and felt her soft but firm grip. "I'm so very pleased to meet you."

"You are?" she answered, not sure what he meant.

"I mean, it's a pleasure . . . not to bump into you like that, but to truly meet you."

"I'm just giving you a hard time, Dan."

"Well, I deserve it."

Allyson looked at him and couldn't believe what she felt. She had heard of that bolt of lightning that would strike when a person met the right one. Should she ask him out for a cup of coffee? Would he be put off by her forwardness? However, she had never asked a man out.

"Are you, I mean, would you . . ."

"Like to get a cup of coffee and talk some more?" She completed his sentence again.

"Yes!" he answered, not letting her know his real thoughts.

He really wanted to tell her how beautiful she was and that he hoped she would not be offended by his compliment. She would probably think it was a chauvinistic comment, and he didn't want to sound like every other guy in the world, like he only wanted to get in her pants. Dan realized he had better stop these run-on thoughts because these thoughts were typical of the male psyche. *What a moron*, he thought to himself.

He had never been like that and had never needed to be like that. He had never looked into the eyes of someone and felt what he was feeling. It wasn't that he had never asked a girl out in high school or his first years in college. He did. He went to many parties and socialized like any other normal male of his generation.

But Dan Adams had always been a polite, well-mannered gentleman, as he had been informed by many a parent. He always thought of others first and knew he had a destiny of his own. He wasn't out to prove to others that he was better as a human being because his family had money. He didn't care about the money. He cared about humanity as a whole and the future of the world.

"Dan?" Allyson asked as she looked into his eyes.

"Sure!" Dan replied, not realizing he was daydreaming.

"Sure what?" she asked.

"I'm sorry. I zoned out for a second. When's your lunch?"

"After this class," Allyson answered.

"Would you allow me the honor of escorting you to the wonderful cafeteria on this side of campus?"

Laughing at his comment, Allyson said, "It would be a pleasure."

"See you after class," he said.

He walked away toward his next class. Allyson watched as he turned the corner of the building. Her heart was beating very rapidly and she hoped the thumping was not visible through her blouse.

Her class was useless. All she could think of was Dan. That bolt of lightning had struck her hard, and she wished the time would go faster. Her mind rambled in many directions.

She wanted to know everything about this man. What were his thoughts? What were his dreams? How did he feel about life and living with her for the rest of it? Where did they think they would go after college? Was she really thinking this? Was this juvenile?

"Wait!" she blurted out loud.

"Miss Rayburn," the instructor asked. "Do you have something you wish to add to the conversation?"

"No, sir," Allyson said. "I'm thinking out loud. I'm sorry."

"Let's keep our thoughts to ourselves, Miss Rayburn," he said as he went back to teaching the class.

The Death Maze

Allyson couldn't believe what had just occurred. She shook her head. She had never allowed something like that to happen in this class, or any class. Ever!

Dan was on her mind. It would be her first real date with the man she might want to hold forever. Her instincts were always correct, but they needed to be dealt with after class. She tried to concentrate for the thirty minutes remaining, as she had a feeling Dan would be outside the classroom waiting for her.

He was outside the classroom waiting for her. He had showed up late for his other class, but it had been canceled due to the instructor being ill. He rushed back, sat down on a bench near the biology building, and tried to do some studying.

It was useless. After they bumped into each other, he had trouble taking his eyes off hers. The green was mesmerizing.

The bone structure of her face was stunning. She had high cheekbones and beautiful full lips. Her nose fit perfectly without the need to change it into the smaller nub that many women of their generation wanted. It was straight and not too large or small. Her eyebrows were tweezed to just the right angle without being too thin or too full. Her makeup was flawless, with all the highlights and color complementing her rich skin color.

There wasn't a strand of hair out of place. Her rust-red hair was cut into layers and bangs. She wore it about four inches below the shoulders.

Dan found the word to describe Allyson: exquisite! She was every man's dream on the outside. Now if she was only the right woman on the inside. Dan wanted this to be right.

Her voice was melodious. It wasn't nasal or whiny and grating. It was refined and well balanced. In his mind, Dan could hear her voice speaking his name. He was in heaven.

"Hi, Dan," Allyson said.

Oh yes, Dan could live with her forever. He opened his eyes and she was actually standing in front of him.

"I'm sorry," he said as he stood up. "I was thinking of you and thought you were talking to me in my mind only. I mean . . ."

"I know what you mean," Allyson said. "I had problems with my class."

"You did?"

"I believe we're both having the same thoughts about each other, hoping that what happened was more than an apparition."

"It wouldn't even matter if it were an apparition. Knowing now that it's real makes it worthwhile." Dan looked at her books. "May I help you with those?"

Allyson handed him a couple books as they walked to the cafeteria. They picked at their meals while trying to find out as much as they could about each other.

Allyson was going to be a lawyer. She was finishing her prerequisites before starting her real classes. In another two years, she'd be in law school at Yale and then on her way to a career as a prosecuting attorney.

She felt that her main strength was the fact that so many in the male-dominated field underestimated her talents. While they were thinking she was capable of just being a law clerk and gopher, she would outwit them and put them under the table. She had no empathy for rich defendants receiving reduced or no sentences because of their connections. She had no sympathy for crooks with poor upbringings. There were laws, and those laws were meant to be followed until they were changed by voters or politicians. Rich or poor, you obeyed the laws.

Dan enjoyed listening to her. When it was his turn, he explained that his aspirations were in the field of chemistry. He envisioned changing the world before it destroyed itself. He had long ago known that fossil fuels would someday be a thing of the past. He stressed that coal should no longer be mined, and that without green energy, the world would self-destruct from too much CO_2 in the atmosphere.

"So tell me about your background rather than your vocational aspirations," Allyson said.

"My background?" Dan asked.

"Yes," she said. "I want to know more about the past. I want to know the man who bumped into me."

"Well," he said, thinking. "I came into this world as a babe wrapped in a cashmere blanket from head to toe. From the first day of birth, I was spoiled rotten."

"You know what I mean," she said, laughing at his metaphors and thinking how marvelous this relationship was going to be.

"My name is Daniel Jeremy Adams," he explained. "I come from New York and I think I want to fall in love with you."

Allyson at first couldn't believe what she had just heard. She reacted with a smile and then a confused stare. When Dan saw her reaction, he tried to defuse the comment.

"That is if you believe at love at first sight. If not, I hope it's love at second sight. If not that, then maybe I could first give myself a good hard kick in the groin, scream a little, and then persuade you to at least give me another chance."

Allyson wasn't laughing. She was smiling. She thought Dan was cute and witty and outright charming.

"I never believed in love at first sight," she exclaimed. "However, you are sure making it a reality for me. If that's what you honestly feel, I'm glad you said it. It was spontaneous and unrehearsed. It was down-to-earth."

Dan didn't know what to think at this point. He couldn't tell how she felt. Was Allyson really glad he said it or was she just being courteous? He had never said anything like that before to anyone. He had never actually felt the way he did when he first saw her and as he did right now. He truly felt that strange ping in his heart and that he needed—no, wanted—to be with her always. She was so unique.

"Well," she said, "in keeping with your honesty, I want to tell you that I think you are very handsome. I feel just as fortunate to have met you. And I was brought into this world wrapped in mink. Cashmere was never in my mother's closet."

Dan laughed. Allyson had a great sense of humor.

"Mr. Adams, you have made this the best day of all the time I've spent on campus to date."

"I thank you very much. I would have hoped that the University of Miami would have been more kind to you."

"It's been a terrific experience so far. I've been able to pursue my goals and learn a great deal. I have a lot of work still left and I'm sure I'll reach my goals."

Dan wanted to know more about Allyson and hoped there were still a few minutes left before her next class.

"Tell me. Is Allyson Rayburn your full name? Or is it some terribly long European title?"

Again laughing, Allyson explained. "I was going to inform you that my mother is of Swedish royalty, but that would be far-fetched. Actually, it is my full name, no middle name or initial. Both of my parents grew up in the US, but their ancestors were European."

"Where are you from?"

The Death Maze

"I'm from Colorado. My folks own a mountain . . ."

"A mountain?" Dan interrupted.

"Not a large one," Allyson tried to explain.

"I'm not sure there are small mountains, Allyson. I know there are hills. Aren't mountains larger than hills?"

"Okay. They own a mountain and a ski lodge and there are lots of people who ski there every year. I'm also a good skier, but really just a modest person who doesn't like to brag."

"And when is your next class?"

"I've already decided that my next class can wait until the next class," she said. "I want to be with you."

"Well, it's Friday and I believe I have completed my day as well. I had a strange ambition to study until dawn." Dan giggled as he said these words.

"Uh huh!" Allyson responded sarcastically. "I'll bet the library even has a chair with your name on it."

"How did you know?"

"I've recently been to the library."

They took their time in the cafeteria and talked all afternoon. They didn't notice the students filing in and out. The world was totally invisible to them.

Dan explained some of his chemistry theories, which left her amazed. Would there be a future for mankind? He assured her there would. Man was very prone to adapt to all situations in any matter of shape or form. Although there would be plenty of arguments, tons of meetings, and almost assuredly a lack of consensus, life would continue. That is, unless mankind had the total desire, and insanity, to wipe itself and all other known planetary life forms out of existence.

Allyson explained to Dan the goals she wanted to reach while in school and upon introduction to the outside world.

She knew of many corporations that had manipulated the laws for their own good while totally ignoring the true realities of the laws. As long as they made lots of money, the corporations didn't care for mankind. It was their way or the highway. Cross the corporations, and you cross the daily functionality of the world.

It was her choice to take it all on. She longed for change. She yearned to ensure that mankind ran corporations and not the other way around. Without the minds of people, businesses didn't exist. She was tired and frustrated of hearing how businesses cheated the middle and poor classes.

The conversations continued until the sun went down. They stared, held hands, and laughed. By the time they noticed dinner was being served, they checked their watches and lifted themselves from their chairs. Walking to the exit of the cafeteria, Dan grasped her hand. He didn't want to let go. Allyson held on just as firmly.

The walkway that led to the dormitories on the east side of campus wasn't long. However, they continued to meander, learning both idle gossip and firm information about the other's family background.

Allyson came from a rich family. It didn't surprise Dan that she held none of the snobbish attitudes he felt most women with money had. She didn't look down on others as servants. She felt that everyone had the inert desire to move in a positive manner. There was nothing negative about her, and her mind was always open to any opinions offered in passing conversation. If those opinions could be substantiated and verified, she was able to determine their veracity whether she felt they were right or wrong.

After all, Dan thought to himself as he remembered the words of his father, *opinions are like assholes. Everyone has one.*

However, Dan did not feel he needed to inform her about his family's fortunes. He did share with her his father's wishes for a son and his mother's abundance of love. He told her he had a sister he adored who was really smarter than he was. He told her he felt he had a lucky streak and he never lost an argument or a bet. He was good with numbers.

Allyson had definite ideas about her future and what she wanted to do to achieve her goals. This was probably why she felt she was able to fall in love so quickly and yet not admit it outwardly. This was her reason for spending almost an entire day with a man she had not known that morning. She trusted herself.

Throughout the afternoon, Dan found that Allyson was well versed in the arts, politics, and philosophies of life according to many but summarized by one: herself. She showed no signs of stupidity or naiveté, and she understood how reason and summarization could benefit a person's overall outlook.

She loved the profession of law. It was for this reason she had come to this southeastern university. Its reputation had thrived on four things: science, law, theatre, and sports. Oh yes, it was growing as a football mecca. The rivalry between the Miami Hurricanes and Florida Gators was becoming huge. The Hurricanes were showing real signs of becoming number one in the country. And Allyson loved football.

Dan explained his reasons for attending U of M. He had always been fascinated with science. He expanded on his world of chemistry and discovering the unknown. He talked about the world of medicine and future cures for cancer, diabetes, and heart disease.

Green energy was then becoming a normal daily discussion in the science world. The Middle East was imposing trade embargoes on oil, and no one knew President Carter would be correct in his opinion that America should no longer be dependent on the Middle East for oil. Putting solar panels on the White House roof had been the correct decision, and it should have led to installing them on all buildings in the country.

Although Dan informed Allyson that he enjoyed the ultimate privacy of his profession, he told her he wanted to be enriched with her presence each and every day. The last eight hours had been unbelievable. He wanted more. The chemistry between them was unmistakable. And he knew chemistry.

Allyson agreed as he opened the door to her dormitory complex. Day one of this new relationship was almost over. They had discovered their new world. It was one they had never known could truly exist.

He looked at her and she stared back. Their eyes met. Dan slowly leaned in and closed his eyes as his lips met hers. Her eyes then also closed and her lips parted slightly. He felt his tongue move into her mouth and hers move as well, both feeling that this kiss was just one of millions that could be. What seemed an eternity was just a few moments in time.

Dan drew away slightly and looked at her. "Thank you," he said.

"For what?" she whispered.

"For you. If I had to bump into you all over again, I'd do it in a flash."

"Me too," Allyson said softly.

They stood speechless for a few more moments as if they had talked each other mute. Then Allyson spoke.

"Would you like to come in with me?"

Dan smiled but wanted to laugh. He thought she had said "come in me," and then realized the full thought.

"Yes, I would."

Allyson smiled and then detected some hesitation. "But . . ."

"But I have a lot of homework," he said slowly.

"Me too," Allyson admitted, only because she did not want to force anything on Dan. Although she did have plenty of homework, she just didn't want to be left alone right now. If not to feel his love, then to have his company. Just to be with him some more.

"I'll see you tomorrow?" she asked.

"At the same cafeteria table for breakfast," he replied as they kissed once more before he turned to exit the dormitory lobby.

Allyson watched as he left and dropped her eyes to the floor.

Dan walked about ten steps before realizing how stupid he was. He turned around and walked back toward Allyson. She lifted her eyes to meet his and they kissed once more.

"Screw the homework," he said.

Allyson didn't need to say what she was thinking: It wasn't the homework that needed to be screwed. She guided him past the lobby and front desk of her dorm. She led him to the elevators, stepped in, and pushed the button to the eighth floor.

After getting out of the elevator, they walked arm in arm to room 802. Day one may have been over. However, evening one was just starting. They read each other's mind and knew that this was not just going to be a one-night stand. Even though there would have been plenty of time to consummate their desire for each other, now was just as perfect a time as any.

Allyson took her key from her skirt pocket and inserted it into the locked door. She turned the handle as she slowly opened the door with her other hand. She led Dan into her room.

The blinds were slightly ajar. The moonlight was all that she needed to see where she was going. Closing the door behind her, she gazed at the image of Dan standing in the middle of the room.

She approached Dan with an incredible ease of movement; he would swear she hadn't taken a step, but glided up to him. She raised her arms to wrap them around his neck. Her face lifted and then her lips once again met his. Her tongue danced around his when she let him enter her mouth.

Dan felt the tightness in his groin and hoped that she hadn't yet discovered that he wanted her so soon. The kisses continued. She was enjoying the fullness and sensuality of the deep connection of their mouths. She loved to kiss, and he enjoyed reciprocating.

Allyson led him to her bed. She wanted to take full control, and they lay down with her on top. While they continued to kiss, she took her left hand and started undoing the buttons of his shirt. As she undid each button, she kissed more of his chest. When the shirt was fully undone, she gently kissed his nipples, which made him rise farther and harder.

She was taking her time. This was to be her moment. She had dreamt of this moment. It played out in vivid fashion within her mind as she completed undressing him. Her kisses followed each removal of his clothing and his hardness excited her more. She felt herself fully wet from this experience.

When she finished undressing Dan, Allyson began undressing herself. Dan tried to help her undo her blouse. However, she gently laid his hands back on her bed. She knew what she wanted to do. It was as if she had performed this a hundred times. In reality, she had only made love twice, but each time had left her defeated.

She had known that when she met the man of her dreams, she wanted to make him explode with anticipation and leave him only wanting more. Now that she knew this was going to happen, her control would guide her to those feelings she had dreamed. Allyson wanted Dan to crave it as much as she did.

Unhooking her blouse revealed the fullness of her breasts. They were round and perfect in Dan's eyes. He felt the incredible urge to come, but fought back knowing there was enough time. He wanted her right now, but knew it would be her moment.

Allyson undid her skirt and let it drop to the floor. When she peeled off her panties, Dan saw that her womanhood had the same rust-red hair that adorned her head.

Dan thought he'd explode. He was feeling wild inside from the excitement of watching Allyson undress. She was nothing less than the epitome of beauty and grace. Her head slightly bobbed as her hair fell across her breasts.

She mounted Dan and let him cup her breasts with both hands. He gently sucked her nipples. Her excitement grew as she felt a rising feeling deep inside her. She hadn't realized she'd be able to come by the erotic touch of his tongue on her nipples. She wanted to cry out, but refused because she only wanted more.

Knowing there could only be additional orgasms waiting for her, Allyson gently guided Dan's firmness into her. She was dripping wet and felt hotter than she had ever felt before. Her movements led him to go deeper. She rode him while tightening with each movement.

She came again and cried out for joy as her movements accelerated. Dan grabbed hold of her and brought her down fully on top of him, and then turned her over so he was now the aggressor on top of her.

He moved with exceptional clarity as his penetrations went deeper. Allyson pushed up and down in concert with his movements. She soon came a third time and let him know she was being satisfied.

It was now time for Dan to reach his climactic moment. Allyson moved simultaneously with him, holding on tightly and craving the gushing feeling. He felt he was going to burst and let out a cry of joy. It came at first with a shot and then a warm gush. Allyson got warmer when she felt her fourth orgasm.

It was unbelievable to her. She could only describe it as pure love. Feeling his body on top of hers made her wish it could never end. She wanted more, but was totally exhausted. Allyson fell asleep with Dan still in and on top of her.

For Dan, this was also a new experience. For a woman to arouse him mentally and physically was nothing short of a miracle. He was ready to reintroduce himself to the Lord Almighty for bringing such a perfect woman into his life. Allyson Rayburn felt like the equivalent of finding the true meaning of life. He would not let this woman get away from him.

When Allyson woke a few hours later, she was under her sheets and there was a note by her pillow. She lifted her head to try and focus on the words. The moonlight was now beyond her windows, so she turned on the reading light next to her bed.

Allyson,
Thank you for this day and this evening. I know I am not dreaming. I have found the woman I want

to spend an eternity with. I pray and hope that what I have just written does not make you want to run to the registrar's office and transfer to the nearest community college in Colorado.

I apologize for not being with you when you wake in the morning and expect to see me next to you. It is something I want to happen every morning. However, I do have a Saturday class and hope to see you at our spot in the cafeteria at 10:00 a.m. for breakfast. I cannot wait to see you. I pray you sleep well.
Dan

Allyson put the letter under her pillow, grabbed her alarm, and set it for 8:00 a.m. It would be enough time to make herself beautiful for her man.

What a wonderful thought! Dan Adams was her man, and he wanted her for an eternity. Her college life had turned out to be the beginning of the best years of her life. Her future with her man by her side would be not only full, but fulfilling. Daniel Jeremy Adams was all hers and she was all his. Allyson Rayburn closed her eyes and went back to sleep.

***

Dan returned from his haze only to realize he was still falling. Why the hell was he still falling? And why had he not asked Allyson for her hand in marriage? What in God's name was really going on?

Was their separation in her senior year a sign of his unhappiness over never again reaching that peak of pleasure? God, how he wished Allyson were a part of his life. He tried to think of her while still falling to focus his thoughts. Or was it the sixth dimension doing this?

Allyson had received a call from her father one afternoon. They were in her room making love. Lifting herself from the bed, she walked to her desk and answered the phone. Dan watched her every move.

"Hello," she answered. She immediately recognized the voice. "Daddy! How are you?"

"Allyson, I have something to tell you," her father said.

Allyson knew it was bad news. She could tell in her father's voice.

"Daddy, what's wrong?"

Dan sat up in the bed and covered himself while listening.

"It's your mother, Allyson. She's had a heart attack."

"What?" Allyson whispered. Dan barely heard it. She was shaking.

Allyson hadn't seen her parents since she had left for college in August. It was now early November and she had been with Dan for almost two years. She was planning on bringing him home with her for Christmas. The plane tickets had already been purchased and arrangements had been made with her parents to celebrate.

Dan saw tears roll down her cheeks. He rose from her bed and put on his pants. He brought Allyson her robe and put it around her shoulders. She turned and buried her face in his chest.

"Allyson? Are you there?" Dan heard her father ask.

A few moments passed before she answered. "Is she all right? What hospital is she in?"

"No, sweetheart. She's not all right. She's dying and wants to see you. I'll take you to the hospital as soon as you arrive."

The Death Maze

"Oh, Daddy . . ." she sobbed as the tears came down faster. Allyson was unable to talk. Dan took the phone from her hand.

"Mr. Rayburn. This is Dan."

"Dan, Allyson's mother is in the hospital. There's not much time. She would like to see Allyson before she's gone."

"I understand, sir. I'll put Allyson on a plane this afternoon."

"Thank you, Dan. Call me back with the flight number and time."

"I'm sorry to hear about Mrs. Rayburn, sir."

Dan hung up the phone and held Allyson in his arms. She was now crying uncontrollably and hanging on to Dan as if it were his life that was about to end. Dan led her to the bed and held her until she fell asleep.

He had heard many stories of how close she had been to her mother. They had done everything together since she was a little girl. While her father was managing the business, her mother took her to dancing lessons from age four to twelve until she decided she no longer wanted to dance.

Then she took tae kwon do lessons for three years when she felt she needed to fend off the boys who were becoming too forward after coming off the slopes. During one winter she encountered a drunken sixteen-year-old who tried to take advantage of her. She managed to kick him in the groin, run to get her father, and have him kicked off the property for a full season.

After tae kwon do, she took cooking lessons and she and her mom tried new recipes, baking everything from cupcakes to cookies, party cakes to pies. Allyson even set up a small area in the lodge where she was able to sell her baked goods and make extra money during the ski season.

When she discovered the field of law, it was all in and nothing else. Her father had been sued for an accident after one skier faked a fall. It turned out that the skier needed extra money to bail a friend from jail who had been arrested for a DUI. Allyson did her own investigation. She knew someone at the hospital who informed her that the accident was a ruse. The skier had never gone to the hospital, and the report had been filed outside the hospital by a part-time worker who had access to the hospital records. After Allyson sent her report to the police, both were incarcerated for a long time.

Dan went to her closet and pulled out her suitcase. He unzipped it and began packing the clothing she would need for her trip. Little did he know it would be her last time at college. A week later, she would have her belongings sent back to Colorado without Dan even knowing it.

Dan then picked up the phone and called the airlines. He made a one-way reservation, since he did not yet know when to schedule her return. He was sure she would call after her mother passed away and would then know when the funeral would take place.

After the plane reservations were made and confirmed, Dan called Allyson's father and gave him the information. Allyson's father thanked Dan for all he had done and said he looked forward to seeing him at Christmas.

Dan sat down on the chair and stared at Allyson while she slept. She was beautiful and looked like a little girl. How he wanted to take her away and protect her for the rest of her life. Somehow he knew, deep inside, this was the end. Something was telling him that once she boarded the plane, Allyson would be gone forever.

He felt a tear roll down his face as he looked at the clock. It was time to get Allyson up and dressed. She needed to be at the airport on time. Dan hated to be late for anything. Even if it meant having his girlfriend leave him.

Allyson opened her eyes before Dan rose to get her up and saw Dan staring at her. She wanted him one more time, but knew that it wasn't meant to be. While she got dressed, Dan carried her bags down to the dorm lobby.

Allyson soon followed, staying close to Dan. He was her protection. He was the shield from all the devils that tried to get in her way. She felt that as long as he was there, her life could only be perfect. Allyson never even figured in a possible death in her family.

The moon was shining brightly outside the dormitory as he led her to his car. She held on to him and squeezed so he would know that she would need him for every interval in life. There was a cool breeze blowing. Dan felt a chill from her body.

They walked past the intramural fields and down a ramp until they came to his red Mustang. He opened the door and gently helped her into the car. When he entered the car on the driver's side, he noticed that she was staring into empty space. He wanted to tell her it was going to be all right, but then decided against it. It wasn't going to be all right. Her mother, and best friend, was dying. She was devastated.

The trip to the airport passed in total silence. He parked the car in the closest parking section next to the terminal and then led her to the ticketing counter and the gate. When it was time to board, Allyson gave him a long kiss, turned, and walked down the ramp to the plane. Nothing had been said for over an hour.

Dan knew it was a sign. However, Allyson turned back and said she'd call him from Colorado and give him the information. She turned the corner again and disappeared.

Dan waited. The gate doors were closed and the plane left the terminal. He saw the plane take off and disappear from sight. When he did leave, it was almost nine o'clock in the evening. Allyson's plane had already been in the air for two hours. Soon she would be with her father. Hopefully she would make it in time to see her mother once more.

Each morning he waited for a call before going to class. Each afternoon, he returned to his dorm room and waited again. Each evening, after dinner, he studied in his room and waited. He hoped he would hear the phone ring before he went to sleep at midnight. The call never came, and he tried to give her the benefit of the doubt, as her mother was dying or had already passed away.

Still, it was uncalled for to totally neglect him and his feelings. He had been there for her. He had taken care of her. He had protected her. Dan tried many times to pick up the phone and dial her number. Each time he put the phone back in its cradle. "Give it time," he kept saying to himself.

A week passed before he took the initiative to go to her dorm room and get some things he had left behind. Dan still had the key attached to his keychain.

As he approached her door, he hesitated at first. A couple of the other women on her floor passed by him and said hello as they recognized him. He politely returned their greetings and then quickly put the key in the lock. After turning the doorknob and opening the door, he stood agog.

It was empty. Dan stared in disbelief before entering the room. He noticed a few books on the desk shelf. The mattress, sans sheets and blankets, rested on the bed frame. The refrigerator, radio, television—all of it—were now gone. He found a notebook he required for one of his classes but hadn't needed until now. When he picked it up from the desk, a note fell to the floor. Dan unfolded the note.

> My love, my life,
> I'll never forget you. One day I'll return and our love will once again be bright. I'm sorry, but my mother's death has totally taken all the life out of me.
> I do love you,
> Allyson

The light within his free fall grew brighter as his memory went from one woman to another. It was as if he was suspended in motion and he was allowed to recall everything. But why? There had to be a firm reason for him to recall the past in such detail.

His mind switched to Ruth. It had been between four and five years since the death of her husband. He had been there the entire time she needed assistance. She had become a wealthy woman because he had fought so hard for her and knew it was morally correct to protect her.

Dan understood that he did not have to be so vigilant when fighting for justice. However, the oil companies were consistent in their vigilance to manipulate the cost of oil and make sure their profits far exceeded the true facts. After all, a barrel of oil that the market said closed at $140 on one particular day did not enter the marketplace the same day. And yet the price one paid at the gas station rose within twenty-four hours. Did the price go down within twenty-four hours if the cost per barrel dropped the next day? Probably not!

There had been no special person in Dan's life during the years between Allyson and Ruth. He had gone on dates. However, before Ruth, he had felt there would never be another woman who would bring him the warmth and comfort, love and companionship that Allyson provided.

Now that Ruth was part of his life, his world had changed and he knew love would one day be a reality. After she moved in with him, it sparked a new fire within him. Subconsciously, Dan knew she needed rest and an assured knowledge of peace of mind. He kept to himself and focused on his work but made sure he was there when Ruth reached out.

What had been buried deep within him had slowly reverberated with a new liveliness. Even with the ground rules they had set after she moved in, Dan grew to feel there was more to care about other than his work.

He knew that Ruth felt it also. She first became a terrific assistant and then developed a friendship with him that would become a lifelong bond. Time was only on their side, and they nurtured each other's private and public well-being. As with any relationship, what began as a spontaneous look grew into a deeper stare. The thankful shake of the hand turned into a hug. The peck on the cheek became the kiss on the lips.

In a sense, Dan had also lost a loved one many years prior to Ruth. They were both dealing with a tragic pain that took many years to heal but always resided within their minds. The hurt only decreases with time. What is supposed to heal all wounds never really does. Life still goes on.

For Dan, it felt like a marriage unconsummated. It was a good feeling to have a woman in the home, as well as a trusted companion. Dan hadn't realized that he wanted and needed female companionship until Ruth moved in.

He began to feel that maybe he had wasted too many years. With Ruth's unfortunate ordeal, Dan made it his mission to begin to try once again. It might even feel good inside, and lessen that stiff, uncomfortable feeling always in the pit of his stomach. Even though he had forgiven Allyson many years ago, he still had that feeling, but this new normalcy was now allowing it to relax.

After many months and then years with Ruth, he felt better about himself. Dan didn't need to shut himself up in his laboratory every waking moment. Ruth helped him get out and have some fun. They went on day trips and experienced as much of the surrounding areas as possible. Getting out at night for dinner or going to a movie theater became a ritual at least twice a week. It was all because of Ruth.

Dan felt his work had more meaning since he was now doing it for someone other than himself. At times, he even waited until Ruth could join him in the lab before continuing. There was a future, and that future was with a new woman who could enrich his life for the eternity he thought he would have with Allyson. Dan's quality of life was no longer "strained," an idea he remembered from one of Shakespeare's plays.

However, he would not have traded the previous years. There are reasons for everything. Dan knew his place in the world and that his work was important. The only thing he lacked was moderation in the quality of time he utilized.

Maybe that was it. Maybe, just maybe, this whole sixth dimension and Apep experience was all for a reason. Could it be possible that this was just a horrible dream to cause him to realize his past mistakes? It didn't seem possible. It was all too real. Besides, what sort of catharsis could possibly be gleaned from an experience as horrendous as this?

He loved Arione and the life he lived there. His life was rich in community achievements. The relationships he had developed over the years were more than concrete: They were friendships to last a lifetime. He had earned respect within his community and the scientific world. Dan was a rock-solid citizen who could be confided in and relied upon by all.

He felt the fall was coming to an end, and his mind drew back to his surroundings. A light began to grow. Dan was sure the landing would come in moments. *Please let it be as painless as possible*, he thought.

He fell into a heavily padded area. He bounced from one wall to another. Each cushion his body touched seemed to throw him to another a few feet away. Dan was sure he hit all four cushioned walls within the area.

Then he stopped. It was as if one of the cushions just grabbed hold of him and held firm until his body ceased moving.

He opened his eyes. His head was positioned so that he was looking in the direction from which he fell. This was good because he wanted to know how far he had fallen and try to ascertain for how long. Dan also knew that wherever he had dropped from would disappear from sight within seconds.

"Concentrate," he said to himself as he tried to make definite eye contact.

He noticed that the ceiling area had a large opening that looked round in shape. He tried to focus on the depth of the opening. He saw a distant fluorescence, but couldn't determine how far away it was. However, it couldn't be more than a few hundred feet.

This was disturbing because Dan had been falling for what seemed to be hours. He could only determine that the

The Death Maze

sixth dimension had made it feel like he had been suspended in time, and the motion of falling was a manipulation of his surroundings. It was kind of like a person standing in the middle of an arena and everything turning or moving except the centerpiece. Dan represented the centerpiece.

The opening did disappear. Dan's new area was only four feet in height and six feet square. He obviously had gone through the correct area. Otherwise, he would be in a smaller enclosure. The maze hadn't decreased in size. Even if it had, how would he have returned to the nursery to find the correct opening?

Dan started to laugh. It wasn't one of those continuous giggling outbursts one had when listening to a funny comic. It was just an immediate realization that he had survived a decision, survived a long fall, and come to understand more about his past.

His flashbacks of Allyson and Ruth were memories of his life with ones he loved. Dan truly wanted to thank Apep for these memories. Apep had allowed Dan to relive two good relationships that had rounded out his life. Both women had brought out only the best in him. Life wasn't about money or things. It was everything that made a person who they were.

Dan looked up again at the now-closed ceiling. He searched for anything that could be construed as a flaw. He wanted to say just one thing. Not finding anything wrong, he simply mouthed the words *thank you.*

Dan then moved to a corner of the enclosure and closed his eyes. He was tired. He needed to sleep. What he had just experienced had left him totally exhausted.

While he slept, Apep watched. Apep never needed to sleep. He only worked to make sure he was always in control. He prepared for the death of Dr. Dan Adams. What lay ahead had already been decided, as all of Dan's decisions were predetermined. Apep was ready.

What disturbed him most were Dan's last words. No one, not even when he had lived in Nubia, had ever thanked him. At first Apep wanted to respond. He couldn't. A grateful attitude was the first out-of-the-ordinary response to the sixth dimension that he had ever seen. Those two small words were more powerful than any Dan Adams had uttered in the sixth dimension.

Apep needed to concentrate on his next move. His preparations were complete. His world was ready for the next chapter.

His thoughts were suddenly knocked askew from what they once were.

Chapter 28

William Barrish lay on his back in bed. He was dreadfully uncomfortable and wished he could turn on his side, on his stomach, into any position other than on his back. Sometimes, he actually rose from the bed and walked around just to get some exercise. But he hated sleeping on his back, and the nurse became upset whenever he rose from the bed.

The pain in his jaw was unbelievable. It constantly pulsed, and felt like it was purposefully taking longer to heal than it should. Even though it was only the day after the fist hit his jaw, he still felt like shit!

He hadn't needed a cast, but he knew the wires were there since he could barely move his mouth. The wires were an excellent substitute for the type of cast that might have been used twenty or thirty years ago. He only wondered once what would have been if his jaw had been broken a long time ago. The wires kept his mouth shut and prevented any movement. This was going to take time, and he knew that time was not on his side.

When he became hungry, the nurses fed him through a straw that fit between his clenched teeth. His food was ground up into a fine liquid and mixed together. If he wanted protein—in other words, meat—sorry, buddy, no can do. You got yourself into this mess, you can wait the eight weeks until it heals. For now, you drink everything.

The television was on, but he wasn't listening to it. He hated reality shows, soap operas, and mostly anything that wasn't the news. He thrived on full doses of politics and local, regional, and world news. He had been hooked on it even as a kid.

Billy, as they used to call him at home, was always a skinny child. He would eat every morsel on his plate and have seconds but still not gain weight. Every member of his family was in good shape. However, Billy was the only one they thought had some sort of disease. Maybe a tapeworm had gotten into his system, his mother thought.

The doctor never worried about it. He told Billy's mother to wait until he hit his teens. Then he should fill out and his skin would no longer cling to his bones. Besides, he was healthy.

Billy was named after his grandfather. He only remembered seeing him a couple times and couldn't really recall him. The two actually played together quite often until Billy was four years old. He learned that his namesake had died on the way to see him. His grandfather had loved him and never missed a week of fun.

They spent many hours at the playground. Billy's first steps and first words were in the company of his grandfather. Grandpa had to inform his parents of these achievements while they worked to ask their son to mimic his feats.

Billy didn't even look like his parents at first. They wondered if there had been a mistake when they brought him home. It wasn't until his Grandfather Warren showed up that they noticed the uncanny resemblance.

Warren William Barrish was very proud when he saw his grandson. The deep, dark brown eyes, wavy hair, and small chin reflected nothing but exuberance when he showed up. His first thoughts were, *This is a child that will move the world.*

He also became upset when anyone called his grandson Bill. William was a strong, masculine name, and Grandfather Warren insisted that Bill be dropped whatever he was around.

Young William wished he could remember this special man. His mother had constantly told him stories of the two of them. William had the pictures and always kept the dream of his grandfather's first thoughts.

His gift as a writer led him to the world of journalism, where he would "move the world." In school, he was a good student. He was fair in sports but mightier with his pen. He developed a column in the school paper called "This Week's Student," and his stories and exposés drew many classmates to him.

Each column gave a short background of a different classmate in his high school. It encompassed the likes, dislikes, favorite subjects, and personalities of each pupil. He never wrote anything negative and always tried to enhance the student's positive aspects.

It actually brought the students closer. They became a more understanding and tolerant body of individuals who needed to get along. In his own way, William tried to prepare his small world of students for the path they were to embark on once they graduated and moved on to either college or the workplace.

He had an uncanny way with others and a certain knowledge of what the world was going to be like after he left high school. Although he wasn't the ideological student always looking for that pot of gold or rainbow, William wasn't the depressed, pessimistic loner, either. He balanced himself evenly and looked upon each event as a new trial with possible rewards.

When William featured the captain of the football team in his first column, he made a friend for life. There were rumors that Eddie Travers was full of brawn and no brains. He barely got by in class, but passed life by being the star of the team.

That all changed when William interviewed Eddie and uncovered a truly sensitive human being. Even though Eddie was big, he was far from dumb. He had ambitions to help others. He wanted to defend those who couldn't stick up for themselves. Eddie wanted to be either a lawyer or social worker. It wasn't about money or prestige. It was about being a good person.

After his first column was written, it wasn't long before everyone sought out William to be his next subject. This was when he thought up the idea of his "Identity Box." Those wanting to be in the column simply had to put their name in the box. Every afternoon, William cleaned out the box and made a list. He would then scrutinize the list and seek out those who had not put their names in the box.

These classmates were the real stories. The ones who felt they didn't have anything to report or give back had the unique stories waiting to be told. Since no one knew who put their names in the box except William, who could possibly object to his choices? Besides, he wrote many articles about a variety of interesting characters within his school.

There was a new hero each week, and it was the middle-class society that pulled it all together. Everyone knew who the king and queen of the prom would be. All the students dreamed of being the exception. The major achievers always stood out in the crowd. However, not all got that chance to shine. It was William who gave those unsung classmates the bit of notoriety that they deserved.

The Death Maze

It was in college at St. John's University that William's pen grew even mightier. His hunger for news grew to the big city. New York had eight million people longing for their chance to come out of their cocoon. It was here that he could write about a world that never slept and a barrage of characters who longed to be the heartbeat of the Big Apple.

Even at college, William faced many dangers and threats. There were always those who wanted to take him down a notch because they saw him as a threat. That was part of the job, as William soon learned.

His senior thesis centered on the lifestyles of black men in Harlem. Knowing that no white man should really set foot alone in Harlem, William set out looking for just one man to help him complete his paper. He found that man: a member of the university basketball team.

He was six-foot-eight and weighed 260 pounds. His name was Herbert Wilson, and he came from a large family with three sisters and two brothers. He also had a record for stealing when he was sixteen.

Seeing the possibilities in Herbert, the judge had told him he could work off his time by paying society back for his crime and becoming a model for others. There were too many kids out on the street who had potential but never had the chance. Herbert could be a prime example of the young black man who made it big by showing others that a little hard work not only didn't hurt, but was rewarding.

Herbert had listened to the judge. He showed his family he would rise above the fray. He studied, earned a scholarship, and won a position on a team that could give him a chance to play professional basketball.

William Barrish won great praise for his thesis. He thanked Herbert for allowing him the opportunity to come into his world and show him a side of life he never would have seen. Herbert went on to play for the Boston Celtics. He sent the judge tickets to the very first game he played. Herbert even gave the press William's name during his first interview. Upon learning of this story, the *Los Angeles News* offered him a position and relocated William to the other side of his world.

William was driving toward Los Angeles after having spent ten days investigating the disappearance of a wealthy businessman when he was almost hit by Lawrence Welles. Ten long, hot days in the Nevada desert was enough for anyone. All William wanted was to return home, write his story, and take a long shower in a city where the hot air clung to your clothes all day long.

The disappearance turned out to be a hoax. He found his subject tied up in a poker game that had been going on for over a week. All involved had made a pact that no one would contact their families until only one person walked away with it all. Prior to that he had spent a few days with a woman.

William was disappointed with himself for convincing his boss, Robert Graves, to give him the assignment. Now it was his dumb luck, and his urge to continue to move the world, that had sent him to the hospital in a small Podunk town.

What was worse was that he now had a hot-tempered hick cop named Richard Dressler on his back who acted like a madman while trying to enforce the laws with his fists. "Those fists," he kept telling himself as he touched his jaw. William needed to think about how he would repay Chief Dressler for his kindness and consideration.

A knock at the door interrupted his thoughts, and Chief Dressler entered. Even though the chief was looking brave and contented, William wondered if he would feel that way had he not been stuck in bed with his jaw wired shut.

"I owe you for this," William said with clenched teeth.

"You already paid me back," Dressler said, showing him the soft cast on his left hand. "Why couldn't you just tell me the truth about the accident? Nothing would have happened to you."

"You wouldn't let me do my job. You forced me to take the action I did. I'm a reporter. Remember?"

"Only too well. And my hand thanks you for all its pain. I didn't know your breed could fight."

"Dressler," Barrish sneered through those clenched teeth, "you're so fucking smug and ignorant. That accident would never have made the front page had you left me alone. Now that I know you're hiding something, it becomes a larger story. Want to know something else? I'm going to make sure it hits page one, center. Then I'm going to send you a dozen copies for your photo album."

Dressler was standing with his good right fist clenched tight. He would have loved to break Barrish's nose and maybe do a number on the rest of his face. He took a deep breath before he answered.

"How come you want to make trouble for yourself? Don't you think you've had enough?"

"Because I owe you and because you're so naive," Barrish said carefully. "I'm going to take this thing to the top. Why don't you look at yourself? You're the one who put the doubt in my head. You're the one who's caused all this trouble."

Chief Dressler walked closer to the bed and leaned over. He was staring directly at William Barrish with his nose so close that one would think it was touching. Dressler wanted to intimidate him. Barrish didn't flinch. He stared back with as piercing a gaze as he could manage. He didn't want the chief to think he was intimidated.

"Barrish," Dressler said, "I personally will take it upon myself to have the pleasure of escorting you out of town as soon as you are released from this place."

"That won't be necessary, Chief," a voice from behind him said. Dressler looked up and turned. Barrish shifted his eyes to the door. Alex Miller was standing there. He had been waiting for the right moment to interrupt the pleasant conversation.

"My client already has police brutality. Maybe I should add assault with intent?" Alex was fishing. However, Chief Dressler didn't know it and hoped that maybe he would go away for now.

"I've got him for reckless driving and withholding information from an ongoing investigation, Mr. . . . what did you say your name was?" Dressler asked.

"I didn't!" Alex immediately responded.

"Reckless driving my ass," Barrish responded to Dressler's accusation.

Dressler turned around to stare again at Barrish, thinking he had the upper hand. As far as he was concerned, he could charge Barrish with reckless driving.

Turning back to the man at the door, Dressler had a question. "Who the hell are you anyway, mister?"

"The name's Alex Miller. I'm from the *Los Angeles News* and represent the man you put in that bed. If you don't mind, I'd like to speak with my client in private."

"And if I'm not through with this man?" Dressler asked.

"Let's just say that for now, you're through. Without representation, you cannot question him or detain him. He's not going anywhere, as you can see. If you need time with him, then you will have to go through me." Alex then walked a few steps into the hospital room and looked at Dressler as if to say *get out*.

Chief Dressler slowly walked toward the door, eyeing Alex with each step. He knew William Barrish wasn't going anywhere. He turned to look at Barrish and saw his mouth turn to a grin.

"I'm not through with you, Barrish," Dressler stated before walking through the door.

Alex waited for Dressler to close the door. When it was a foregone conclusion that the door was not going to close, he walked over to it and closed it. He wanted privacy with William, and to make sure that no one would listen in on their conversation. He also checked for any listening devices that might have been stashed in the room when William was asleep.

"What are you doing?" William asked.

"I'm checking for bugs," Alex said.

"You're kidding, right? In this hick town?"

"I check everywhere, kid. It's a habit, and one that's helped me in the past," Alex informed him. "You don't know where that cop is from or if he's even a hick. Besides, he may have his story down pat. That's what we need to do now."

William had known of the famous, or infamous, Alex Miller for a few months now and was glad he had come to help. Alex Miller was highly respected in the newspaper business. He had begun as a delivery boy when he was only six years old. His father had taught him the value of each nickel he earned. Before Alex had graduated from elementary school, he had almost one thousand dollars in the savings account his dad had opened for him.

The love between a father and his son is precious. After Alex's mother walked out on them, Alex turned to his father for everything. He listened carefully to each word his father uttered. Every lesson in life had a reason, and every reason needed to be stored in the memory. It was good if one learned each lesson without repeating it. However, it was also not practical to think that all lessons would be remembered throughout life.

Alex had a really good memory, though. He was able to understand the idealism behind each forked road that would enter his life. He learned to be self-sufficient and expected help from only his closest family, his father. Most of the help came in the form of small speeches. However, when really needed, his dad's outstretched arms were always there for anything else.

"If you listen to yourself," his father would say, "you only have yourself to blame. Never take it out on someone else."

When Alex asked what "it" was, his father simply explained that "it" was all the consequences and truths that could be rationalized and reasoned from within. "God gives us this freedom," his dad would say. "Never question God, and always know that he is there for you."

At first Alex did not understand what his father meant. Even though he rarely went to a church or temple, growing up with this knowledge made him a stronger person. He became devout in his beliefs without the formal religious background. He grew to be a good man with strong convictions and attitudes. These were the ideals that he lived, and they were the reasons for his success.

When Alex entered his high school years, he was the only one of his classmates who had formulated definite ideas about his future. Some of his schoolmates taunted him about the short stories he consistently wrote. His writings included all genres, from poetry to prose, documentary to fiction, the known to the unknown.

The Death Maze

His flair for the English language rescued him from many a dilemma. Like the time the principal called him into the office to reprimand him for arguing with his teacher in front of the entire class.

"My situation, Mr. Deavers," Alex had explained, "was crucial in the development of my argument favoring the main character for the hanging of the cat and the burning of the draperies. This was a troublesome period in the life of the antagonist. This was the basis for the benevolent, uncompromising behavior that led him to become a superlative creator of literature in a turbulent time in society. That was the reason I acted the way I did. To make my statement. It was supposed to be a part of the report."

Not having read the book *Black Boy* by Richard Wright, Mr. Deavers dismissed Alex and later talked with his teacher regarding the art of debate in the classroom. Alex was entitled to his opinions, and this woman was simply going to have to adjust to each student's own individualism and intellect. Stifling them could hold them back, and retribution with a bad grade could be detrimental to their future studies and careers. Her mind needed to be more open in these drastic times of change. If the teacher wanted more control, she should simply make everyone read the same books.

Alex Miller was also an above average athlete. Although his five-foot-nine-inch frame wasn't tall enough to meet the standards of the basketball team, he commanded the qualities of a real fine halfback on the soccer team. He was naturally left-footed and played the game with skill. Whether on defense and fighting for control or on offense assisting the scoring of points, Alex was able to be in the right place at the right time.

When Alex was seventeen, he was placed in charge of distribution of his own area for the local newspaper. Eight younger children delivered for him. His bank account grew and he saved a lot of money. By the time he enrolled in college, he had enough for three of his four years of education. It was more than enough, since his father had been saving and preparing as well.

He dated a couple girls, but none of his relationships were ever serious enough to take him away from his goals. Alex Miller knew he wanted to be a journalist.

Directly out of college, he was offered a job as a cub reporter for a large Midwestern newspaper. Jumping at the chance to learn, Alex Miller went to Chicago and the *Chicago Herald*.

During eight years reporting on politics and corruption in a hard-edged, seedy city, Alex uncovered many on the take and many lobbyists who needed to be knocked off their high horses and brought down to street level. He witnessed stacks of envelopes being given under many tables. He was assigned many jobs outside Chicago as well. He required a well-rounded, real-life education.

There was an attempt on his life that left him in the hospital for two weeks. It was part of a set-up designed to bring down a top union official. With cameras watching and recording cables ready to take down every word, Alex Miller walked away with his life intact and his own column at the *Los Angeles News*.

Having now been employed for over twenty years at the same paper, Alex enjoyed a great deal of freedom. He spent many hours preparing his column and had an abundance of stories ready for print when he accepted the invitation from his editor, Robert Graves, to go and help William Barrish.

Alex Miller was now in his late forties. He was tan and had a slight extra in the stomach and a bit of gray on the sides, but he was ready. It had been a long time since he had encountered the pressures of what William called a "small-town cop." He was actually looking forward to ruffling a few feathers. His juices were flowing when he listened in on William and the chief's short conversation.

In the end, the grim outcome of this situation would remain with William for the rest of his life. However, Alex Miller would reach a new height. A new story would be told. William Barrish would receive a plaque on Alex's behalf.

With the door now closed and the room checked, Alex felt it was safe enough to converse with William.

"How's the jaw, champ?" Alex asked as he faked a small punch.

"It hurts, Alex."

"Even though I know the answer, I still need to ask. Were you driving recklessly?" Alex saw the look in William's eyes and asked his next question. "Or is that the way they keep you around this town?"

William wanted to laugh but couldn't. He saw the sarcasm in Alex's look.

"You guessed it!" William took a moment before continuing. "How long have you been representing the paper?"

"As long as I could remember getting away with it and getting others out of trouble. I'd better keep my voice low. I know I don't have to worry about yours."

"Why?" William asked. "You just checked the room."

"We don't know where the gestapo is hiding, buddy boy. The way your luck has been going, we'll both be in this place if the fist hits another wall. And I do not want that wall to be my jaw."

"I can understand the feeling, Alex. Been there! Done that!"

"Look, William, if we can find out what's going on in this town before what's-his-face wises up and calls the paper to find out who I really am, you'll probably end up with one of this year's top stories."

"You mean we," William chimed in. "I want to share this with you. After all, you may end up just like me. We can be bookends."

"We'll talk about that later. First of all, what have you learned so far?"

"Not a whole hell of a lot. Except I know a dark secret is being kept to the ground. No one seems to be talking to any strangers. Especially if that stranger is a newspaper reporter. Although there is one doctor who gave me the shut-up signal."

William was getting tired and Alex could see it. His jaw was hurting. However, Alex needed to know a bit more.

"Can you just give me a little more before I leave you alone for a while? Bring me up to the point where you got your jaw broken. Oh, and don't leave out any of the gory details."

William began telling his story for the third time, up until the gory detail of his head leaping up from his body and slamming down. He couldn't remember much of what happened afterward.

Alex listened with great interest and even felt the pain when William talked about the fist hitting his jaw. There was something about the car that didn't set in well. Why was the woman running away from the hospital? What happened to the guy in the car? What was his name? Where were these details leading? What did the woman have to do with what they were hiding?

Too many questions and not enough time right now, Alex thought. He saw that William needed to rest and told him he'd give him a few hours. Alex wanted to question Dr. Shirley Anderson, but hadn't decided whether to do this with or without William by his side.

"I'm just going to get a bite to eat and let you rest for a while, William."

"Thanks, Alex. By the way, you can call me Will. I don't mind."

"Will it is! As long as it doesn't turn into a 'won't,' then I'm all in. Just keep it level and up front."

"Thanks. See you after I rest and you eat," Will said as Alex began walking to the door.

Alex turned to Will before opening it. "I'll bring you back a hamburger. Want cheese on it?"

"Funny!" Will stated. "Make sure you grind it up with the chocolate milkshake and fries."

"Now that's disgusting."

"You started it," Will replied as Alex closed the door.

Chapter 29

Dr. Samuel Ryan and Dr. Allyson Rayburn had followed Bone in their car after breakfast. It was to be their first time in the house and they did not know what to expect.

What really had Allyson spooked was that it would be the first time she had had any actual interaction, surreptitious or not, with Dan Adams since she had to leave college due to the death of her mother. The tightness in her stomach was intense. At one point, she thought she would lose the food she had just eaten.

So many thoughts were going through her head. She was constantly remembering the good feelings and highlights of those wonderful, too few years they had spent together. Even though it had only been a couple years total, there was a permanent lock that refused to let go.

Allyson had carried this up until now. She had purposely read everything she could get her hands on about the career of Dr. Daniel Adams because she still pined for her long-lost love and the relationship that she had allowed to discontinue after the death. The only question that persisted was why. She tried over and over again to find reason for this unfulfilled void in her life. Even though she had vague ideas, Allyson never solidified them. *Why didn't I call or go back?* she kept thinking to herself. *What was I afraid of?*

Her career had been inspired by the man that she had never stopped loving. She knew that she needed to change careers after her mother's death because she did not want to see her father die of a broken heart. Allyson cared for her father for two years even though he was a healthy man.

She quickly settled into a daily routine, but knew her father was still vital. When he stood up and finally took control and said she needed to continue with her life and that he would be all right, tears of joy streamed down her face.

Allyson hugged her father and left for the afternoon. She registered at a local college, transferred what course credits she had, and chose all the prerequisite courses she would need to make chemistry and pre-med her new majors.

Her grades were nothing short of As, and Allyson graduated in two and a half years. She entered graduate school, and after another two years, she had a master's degree in chemistry and began going for her doctorate.

Her life was moving quickly, and the last two years flew by. Nothing got in her way, and she dedicated her time to finishing her goal without any interruptions. When she did complete her doctorate and pass the boards, Allyson accepted an offer at the University of Colorado's Denver Medical Center.

She immersed herself in her work until she felt ready to apply to UCLA for a position with their chemistry department. She had been working there for many years now. Allyson was comfortable and ready to research her former boyfriend.

Now that she was here, Allyson was full of pain and joy. Her pain was obvious. Dan Adams had disappeared and she had been asked to assist in finding him. Her joy was that she was actually in his home.

She could smell him even though he had been gone for days and the smell of smoke had taken over. She could see him in the pictures that had been placed around the home. She could hear him as her mind envisioned what he would be saying while living there. She knew she would touch him when she and her colleague found him and returned him to his home.

"Allyson," Dr. Ryan said for the third time.

Allyson got out of her dreams and realized she was standing with her colleague in the living room.

"Yes, Sam," Allyson responded, her mind a bit clouded by her surroundings.

"Are you all right?"

"Yes, Sam. I'm okay. I just need some air."

Allyson walked out the front door, took a couple breaths of fresh air, and reached into her pants pocket. She pulled out a handkerchief, dabbed her eyes, and replaced the handkerchief. She opened the front door and walked in. This took all of two minutes.

"Okay," she assured Sam as he and Bone stood in the hallway. "I'm fine. Let's go see the lab."

They walked through the house. It looked the same as when Bone and Chief Dressler had seen it. The lab was a mess.

Doctors Ryan and Rayburn couldn't believe what they were looking at. First was the hole in the ceiling. Nothing like this should happen, they both surmised.

Staring at the hole, Dr. Ryan spoke first. "What do you think?"

"I'm not sure," Allyson said. "My first thought is that this was not caused by a chemical explosion."

"Why do you say that?" Bone asked.

"First of all, I don't smell any chemicals. I don't see any liquids out of place." Allyson looked down at the floor and saw the car under a table and the apparatus affiliated with Dr. Adams's work. "Sam! Look at this."

Dr. Ryan walked over to Allyson and saw the equipment. "Is this what you were telling me about in the car?"

"I believe so," Allyson confirmed. "Bone, is there anything in the back to look at?"

"Sure is," Bone confirmed. "Dr. Adams owns a lot of land. The entire area has been fenced in because of what he was working on. He even had Ruth Putnam helping him."

"Ruth Putnam?" Allyson questioned.

"She's the woman who's been living with Dr. Adams for some time now. He helped her a few years back and then they became involved."

Another jolt hit Allyson. She had no idea that Dan was with someone. She needed to be discreet in asking questions. Allyson didn't want to give Bone any indication that she was here for any other reason than to find Dr. Adams. She could learn plenty by talking around the subject and slipping in other remarks and concerns.

"According to the story," Bone continued while walking toward the back door, "Dr. Adams was working in the lab and just disappeared into thin air."

They walked outside and saw a large facility. It was obvious to both Allyson and Sam that Dan Adams was working on some sort of geothermal energy project. Everything was in place. The monitors on the pumps were still working as Allyson inspected them.

"Sam, do you see anything out of place here?" Allyson asked. She felt very confused.

"Allyson, I don't think we're looking in the right place. I'm very uncomfortable right now."

"I feel the same way." Allyson looked at Bone. "You said he just disappeared into thin air?"

Bone acknowledged the question as he walked toward her. "Yes, ma'am. Just disappeared. No sight of him."

"What about a time warp, Sam?" Allyson asked.

"But why would there be a hole in the ceiling?"

"Maybe the energy released caused the hole," Allyson surmised.

"If he was in the lab, I could understand that. If he disappeared out here, then I'm baffled," Sam Ryan explained as he kept walking around the geothermal area.

He didn't even notice stepping over the covering of the hole. The moss and grass had grown a bit since Dan disappeared, and the hole was slightly camouflaged.

"I'm a bit confused, Dr. Rayburn," Bone said. He grabbed his speaker radio to call his boss. "Chief? Come in, Chief."

"What's up, Bone?" Dressler asked.

"You need to hear this. I'm at the house with the doctors from UCLA." Bone kept the speaker open and let Dr. Rayburn speak.

"Time warps are a state of being out of true in plane or line, or a mental twist or aberration. It's a different level of being," Allyson Rayburn explained.

"I'm not sure I understand, Dr. Rayburn," Dressler said.

"I know I'm confused," Bone added.

"It's quite simple," Allyson continued. "Our bodies are in a certain area of time and being. If it were possible to change our motion of time to a different level or state of being, or a diversified alternative unlike time as we know it, we could change the warp of time."

"It's not just chemistry," Dr. Ryan added, "it's also physics. However, this includes areas of both sciences. They overlap in many ways."

"Could a change in time or being cause an explosion and thus have created the hole in his lab?" Dressler asked.

"Absolutely!" Allyson replied. "If Dr. Adams did not know of the time warp or its cause, then he had no way to contain any ramifications determined by the testing. He may have thought he was working on X and actually produced Y."

"The only thing we need to identify is where the change or time warp began. We need the physical area if this is true," Dr. Ryan explained.

"You mean an actual place in or outside his home?" Bone asked.

"We've already searched the grounds," Dressler chimed in.

The radio went dead for a few moments and all four of them thought. Bone walked slowly around the backyard before the signal came back in. Doctors Ryan and Rayburn wanted to get back into the house and look again.

"Bone," Dressler said, "I'll get back with you shortly. I'm working on things here at the hospital. Out!"

Bone accompanied the two doctors back into the lab. They studied the hole to determine if the explosion had gone straight up and created a round hole, or a hole that was splintered in many directions. The good news was that it was splintered in all angles. The bad news was that they couldn't determine the origin of the explosion. A round hole would have meant that the area of experimentation had been below it. They had already determined that there was nothing below the hole.

"Let's look at this in another way, Allyson," Dr. Ryan said.

"What do you mean, Sam?" Allyson asked.

"There are many passageways through time in the atmosphere. When one hears a sonic boom, like when the shuttle returns to earth, the speed of sound has been broken. If Dr. Adams was traveling faster than that, it may have broken open a warp or hole. What if he did his experiments somewhere outside and his residue was not fast enough to catch up with the actual speed . . ."

"I think I understand, Sam," Allyson interrupted. "You're suggesting that the hole was caused not by Dan Adams, but by what was behind him trying to make up the distance between the speed of his actual body disappearance and what trailed him."

"Kind of like *Star Trek*," Bone uttered. They looked at him. "You know, when Captain Kirk says 'warp speed' and the ship bursts forward and the little black lines on the screen indicate from where the *Enterprise* began and then move forward to catch up."

"Exactly, Bone," Dr. Ryan said, smiling. "Good analogy."

"So where is he?" Bone asked.

"What do you mean?" Allyson asked.

"Is he thirty years in the future or one hundred years in the past like in *Back to the Future?*"

"He could be in a different dimension in the current time frame, Bone," Allyson stated. "We don't know whether it's past, future, or present!"

They all stared at each other as she finished her comments. The situation was terribly frustrating and disheartening, especially for Allyson. She wanted so much to find the right answers and the simple measures that would reunite her with Dan.

"Then where is he?" Bone asked once again.

"I wish we knew," Dr. Ryan answered.

"No one has been able to succeed in a time warp experiment, Bone," Allyson added. "That's years away from discovery."

Allyson did not know if Dan was working on time warps. She only knew of AGE. Nothing concrete had recently been written on time warps, either.

Allyson knew Dan would never say anything about his work unless he had a major breakthrough. She hoped it wasn't a time warp. However, if it were, Dan was probably caught in it.

If he were safe and just hiding out somewhere away from the news media, Dan would return when he was ready and when the work was completed. Allyson prayed he was safe. Just think of it. A time warp breakthrough. Or AGE. Dan would surely get the top prize for this.

Little did Allyson know, the top prize was to continue living.

Chapter 30

Alex left Will's room and walked down to the nurse's station. When he got there, all talk ceased between the three nurses. They all stared at him as if his aftershave was the wrong scent. A joke materialized in his mind about a guy asking a beautiful woman out who laughs because the zipper to his pants is open. Alex quickly lowered his eyes to his zipper and was relieved that the zipper was closed and secure.

It was a shame, he thought. Two of the nurses were attractive enough to take out. The taller was blonde and blue-eyed. Her nametag said Trisha Seward, RN. The second was a bit shorter, but more striking in color. Her light-brown hair was styled in a layered shag. Her eyes were deep brown, almost black, and her skin was beautifully tanned. Her nametag said Melinda Torres, RN.

Now this is a woman, he thought. Alex made a mental note to get Melinda's phone number after this assignment was completed. *Would she want to relocate to the city?*

The third nurse was middle-aged with a few more lines on her face. She looked like the head nurse type, and was obviously more experienced in the job. He was glad there was a wedding band on her left hand. She had appeared to be giving orders before he walked up. Her nametag said Emily Hodges, RN.

The Death Maze

It was then that Emily approached Alex. He had hoped it would be Melinda. He didn't know that the three of them had been talking about Will and him.

"Can I help you?" she asked.

"You sure can," Alex said, wondering if Melinda would want to go out. He came back to life after the brief daydream. "Are you in charge?"

"Yes, I am," she assured him.

"Well, I'd like to find out how to get William Barrish released."

The three just looked at him, baffled. He obviously did not know that Dr. Shirley Anderson had to approve the release.

"Okay," Alex said, breaking the silence. "If I can't get the release, how about the phone number of Melinda so I can call her later in the day?"

Melinda turned red over her tan. Trisha smiled and laughed to herself, while Emily didn't move a muscle in her face.

"Okay. Enough sidebars for now," Alex said while moving his eyes from one nurse's face to the next.

"I'm sorry, sir. Dr. Shirley Anderson must first see her patient and approve a release," Emily stated.

"And where can I find Dr. Anderson?" he asked.

Melinda immediately stepped forward and looked into Alex's eyes. "I'll go and get her, sir."

"Alex," he told her. "Name's Alex Miller."

"Thank you, Mr. Miller," Melinda replied. "I'll go and get Dr. Anderson." Melinda left the station and Alex's eyes followed her every move.

"You'd better put your eyes back in their sockets, Mr. Miller," Emily stated. "Don't you know it's not nice to stare?"

243

"I'm terribly sorry," Alex said, not really meaning the apology.

Little did Alex know that Emily thought he would go nuts when he saw Dr. Shirley Anderson. Emily thought she was more beautiful, more poised, and much smarter than the nurses, a better match for this out-of-town hunk. She was also closer to his age.

Emily had to admit that Alex was very handsome. Dr. Anderson would be perfect for him. She had known Shirley Anderson for a long time. They were good friends and she was always wondering what Shirley was waiting for in a man. Shirley could have anyone she wanted. She didn't need money, cars, a house, or anything . . . other than a steady man.

Shirley once told her that she had a secret admiration for one man. She was never able to say anything to him. They were actually friends, but Shirley never informed Emily of his identity. Emily just assumed this mystery man was married and unattainable. But why couldn't she move to the next prospect?

Emily wanted to see Alex's face when Shirley Anderson walked up to the nurse's station.

Melinda Torres returned and informed Alex that Dr. Anderson was with a patient and would be here shortly. She then moved back to a chair at the station.

"Thank you," Alex said. He looked at Emily and thanked her also before returning to Will's room.

Emily's only thoughts were *just wait*.

When Alex entered Will's room, Will was watching television and bored as hell.

"What about the release?" he asked.

"I'm waiting to speak with Dr. Anderson," Alex informed him.

"You'll like her, Alex. She's terrific, and I think she wants to say more about the accident."

"What makes you think that?" Alex asked.

"She was the one who gave me the look to be careful and shut up."

"And you didn't," Alex stated simply. "First rule, Will, *is* to shut up when the good doctor says to."

"I know that now, Alex," Will said through his teeth.

There was a knock at the door and Dr. Shirley Anderson walked in. Alex did keep his eyes in their sockets, but he was going crazy inside his body. This woman was everything he had heard about and more. His only questions were why she wasn't taken and where such a small town got so many beautiful women.

Walking past Alex, Shirley went to Will. "How are you feeling, Will? How's the jaw today?"

"Stiff! Wish I could open my mouth."

"Not for at least six weeks, I'm sorry to say," Shirley informed him.

"This is Alex Miller," Will said as they shook hands. "Alex was sent from my employer to help . . . in getting me out of here."

"Actually, to make sure he was okay and to help in any way I could," Alex added while giving the eye to Will. "I'm pleased to meet you, Dr. Anderson. I've heard a lot about you."

"Only good things, I hope," Shirley interjected.

"All of the gossip was positive," Alex shot back. "However, no one told me you were so beautiful."

"Thank you," Shirley stated as if she'd heard it before and wanted to keep it to business. She was admiring Alex Miller in her mind. Emily had given her the ten-second impression before coming into the room. She felt she needed to keep it professional on the first meeting.

"What do I have to do to break Will out of here?" Alex asked with a grin. "Not that breaking him out would be the best thing for him. But there is some work to do, and I would make sure he is safe."

"I have no problem giving you the release as long as you make sure he doesn't try to remove the wires in his mouth. After all, we wouldn't want his jaw to drop to the ground. Would we?" Shirley said dryly but also jokingly while looking at Will.

"Huh?" Will managed to grunt.

"Just kidding, Will," Shirley said. "I need to keep you aware of the tenderness of your jaw and to remind you not to chew for a long time. Everything must be through a straw for a while."

"Aren't I the lucky one?" Will said sarcastically.

"I'll let him get dressed and bring you the release, Mr. Miller," Shirley said before leaving.

"Call me Alex. Please," Alex replied before motioning to Will that he'd be right back.

He followed Shirley into the hallway and called out to her. She turned and walked back to him.

"Dr. Anderson," Alex said.

"Call me Shirley. Please," Shirley said in a mocking reciprocal manner.

"Shirley! Thank you! I wanted to know the status of the two individuals who were in the accident. Are you able to give me any information?"

Shirley looked into his eyes and saw the professionalism he now exuded. She had a feeling Alex was not the lawyer he had claimed to be. She also had a feeling he was here for a much larger role. She figured that Will, the younger of the two, needed a more mature, seasoned veteran. Alex was definitely that individual. However, he was smooth and even-mannered and had the ability to find jocularity in all situations. He was quicker than Will. She liked that and sensed the same understanding she had with Will.

"I'll be happy to tell you some things. Others you must find for yourself," Shirley said.

"I'll appreciate any and all information you may have."

"Ruth Putnam is doing fine. She's resting right now and shouldn't have any trouble recovering."

"I also know there was a man involved. How is he doing?"

"He passed away. Never regained consciousness."

"Any identification on the body?" Alex asked.

Shirley motioned for Alex to step closer. She wanted their voices to be lower.

"Look. I don't think you're a lawyer," she said softly, looking down at the floor and back up to his eyes. "I want you to know about . . ."

"About Chief Dressler?" Alex finished the sentence in the same low tone.

"Yes!"

"I've had trouble with these types in the past. I use the lawyer bit to put them off guard and hope they don't have the time to check up on me. As long as Chief Dressler thinks I'm a lawyer, it keeps him on his toes."

"I want to help Will in any way I can because he was treated unfairly," Shirley explained. "I've never seen the chief act that way. However, it showed me the type of man he can really be. Just be on your guard."

"I intend to be," Alex assured her.

"Excuse me, Dr. Anderson," Melinda interrupted. "The release is ready for your signature."

"Thank you, Nurse Torres," Shirley replied. She signed the release and gave Alex a few instructions about Will's care.

Melinda took back the release after it was signed and gave Alex a copy. She smiled at him and left.

Alex was about to go back to Will's room when he felt Shirley's hand on his forearm.

"Look," Shirley said. "We must talk further."

"I agree," Alex said. He looked directly into her eyes before opening the door to Will's room.

Shirley stood by the door for a few moments before realizing she was alone in the corridor. She walked back to the nurse's station and up to Emily, who was now alone. The other two nurses were checking on patients.

"An interesting man," Shirley said to Emily.

"Good looking, too!" Emily shot back.

Shirley Anderson left the station and walked back to her office. She needed to get ready and be prepared to drive over to Dan Adams's house as soon as Dressler called her. The two doctors from UCLA had been there yesterday and would be there again today. She had to remind Dressler that he had agreed to let her be a part of the search.

Her next thought was what her friend, Emily Hodges, had said about Alex Miller. He certainly was a good-looking man. He could easily be a person she would want to know better in every sense of the word.

The telephone rang. It was Dressler.

"Have they started yet today?" she asked.

"Not yet. However, if you want to be included, I'd suggest you get over here right away," Chief Dressler said dryly.

Asshole, she thought. His demeanor had changed 180 degrees since Will arrived on the scene. She now knew she could trust Alex and had decided to tell him everything she

The Death Maze

knew about the case. Not only would they get a good story, but she would get even with Chief Dressler for treating her like an outsider. If anyone deserved a good kick in the balls, it was him.

"I'll be right over."

"By the way," Dressler added, "how's Ruth Putnam?"

"She's fine. She's getting all the rest she needs."

"What have you done with the Welles body?"

"I've burned it, Chief," Shirley snapped. "What do you think I've done with it? It's still here in the hospital morgue waiting to be claimed."

"Okay. I'll contact the next of kin. What about Barrish?"

"What about him?" Shirley asked back.

"You're a pain in the ass, Shirley," Dressler said loudly. "Can't you give me a straight answer without asking another question?"

"I've released him to Alex Miller," Shirley answered.

"What do you mean you've released him to Alex Miller?" Dressler was about to have a fit.

"I mean I just signed the release. I have no reason to keep him here against his will," Shirley explained. "Besides, Alex Miller said he would be responsible for him. They will not leave the area. Why do you want to keep him here?"

"Because I don't want any trouble." Dressler's voice was a bit louder now. "Those two will probably cause a huge mess. Furthermore, I don't want anything in the papers."

Shirley Anderson wanted to rip Dressler's hide right off his body. He was being so pigheaded. He didn't realize that with a bit of professional diplomacy, he could have lowered the radar on this story.

She had known Richard Dressler for many years and had never seen this side of him. It was like night and day. How

249

could he have lasted as chief of police of Arione and Vera for so long? *Just wait until the next election,* she thought. *If he runs unopposed, I'll run just to make sure he sweats.*

Then she realized it had to be Dan Adams. They were very good friends, and as long as he was around, there was no temper. Dan was the diplomat, the bravado. Dressler was making up for the loss of his outside trumpet. Without Dan, Chief Dressler needed to blow the horn a bit louder.

"Are you listening to me, Dr. Anderson?" Dressler yelled.

"Look, Chief," Shirley said, trying to hold back her anger. "If you would explain the situation to William Barrish and Alex Miller in a pleasant tone of voice and a diplomatic demeanor, maybe they could assist you in keeping it from the papers until there are more answers."

"I'm doing—" Chief Dressler stated before Shirley cut him off.

"By acting in the manner you are, they are only going to rebel against you and realize there is more to the story than what you are trying to leak out."

"My job—" Chief Dressler tried again.

"Face it, Chief! You certainly haven't expressed or displayed any understanding on their part and haven't been the epitome of kindness."

"Are you through lecturing me, Dr. Anderson?" Chief Dressler asked.

"I did not mean to lecture."

"My job is to enforce the law as best as I can, Shirley. No one, not even you, will tell me how to do my job. Do I make myself clear?" Dressler sternly stated.

"Only too clear," she said. "I'm just glad that my job doesn't require me to face the electorate of the Arione and Vera constituency." Shirley slammed down the phone.

She took a few long breaths before leaving her office. She didn't want anyone to see her in an angry state. Knowing the drive over to Dan's house would mellow her out, she tried to put the conversation with Chief Dressler out of her mind.

Dressler cursed a half dozen times before realizing that Shirley Anderson had hung up the phone. Then he cursed once more just for the hell of it.

He was steaming. Not because Barrish and Miller would be God-knows-where. That was something he could contain. It was because the good Dr. Anderson had hit upon a tender vein. If he didn't start playing the game the way it was supposed to be played, he could lose the respect of the entire town and lose control of the investigation.

Chief Dressler really did believe that keeping the story out of the papers was the proper decision for both towns. He imagined there would be total chaos if the story were to get out. There could be hundreds, if not thousands, of quacks and kooks driving in from all points of the country to see what could be a freak show.

He had been in charge of the small but terrific police force for a long time now. There had been the normal car speeders and minor misdemeanors over the years. However, there had never been murders, gang problems, major drug busts, or any of the multitudes of problems that plagued larger cities.

Now two individuals wanted to write about it. It was unfortunate that it was going so badly, as one had accidentally stumbled upon the situation by trying to be a Good Samaritan. Chief Dressler really was sorry he broke William Barrish's jaw. He just needed him to understand that there was one person in charge, and that his directions were to be followed and implemented.

Dressler couldn't understand why he was being castrated by Dr. Anderson and who knew how many others. He didn't want to become the heavy. Someone had to be in order to keep the town secure. He felt that everyone understood what could occur if things got out of hand.

If anyone was to be the fall guy, it should have been William Barrish. Now that Alex Miller had teamed up with him, there were two bad guys. They were the ones who could change their small, tranquil towns into hostile, chaotic sideshows. They were the ones who should be run out of town. They represented an outside influence that Arione and Vera did not wish to have.

Dressler needed to change the course of the situation. He didn't feel he needed to appeal to everyone. His deputies were on his side. Ruth Putnam and most of the other residents were behind him. Most of the residents just wanted to know the whereabouts of Dr. Adams. They had known him as a wonderful member of their town and knew he cared for them as well.

It was just Dr. Shirley Anderson and maybe a few others who were rattling the cages. Shirley wanted to be involved, and so he had called her. What more could he do for her? He made a mental note to talk with her when she arrived at the house.

He decided that once she did arrive and the other two doctors were working, he would leave Dan's house and call a town meeting. He would reach out to the town for any assistance they wished to give in this complicated situation. Dressler would let Arione be a part of its own destiny. His only restriction would be to keep it within the means of the law. Dressler preferred doing this within his department's arena. He figured most would want it that way.

Dressler did want William Barrish and Alex Miller out of town. That was a no-brainer. However, kicking them out of town would only cause innuendo and idle chatter from their newspaper. The next step would obviously be the lookie-loos and crazies coming into the desert. He really needed to solve this case for a positive response in the news.

Dr. Shirley Anderson was a different matter. Dressler was allowing her the access she wanted. After all, she was a good physician and friend of Dr. Dan Adams and Ruth Putnam. She was sincere in her quest to be a part of the investigation.

However, she was allowing Barrish and Miller the free reign they required to snoop all they wanted. Her recent release of William Barrish gave them *carte blanche* to move about town, ask any and all questions to whomever they desired, and put unnecessary stress on the population.

The townspeople were going to bombard him in his office. For this, Chief Dressler decided that if Dr. Shirley Anderson continued to act as she did, he would do whatever was needed to ostracize her. The blame would go to her.

He was glad to have taken the time to think about his next moves. Putting all items into place gave him the peace of mind he needed to get his friend Dan Adams back, get that positive report in the newspaper, and have the confidence he always had when running for election every five years.

Chief Dressler exited the police station and got into his car. He drove over to Dan's house, where Doctors Ryan and Rayburn would begin their second round of discovery. Dr. Shirley Anderson was on her way. He was sure they would welcome a third mind into the perplexing puzzle.

Dr. Allyson Rayburn knew that going over the notes again would be tedious, since they had found nothing the first time. However, this time she wanted to dissect every note to avoid missing any morsel of information she may have overlooked.

If it had been a time warp, Allyson would want to mimic each of Dan's moves until just before the final moment. This would have to be done one step at a time, as she didn't want someone else caught in the same place Dan might now be. As far as she was concerned, she would take control.

Allyson remembered Sam Ryan saying he felt uncomfortable outside the lab. Little did she know that discomfort was mild compared to other feelings she would experience.

Chapter 31

There was no way of knowing how long he had been asleep or what day of the week it was. When Dan looked at his watch, he saw that it had stopped at 9:42 p.m. on Tuesday. Right now he didn't care if it was Tuesday, Wednesday, or even Saturday. He only cared that he was still in the maze and not at home, still fighting for his life and not with the woman he wanted to spend the rest of his life with.

His stomach was growling again and his throat was dry. He had only eaten once since he had entered the sixth dimension. He could still taste that meal and thought about the aroma of the food, its texture, and its taste. However, he was amazed that he had not had even the slightest thought about the release of the food at the other end of the human body. Dan had not needed to go to the bathroom since his ordeal began. He wondered why.

He also knew that Apep could end his hunger cravings once and for all just by killing him. He could make him suffer even more by starving him to death. Wouldn't that be a wonderful thing to watch? Apep's thirst for suffering could be extended for days while his body withered away.

Maybe Apep didn't have a number of days on his agenda. Maybe there was something more devious about this world that couldn't handle the presence of human beings for more than a certain amount of time. If that were the case, Dan figured he hadn't been asleep more than a couple hours. Could he have been here longer than twenty-four hours? He did not know.

Forget it, he thought. If Apep really wanted him dead, he would have expired a long time ago. It was the sixth dimension and Apep that were putting him through this hell. The least he, or it, could do was supply him with food and drink when he needed it. He had to go through this ridiculous maze in order to die for him. Dan wanted nourishment and he was going to ask for it.

He tried to stand, but bumped his head before rising about a foot. Dan had forgotten about his surroundings while debating the food issue.

While sitting down again, his mind played tricks and tried to recall, once more, the unfortunate events that had plagued his mind and body.

"Nope!" Dan sighed aloud. "I just do not believe or understand why this is happening!"

Where was the disruption in this world? What had he altered in order to be here? How had he caused a problem by accidentally—and the word "accidentally" stuck in his mind—appearing in the sixth dimension?

Apep, the lethal king of the sixth dimension, never occupied even a morsel of the space through which he traveled. Maybe Apep was the only entity in the sixth dimension. His loneliness was interrupted by the presence of another in his world.

That was it! Apep was the only entity left in the sixth dimension and needed Dan Adams as his pawn, his robot, his clown. This was just entertainment to him. It was a slight alteration within an unseen world, and when he was finished, he would discard a live human being that his sick mind considered just another toy.

Dan was terminally baffled. His mind was always tired, and his imagination was running wild. He couldn't really blame himself for his thoughts. Throughout the maze, there had been no interference or interruption imposed within the magnitude of the sixth dimension.

What did Apep look like? Would Dan be frightened by his appearance? Was he some kind of intellectual yet hideous deviant with four arms, three legs, two noses, and mystical antennae that sucked out life from a single touch?

Dan decided to wipe out all these ridiculous thoughts from his mind and face his dilemma by beginning anew. He was in the smallest, most confined area he had been in yet. It was uncomfortable and he was closer to death.

That was the way he felt. He couldn't disconnect his mind from any of his thoughts. If he could, it would be a terrible thing to waste. The mind was capable of doing anything.

This sudden, odd feeling now disappeared. He had felt this way many times while in the maze and was sure he would feel this way again. Done! Finished! Over!

Dan put his hands to his face and felt the moisture on his hands. He dried his hands on his pants and rubbed his eyes. They were tired and felt red.

While the rubbing seemed to help arouse the old eyeballs a little, he knew it was just a temporary fix. He felt pressure in all areas of his body. It was like dropping a person who had never been in a pool and telling them to swim.

Dan looked at his hands and arms and saw scrapes, cuts, bruises, black-and-blue marks, and sore muscles from the different passageways he had crawled and climbed through. Images came into his mind like flashes of pictures on a computer program.

He had acquired some of those bruises and marks by throwing the crib and bassinet around the room. That devilish nursery! Dan could only think of it as a living hell or a place to retreat when one wanted to rehash ill memories. Only he didn't have bad memories from his childhood.

Dan tried to get comfortable. Even though he had just awakened, his fatigued body required some rest. He lowered his head, closed his eyes, and tried to bring his body into a state of meditation.

He relaxed his muscles and tried to bring his mind into a state of unaltered transition. Closing his eyes, Dan inhaled three times and then exhaled slowly. Focusing on a small ladder within his head, he saw himself climbing a dozen steps to the tip of his head.

Dan saw himself, as if in a dream, lift a small latch inside his head and unlock a trapdoor. Opening the door, he stuck his head out to view a galaxy of stars. They were bright and picture-perfect.

He stepped farther up and brought his entire body out from within his head as his meditative state became full and functioning. Reaching down to the trapdoor, Dan closed it and saw himself on top of his own head looking out at the wonder of the heavens. The stars were never ending. The lights were vibrant and, for now, felt real.

Dan felt a sense of nirvana. He knew he could travel anywhere in God's universe. He knew he would be safe. What had put him in his state of security was his cord of life. That thin, tough silver membrane would keep him physically alive, as long as it stayed attached to him. If it severed, he would stay in his meditative state, comatose, and never return or wake up. He would be considered dead, and Apep would lose his entertainment in the form of Dan Adams.

The Death Maze

Dan loved this. He had learned about meditation after college and practiced it many times. It kept him alive and refreshed. It allowed him to push through his science and still cling to his beliefs of an ultimate entity or being. He truly believed in God. Although in his mind, all the stories he had read in the Bible were just that, stories, Dan knew they were the guidelines for a just and decent human life.

Dan looked out into the universe of stars and simply thought about where he wanted to go. He wanted to look at a place as serene as a garden with a distant lake. He wanted to smell the aroma of roses, carnations, petunias, and lilacs. He knew the path to the lake and felt like his legs didn't need to walk. They simply floated while he embraced the sights of wading birds, flamingoes, jumping fish, and so much more.

It was beautiful to just relax. It was a striking change from the previous dimension. Dan took in all the wonders of his surroundings and wished he could stay in this state forever.

Only he couldn't.

When it was time to return to the top of his head, Dan simply reversed his steps and allowed the cord of life to coil back. His movements were exact. The timing was just as Dan wanted. The rule of thumb was that there was no time. This was Dan's meditative state, and he controlled it as he pleased.

Once back on his head, Dan opened the trapdoor and stepped in. Before closing the door, he took one more look out into the universe as he had previously seen it. It was simply outstanding.

Slowly descending the twelve steps, Dan soon found himself totally back in his body. His breathing was even and refined. His fatigue was gone. He felt refreshed and ready to continue. In his mind he counted to three and then slowly opened his eyes.

He was back. Although it had felt like hours, he had actually been in his meditative state for only thirty minutes. He felt fully rested.

Dan carefully lifted his head and stared at the low ceiling. It was that incorrigible hospital white he so despised. One would think that torture didn't have to be so boring. If he was going to be tortured, he should at least be able to design the colors of the room he would inhabit.

This made him chuckle. Torture and colors! Such a travesty!

He lowered his head as his eyes strained to focus on a tiny object in one corner of the tiny space he occupied. Moving closer, Dan strained to see exactly what it was.

It looked as if it were a dead bug. It was a dark stain in the form of an ink spot.

Dan moved his eyes to the left. He saw another dead bug or ink spot in the opposite corner. Although these images looked like dead vermin, there was something about them that was different in the smallest, minutest sense.

Dan brought his hand over both objects, making sure he did not touch either one. This could be his next decision, and either his fourth mistake or another success. He just didn't know and wanted more assurance.

He looked at every corner of the enclosure. His eyes zeroed in on each ninety-degree angle in the floor and ceiling. Dan faithfully scavenged every inch just to make sure these two drops—or dead ants, ink spots, or vermin—were the next choice.

He then brought his right hand over the spot to his right. That area felt a bit cooler than the rest of the enclosure. Dan wondered if this was abnormal or not.

He brought his right hand back to his body and stretched out his left hand. As his hand got closer to the spot to his left, he felt the warmth. The temperature was definitely different.

"This is it," he concluded out loud. This was the choice that could bring him from his third to his fourth *faux pas*. It could be four down with only one to go, or another triumph that would continue his maze travails. Which was really worth it?

Dan gently extended his right hand to the right. "BUG!" he called out. "I'm calling you a bug. Okay?" Dan said out loud without yelling. He was not angry. He was not frustrated. He just didn't know what to call it anymore because there was no word he could find.

His forefinger and middle finger pressed down. He felt the coolness grab him and hold on. He tried to bring his fingers away from the object, and needed to jerk them before it let go.

Dan thought it very weird . . . at first. The he realized that nothing should be thought of as weird in this place. Why nothing had lashed out at him before was something he hadn't contemplated. Now, he would make it an anticipatory rite as long as he remained in the sixth dimension. "Anything and everything" would be his motto

Then he thought he felt it. It was ever so slight. The change in his stomach was minimal. The tenseness in his bones felt like locks being secured.

It then jumped to its height. It rumbled and rolled. The walls moved inward, forcing Dan to squeeze further into a ball. The ceiling lowered one inch at a time.

Dan hurried to search for the other bug. At first he was disoriented because he couldn't find the bug. It had disappeared. Maybe the ceiling had lowered or the floor had raised so he couldn't see it anymore.

He pressed down into the corner where he thought the bug was and pushed with his left thumb. Dan felt his way to the next corner and pressed again. He finally moved his right hand to the last corner. Dan then pressed down a fourth time. Nothing happened.

The ceiling continued to fall slowly. There was no way to freedom. This was it.

"This wasn't the final choice. APEP!" Dan yelled. "This can't be it. This is only the fourth mistake."

Dan wasn't incorrect. The walls suddenly stopped moving. The ceiling ceased dropping two feet from the floor. Dan felt like a crushed tomato and thought his blood would ooze from his veins.

Now lying on his stomach, Dan was relieved that he was still breathing. He did what he thought he could never do, and that was sincerely pray. It wasn't meditation or just the mindless words many say in place of prayer. Dan really prayed to God.

He thanked the Lord for his life. He recited the entire verse of the Lord's Prayer, and though he wasn't originally of the Christian faith, he happened to enjoy this verse and its words of sincerity. They made him feel better. They even prepared him for what he felt was the inevitable.

When he was finished with his many prayers, Dan again lifted his hand to where he thought the correct bug would have been. He felt a small object.

Lifting his eyes, he saw that the bug was once again present in his sight. Depressing it one last time finally produced results.

The right wall disappeared. It vanished completely, leaving a pitch-black view. He couldn't tell if it went for three

The Death Maze

feet or thirty feet. However, he felt and knew this was leading to the final decision.

Dan dropped his head and closed his eyes again. He quickly thanked the Lord for another moment of life. Even if he were correct that this was the fourth mistake, the prayer to God was worth it. It made him feel better inside and out.

He then noticed his hunger was gone. The rumbling in his stomach was not because he wanted to eat, but because he wanted to puke. His stomach rolled, and he did everything to suppress the spasms that he thought were to follow. He waited, but nothing came. For that, he was again thankful. What more did he need to do?

He looked again into the darkness that called to him. Dan knew he would have to crawl into it and did not relish the thought. What if he just stayed where he was for a while? For some reason, that was exactly what Dan wanted to do for the time being. His intuition told him that he needed another thirty minutes to compose himself. He required a bit more time before proceeding into the abyss.

Right! It was not going to happen!

The floor beneath him started inching toward the dark like a conveyor belt. The side of the enclosure began pushing him forward as it moved with the floor. The movement was subtle, but just enough for Dan to realize that he would be in total darkness within a few minutes.

To hell with it! Dan thought. Since there was no pain involved, he let the floor and wall continue to move and push him. When he entered the black space, the wall disappeared and the floor seamlessly changed color from white to black.

This could be the worst part of his entire ordeal. This was where the mind did whatever it wanted because there was no visual. The mind does weird and crazy things in the dark. It fantasizes about everything and anything. It maximizes and minimizes any idea. It frees itself from all reality because every synapse in the brain is working.

There are those who go totally nuts when confronted with the dark. Some end up in asylums. Some become idiotic; others become macho. Isolation is a good form of darkness. And then a few let it go with the understanding that the dark eventually goes away.

Dan, as a rational individual, never had problems being in the dark. However, that was in his three-dimensional world. This was the sixth dimension, and it was controlled by a madman. Dan didn't know what to expect. Darkness, like war, causes the mind to retreat at the moment something is heard. The moment movement is felt.

Dan decided he hated it. This was definitely not his best moment, and he wished he could have left himself for dead in the previous lighted room. Everything would be over by now.

His pupils were open to their limit, begging for the slightest ray to enlighten them. Any morsel of light would ease the tension. Dan knew this was not eternal, but hoped it would not go on too long. Apep had found a weakness in Dan Adams.

Dan lifted his hand upward. He wanted to actually feel the ceiling. He confirmed it was approximately two feet high. The width was around three feet. He could feel angles, so he knew he was still inside an enclosure.

What he did not realize was that he was still moving.

Chapter 32

"Dr. Adams," a voice said in the darkness. Dan recognized it, but still jumped. He knew he would eventually hear Apep's voice again. He just didn't think it would be until he actually made his last decision. Maybe this was it.

"Where are you?" Dan said, hoping that he would finally be able to see him.

See him? He was in the dark. Was Apep going to appear in an illuminated state?

"I'm right here in the sixth dimension. As I have always been," Apep said in his normal bass voice without altering his pitch or tone.

"I'm sure you have followed my every move," Dan said sarcastically.

"You know I have, Dr. Adams. I haven't missed a beat."

"Wonderful! I'm sure you've been entertained."

"Actually, your movements have intrigued me. Quite different from the others," Apep replied.

"Others? There have been others?"

"You will actually get to meet the other two shortly. After you make your final error, you will join them."

"You're so sure I'll make the wrong choice?"

"It's already been predestined," Apep assured him.

Dan didn't know what to think. If it was already a dead issue, then why put him through this? It didn't make sense. However, Dan would have to go through it all.

"Predestined by whom, Apep? You? You're now informing me that all this was known from the beginning? Then why put me through it?"

Dan tried not to raise his voice. He knew it only inspired Apep to be even more evil. Apep feasted on his anger.

All of a sudden, thunder and lightning broke through the darkness. The lightning passed just above Dan's head. Its illumination briefly showed the dimensions of Dan's enclosure. It made Dan jump, and he slightly hit his head.

"What was that all about, Apep?" Dan said, his voice rising a few decibels.

"It was just . . ." Apep stopped.

It suddenly became silent. Deathly silent.

Dan waited for an answer and somehow knew not to ask again. Something was not right. Something had interfered with Apep's schedule. Dan tried to think.

Apep was thinking also. What had just occurred had happened only twice before. The first time was when Mr. Chou entered the sixth dimension. That was how many years ago? Two hundred? One hundred? Fifty? Apep tried to remember, but he couldn't recall. The second time it had occurred was when Stanley Moser entered in the early 1900s. Was that the right timeline?

Apep lost his train of thought and wondered what was going on. Maybe Stanley Moser was first and Mr. Chou was second. Why couldn't he remember this? He tried to think of how long he had controlled the sixth dimension. He had arrived 2,500 years ago. Wasn't that it?

The Death Maze

Apep didn't like the thunder or lightning. He had no explanation for it. It was surreptitious. It came from nowhere, and Apep couldn't anticipate or control it. He needed to get back to Dan Adams. However, he also needed to be composed.

No!

Apep needed his voice to be composed. That was it! He needed to modulate his voice. The silence was now a good minute old, and he was sure Dan Adams would speak in a more agitated tone.

"It was—"Apep started to say.

"Good to know you're still around," Dan interrupted.

"I have always been around," Apep stated.

"What was that for?" Dan asked.

Apep spoke quickly. "You're afraid of the dark, Dan Adams? I decided to illuminate your area slightly. Make you jump a bit."

Somehow Dan knew this was not the truth. Apep was speaking a bit more quickly than he normally did. Dan knew he did not have the answer. Still, Dan didn't want to ask about it anymore. He wanted to know other things.

"How have my movements intrigued you?" Dan asked, going back to Apep's previous statement.

"You have been more of the mind. Your thought processes are deliberate and well conceived even when agitated."

"Glad to know I've been able to process my choices with such clarity for you," Dan replied. "I'm sure my last decision will enthrall you."

"I'm looking forward to it, Dan Adams."

"So what else do I need to know?"

"You already know that the ceiling is now two feet tall and the walls are only three feet wide."

"So tell me something that I do not know," Dan stated with a bit of sarcasm.

There were reasons for the extra conversation. Dan knew something was not right. Apep had been startled. Dan needed to get him to speak so he could try to understand or interpret any indecision in his voice.

"You have come to the final point in your journey," Apep continued. "We want you to crawl to your last decision. I am certain you will reach it shortly."

Dan did hear it. He wasn't sure Apep realized what he had said. It was the first time he had said the word "we," and Dan knew this could be a slight break. There had never been a "we" in any of their past conversations. Apep had always been in control. What had caused him to lose that control?

"Upon your arrival, you will encounter two light switches," Apep explained. "One will lift in an upward motion. The other will move in a downward motion."

"Sounds obvious to me," Dan interrupted again.

"IT IS OBVIOUS!" Apep said, raising his voice.

Wait a minute, Dan thought. This was also a relative first. He had never heard Apep get upset. He was always cajoling, jesting, or speaking simply. His voice was always controlled. Dan knew that something was definitely off-kilter.

"Will you interrupt again, Dan Adams?" Apep asked in a normal tone.

"Obviously not! Please continue," Dan replied, knowing he could arouse him and possibly gain the upper hand.

"If you choose correctly, on the opposite side of your choice will be a large tube that will transport you back to your dimension."

"Why are you doing this to me?" Dan asked.

"You are a dangerous man. It's that simple."

The Death Maze

"Well, then, please explain the simplicity of it all," Dan responded. "How could I possibly be dangerous to one as powerful as you?"

"Thank you for your kind adoration. I rarely hear it."

"That wasn't adoration, Apep. That . . ." Dan caught himself.

"I'll be happy to accept it as adoration," Apep said.

Dan couldn't understand Apep's manner at this point. He did want to know how he was dangerous and knew Apep would soon explain. However, Apep's entire demeanor had changed, if ever so slightly. This could cause extra pain in reaching his final destination. Or it could be a quick crawl to where he would pick the wrong choice and end his life.

"You created a device that would not harm. This is as you intended," Apep began to explain. "However, your device was built adjacent to a portal that leads to the sixth dimension. This was the second time this portal was opened, though it was thought to have been permanently sealed. As I explained before, there were two others before you." Apep stopped for a moment.

"I need to ask a question," Dan gently interrupted.

"You may ask."

"You say my device would not harm."

"Correct!"

"If you knew it would not harm, then why retaliate against me?"

"There would be many later on who would want to alter or adjust or interfere with this device. This could actually exacerbate the opening of the portal and cause it to be continuously ajar. Prior to your accidental opening of the portal, it had remained unaltered for almost one hundred years. It must be kept closed for all eternity."

"I still do not understand the retaliation against me. Why not let me go back and close the portal? Why not make it so no one could open it again?"

"Our dimension has no use for the human sect. I do not want any opportunities for it to be opened again," Apep explained.

There it was again. Apep used the plural term "our" instead of the singular "my." It was another mistake that Dan was sure Apep had not noticed.

"Human beings are by nature ruinous, deadly creatures fending off each other for power and wealth. You do not care for the welfare of other species that harbor different points of view or means of life."

"And what about you, Apep?" Dan shot back. "Do you care? I have been tested and put through hell trying to understand what I did wrong. If you can see what I was building, then you know that it can be used to expand the means to avoid destruction of the atmosphere. Without experimentation, world powers would continue to push the earth's limits and threaten global annihilation to raise their bottom line and profits."

"I control the sixth dimension, Dan Adams, for the purpose of continued life free from all outside influence and germinal exposure. Your experiments, and now your knowledge of my world, could only lead to further educational influence. More will come."

"I'll stop it if I can be given the gift, by you, to go back home," Dan assured him.

"You are a scientist, Dr. Adams," Apep explained. "Knowledge is king to you. My world is without the lies and distrust you have displayed in the maze. I was able to analyze your reactions to all you encountered. Once you explain,

The Death Maze

or try to, the more you will want to know. I cannot trust what you say. If I cannot control, my world will be your next victim. More will actually want to come."

Apep tried to get Dan off balance. He really wanted to do to Dan as he had done to the other two. They had been easier targets. Dan was the intellectual, the thinker. Apep needed Dan more than he needed to go back to his home. Dan was his study and could prepare him for the possibility of more entering the sixth dimension.

Dan was now stumped. It sounded as if Apep was not going to agree to anything, even if he successfully beat the maze. He required a more thorough processing while moving on to his last destination. Dan needed to outwit this monster.

"My world has one ruler, Dr. Adams," Apep explained. "I do not allow egos to contaminate it, as in your world. The feeding of the mind builds our capacity. We do not cause the destruction of another breed simply for sport."

"Where are you going with this, Apep?" Dan asked, desperate for the final confrontation. He understood now that there had been more in this world. But how many?

"I wish to inquire how many species have been wiped off the planet Earth since the beginning of mankind?"

Apep waited for an answer and knew he would not get one. Dan didn't want to answer, because it was all relative to the factor of time and progress. All creatures were not equal. Only mankind was supposed to understand and know this. And yet they were killing themselves as well, due to unwarranted greed and an insatiable thirst for power.

"You cannot answer that because you honestly do not know," Apep said.

"I don't know, because the selfishness of my species . . ." Dan's voice trailed off. This really affected him. Apep was beginning to sound—and he wished he did not think this—correct.

"Would it not surprise you to know that thousands of types of creatures no longer live on Planet Earth because of man?" Apep asked. "Ever since the dawning of mankind, his destruction was imminent. Man does only for himself without giving back and looking at the beauty of the world that surrounds him."

"My world isn't totally like that," Dan replied. "There are many countries that wish to destroy other people's way of life. There are egomaniacal individuals who long to rule and rob others in the name of greed and humanity. There are the gangs that espouse a cause and trash people's souls for the purpose of control and money. However, there are many more who appreciate a *cause célèbre* for the purpose of helping and arousing large crowds to benefit mankind."

Dan didn't know if he was getting through to Apep. He was struggling in his small enclosure and trying to justify his world to one who truly hated himself.

"Enough talk!" Apep commanded, obviously through with Dan's preaching.

"NOT ENOUGH!" Dan shouted back, not knowing he'd had it in him. "I've listened to you and gone through your silly trips for the benefit of your twisted ego and entertainment. If I'm going to be put to death, you should have the patience to listen to my words."

Suddenly another spark of lightning twisted around Dan's body without touching it. Then thunder followed. Dan didn't jump as high this time, as he had anticipated something was about to occur.

Apep tried to speak, but was kept silent by his disdain for this unaccounted thing he could not control. He needed to again compose his thoughts, and decided to let Dan finish his soliloquy.

After a few moments of piqued silence, Dan was able to continue. "There are individuals in my dimension who enjoy keeping the masses at bay. These are the same nouveau riche whose attitudes and lifestyles are only for the elite. They get all the benefits and enjoy the comforts of life while watching and feigning disgust as others suffer for their meager means.

"There are creatures whose hope for survival rests in the hands of men and women hoping to push back the terrible industrial triumphs of the twentieth century. Others feel it's their turn to live life beyond its fullest and do not wish to adapt to reality.

"We have the questions and we have the answers. What we do not have are all the means to make matters better as individuals. We need the entire cooperation of all. Mankind acknowledges it excesses. Only there are those who feel they should live forever with these excesses.

"There is so much power in the world today. It is because of this power that the world remains intact. Power is not in the hands of one person who could push a button at the whim of one psychological nutcase. Since others have power as well, treaties keep the mighty at bay. It's those who do not wish to follow the same rule of law who cause such overblown reactions."

The enclosure was silent. Dan at first did not realize he had spoken for so long. He was passionate and reactionary at the same time. He words brought him to fatigue, and he knew he had meant every one of them.

Having grown up as one of the rich, he always felt he should give back. This was why he always watched over and tried to protect those who could not fight back.

He felt his purpose was to reach into the depths of his mind and try to create a world that was better for the next generation.

Now he wondered if Apep was truly listening. Did he really care what he felt inside, or was it all just a bunch of crap? Did he know that sooner or later Dan would eventually tire of the speech? Dan just waited.

"By killing me, Apep," Dan finished, "you do the same as mankind does. It's the same thing you abhor."

That was the trump card Apep had been waiting for. The one line that could totally nullify Dan's entire speech.

"Not really," Apep said with some pleasure. "I enjoy being the hunter and watching the hunted."

"Terrific," Dan uttered under his breath.

"A wonderful speech, Dan Adams. Very touching," Apep expanded. "However, my world does not survive well with human beings dropping in on it. You are dangerous to the sixth dimension and must suffer whatever consequences it holds. That is, unless you complete and beat the maze."

More silence as the enclosure slowly became slightly illuminated. Dan could see his hands.

"How do I know both switches aren't deadly?" Dan asked.

"That hasn't occurred once since this all began. Has it?" Apep replied.

"What if I refuse to choose, Apep?" Dan asked in total exhaustion.

"I will leave you in your small enclosure to die. Good luck, Dan Adams," Apep said. Dan's world became silent once more.

He sincerely enjoyed the banter with Apep. Dan was hoping Apep also appreciated the conversation. He realized

The Death Maze

they could both learn from each other. Seeing each other eye to eye? That was another situation. They were so much alike and yet so different.

Well, duh! Dan thought. *Where did that thought come from?*

"Hello?" Dan called out.

No answer.

There wouldn't be an answer. If he decided not to crawl, Dan would be left to die. It was simplicity at its best.

He looked down the small enclosure, trying to see where he was about to crawl. Dan couldn't determine the end, or even if there was an end. He only needed to realize that he should start crawling. He would not find out his fate until he took those first few inchworm moves.

So he began once more, one final time.

The lights were dimmer than two minutes ago, and Dan was unable to determine what his hands would touch. His mind wandered off on multiple tangents. It thought of a song he heard as a kid called "Spider on the Floor," sung by an entertainer named Raffi. Now why in the hell would an entertainer for kids traumatize kids about a spider on the floor about to get on a child? That was the only song he skipped when he listened to the tape.

The second song was funnier than the first. It was called "Spiders and Snakes" and sung by Jim Stafford. Dan enjoyed that one and tried humming it as he crawled.

"I remember when Mary Lou said you wanna walk me home from school . . .

I don't like spiders and snakes and that ain't what it takes to love me

You fool you fool . . ."

Dan began feeling a chill. It was as if the tunnel and his enclosure were coming to an end. He felt around for a light, a switch. Anything that might signify this was the end.

There wasn't anything. His enclosure and size remained the same, and he kept crawling along. His long journey was far from over.

Before he reached the pinnacle of his many choices, there would be at least one mile of blistered hands and a raw stomach. His joints would cry out from pain. Sweat would drip continuously, and the stinging of his eyes from his tears would slightly bloat his face.

Dan's only concern was to reach the end. He didn't care about death anymore. In fact, he welcomed it. It might actually be a relief after this nightmare. Only God knew how much he had to endure.

The idea of burdening Apep with his corpse gave Dan a wonderful feeling. But what would it mean to Apep? How would he feel, knowing he had killed another human being? Would he be his third? Did Apep even have any feelings? Did the sixth dimension have any scruples?

Probably not.

Dan heard thunder once more. But was it in the back of his mind or actually within his enclosure?

Chapter 33

Shirley felt good. No, she felt great! All her anxieties and stress were gone now that she was able to regain the real freedom she had lost when Chief Dressler put her into a corner regarding Alex Miller and William Barrish. Hanging up on the chief of police was therapeutic. It was a catharsis she hadn't felt since college.

Shirley was one of two female students in a med school with 108 males in her class. The two of them experienced constant tests of anguish and chauvinistic taunts, as the men thought they were fair game.

Robin Brooks was Shirley's roommate. She was a plain Jane with brains who came from a small town in the Midwest. Robin had never experienced such cruelty. Before coming to med school, her hometown threw a party for their soon-to-be new doctor. In four years, she'd complete her graduate program and residency and be able to go home to minister to the sick and needy. That was her calling.

The friendship between Shirley and Robin was close. So close that rumors of "lesbian bitches" on the campus escalated out of control. In the 1970s, with tolerance being a more open subject, one would have thought this couldn't happen.

However, it did. After six weeks of constant jeers, hoots, and hollers, Robin decided she couldn't handle the pressure anymore. Graduate school was hard enough without the persistent taunts. She gave Shirley a deep hug and left in the middle of the night for home.

There were some who said she had a nervous breakdown. Others opined about her lack of devotion and desire to be a doctor. The medical profession only wanted serious students who could advance the profession into the next millennium. Shirley knew that Robin had the drive to become a brilliant doctor. She certainly had the grades. Otherwise, she would never have been accepted to the college she had chosen.

Shirley knew better. And she planned for a year and a half to get her revenge. It would take a steady hand and focused eye to continue with her studies and get to know her deviant classmates. By the time she was finished, her name would be infamous. And yet no one would know it was really her who caused so much trouble.

Shirley became the model classmate. She played her part to the hilt. Every day was spent with these disgusting pigs to show them that she was a woman who could handle stress and also put these bastards in their place.

Her plan started with finding the most vulnerable of all the males in her class. Poor Terry Meyers! He not only looked as if he had never touched a woman, but admitted one time to Shirley that he was indeed a virgin.

Their friendship grew, with Shirley giving Terry false confidence. Terry would thrust his chest out and falsely claim that Shirley was his, and declare that no one should argue with him or touch her.

What was even funnier was that most thought it was real. Shirley refused to be alone with anyone but Terry. He was academically smarter than most in their class, but also the shortest besides Shirley. And Shirley took advantage of it.

The Death Maze

They spent many hours in the library and equal that amount of time with their required lab work. When Terry wanted to go to his room or even Shirley's room, she quietly refused and said her degree and studies were more important. They would have plenty of time after they graduated and she could begin to devote all of herself to him.

In the meantime, Shirley acquired the friendship of Ramona "Boobs" Pinkerton, as some men called her. Ramona had enough for two well-endowed women. Shirley had met Ramona in the local bar in town, of which she was the owner.

Shirley became a frequent customer and spent enough time with Ramona to unfold her entire plan by the end of the first year. Ramona was perfect as her coconspirator, since she actually hated most men. This would be her payback for the cruelty she had to deal with when growing up with the largest breasts in high school.

Ramona had a beautiful face and full figure. She just also had these huge knockers that got in the way all the time. Breast reduction was an option that never materialized. A year after purchasing the bar, Ramona had actually met the man of her dreams, and they were still together after many years.

With the approaching deadline coming into full view, Ramona planted Natalie "Ginger" Holly in her bar. She was every man's wet dream, and the perfect tease. Ramona had her come to the bar every weekend for two months to get to know the patrons—that is, victims.

Little Terry Meyers never saw it coming. His first reaction to Ginger was nothing short of an open mouth and a bit of drool dropping from his lips. Ginger had him tied around her little finger by the end of the first meeting. Before the end of the night, the bait was set.

Ginger wanted Terry in her apartment, which she had leased for only the two months, one week before the graduation ceremonies. He could bring as many of his friends as he wanted, but only one man at a time could truly "stick it in her." The price was forty dollars a pop.

Terry exited the bar and blabbed it to every one of his 107 classmates. Naturally no one was to inform Shirley of the encounter, since she belonged to Terry. He was just so horny that he couldn't keep it in his pants long enough to wait until Shirley was ready.

Everyone gathered at Ramona's bar over the course of the two months that Ginger was there. She played all of them like the true "doll" she was. She teased and pursed her lips like a pro on Forty-Second Street and Eighth Avenue in New York City. Ginger also made the appointments so she could time this perfectly. She could have all 108 of them and be done by late Friday or early Saturday.

By the end of the first month, all 108 males had made their appointments. Ginger asked for the money in advance. When all had paid, Ramona put the money in a wooden box for safekeeping. There was $4,320 waiting to be split by Shirley, Ramona, and Ginger.

The magical night approached. It was one week before graduation, and every male was eager to let out a little pent-up frustration. This last semester had been tough on most of them.

They lined up outside Ginger's place. No more than twenty men could congregate at one time so as not to arouse suspicion, so they needed to keep to the strict schedule.

Terry was first. Ginger opened the door and showed him to her boudoir. The lights were low and Ginger undid her robe to show her fantastic, perfect body. She writhed and

The Death Maze

stretched out her arms to let Terry know she wanted him . . . NOW!

Terry played with the zipper to his pants and had trouble, at first, getting it down. The lump under his shorts was becoming difficult to contain, as it only grew at the sight of such a beautiful woman. He stumbled while trying to remove the pants before gently placing himself on top of her. Before he had time to insert his entire manhood, Terry let out a scream and emptied the sticky liquid. In no more than thirty seconds Terry was finished.

Ginger gently told Terry he was great, "just the best," and asked him to let the next future doctor in as he exited her place. Terry's reaction was one of a dreamy-eyed buffoon. He found his pants and stumbled as he put them back on.

Walking out the door, Terry let the next customer in and began bragging to the others how great it felt. Phrases like "she was perfect" and "the best I ever had" seemed to be the reaction coming from his lips. "Remember, do not tell Shirley," was his final comment.

Everyone patted Terry on the back and thanked him for this experience. He was their local hero, and they'd all celebrate at graduation in a week. This would definitely be a memory of a lifetime. It was a story they would only tell between themselves.

Shirley was at Ramona's bar that evening and all they could talk about was Ginger and her devotion to helping them get back at these bastards. It took a year and a half of planning, and the final day was almost over.

"I'll miss you, Ramona," Shirley said.

"Me too, Shirley," Ramona replied.

"Did you mail all the envelopes?"

"They were mailed out this morning. They'll get the news tomorrow."

"What about Ginger?" Shirley asked.

"I gave her the name of the doctor you recommended," Ramona responded. "She already contacted him and made an appointment for Monday. This weekend is one she can truly appreciate doing her work."

"I owe you a lot. You know that!"

"You owe me nothing, kiddo," Ramona stated as she bent down to give Shirley her share of the money. "I already gave Ginger her third."

"Why don't you and Ginger . . . split it up?" Shirley said. "I got my revenge and really didn't want any of the money."

"How about I just give Ginger the entire amount? She'll need it for later!" Ramona said. "Besides, helping you get back for Robin was worth all the planning." Both of them just laughed.

The next day, all 108 men woke up in the late morning. It was the weekend and none of them really wanted to do anything now that classes were over and graduation was just around the corner. They congregated at a breakfast diner and talked about the previous night while eating hearty meals and drinking lots of coffee.

Terry Meyers went to pick up his mail after the meal. There was only one letter in his slot. He reached in to retrieve the letter and then closed the mail slot. There was no return address on the letter. He had no idea who it was from.

He opened the letter, read the contents, and quickly threw up his breakfast on his shoes. He bent down to wretch again and somehow managed to scream a four-letter word starting with S and ending with H I T.

Dear Terry,

    I am pleased to inform you that last night was wonderful. I was able to satisfy my every dream. However, I need to inform you that I have a bad case of syphilis and crabs and will begin treatment on Monday. While I know this will not last forever, I wanted you to know how wonderful it is that you could catch it from me. Do you know the words to "For I'm a jolly good fucker"? If you didn't before, I'm sure you do now.

    Screw you,
    Ginger (Robin's friend)

That year saw the largest epidemic of venereal disease on campus. All mouths from the med students were silent for quite some time.

***

Shirley laughed out loud as she opened the door to her car and got in. She started the engine, put the car in drive, and drove toward Arione. She was looking forward to assisting Doctors Ryan and Rayburn and hoping that something could be done to locate Dan Adams.

Her mind quickly drifted back to Ramona and Ginger. It was because of these two women that she had the guts to stand up to Chief Dressler this morning. No one was going to belittle her ever again.

Then her mind drifted in the direction of Alex Miller. He seemed like a terrific individual with a good sense of humor. She wondered why he had never married, but quickly figured that he enjoyed traveling for his work.

Still, he was handsome and certainly cared for his fellow workers. She had that inner feeling that he could be trusted. What was going on in Arione was a real dilemma and mystery. Alex Miller and William Barrish were only doing their jobs, and she was sure that if they were properly informed, they could be convinced to release only what was valid at the time. Give them exclusivity and they would shut their mouths and put down their pens.

Shirley felt that she could also be very interested in Alex Miller on a personal level. He excited her and was alive with a great imagination. There weren't many men in Arione or Vera who had the combination that Alex possessed. Dan Adams was already spoken for. Many others were married. In two small towns, how many good fish could there possibly be?

Now that there was fair game in town, and one of them was obviously quite mature and seasoned, Shirley felt she should let herself be known to him. As long as he was in town, the possibilities were endless.

"You two can come up for some air if you like," Shirley said to the windshield.

Alex Miller and William Barrish lifted themselves up from the back floor and sat down on the seats as humans normally would.

"You knew we were here?" Will said through his teeth.

"I wasn't born yesterday, Will," Shirley replied.

"And I'll bet you're driving to Arione," Alex chimed in.

"No need to bet, Mr. Miller. Besides, I usually win when I bet."

"I'll bet you do," Alex confirmed.

"You want to know something, Will?" Shirley asked.

"Sure!"

"Ever since you arrived on the scene and revealed your professional identity, I knew Dressler would have trouble keeping the story from appearing in the newspaper. Before you arrived, no one knew. And probably no one would ever know," Shirley explained.

"Know what?" Will asked. "I still don't know what is truly going on."

"Would you mind revealing the entire story to us, Dr. Anderson?" Alex asked.

"When you begin calling me Shirley, I will."

"All right, Shirley. But please call me Alex, so we'll be on the same level."

Shirley looked in the rearview mirror and eyed Alex. She definitely liked what she saw. This could truly be a refreshing and promising new start for her.

"I'll tell you what you need to know if you promise me one thing," Shirley stated.

"And what is that?" Alex asked.

"That you do not reveal your sources and hold all news for at least twenty-four hours before printing it. Agreed?"

"Why twenty-four hours?" Will asked.

"It would make it harder for Dressler to pin the released information on you. Is that correct?" Alex asked.

"You read my mind," Shirley said.

"First, you should realize that a good reporter never reveals his sources. I never have and never will," Alex explained. "Second, you've got a deal. And third, let's talk about getting together. It would be my pleasure to get to know all about you."

"In my mind," Shirley smiled, "we already have."

As the car sped toward Arione, Shirley narrated the entire ordeal up to the arrival of one Alex Miller. Will listened and tried interrupting a few times before being cut off by Alex. All the questions had to wait. The most important thing was to figure out the whereabouts of Dr. Dan Adams.

Prior to arriving at the edge of Arione, Shirley instructed both men to drop to the floor of the car. Dressler was to meet her at the house. They would need to sneak in if they wanted to speak with Dr. Ryan and Dr. Rayburn.

When they arrived at the house, Shirley quickly exited the car and walked toward Chief Dressler and his loyal Officer Bone.

"Hello, Chief," Shirley said with enthusiasm.

"Shirley," Chief said.

"Dr. Anderson," Bone followed.

"Let's go into the house," Dressler stated. "You need to meet the others."

Dressler accompanied Shirley into the house while Bone waited outside.

"Deputy Bone is not coming with us?" Shirley asked nonchalantly, noticing that only Dressler was behind her.

"I'm having him wait for someone," Dressler said smugly.

Once inside the house, Shirley felt her insides tingle, her heart begin to speed up, and a million goose bumps rise to the surface of her skin. She hadn't felt like this since Ginger took on her chauvinistic male classmates.

Dressler led her from the hallway through the living room. Shirley noticed that nothing seemed out of place. It was as if no one had lived in the house for a while. *Where is the problem?* she thought.

Walking through the living room and into the hallway before the lab, something began to change. It smelled different. She sensed an aged feeling hanging over her head.

She looked up but saw nothing new. She dropped her head to look at the floor. Nope! Nothing out of the ordinary.

When Dressler opened the door to the lab, it hit her. It stung her eyes, and she rubbed them. She looked at the ceiling and saw the hole. Shirley had never been in Dan Adams's laboratory. Whatever had happened to him must have been devastating. She hoped that he was still alive, wherever he might be. *That's what I'm here for*, she thought. *To help locate him and bring him home.*

There was very little glass on the floor. The debris from the roof had been swept to one side of the lab.

"Dr. Shirley Anderson," Dressler said. "I'd like you to meet Dr. Samuel Ryan and Dr. Allyson Rayburn."

"It's a pleasure to meet both of you," Shirley said, extending her hand.

All three shook hands and got through the normal formalities very quickly.

"I'm going to leave the three of you to your work," Dressler said. "Officer Bone will be outside. If you need anything, just ask."

"Before you leave, Chief Dressler," Allyson began, "I want you to know this is not going to be as simple as I thought."

"And why is that, Dr. Rayburn?" Dressler asked.

"Well, there are only four pages of notes here. Where would all the others be?"

"The last time anyone entered the house was when you, Dr. Ryan, and Officer Bone came in yesterday," Dressler explained.

"Did he keep his notes somewhere else?" Dr. Sam Ryan asked.

"Not to my knowledge, Dr. Ryan. You have the run of the place and may look to see if he kept other notes. Just please try not to disturb anything that doesn't relate to your work," Dressler stated before leaving.

The three doctors looked at one another. It was Shirley who broke the ice.

"May I see the pages?"

"Of course," Allyson said. "What's your specialty?"

"I'm a doctor at Vera Hospital. I've been treating Ruth Putnam, Dan's—" Shirley rushed for the correct word. "—friend and roommate, since this all happened."

"I see," Allyson said.

"I've known Dan for quite some time now," Shirley continued to explain. "Arione and Vera are sister towns, and everyone knows everyone else."

"Do you see anything in the notes that may suggest what happened?" Dr. Ryan asked, hoping to break the small talk.

Shirley led her eyes to the notes. On the pages were a few drawings of a geothermal energy plant, how it was to be installed, and what it could do. Next to each drawing were descriptions of each phase of the plant and where the energy was to be made and kept. Information on how the energy was retrieved and put into the vehicle was on the last page. At the bottom left side of each page were the initials AGE.

"What does the A mean in AGE?" Shirley asked.

"We believe it stands for the word *alternative*," Sam said.

"It looks as if he was working on a way to convert steam into energy for the purpose of running vehicles," Allyson added.

"I see," Shirley said, nodding her head. "Dan was working on a system for vehicles to get better energy and mileage than they would with gasoline. These vehicles would also burn totally clean, with no carbon emissions. It makes sense. But what does that have to do with a bomb?"

"Who said anything about a bomb?" Allyson asked.

"No one. It was just the rumor floating around," Shirley said. "I expected to see more of a disheveled lab and home. This place looks too clean."

"Let's walk out back," Allyson commanded. "Dan's experiment on alternative geothermal energy is quite impressive. We believe he was almost completed when he disappeared."

Allyson led the three to the back door and walked out.

Chapter 34

Dressler gave his orders to Bone, got into his car, and left. He had more pressing matters to attend to and wanted to get started as quickly as possible. It never crossed his mind to look in Shirley Anderson's car. On his mind was the meeting waiting for him at the station. Once he had the approval of the town council, he would find Miller and Barrish and lock them up until he could figure out how to get them out of town.

He was still pissed at Shirley for signing the release and letting William Barrish leave the hospital with Alex Miller. Who knew where they were at this moment or whom they had talked with. Hell, he had no idea if anything was yet in print or about to be. He just hoped nothing had transpired, or there would be a caravan of cars on their way to see the crazy towns of Arione and Vera.

Bone opened his car door and prepared to take a nap. With his boss gone for at least a couple hours and knowing it would be a long day, a quick nap called out to him. Arlene had been real good to him ever since he said they could get married when this case was solved. He hadn't had a good night's sleep in the last few days.

About fifteen minutes later, Alex and Will heard snoring coming from Bone's car. It was the perfect time to make their move and get into the house. They raised their bodies from the car floor, and Alex lifted the door handle with great ease. He was sure that any excess noise would wake Bone, and he didn't want a confrontation at this point. Alex knew Bone would recognize Will. But Alex had a plan, since he had not yet been introduced.

Alex quietly opened the back door on the driver's side, and they crawled out of the car and scrambled to the house. Will was nervous and excited with the thrill of it all. Alex knew how his friend felt, but still warned him not to be overly excessive with his movements. The slightest error would probably put them in jail.

Alex looked at Will when they got to the door. He put his forefinger to his mouth, telling Will to stay quiet. He had been in this situation a few times over the years. It made him remember his first big assignment.

***

It was a murder case involving two eighteen-year-olds from Chicago. One of the kids, Russell Austin, had turned out to be a psycho. He had stabbed and hack-sawed his friend to death, and the police had arrested him. Alex convinced his boss to give him the assignment and was warned not to get into trouble. His boss wanted Alex to find out if the kid was really a psycho or just putting up a front to avoid the electric chair.

Alex wanted to be the first to get inside the jail. The kid wasn't going to talk until he went to court. His lawyer had told him to steer clear of the press. The goal was to plea insanity to avoid doing hard time in jail. Life would be better in an institution instead of with a prison full of hardened criminals. Even though he was legally an adult, the courts would be more lenient on a younger individual.

Alex felt that if he could scoop everyone else, there could be a promotion and a fat raise. As he was in his early twenties, perhaps he could convince the kid that he had nothing to fear from him. Alex just wanted to get the real story, not the sensationalized one. "No pain, no gain" was his motto.

An appointment was made to talk with Austin without the knowledge of his lawyer. Austin wanted his story to be told before going to court.

A few simple matters had to be settled before Austin agreed to the interview. First was that the interview would be in a room with no bars. There needed to be a desk and two chairs. Second was that a police officer would be stationed outside the room so the conversation would flow smoothly. Austin would talk and answer questions for no more than two hours without a break before being taken back to his cell.

Finally, Austin wanted there to be no recording devices of any kind. Alex should bring a pad of paper and a pen. He was expected to either write down everything or remember it. Austin did not want any surprises when he went to court. A recording of his voice would confirm it all, but the written word could be disputed as a slip of the mind or a misunderstanding.

Everything was settled. The interview was going to take place on a Friday, as the Saturday paper wasn't as important as the Sunday edition. Austin wanted Alex to write on Saturday and publish the story on Sunday. It would be front-page news, with Austin's picture in the center.

Alex's adrenaline rose and he felt a rush throughout his body. He knew that this would be his story of the year. He would never forget this experience, and he hoped his hand wouldn't shake when he took his notes.

The Death Maze

Alex entered the police station. He removed his coat and handed it to a police officer. He was asked to empty his pockets of all his personal items and leave them in a small box. He was only allowed his pad and pen.

Young Alex Miller, reporter for the *Chicago Herald*, entered the room, sat down in one of the two chairs, and waited.

A few minutes passed before the rear door to the room opened. Alex stood as Russell Austin, a curly haired, five-foot-ten, eighteen-year-old kid wearing an orange jumpsuit, entered. His wrists and ankles were cuffed and he was followed by two large guards.

Russell sat down in the other chair as one guard removed the handcuffs. The guard then bent to his ankles and removed the ankle cuffs. Then both guards left the room through the door they had entered. One guard stood at the door and watched through the door window. A second guard watched through the window of the other door.

Russell slowly got up from the chair. He looked at both door windows, making sure the police knew he had no ulterior motive for standing up. Both men were allowed to walk around the room. They were not allowed to shake hands or touch in any manner.

Russell walked slowly around the room and looked into every corner and crevasse. He looked at the ceiling and lighting in the room for a good thirty seconds before lowering his head. He then sat down again and looked at Alex.

"Ever think people are consistently watching you in every corner of every room you enter?" Russell said very calmly in a near monotone.

Alex just looked at Russell, trying not to stare but to appear normal.

"I'm not sure I understand," Alex replied.

"They're watching, you know," Russell calmly stated.

"I know they are. There's a cop at each door," Alex assured him.

"That's not what I mean."

"What do you mean?" Alex asked.

"I mean they're watching us. They're judging us. They're CONVICTING US!"

Alex waited for a moment. He thought that maybe the guards would rush into the room and put Russell's cuffs on again. He really didn't know if he was safe or not. Russell could easily grab him or punch him in a split second. Alex remained in his seat.

"Why do you say that?" Alex asked after a few moments.

"Because every word we speak is written down somewhere. Whether it's in our mind or on some piece of paper, it's there," Russell explained. He then opened his mouth as if wanting to continue, but said nothing.

Alex waited.

"I was once told that when a person dies, they see everything they have done before they meet the maker. Do you think that's true?" Russell asked, staring at one wall.

"I honestly have never thought about it before," Alex replied.

"Before I killed my friend, I saw God telling me it was time."

"Time for what?" Alex wrote the word *time* on his pad.

"It was time for him to die," Russell stated simply, now looking at Alex.

"Why would God ask you to kill your friend?"

"Because . . . it . . . was . . . time!"

"Do you believe now that God told you to kill your friend?" Alex asked.

"I don't hear him anymore."

"What do you hear?"

"I hear the laughter."

Alex waited before he spoke. He needed to watch Russell's reactions. He wanted to make sure his reaction to any of Russell's movements would not be misconstrued as a threat.

Then he saw Russell's face change. It became softer. The lines seemed to disappear. Russell sat down, looked at Alex, and spoke in a normal voice as if nothing had yet been said.

"You're Alex. Right?"

Alex waited for a split second before replying. "Alex Miller. From the *Chicago Herald*."

He did not know what had just happened, but knew he needed to just go along. Alex wanted to write something down, but knew his memory would serve perfectly.

"So you want my story. Well, you ask the questions and I'll give you the answers," Russell said like a normal eighteen-year-old.

Alex looked at him for a few moments before beginning again. He was not sure what he had just witnessed. He was sure that Russell would end up in an institution and avoid all jail time.

The two hours went by quickly without another incident. Russell was eager to explain that he couldn't remember what he had done. He had been having a good time with his friend. All he remembered was the police picking him off the floor and dragging him away from his dead friend.

The hacksaw was in his hand. His blood was mixed with his friend's blood. He told the police that God had instructed him to kill his friend.

At the end of the interview, Russell stood up. Alex saw his face change again and the lines appear once more. Russell jumped on the table and yelled.

"SOCIETY SHOULD BE REPRIMANDED FOR ITS CRUELTY AND NEGLECT OF OUR YOUNG ADULTS."

Russell reached into his pocket, grabbed something, and opened his mouth. Whatever was in his hand, he put in his mouth and swallowed. This was all before the guards had a chance to rush in, push Alex aside, and try to get Russell down from the table.

Russell then began to fall. The guards caught him before he hit the floor. Alex stared at Russell as he was led out of the room. The last he saw was foam coming out of Russell's mouth.

Alex waited at the police station until he could find out what happened to Russell. When all the commotion was over, a police sergeant came up to Alex to inform him that Russell Austin had died. The pill he had swallowed was a cyanide tablet. There would be an investigation into how he had gotten the tablet.

It was a long, tiring day for the young reporter. His body moved as if it knew where to walk and what to avoid while walking.

He looked for the first bar on the way home and went in. He needed a drink. He needed two before he could take out his pad and look at his notes. As he reread the notes, he remembered everything that went on between the sentences.

Friday afternoon would turn into Friday night before Alex found himself opening the door to his apartment. He took off his coat and sat down on his couch.

The next morning, Alex woke up on the couch with the same clothes on. He was so tired. He was numb. He took off all his clothes, went to the bathroom, and took a long, hot shower.

When he was finished, he put on a pair of jeans and a White Sox T-shirt. He sat down on the couch, picked up his trousers from the floor, and took the pad of paper and pen from his pocket. He reached for a larger notebook on the table in front of the couch, opened to the first page, and began writing.

The morning sun that shone through the window shifted with each hour that Alex wrote. The light in the room grew dimmer as the sun began to go down. When Alex was finished, it was five o'clock in the evening.

The phone rang. Alex picked it up. It was his boss. Alex listened.

"It's done," Alex said. "It will be on your desk in the morning."

"Tomorrow's Sunday, Alex," he heard his boss say.

"It'll be there anyway, boss."

"You okay?" his boss asked.

"Fine. Just so tired."

"Get some sleep," his boss said before hanging up.

Alex went to the kitchen and opened the refrigerator. There was one beer and a bottle of soda, a package of hot dogs and buns, and a jar of pickles. Alex grabbed the beer and closed the refrigerator door. He opened the beer and drank its entire contents in one gulp.

Alex then went into his room and fell asleep.

***

Alex's mind returned to the present and he looked at Will. Will seemed anxious and ready to pounce forward. Alex took his hand and laid it on Will's shoulder.

"Easy, Will. Let's take it one step at a time and try not to screw this up."

"I'm ready when you are," Will assured him.

Alex hoped the outcome of this adventure would be totally different from his first major assignment. He never had never forgotten about Russell Austin. His mind wouldn't let it go.

However, Alex also felt that surge of energy, that rush from inside his veins. He and Will started toward the door and immediately entered the house, making sure the door opened and closed without a sound.

Once inside, they looked at everything. Will knew that the layout of the house would be important and made sure to remember it. It was already second nature for Alex to remember.

They heard voices in another room. They slowly moved in the direction of the sounds. Reaching the hallway before the lab, they saw that the door was open.

"Hold it right there," Bone ordered from behind them, startling them both.

Both turned their heads and stared at the barrel end of Bone's gun.

"Do you mind explaining this?" Alex asked, as if Bone were crazy to pull a gun on them.

"Just tell me what the two of you want and why you're in this house. Then, maybe, I'll explain the gun."

"We were looking for Dr. Anderson," Will said a bit loudly, hoping Shirley would hear.

"Are you from the hospital?" Bone asked. "Wait! Aren't you that reporter who got his jaw broken by the chief?"

It was Alex's cue.

"That's right, Officer. Dr. Anderson asked me to bring him here. Posthaste!"

"Let me see your identification," Bone demanded. "I was told you couldn't leave the hospital. How did you get out?" Bone took a few steps closer.

"I seem to have left my hospital identification in the car," Alex said, checking his pants pockets. "If you wouldn't mind me getting it, I'll be right back."

Bone took a few more steps closer. He didn't trust these guys, but was confused. If this man was from the hospital and Dr. Anderson did send for them, he could be in big trouble for aiming his gun at them. On the other hand, if what the older man said was a lie, the chief would be proud that he had caught them.

Bone kept the gun pointed on Alex and Will. They were eyeing him as much as he was keeping them in focus.

Just then, Dr. Anderson came into the room. She saw the gun and quickly reacted.

"Officer Bone, what the hell are you doing?"

Bone was startled. He had not expected Dr. Anderson to react like this.

It was the perfect moment for Alex. Moving quickly, he grabbed Bone. They both fell to the floor. Will rushed to help Alex so the gun wouldn't go off. Will stepped on Bone's wrist, and Bone yelled and let go of the gun.

Bone tried to punch Alex but couldn't move fast enough. Alex knelt on Bone's other wrist and threw a punch at Bone's face. Bone's head cocked backward and hit one of the side tables. The impact didn't break the table, but it did knock Bone out cold.

Shirley rushed in to check on all three men.

"You're all animals," she declared.

"You saw the gun," Will said in his muffled voice.

"He's only knocked out, Shirley," Alex chimed in. "He's not dead."

"I just didn't expect any violence. I hate violence."

"I'll remember that on our first date," Alex confided to her.

Shirley checked Bone's head and felt a large lump developing on the back of it. Bone would certainly be groggy when he woke up. His breathing was steady. Shirley knew that he'd have a bad headache.

"Let's move him to the couch," Shirley ordered.

"We need a rope," Alex said.

"For what?" Shirley almost yelled.

"To tie him up," Alex explained. "When he wakes up, he'll want to arrest us. There's too much at stake here."

"You said the story was important, Dr. Anderson," Will added.

Shirley was frustrated. She looked at Alex, then Will, and then back at Alex. "Fine! Get a rope. But don't tie it too tightly and cut off his circulation."

"You heard what the doctor ordered, Will," Alex said. "Let's go find a rope."

Will and Alex found the kitchen and rummaged through the drawers. It wasn't long before they returned and tied up Bone.

"Grab the feet and I'll grab the shoulders," Alex ordered.

"For what?" Will asked.

"We're going to put him in his car. It'll be safer for us."

Shirley just looked at Alex and walked back into the lab. Alex and Will carried Bone outside to his car and lowered him onto the front seat. They closed the car door and started walking back to the house.

"Wait a second," Alex said. He walked back to the car, taking a handkerchief from his back pocket. He opened the door and stuffed the handkerchief into Bone's mouth. After closing the door one last time, Alex and Will walked back to the house.

It wasn't long before Alex went outside again. This time he had Bone's gun in his hand. He walked to Bone's vehicle, opened the door a third time, and gently placed it in its holster. He knew it would be strange for Bone to wake up and explain that two men overpowered him with his gun still in its holster. Chief Dressler might even ask why Bone hadn't removed the gun when he first confronted them. It would be funny to listen to the explanation Bone would have to give. Alex loved his job.

Chapter 35

Apep was now waiting for the final decision. It would be the last moment that he would have to endure Dr. Daniel Adams. He had watched and thoroughly enjoyed all the choices Dan made. Apep had been entertained when he viewed Dr. Adams's past, and he wondered why he would question life ending the way it would. Apep truly loved his power. Didn't Dr. Adams know that everything was predestined?

This man, Dr. Daniel Adams, was one smart human. Much smarter than Apep had been in his last incarnation as a human being in the lands of Egypt and Nubia. Then again, life was much more complicated in the twenty-first century, and there was more opportunity for knowledge. It would have been a great challenge if this man had lived at the same time as he. It would have been splendid if Apep had been allowed to incarnate in the same century as Dan Adams.

Maybe things would have been different. Maybe he would have put his sorcery to better use and benefited mankind. Just maybe he would have been able to work with this man and turn the world upside down. The two of them would have ruled supreme. They would have been wealthy. But hadn't Apep realized yet that everything was predestined?

If Apep had the power, he would turn back time and transfer this scientist to his era. Just think of the power they could yield. Think of the innovations he could have introduced to make life wonderful for themselves and possibly all. Apep could have been a hero instead of a menace and pariah.

Why, oh why, are the gods so cruel to me? he thought. Apep only wanted the things that every man wanted.

Predestined, Apep. Predestined!

In his time, the monarchy and the elite were pitted against the peasants and working class. Everything went to the monarchy. As long as the rulers made it seem that the underclass existed only for them and the peasants lived to serve, things went well. Any uprising, and the monarchy made life a living hell. That was the way it always had been. Apep thought that was the way it always would be.

However, Apep was right in the middle. He had tasted the sweet life because he served with powers just above the peasants. His advice and magic was needed by the monarchy. He was given just enough, but held back from rising to what could be his true stature.

That was why he rebelled. Apep, at the time, felt that everyone deserved to rise to any level. But he also knew that he could elevate himself above the masses by studying the powers of the mystics. His life would be better if he showed the king his strength through magic and sorcery. He would be a valuable asset. He was a valuable asset.

And that was why his incarnation was destroyed. Apep didn't truly understand that he posed a threat to the one family that allowed him to become who he was. Apep hadn't known that he had been created for the monarchy.

When he first arrived in the sixth dimension, Apep didn't understand why he was there. He needed to learn on his own. He reached out to understand what boundaries he could ascend. He strived to incorporate his powers with that of the sixth dimension. He suffered. He reasoned. He compromised. He learned. He understood. He grew. He rose to become its master.

But master of what?

PREDESTINED!

Apep was all of a sudden tired. He hadn't felt this way for so long.

Apep had the power to look back in time. It was something he hadn't done in over a thousand human years. He wished he could alter what he saw, but it never changed. He would only be able to learn from it.

And now he decided to do it . . . again. He needed to relive all he had forgotten. Being in the sixth dimension had suddenly made him feel alone. And indeed he really was.

Using all his powers now, Apep traveled. He went back one hundred years. He crossed the previous millennium. The faster his thoughts traveled, the quicker he moved. He suddenly stopped.

Apep saw his home. The seven were with him. His perilous end in the caves quickly passed before his eyes.

This was not what he wanted to see. Apep decided he wanted to see the beginning of the new world. His mind moved to the shores of New England. In a flash, Apep was there. The building of a new world.

Then he saw the guns. The expansion of the new world was a natural progression, but there was so much death. Freedom, something every human wanted, was costly. The settlers' ideology seemed worth the cost of human life. Apep smiled inside.

The Death Maze

The war for independence, the Civil War, World War I, World War II, the Korean War, Vietnam, the first Middle Eastern war, the second Middle Eastern war. It seemed to never end.

Apep drooled at the devastation. His mind went wild at the sight of these experiences. Humans learned nothing from the past. Apep felt it was always someone wanting to be supreme over someone else. It was his ideology.

The human race prided itself on creating greater and more powerful means of destruction. The smarter mankind became, the greater the educational and scientific results. But the more devastation that could be brought into the world, the sooner the end would come. No one seemed to learn the true lessons of life.

Even though Apep had an idea of why he had been sent to the sixth dimension, he never knew for sure. Apep thought it was because of his selfish knowledge to understand and control. He thought he was the master. He was not. It was predestined.

The sixth dimension, indeed, had its own heartbeat. It had its own reason for being. It was truly a dimension of tolerance and understanding. It was not directly tied into Apep's huge ego. It could and eventually would challenge the mind of Apep and show the causes and effects of the oneness of God. Apep would have to be responsible for his actions.

There was a side to the sixth dimension that was never revealed to Apep. It was actually a rival and parallel world where nothing but peace prevailed. Living side by side with its three-dimensional brother, it longed to see that the Earth would become a place where harmony and peace were eventually one.

Apep was brought to this world specifically for this purpose. It was rare that someone was deposited into the sixth dimension to learn. However, Apep was the exception. He was a human who needed to learn kindness, consideration, and humanity. At the time when Apep had lived, he had been the worst of the worst. And he hadn't been learning even up to this point.

The sixth dimension never understood why mankind needed the benefit of knives, guns, bombs, and nuclear destruction. War was everywhere. Destruction went back as far as man existed. Why the human race had even been allowed to develop these weapons was discussed between the true inhabitants of the sixth dimension.

Not one century went by that war didn't happen. Peace could not be a part of its chemistry.

This was a sad state for the human population. Time was not on their side. Their existence on Earth was only a miniscule span of time compared to the length of time the universe had been. God's greatest creature could eventually destroy itself.

It was shameful that the human body could not exist if a bullet entered and destroyed a vital organ. The sixth-dimensional mind could hinder a bullet from even passing through the air if it wanted. It was just a simple thought process.

In the sixth dimension, the mind was the total existence. It was fully functional. The average mortal or human being only used approximately three-tenths of his or her brain. The genius was thought to use five-tenths at most.

If humans could learn to operate the total brain, they wouldn't need the body. It was just holding them back. Maybe that was why the average life span for a human was sixty-five to eighty-five years in the current means of time. The body deteriorated, not the mind. And war only shortened the existence of so vital a creature of God.

The family concept was different among human beings than it was among those in the sixth dimension. In the sixth dimension, family was not conceived through intercourse. How could it be? There were no bodies. This was done, as everything was, with the mind.

In order to introduce "addition," as it was called, one mind needed to be at rest for a period of one human day, or twenty-four hours. Every entity, or mind, in the sixth dimension was asexual. Each representative of the sixth dimension was able to literally do anything it conceived of. The mind was endless.

During the period of time of addition, the mind lowered its level of support by only one degree of its total use. That simple degree would drop from the mind in the twelfth hour, the halfway point of the period of rest, and now be a manufactured attachment. It developed into a single thread from the adult mind. In the latter half of the rest period, the nutrients and characteristics of the sixth dimension were fed to the new addition being formed.

At the end of twenty-four hours, the thread would be severed from the adult mind, allowing the addition to incorporate into itself. The new mind, in development, would then be introduced into the dimension. The mind that had introduced the addition would leave its creation, giving it a chance for the second stage of introduction or education.

Over the next six months in human terms, the new, or novice, mind would be under the control of one of the Elder Minds. The life of an Elder Mind would end at the conclusion of the education process of the new mind. At this point, the Elder Mind would have reached its living term of approximately four centuries, and would then move to the upper Level of Understanding.

A second thread was connected by the Elder Mind to the new addition. It was here that all knowledge and understanding would be transferred. The learning process would include all aspects and traits of living, which included voice attenuation.

The traits of living incorporated the history of the universe, the hows and whys of living in the sixth dimension, and an understanding of the dimension's main purpose, which was defined as simply "cause and effect." This would allow for the observation of its brother dimension and the education of the Earth planet and its inhabitants.

Voice attenuation was briefly incorporated for one purpose: communication with a human being. This was completed by an Elder only when absolutely required. This had only been done once since the creation of the sixth dimension by the Supreme Power, as they called it. Humans called it the power of God Almighty.

By the end of the six months, the new mind would have grown to its full capacity. The Elder would then order the new mind to sever the thread. This would begin the end of the Elder. It would simply shut down and drift to the Level of Understanding it had earned.

In human terms, when someone dies, the soul rises. Many believe they are going to heaven to be forever eternal with God. Others do not believe, and think the end of life is the end of everything. There's nothing beyond the human incarnation. "Ashes to ashes," as the prayer goes.

The Death Maze

Still others believe that the soul rises to the Level of Understanding achieved while having been incarnated in the human form. A truly devout individual who only did good for man might reach the height of heaven. This was their belief and understanding according to the laws their religion had taught.

A despicable individual may be relegated to what they believed was a hell of fire and brimstone. This place called hell was the farthest from heaven or eternal bliss. It was all a matter of Level of Understanding, as the minds of the sixth dimension knew it to be.

One thing the sixth dimension did understand was the existence of other beings from alternate dimensions and galaxies. The universe was eternal. To believe that man, or mind, was the only entity within the universe was simply narrow-minded. This was the reason for the great wisdom within the sixth dimension. True understanding and tolerance were natural within its world. It was rare that an Elder would interfere and object to intolerance.

Unbeknownst to Apep, he was on the verge of hearing a voice of an Elder for the first time. After twenty-five hundred years, Apep still had not learned the true meaning of why he had been brought to the sixth dimension. It was supposed to be a wonderful time of education and fulfillment. He was allowed to remain in the sixth dimension as long as he existed solely for the purpose of development, growth, and evolution. Apep thought he had evolved to be master.

The minds of the sixth dimension were quickly tiring of Apep and his twisted ego. The sixth dimension gave him the means to be challenged and to hopefully change. However, Apep hadn't changed. He thought that he had changed somewhat in the beginning. As he grew to understand his position, Apep fooled even himself. What he thought was growth had actually been a neutral educational process without justifiable expansion. Apep should have been more understanding. He only became more intolerant.

When the first human accidentally arrived, it was a means to establish a new entity never before allowed. Apep, at first, didn't understand how this could happen. He wasn't prepared to see someone from the world he had come from. He toyed and played with this person and enjoyed what his demented mind had created from the past. His understanding and compassion from all his years in the sixth dimension were suddenly lost. Apep failed the first human.

Then there was a second. The sixth dimension didn't understand how this could occur. It was unforgivable. And yet it was an opportunity to undo what had been done to the first. Apep could have risen to the challenge. Becoming a forgiving soul could have earned him accolades from the Elder Minds. He failed once again. He embellished the misery of the poor soul who had accidentally entered through a portal thought to be sealed. The outcome was the same as the first. Without him knowing, it almost destroyed the entity know as Apep.

However, the Elders decided to give him a final chance. Something was causing them to allow him to exist for additional time in the sixth dimension. Although the minds could conclude the decisions were for the benefit of one relentless, uncaring, demented soul, they already knew the predestined outcome would be failure. Maybe, just maybe, Apep would surprise them.

Now there was the third. All portals should have been closed. How could this have occurred a third time? It was unheard of and uncalled for. However, they hoped that

Apep would do the right thing. They were watching and judging. They were ready to move and interject if needed. Would Apep show surprise compassion? Would this save his soul?

The sixth dimension did not enjoy his destruction of the two humans who had previously entered it. Mr. Chou and Stanley Moser may have been eliminated by Apep. However, the sixth dimension had intervened, without Apep knowing, prior to their bodily end.

Apep's decision for the outcome of Dr. Adams would possibly be his last decision. Maybe it was time to reintroduce Apep into the level of understanding he only knew. Maybe he needed to be lost until his soul realized it had done wrong in the Universal Source of Understanding.

For now they could only watch.

In the peaceful world of the sixth dimension, Apep had introduced pain and suffering. His mind had reversed two and a half millennia of learning in a matter of one hundred years of sick recall. His ego was too great. His pride too passionate.

The sixth dimension knew what to do. It just required the patience to observe the finality of the human known as Dan Adams. The minds would watch every step of the way. They were prepared to interrupt when the time was right. Even the last millisecond could be altered.

Apep could be in his last allotment of time.

Chapter 36

Chief Dressler arrived at the police station, opened the door, and saw that all five members of the town council were waiting for him. The meeting would be in the back room of the station away from the main office. One of his deputies waved to him from his desk, and he waved back with his good hand as he walked past the main desk and motioned that he would be in a meeting. It was understood that there were to be no interruptions.

Three of the five members of the town council were as closed-minded as could be. This suited Dressler very well, considering the subject he was to present. He needed full cooperation.

There was Stan Chertoff, a real estate developer in charge of overseeing new development for Arione and Vera. Pete Burgess was the principal of the Arione-Vera Elementary School. Alvin Doolittle was the owner of the General Depot Goods & Services.

Everyone in town could get just about anything they wanted at Alvin's store. He made trips to Needles and Barstow, California, once a week to look at any and all new trends, clothing, housing needs, and memorabilia. He prided himself on great service, good prices, and a friendly voice. Alvin loved to talk. There was also a back-door poker game every Wednesday night in Alvin's rear storage area.

The Death Maze

Chief Dressler looked the other way as long as no one lost too much and no complaints were registered.

The other two members were very open-minded individuals. Reverend Dennis Hobbs needed no introduction, since he saw most of the residents of both towns every Sunday at the Church of Christ. His sermons usually stuck to topics of everyday life and the dealings of rural and suburban life. They always included the weekly teachings of the New Testament. Rev. Hobbs held a Bible study once a week on Thursdays, after the back-door poker game on Wednesday.

Finally, there was Crystal Nelson. She was the only woman lawyer in Arione and Vera. Although her office usually handled minor cases, she also had an office in Needles. This kept her very busy. Arione was her home; it was where she got away every night from what she considered a busy city. Crystal also kept the notes for each meeting.

Chief Dressler began. "Let the record show that this meeting took place on this day . . ."

"Forget the formalities, Chief," Stan Chertoff interrupted. "Just tell us why we're here. I have a business to get back to."

Stan was the most arrogant member of the council and the most impatient. Dressler knew he would have problems with him. He just never thought it would be while he spoke the first sentence of the meeting.

"This meeting concerns Dan Adams," Dressler informed the group in as respectable a voice as he could manage. Even though Dan was Dressler's closest friend in town, the meeting needed to be directed toward the manner of the probable interference. The chief did not want to lose his anger too soon and didn't want his relationship with Dan to cloud the council's decision.

"Has he been found yet?" Rev. Hobbs asked. "I've said many prayers for his safe return."

"I know that Ruth would thank you for that, Reverend Hobbs," Dressler said. "She's still in the hospital from the last accident. But no, he has not been found yet."

"Let's get back to the reason for the meeting, Chief," Stan blurted out. "I have my business."

"Two reporters accidentally arrived on the scene due to a car accident. They believe there is a greater story in the disappearance of Dr. Adams and want to nose around. I do not believe this would be the best for the town."

"Come on, Chief! A couple reporters?" Stan asked with continued impatience. "Kick them out of town, lock them up, whatever you want."

"I need to know that I would have the backing of the council. There are constitutional rights at stake here," Dressler explained.

"Screw their rights, Chief," Stan interrupted again. "Let me get back to my business."

"Stan," Dressler said in a raised voice. "Pardon my language, Reverend, but screw your business, Stan."

Stan Chertoff rose from his chair and walked right up to Dressler. His face was red. Because Dressler had insulted his business, he felt he had been personally insulted. Arione and Vera were his babies, and bringing new residents was the lifeblood of continued growth and prosperity. Without it, towns out in the desert died after a single generation.

As far as Stan was concerned, business was definitely the first priority. He had only run for the position on the town council because his wife had nagged him about getting involved and being someone important.

In Stan's eyes, the town council was small beans. There were only supposed to be four meetings a year, or one every three months. This was Stan's second term on the council, and there had already been three meeting in the first four months. He couldn't wish hard enough for the year to end.

In the next election, Stan would have his wife run instead of him. He would personally put her name on the ballot. If she were so concerned with public affairs, let her tolerate Chief Dressler and the rest of the council members.

The argument between Dressler and Stan didn't last long. Crystal Nelson let out a long scream that immediately turned both men's heads in her direction.

"Do you mind explaining your sudden outburst of insanity?" Dressler asked.

"Not particularly," Crystal responded smugly. "However, it did get you two pigheaded idiots to stop arguing so we can get on with the meeting."

"The meeting's adjourned as far as I'm concerned, Miss Nelson," Stan said and began to walk out. Before opening the door, he turned back to the other members. "Do whatever you want with the reporters. I don't care if you lock them up and throw the key away." Stan left the police station.

Alvin Doolittle finally spoke. "Can we still have a meeting without all five of us?"

"Absolutely," Dressler proclaimed. "Stan gave us his thoughts."

"They could be misconstrued in a court of law," Crystal announced.

"We're not in a court of law," Dressler protested.

"If we act irrationally and out of the concerns for public safety and the town, he could say that his thoughts were taken out of context," Crystal explained.

"Why don't you explain the full situation, Chief?" Rev. Hobbs said in his natural ecumenical manner.

The four remaining members returned to the chairs they had originally taken before the commotion started. Chief Dressler walked to the front of the room. He took a few moments to gather his thoughts before speaking. When he looked at the four remaining council members, he saw that Crystal was writing some notes down. She looked up at Dressler, stopped writing, and was ready to begin again.

"As I was saying, I'm not for allowing these two reporters to write a story and make Arione into some kind of zoo for curious onlookers. The minute this story hits the paper, this town will be filled to the brim with all sorts of weirdos. What I would like to do is escort them out of town. A second solution would be to give them exclusivity in return for no stories until I'm ready. Any rebuttals?"

Chief Dressler was amazed he got all of it out. As he spoke, he realized what he said was rational and not out of the ordinary. He knew that many stories were written only after the problem was solved. He didn't know if Miller and Barrish would agree.

"I have one question," Crystal announced. "How did the press come upon the story in the first place?"

"By sheer accident, Miss Nelson," Dressler began to explain. "In the shortened version, there was a car accident between Vera and Arione. It involved Ruth Putnam. The other car just happened to be driven by a reporter for the *Los Angeles News*."

"Talk about flukes," Pete Burgess stated, finally opening up his mouth. "I wonder what the odds are for that to occur."

"Remote, I'm sure," Dressler answered.

"Do you believe these reporters would really cause problems?" Pete asked.

"I believe reporters only care about getting the story, Pete," Dressler explained. "When they smell a good one, it's all about getting the hook for the public interest, writing it, and rushing it to print. Any mistakes or unfortunate miscalculations they write a statement, retracting the incorrect sentence later before going on their merry way."

The four council members looked at one another. They thought for a few minutes. Crystal Nelson pondered the legality of the City of Arione taking action against the reporters. How hard would it be for a small town to sue a large newspaper should it cause great distress on the population or an individual of their fair town?

Pete Burgess only thought about the safety of the children of both towns. He didn't know the legalities concerning a reporter's need to question a minor. He wondered if he should say something to the teachers and advise them to talk to their students.

Alvin Doolittle knew business would be brisk. He wondered what sort of T-shirt would be respectable to sell should the crowds arrive.

Rev. Hobbs only cared for the moral aspect. There would possibly be interference with privacy. No one could speak for Dr. Adams. But what about Ruth Putnam? What would it do to her? Had anyone asked her how she felt? He needed to pray on this.

Chief Dressler saw that they were all contemplating every avenue according to their interests. However, he needed to know where they stood. Time was not on his side with Miller and Barrish running around.

"Do I have agreement on keeping the reporters out of town?" Dressler asked.

"I'm for keeping this town safe from all outsiders," Pete Burgess announced.

"Except for the weekend business that always comes, I agree," Alvin Doolittle said.

"What about you, Reverend Hobbs?" Dressler asked.

"I do agree that it's important to keep the town safe. You have my vote."

"That leaves you as the last vote, Miss Nelson. What do you say?" Dressler asked.

"I'll make it unanimous, Chief," Crystal stated. "I'm trying to weigh both sides of the legal issues. The courts usually take the side of the city."

"Great! I call the meeting to a close and ask that the notes be distributed to all members as usual, Miss Nelson," Dressler said. He started for the door.

He needed to get back to the house.

Chapter 37

Dressler walked out to his car eager to get back to Bone. He felt great knowing the meeting went exactly the way he hoped it would. Now he had the backing of the full town council and was able to gather up Miller and Barrish. He would present them with the option of leaving town or securing exclusivity. Either way, they would not be able to report or print on anything until given the go-ahead. He wondered if a jail cell would look good to them if they objected.

It was only a few minutes to the house. There was a terrific breeze blowing from the west, which added some comfort to the heat of the day. Dressler didn't care how hot it had become. With the meeting over and the results in his favor, it could have been 125 degrees and he still would have a smile on his face.

After parking in front of the house, Dressler got out. He noticed Bone's car and was glad he was inside the house watching any and all testing. Then Dressler walked up to the front door, opened it, and entered the house.

"Dr. Anderson," Dressler called out. "Is there any news to tell me?"

Dressler waited only a moment before calling out again. "Bone! Where are you?"

Shirley Anderson walked out from the lab and into the living room area, meeting Dressler.

"Did you say something, Chief Dressler?" Shirley asked.

"Yeah, I did," Dressler replied. "Where's Bone? Any good news?"

"Haven't seen Bone since this morning, and no news yet." Shirley looked straight at him and put on her best face, knowing that the chief would go off once he found out what had really happened to Bone.

"His car is in the front of the house," Dressler announced. "Maybe he's walking around the property." Dressler was about to go out the door before he turned and asked a question. "Is there anything you need?"

"Actually, there is. We'd like some coffee."

"Why don't you just use the coffee maker in the kitchen?"

"It's not our house, Chief," Shirley explained. "We weren't sure if you'd object."

"I thought I said it would be okay this morning." Dressler was growing impatient. "You haven't seen him since this morning?"

Dr. Allyson Rayburn walked into the room and saw the chief. She looked tired, like she needed a break. Dressler saw on her face that things weren't going well.

"Chief Dressler," Allyson said, "good to see you."

"Thank you, Dr. Rayburn," Dressler replied. "Have you seen Officer Bone? Is he walking around the back?"

"I haven't seen him since we began working this morning. However, I would love to take a break and go get something to drink. It's been a long morning," Allyson explained.

"So I've been told," Dressler acknowledged. "I'll go find Officer Bone and have him bring some sandwiches and drinks." Dressler started for the door. "Something doesn't smell right," he said, almost to himself but loud enough for the two women to hear.

Allyson and Shirley looked at each other and then walked back to the lab. Shirley had not said a word to the other two doctors concerning Alex Miller and William Barrish. Now she didn't even know where they were and knew it was better that Allyson and Dr. Ryan were kept in the dark.

Dressler got outside and stood on the porch before moving toward Bone's vehicle. He looked out on the horizon and took in the view. The surrounding desert and hills were magnificent. He never tired of watching the wonder of it all. He truly loved caring for Arione and Vera and was proud of what they had become.

The breeze now felt even better than it had two minutes before. Even though the heat from the sun baked in the middle of the day, the desert always offered a relaxation he couldn't feel in a big city. Cities had too many people, too much traffic, and way too much crime. Chief Dressler was glad he had moved away many years ago.

He brought himself back to the present, leaving his daydreams behind. Dressler knew Bone would never leave without informing him and was becoming irritated at not knowing where the two reporters were. He hoped they wouldn't go back to the hospital and look for Ruth Putnam. She needed all the rest she could possibly get before returning to her empty home.

Dressler walked toward Bone's car and immediately heard muffled sounds. He picked up the speed of his walk and stood baffled by the sight in front of him. He opened the car door, dragged Bone out, and saw sweat dripping from his face.

Dressler wanted to rip the handkerchief out of his mouth. Instead, he banged the car with his good hand, the one without the cast, and then began untying him. Once the ropes were off and the gag removed, Dressler wanted answers.

"Thank you, Chief," Bone exclaimed. "I'm sorry . . ."

Chief Dressler raised his good hand. Instead of going off on Bone, he took a couple deep breaths. He needed to remind himself that he had just come from a successful meeting. It really didn't make a difference now how long it took, as long as he was able to do what was required to succeed. Miller and Barrish were now impeding an ongoing investigation. Any attempts to interfere would result in arrest.

"How the hell did you get tied up?" Dressler just asked. He did not yell or go off on his sweaty, smelly officer. He already assumed Miller and Barrish were not at the house. That was a bad assumption, and Dressler would realize it later on.

"There were two guys, Chief," Bone explained, overly anxious due to the situation. "I never saw the older one before. I recognized the younger one a bit late. They were in the house in the living room. I took out my gun and they jumped me."

"When did they show up?"

"Just after you left this morning to go to the meeting," Bone said. He decided to inform his boss how he truly felt now that he'd obviously had time to think. "You really should have informed me what's going on, Chief. I mean, I could have been better prepared."

"You're absolutely right, Bone," Dressler admitted. "I didn't think you were up to the task. I apologize. The fact is you're well prepared to do the job I asked you to do when you first arrived."

"Thanks, Chief. I really appreciate the vote of confidence."

"The second man is Alex Miller. He says he's the lawyer for the paper. I think he's just a well-seasoned pro who outsmarted an old cop like me."

"Chief, he's slick and talks real well," Bone admitted. "Anyone could have been fooled."

"Well, we need to keep our eyes alert and be more aware," Dressler stated. "Call in to the restaurant and order some sandwiches and drinks. By the time you get there, they'll be ready to bring back to the doctors. I've got to go back in the house and question Dr. Anderson. She has to know something."

Dressler started for the house and turned his eyes back in the direction of Bone. He noticed Bone's gun in its holster. Bone looked at his boss with a blank look.

"What's up, Chief?"

"I thought you said you took out your gun and the two men overpowered you."

"I did," Bone said.

"Then why is your gun still in its holster?" Dressler asked.

Bone looked down at his side and saw the gun. He looked back at his boss. "I haven't got the slightest idea how it got back in the holster, Chief."

"You were knocked out, Bone?" Dressler asked.

"Yeah, Chief," Bone replied.

"Do you think maybe they put it back so they wouldn't have to worry about the possibility of being caught with a stolen weapon?" Dressler asked.

Without hesitation or wanting to appear stupid, Bone looked at his boss and smiled. "I believe you must have the correct presumption, Chief. That's exactly what they must have done."

Dressler just shook his head. "Yeah! Well, I'm going back in the house. Call for the food," Dressler said and left.

Bone knew better. Watching Chief Dressler walk to the house, he decided that if he met up with Miller and Barrish, he would tell them to freeze and come with him to be questioned at the police station. If they didn't listen, he would fire one round into the air as a warning. If that didn't work, someone would take a bullet in the leg. He was not going to be outmaneuvered again. He needed to be better at his job.

Bone then got in his car and started the engine. Putting it in gear, he picked up the phone to call the restaurant. He suddenly became determined to see justice done and wanted the reporters as much as Chief Dressler.

Inside the house, Chief Dressler was in the lab speaking to all three doctors. He wanted to explode, but knew better than to keep his temper from reaching what could turn into a tantrum.

"I have asked you in the past, Dr. Anderson," Dressler explained, "not to interfere with my work. I now ask all three of you to watch out for these two men."

"What do they look like, Chief?" Dr. Ryan asked.

"You can't mistake them, Dr. Ryan. One's around twenty years older than the other. They're reporters. They're trying to find out why I want this story kept out of the papers. I'm now prepared to offer them an exclusive if they leave it alone until we have all the answers."

"Why can't you just give them the benefit of the doubt, Chief?" Shirley asked. "Give them a little leeway. Maybe they'll see the sensitivity of this story and understand."

"One speaks in a muffled voice," Dressler explained, totally ignoring Shirley's comments. "His jaw is broken and wired shut. Right now they're wanted for assaulting an officer of the law. If you see them, you're to call me or the station immediately."

"You can't be totally closed-minded about this, Chief," Shirley added.

"If you fail to notify my office, I may have to consider the possibility of you being an accessory to the crime for harboring a fugitive," Dressler continued, still ignoring Shirley's pleas but pointedly speaking in her direction. "I also have the full backing of the town council to arrest them on-site for interfering with a police investigation. There is no leeway."

"I'll let you know if I hear anything, Chief Dressler," Dr. Ryan said.

"Thank you. Bone is getting you sandwiches and drinks. He should be back in a few minutes. If there's anything else, please let me know."

Dressler walked out of the lab and smiled. He had been able to hold his anger and get the upper hand on Shirley Anderson. He left the house, got in his car, and drove off.

Shirley couldn't believe what she had just witnessed. She had been so sure that Dressler would lose his temper and go off on her. Chief Dressler was again acting like the man she'd known for many years. There was a total dichotomy in his behavior.

Shirley walked out of the lab and into the living area. Alex Miller and William Barrish had heard the entire conversation from somewhere in the kitchen, where they were hiding. They walked into the living area and met Shirley.

"I can't believe what I just heard," Shirley said.

"Why can't you believe it?" Alex asked. "This is quite typical when a reporter tries to get the scoop and put the authorities in an awkward position. The public has a right to know."

"You could be put in jail for even writing the first sentence," Shirley stated, looking into Alex's eyes.

"Hey, I'm not thrilled either," Will said. "I've got more at stake here. I still owe that crazy bastard for this," he said, pointing to his jaw. "I not only deserve the story, I want this story."

"He did say something about an exclusive," Shirley reminded them.

"He's got no one else," Alex chimed in. "Besides, we can get at things before he finds out where we've been. He didn't believe we were still in the house. Otherwise he would have checked."

"He has a lot of connections, Alex. He knows the right people in Needles and Barstow. He also knows the powers that be at the Los Angeles Police Department. Just be careful." She turned to Will. "Do me a favor, Will. Try not to speak so much. It only hinders the healing process because you're still using muscles in your jaw. Remember, four to six weeks."

"I'll try to do what the good doctor orders," Will said reluctantly.

"I've got to go back to the lab," Shirley stated. "I don't want to get the other two doctors in trouble. If they know you're here, Dr. Ryan will call Chief Dressler. I'm not so sure about Dr. Rayburn. I think she would be on my side."

"We'll go question Ruth Putnam," Alex informed her. "I believe that maybe she can answer some questions."

"I'll phone ahead of you and let the nurses know to give you access to Ruth. It'll be easier if they know I've given the authority," Shirley said. She walked back to the laboratory.

Just then they heard a car stop in front of the property. Alex and Will went to the front window and saw Bone get out of his car. He opened his back door and pulled out a bag with the sandwiches and drinks.

"How do we get around him this time?" Will asked Alex.

The Death Maze

"Here's what we'll do," Alex said, and then whispered into Will's ear.

"Are you out of your . . ." Will said.

Alex left the room immediately, followed by Will. They rushed through the kitchen. Alex stopped and found two brooms before opening the back kitchen door. They raced to the side of the house.

Alex handed one broom to Will and told him to go back to the kitchen door and jam it into the outside handle of the door and the doorjamb. Alex was sure it would give them time to get away and drive to the hospital.

"I also saw a bucket as we ran," Alex said. "Place the bucket right next to the door."

"He'll see it," Will said.

"If he sees us, he'll panic and race to the door, find it jammed, and try to force the door open. Once he gets it open, he won't think about another object blocking the way. Just do it," Alex instructed.

"But . . ." Will objected.

"Go!" Alex ordered.

Watching as Bone opened the front door and entered the house, Will left to do exactly as Alex instructed. He easily found a bucket and picked it up. He then closed the front door.

Alex quietly walked to the front porch. He heard Bone call out that the sandwiches and drinks had arrived. Alex then tiptoed up the front porch steps and jammed the other broom through the door handle and into the doorjamb. He saw a medium-sized potted plant on the porch, picked it up, and moved it next to the front door.

Rushing back to the side of the house, Will saw Alex running to Bone's vehicle. Alex opened the front door and saw the keys in the ignition. Taking the keys, he locked the car and closed the door. Alex then tossed the keys under the car and ran to Shirley's car.

Will then also ran to Shirley's car and got in.

"Doesn't anyone lock their cars out in these hick towns?" Alex asked Will as he started the car.

Bone heard a motor turn over and went to the front window. He saw that his car was untouched and looked at the car in front of his police vehicle. Alex and Will were in the car and beginning to pull out.

Bone ran to the front door. He turned the handle, trying to pull the door open. It wouldn't move. He tried a second time, tugging harder. He heard a small cracking sound but was still unable to get the door open.

"C'mon, dammit!" Bone said to himself as he tried a third time.

After running to the kitchen's back door, Bone turned the handle and met the same fate. Though he tugged harder with each attempt, he was still unable to get the door open. He didn't even hear a cracking sound at the back door.

Bone took a step away from the door. He took out his gun and pointed it at the door. He then realized how stupid his actions were and changed his mind. Returning his gun to the holster, Bone raised his foot and kicked the door, knowing this frustrating attempt would do nothing since the door opened into the house.

He then rushed back through the house. He approached the front door, grabbed the handle, and took in a deep breath. With all the strength he could muster, he tugged the door and heard another crack.

He repeated his actions one more time, and the door flew open, hitting him in the face. He fell backward and caught himself from falling to the floor. He felt blood begin to run from his nose, but was too caught up in the adrenaline of trying to catch Miller and Barrish.

Trying to run, Bone stumbled forward and then picked up speed. His right foot caught the back of the potted plant and he tumbled forward, falling down the porch steps. When his body stopped moving, he tried to lift his head but couldn't. He was out.

Chapter 38

Chief Dressler was back at his office, planning his next move. He still couldn't believe he had been able to hold his temper. It had totally caught Shirley Anderson off guard, and he was very proud of himself. It was rare that he could pat himself on the back.

Now what should he do with Miller and Barrish? What would the sheriff have done back in the good old days? He knew he would have made a great 1800s sheriff in a town like Dry Gulch or Virginia City. Law and order was cut and dry.

He could order a "shoot to kill," but then thought that to be a bit drastic. Miller and Barrish hadn't really harmed anyone. Imagine the newspaper reports that would come out if he actually had the two reporters shot. They would be devastating to both towns. The publicity would be beyond imagination.

Dressler came back to reality and resigned himself to forgetting about the old days and living within the laws of the twenty-first century. It was hard enough getting through a normal day without having someone think you were nuts for wanting to be a sheriff who lived over one hundred years ago. He needed to think about his next move.

It was obvious. He would issue an all-points bulletin and have his Vera substation place a deputy at the hospital. Bone was at the house and free from his restraints. A third deputy would be placed at the Arione Motel. If Miller and Barrish wanted to speak with Dr. Ryan or Dr. Rayburn, they would be arrested prior to knocking on the doors of their rooms.

Dressler was sure Shirley Anderson was not on his side. It was evident in two of her actions. First was when she released William Barrish from the hospital knowing that he wanted to question him further and actually detain him. Second was when she said she did not know of their whereabouts when asked at the house. Dressler saw the slight hesitation in her eyes. If nothing else, he knew when someone was lying to him.

He looked at his desk. It was cluttered with reports and information on Dan Adams. A few memos written by his desk clerk said that a couple had seen Dr. Adams in Needles in a bowling alley. A second reported seeing him fixing a blown tire on the way to Las Vegas. Dressler immediately dismissed these.

There were numerous inquiries concerning Ruth Putnam. They were mostly from the members of the church sending their best for a speedy recovery. A few were condolence remarks written under the assumption that Dan Adams had passed away. Dressler threw these into the trash. He didn't understand how the ridiculous rumors had started.

Back to the immediate concerns. Miller and Barrish would definitely be arrested. Assaulting one of his deputies would not go unnoticed. No matter how decorated a reporter might be or his or her degree of overzealousness, no member of the police force deserved to be ridiculed or harmed while doing his or her duties according to the law.

This was where Dressler's anger could get out of whack. Talking to the town council had been therapeutic. It had brought him away from the irresponsibility of his anger.

Thinking about what these two had done to Bone irritated him. He wanted revenge.

And he couldn't get it while sitting at his desk. He rose from his chair and instructed his desk clerk to get one of the deputies over to the motel.

"Have them watch for Alex Miller and William Barrish. They're to be arrested on-site and brought into the station. If they ask for the charges, tell the deputy the charge is assaulting an officer of the law. No questions asked. They can make their one phone call from the station."

"Got it, Chief," the clerk said.

"Also call the Vera substation. I want a deputy stationed at the hospital. Same reason."

Dressler left the office. He got into his car and drove to see Bone.

When he got to the house, Bone was nowhere in sight. Dressler got out of his car and immediately checked the inside of Bone's vehicle. He was pleased that Bone was not tied up inside. He then moved up the walk. When he saw the front door, Dressler began to run.

The door was open and he raced through. He saw Bone in the living room being attended to by Shirley Anderson and Dr. Rayburn. Bone's nose was twice the normal size, and large black and blue marks were under his eyes. There was cotton stuffed in both nostrils, and Dressler could see signs of dried blood.

Dressler took a deep breath. Shirley Anderson looked at Dressler and waited to hear the questions.

"Should I guess?" Dressler asked.

"Only if you want to, Chief," Shirley responded.

"I was talking to Bone," Dressler said sternly.

"I saw them, Chief," Bone said in a weird, muted voice.

"Okay," Dressler sighed. "Where?"

"I was in the house and they were in Dr. Anderson's car driving away," Bone explained.

Dressler turned to Shirley. "Did you know they were taking your car?"

"I had no idea it was gone until after Bone informed me when he awakened."

"Did I miss something?" Dressler asked. "Awaken from what?"

"It appears the two reporters jammed the front and back kitchen doors, Chief," Dr. Ryan said as he walked into the living room.

"I tried tugging at the door and it flew open in my face," Bone explained. "Then I ran and fell over a potted plant placed in the doorway."

"I walked into the living room," Shirley stated, "saw the front door open, and then saw Bone on the ground. I helped him up and took him inside the house."

Dressler needed only a few seconds to determine what he would do. He brought his attention to Bone and then back to Dr. Shirley Anderson.

"Dr. Anderson," Dressler announced sans anger. "You are going to inform me where Alex Miller and William Barrish are or else I'll have to put you under arrest."

"And why on earth would you arrest me?" Shirley asked, keeping her cool.

"You have assisted in letting two individuals who assaulted my deputy get away. I'm not sure I believe that you did not know about the car. However, I do know that you were aware of their whereabouts when I asked you this morning."

Shirley spoke above the normal pitch of her voice. "Are you accusing me of lying to you? Do you think I would go out of my way to block your precious ego in keeping this story out of the papers?"

They all looked at her. Dr. Allyson Rayburn wanted to say something. Dr. Sam Ryan wanted to get back into the lab. Bone wanted to object to his boss, but knew better. Dressler just stared and let her get angry. He knew it was the guilty who first raised the level of discomfort.

"I actually do," Dressler then admitted.

"What are they, Chief? Do you consider them fugitives running from the law?" Shirley asked, still in a higher than normal voice. "They're not prisoners."

"They will be, Dr. Anderson," Dressler announced. "Right now I have one of my deputies at the motel and one at the hospital watching out for them. They have instructions to arrest them on sight. They'll be brought to the Arione jail and booked for assault."

"They were doing their jobs, for God's sake," Shirley yelled.

Dressler had enough. He allowed his voice to rise to the same level. "Their jobs do not include tying up an officer of the law and knocking him out. They do not include stuffing a handkerchief in his mouth, Dr. Anderson."

"Well, breaking William Barrish's jaw and threatening him for trying to ask questions should not be a part of your job," Shirley shot back. She then lowered the sound level. "Can't you understand that from the time you caught him on the phone in the hospital, the paper already had the story?"

Dressler just listened. Something was getting to him, and he now seemed to understand. He looked at Bone and then turned back to Shirley.

"Has anything out of the ordinary happened since?" Shirley asked. "Has Arione been bombarded by the paparazzi and the weirdos you so warned everyone about?"

Dressler walked to the front door. He looked out to the horizon, where the western ridge of Arione and the desert melded together. He tried to gather his thoughts, as he sensed that even Bone was agreeing with Shirley.

Bone had been tied up, gagged, knocked out. He had then been bruised, bloodied, and knocked out again. Still he seemed to be rational enough not to harbor any bad feelings toward Miller and Barrish. Why?

Here he was, totally at ease. Bone had been hurt. Dressler thought his stature, or ego, as a police officer had been bruised. He would think Bone wanted revenge. But Bone showed no sign of vitriol. It was all part of growing in the job and learning that some lines needed to be bent.

Bone was totally different from when he had first arrived. He was eager to make nothing but a good impression. He followed the law to a tee. He never missed a court date when a ticketed driver contested a citation. He had all his facts straight. He was a model . . . Dressler was ashamed to admit it because maybe he no longer was . . . a model police officer.

It was a time when the world was totally upside down and the normal was no longer the norm. It was a world in which it seemed everything couldn't be explained and the unexpected happened only to the innocent. In the crazy, mixed-up, fast-paced world where the Internet announced news before the old, reliable newspapers did, Dressler grew suddenly tired. He stepped outside to the porch.

"I'm going back into the lab, Allyson," Dr. Ryan announced. "If we do not have something to report by the end of the day, I wish to leave and return to Los Angeles." He walked into the laboratory.

Allyson just sat in one of the living room chairs. She stared at the pictures in the room and saw the image of the man she still loved. She longed to understand where he had disappeared to and knew she had to remain in Arione if she were ever to see Dan again. Allyson decided she would not return to Los Angeles with Dr. Ryan.

There was a bowl of cold water next to Bone. He was dipping a face cloth in the bowl and then holding it to his nose. Shirley had told him to continue putting cold water on his face to keep the swelling down.

Shirley was looking out the front window at Chief Dressler. His movements were slow. She didn't know what he was thinking. She wanted to step outside next to him and find out.

It was then that Dressler walked back into the house. He stood in the foyer and looked at Allyson, then at Bone, and then finally at Shirley.

"I guess all I need is a smart woman to tell a pigheaded bastard like myself to come down off his high horse," Dressler said.

No one said anything.

"I'll call off the hunt," Dressler then announced.

"Thank you, Chief," Shirley said.

"I just want to know what happened to one of the residents of my town and my close friend," Dressler added.

"I know we all do," Shirley agreed.

Chapter 39

Dan had been crawling for what felt like an eternity. His hands were blistered and his body was dripping with perspiration. The illumination in the maze was minimal at best. All in all, he felt like shit!

He tried to figure out how long he had been traveling and how far he had gone. He couldn't believe it might only have been fifteen or twenty minutes. Even though he needed to rest frequently, he knew he had been crawling for at least a few hours and maybe a mile or two. Either way, it was way too long for him to be on his hands and knees—or stomach and knees, as Dan had to change positions often.

He felt his eyes straining and knew they had to be bloodshot. They were even playing games with him. At one point, Dan was sure he saw the end, but when he reached that point, the image disappeared. Little did he know that Apep was creating little mirages as he inched forward.

Even though Apep wanted Dan to reach the end now, he loved watching this mere mortal crawl and suffer. As despicable as he had been in Nubia and ancient Egypt, Apep was now even more of an insufferable and maniacal monster, as he was fully aware that his powers had become far superior.

Dan's clothes were drenched with sweat. Perspiration dripped from his head. Wiping his brow on his sleeve was almost useless, since more sweat dripped down a few seconds later. When the drops stung his eyes, Dan simply shut them and waited for the pain to subside.

He constantly longed to rest and never realized this could be so difficult. At one point he stopped for what felt like thirty seconds. His body then jerked, moving forward again.

However, his mind was preparing itself for the final decision. He knew he would soon confront the two switches Apep mentioned. *When, dear God, when will it come?* Dan kept thinking. *Just let me go without too much pain.*

As he inched his way through the final stretch of the maze, Dan kept checking the circumference and height of the enclosure. He needed to make sure it had not decreased in size. His reasoning was simple. Apep was not without further gimmicks or changes. Many disguises could be left in his warped mind.

Through constant examination, Dan was sure the size of the maze had not changed. However, he wasn't convinced that his confines hadn't been manipulated by Apep. After that last conversation, Apep's manner had altered. Dan remembered the silence when the lightning and thunder materialized. He was sure Apep had not caused those effects.

There was the unintended use of plurality in his words. Maybe Apep was just having his own brain farts. Dan remembered going through similar moments when he worked too many hours without a break.

However, Dan did not know if Apep could become tired in his own world. Without the physicality of a body, was Apep capable of feeling muscle fatigue? Then again, Dan didn't even know if Apep could materialize into the physical.

The sixth dimension never revealed all its cards. Voice and thought could actually be only a portion of this world.

"Now I know why I'm tired all the time," Dan said out loud. "I'm thinking too much and letting my mind wander. Stop it now! Stop it. Stop it. STOP IT!"

Dan did stop. He halted and took a rest again. He laid his head on his folded arms while his outstretched body just ceased to move. He said to himself that he only needed a few moments. He let it all go.

While he rested, the Elder Minds of the sixth dimension observed him in earnest. They were aware of Dan's movements. His struggles were beyond the torture they had previously witnessed. They admired his strength, physical and mental. He was at a different level than Apep's previous victims. The human being had grown.

However, the Minds were even more attuned to Apep's attitude and were quickly becoming tired of it. This was not the world they had set out many millennia ago. The sixth dimension was a place of intellectual superiority where peace and prosperity were to reign supreme.

Apep had come to them for a purpose. His schooling left him craving more, though he was unaware of this. He surpassed the expectations of the Minds. They knew he would eventually be reintroduced into the human world, and his reincarnation moment had been set. The Minds were proud when Apep's soul grew and understood it was time to be a productive incarnation.

Then the portal opened and Apep's thirst to conquer reappeared. It was as if he had not even been aware of the time he had spent in the sixth dimension. Apep suddenly lost his peace. His madness was no longer relegated to the ancient past of his world. His cravings reemerged more strongly as he took it upon himself to control the outcome of his first victim. With his powers of the sixth dimension, the Elder Minds only hoped Apep would do the right thing.

***

Stanley Moser was just a kind, likeable soul. He had never hurt anyone and always went out of his way to offer a helping hand if needed. Everyone liked Stanley and asked about him after he left.

His travels to the desert in the early 1900s were always a mystery, because Stanley never talked about himself. The only thing he did say was that he believed in God and that God was his personal guide. Every night before he went to sleep, Stanley thanked God for another day. He prayed that if he woke the next morning, he would once again thank the Good Lord for his peaceful and restful night of sleep.

Stanley never said a mean word about anyone and never raised his hand against another human being. He always asked if there were odd chores needing to be done and completed tasks for the wages agreed upon. He never took more, and sometimes knew that the agreed wage was more than the person could afford. In some instances, Stanley even gave back part of his wages.

Stanley had a direction and always moved in it. When he found the three hills west of Needles and due east of Barstow, some of his dreams at night ceased. He reasoned this was God's way of telling him that he had reached his intended piece of ground.

He began to dig his hole, and soon knew that the depth was right. He'd had dreams of digging for a fortnight before discovering the first of many silver nuggets. The metal box he purchased soon became full, even though his dreams told him he had barely scraped the main vein.

All of Stanley's actions were for a purpose. Stanley remembered that purpose as he made his promises and vows to God every night.

After he topped off the metal box with the last nugget, Stanley buried the box and tied the shoelaces to the handle. He then placed a third shoelace around a bush branch and drew an arrow on it to show the direction of the metal box.

As he left the hole each afternoon, Stanley covered his hole and made markers to remind him where to reenter the next morning. He would then walk back to his tent-covered camp area and prepare his dinner. Stanley felt truly blessed.

Had Ben Stanton, the reporter for the *Needles News*, ever entered the hole he believed Stanley had dug, he would unfortunately have met the same fate as Stanley. He first would have found an even larger box placed into the dirt behind the fifth rung of the ladder. In fact, at the bottom of the ladder, approximately five feet behind the lowest rung and neatly camouflaged to look like plain dirt, Stanley had placed twenty-two shoeboxes filled with silver nuggets. They were worth a fortune. However, Stanley was not ready to deposit his finds.

As long as Stanley had his dreams, he would keep digging. If ever the dreams ended, this would be Stanley's cue that God wanted him to move on to the next assignment. Stanley knew that God would inform him what he was to do through the next set of dreams. Unfortunately, Stanley opened up the portal to the sixth dimension.

Ben Stanton never realized how close he came to meeting the same fate. All he believed was that Stanley had not been around the day he came to show him the article he had written about a lone, young silver miner. Ben never came back to the hole, never heard from Stanley, and never told anyone about the metal box he had found.

The hole, over the years, filled with dirt and mud from dust storms and rains. Dan and Ruth could have dug on the side of the house and found the metal box with the shoelaces tied to a lone bush branch now buried a foot beneath level ground.

From the moment Stanley first opened his eyes in the sixth dimension, the Elder Minds watched his every move. They were worried about Apep and what he would do, since it had been so long that he had encountered a human incarnation. Would Apep pass the tests? It was like being newly reborn without knowing you had a physical body. They felt Apep's cerebral movements approach Stanley. It was an uncomfortable event, and they monitored it carefully.

Stanley's head moved slowly and he tried to figure out his whereabouts. Apep had made Stanley's surroundings look like he was still in his silver mine. Stanley lifted himself and walked to where he thought the ladder would be.

"Can I help you?" Apep said.

Stanley looked up, thinking the voice was coming from the top of the hole. "I'm down here," he yelled. "I think I may have fallen."

"Don't think," Apep ordered. "I'll do all the thinking for you."

"I'm not quite sure I get what you're saying," Stanley said in a nervous tone.

"Then let me explain it to you," Apep stated.

A light appeared from behind Stanley and a rattlesnake materialized from the light. Stanley turned his head toward the light and saw the snake. At first he didn't move.

The Death Maze

The Elder Minds weren't pleased with Apep's statements or his reactions to poor Stanley. They first needed to understand how the portal had opened, and quickly put the onus on Stanley even though he could not imagine what was involved. He had inadvertently dug into the silver vein, which crossed a section of dimensional overflow. This was a very rare phenomenon.

There were only three overflows on Earth's three-dimensional plane. Egypt had found the first with Apep's dungeon pit. Now Stanley had accidentally discovered the second. The third had yet to be discovered when Stanley entered the sixth dimension.

The Elders were glad the second portal had been found. They could now work to close the opening. The opening in Egypt had been sealed when the Nubian prince ordered the hole to be refilled. After two and a half millennia of weather changes, it was now buried in one hundred feet of sand.

Stanley had been told about rattlers in the area and instructed on what to do if he ever came upon one. At this junction of his life in the desert, Stanley was not remotely afraid of one.

He took his knife from his back pocket, took careful aim, and then threw it. The blade lodged itself into the head of the rattler, which quickly ceased moving and died.

"Excuse me, sir," Stanley said as he looked up toward what he thought was the entrance to the hole. "Would you mind sending down the ladder? I thank you for my dinner tonight. God bless you!"

The Elders were impressed. Maybe this would be it for Apep, and he would go his merry way and leave this poor soul alone. Apep didn't, at this point, have much longer before his reincarnation. He just needed to continue to learn and advance.

Apep was having none of it. He didn't believe this human was not afraid of snakes. Everyone had been afraid of snakes when he had lived. They were evil and ugly. This was Apep's reason to transform and live as he had. An attacker emits power when he creates fear. Stanley showed no fear. He did not realize he was being attacked.

"I'm impressed with your survival skills," Apep said.

"Thank you, sir. Would you mind sending down the ladder?" Stanley asked.

"Your ladder is not a part of this world," Apep stated.

"I'm not sure I understand. I'm tired and would like to come out and prepare my dinner."

Poor Stanley! Apep was going to love killing him.

The Elders became very disappointed when they realized that Apep would not do the right thing. Stanley was just a victim of happenstance. It was coincidental that the overflow landed within his silver mine. It should never have occurred.

When the Elders understood that Apep was going to kill Stanley, they melded together to offset the final outcome. They had to allow Apep to believe he had killed Stanley in order for him to drift away thinking he was still superior.

Stanley waited, hoping the ladder would appear. He never realized his life would end in the hole he had dug, much less another dimension. It wasn't part of what God had sent him to do. Then he felt the bullet enter his chest.

Maybe God was angry that he had filled so many shoeboxes. Maybe he was angry that he had not completed what he thought was his mission. Maybe he should have taken the shoeboxes and deposited them to be weighed. The money could then be given for his ultimate mission.

Apep knew it would be easy to materialize the gun out of nowhere. He had seen guns develop over the years. He knew this slow-witted jerk would grab for the gun and lower it away from his head. Apep knew the bullet would discharge a fraction of a second after Stanley grabbed the barrel.

When the bullet entered the skin and Stanley jerked, Apep laughed and then left, believing his crime was successful. But there was enough time for the Elders to intervene. They had anticipated Apep leaving too soon, and drew 100 percent of the energy moving toward Stanley's heart.

The bullet had actually pierced Stanley's chest and then stopped. Stanley had jerked, Apep had left, and the bullet had reversed itself out of Stanley's body. The heart had never been injured.

However, the Elders didn't realize the shock that Stanley would experience. He dropped to the ground, as his mind thought he had been shot in the heart. Stanley lay motionless.

The Elders secured Stanley's body by encircling a mystical enhancing shield around it. They dropped his temperature to freezing. Then they lifted him, securing his body so no other shock would come from within or without the realm of the shield.

They put Stanley in suspended animation and secured him away from Apep. Apep would never know what happened to the body.

***

Dan woke up feeling he had been moving the entire time he slept. "Couldn't have been," he said to himself. Apep hadn't been assisting his movements in any way. Why would he start now?

He began inching along once again, now that he felt slightly rested. He had some unusual thoughts while resting. Things that brought him back to his movements in the maze. If ever he escaped this mess, he would have many hours of serious thought about the meaning of all the situations he had been in.

His mind wandered back to the nursery room. It was strange that Apep would bring him to his early childhood. The entire dramatization was impressive, especially the accuracy of the room. How could that occur? Was the sixth dimension a direct parallel to his own three-dimensional world?

Seeing Ruth in the hospital and even his own house, right before his eyes, was mind-boggling. The images and effects that were brought forth from his memories were uncanny. But what did they all mean?

There had to be some reason for remembering the only two women he had loved while falling in the chute. What was Apep trying to tell him? Or was it just Apep's sick sense of being and need for constant misery that compelled him to have Dan recall his heartbreak?

Dan upped his speed. He felt a new sense of urgency to meet his final decision. The enclosure turned to the right about forty-five degrees and then turned at another forty-five-degree angle to the right. It straightened and continued. The temperature felt hot and then cold. The texture of the floor turned from smooth to coarse and then to smooth once more. The height and width always remained the same.

Dan looked into the distance and saw it. Two beams of light were shining on two objects about fifty feet ahead of him. As he approached, he saw two switches, exactly as he was told he'd see. Both looked the same. One would move upward and the other downward. Which to choose?

Suddenly Dan stopped. He was only twenty feet away from his last choice. Why did he stop? Why did his body cease to continue moving forward? Dan felt something was holding him back.

"Choose wisely," a small voice told him.

"What?" Dan asked in a whisper.

"Think before you decide," the same voice said in a soft tone.

Dan didn't say a word. He listened for more. Was this Apep talking? Was it his inner mind speaking to him? He waited.

"Slowly move forward. Think while moving," the voice instructed in Dan's inner ear.

Dan crawled slowly. He realized it was not Apep. But if not Apep, then who? Was it someone else reaching out?

Dan stopped moving about ten feet from the switches, closed his eyes, and let his mind work. He tried relaxing his body so he could meditate. All he needed were a few precious seconds. The quiet and calm allowed him to climb the steps needed to get out of his body and into his comfort state of consciousness.

He opened the trapdoor within. He stepped out and closed the trapdoor. He felt the silver cord of life attached to him as he attempted to move. Then he heard it.

"Stay still," the voice said. "Do not venture beyond your body."

Dan's inner consciousness looked around. "Why can't I see you?"

"You do not need to," the voice said. "You only need to listen."

"Who are you?"

"Just listen," the voice commanded.

Dan did not waver from his position. He kept the trapdoor directly beneath him in case he needed to quickly move back into his body.

"I am from the sixth dimension," the voice explained. "Apep thinks he controls. And yet he does not. He needs to continue to learn and move on. The Elders are here to assist."

"I do not understand," Dan's inner mind replied.

"Go back and choose carefully," the voice instructed. "We will be there. We cannot interfere at this point for reasons that must remain unexplained."

Dan said nothing. He didn't know if he should trust this voice because he didn't know if it was Apep trying to trick him.

"Go back and decide. We will be there," the voice said again before going silent.

Dan waited for a while before opening the trapdoor in his head. He climbed down the steps inside his body. He woke from his meditation to confront the two switches.

Dan stared at both of them, his mind turning. He wanted nothing other than to pick the correct switch. He pleaded with himself to find all the reasons to pick one switch over the other.

Arione became a vision in his eyes. There was some connection he never made. How did his experiment cause him to enter into this world?

He thought about the beginning of this turmoil, this nightmare. His mind raced back to his first moments in the maze. Those five white walls, Apep's first words, and the introduction to the sixth dimension.

The Death Maze

"What does it all mean?" Dan said to himself.

The two switches were like the entrance to the Kingdom of Oz. They were the keys to the opening of the pearly gates. The correct switch would lead him back into the arms of the woman he loved and had long ago decided he wanted to be with for the rest of his life.

This was it. There weren't any more decisions after this. The long journey was over. He had succumbed to the kaleidoscopic effects of the hallway, the narrow tunnel where he needed to first crouch on all fours, the nursery, the chute, the mirrored room, the strange meal that appeared when his hunger called, the screens that lowered themselves from the endless ceiling, and the long tunnel only two feet in height and three feet in width.

Dan had felt heat, cold, and tremors that had rolled him from one side of a room to the other. The unexplained lightning and thunder that left Apep silent. And lastly, the small voice of the Elder.

He had a feeling there would be nothing else to stop him from returning home.

Dan reached out his hand. It shook from excitement. It trembled from fear. He closed his eyes and chose the switch that moved up.

Chapter 40

Alex and Will sped down the highway the short distance to Vera. The hospital was adjacent to the exit and Ruth Putnam was in that hospital. They only prayed that they wouldn't see Chief Dressler or anyone who might recognize them or know of them.

Talking to the only person who might know the true story and reason behind the disappearance of Dr. Adams was their only reason to remain in Arione or Vera. Once they had some idea of what was truly going on, they could outline the main body of the story and then put it together away from both towns. They could send the story to their boss from Barstow to the west or Needles to the east. It all depended on their understanding and if they needed to return to Arione.

Will wondered if Bone had broken through the broom handles wedged in the doors. He hoped Bone had not been hurt too badly if he had fallen over the bucket or flowerpot left in front of the doors. The he wondered what the penalty could be if Bone did get hurt and Chief Dressler pressed charges.

Alex parked the car in a parking spot reserved for doctors. He was driving Shirley's car. What did he care? He knew Shirley would contact them if there were any problems once they left. They exited the car and walked to the front entrance of the hospital.

"You think we'll be fine talking to Ruth Putnam?" Will asked.

"I believe we will be successful. That's how I always think, Will," Alex told him. "A positive attitude always produces good results. Even if I'm not successful in all my attempts, I've still accomplished something."

"I'm beginning to understand more and more," Will admitted. "It becomes easier with every step. Doesn't it?"

"You don't even need an answer to that, Will."

Alex didn't even think about not getting to Ruth Putnam. Doubt was never a part of his overall outlook as a reporter. He needed the story. Ruth Putnam was the lead. He would follow his path to the lead. It was that simple.

What wasn't so simple was Shirley Anderson. She was putting herself at risk by going up against Chief Dressler. She had definite roots in both towns. Her future could be in jeopardy if Dressler wanted to pressure her.

If that turned out to be the case, he thought Shirley could have a future in Los Angeles with him. She had chutzpa! Balls! Shirley had the guts to make it anywhere she wanted. Alex hadn't met anyone like her in a long time. And the remarks in her car on the way to the house earlier had to mean something. He had a gut feeling. His gut feelings were almost always worth following. Would she follow as well?

As soon as this assignment was over, he decided that he'd ask his boss for some time off and return to Arione. It would be a definitive moment in his life to have a woman tie him down. Shirley was that special and unique. This would be his perfect relationship. One he'd really longed for for some time, but only just acknowledged. But first, this mess needed to end.

"Alex," Will asked. "Are you okay?"

"Yeah! I'm fine. Just have more on my mind than I originally planned," Alex admitted. "Why?"

"You had this look on your face as if something was hurting and pleasurable at the same time. It was weird."

"Let's just leave it as weird," Alex said as they entered the hospital.

They passed the front desk and went to the stairs. After walking up one flight, they turned in the direction of the nurses' station and saw Nurse Emily Hodges. When she saw Alex Miller, she smiled.

"I was right, wasn't I?" Emily asked Alex.

"Absolutely! I believe you are amazing," Alex assured her.

"You're not telling me anything I don't already know, Mr. Miller," Emily said.

"You may call me Alex. All my friends do."

"Well then, Alex," Emily responded, "please feel free to move on. Just be quiet and respectful. Don't agitate Mrs. Putnam."

"No problem, Emily," Alex said. "Will and I will try to be quick and let her rest."

"Mr. Barrish?" Emily asked. "How is your jaw?"

"Hurts, but Dr. Anderson said it would take time," Will admitted.

"I hope you understand that only with time will the jaw heal successfully," Emily explained. "Try to limit the speaking. Let your associate do that for you."

Just before Will responded, Alex interrupted. "He understands. And I understand."

Before they started walking to Ruth's room, Alex looked at Emily and winked. "By the way," Alex added, "if the police show up, will you let us know?"

"In a heartbeat!" Emily answered, winking back.

They walked to Ruth's room and stopped before opening the door. They took one more look at each other, and Will took a deep breath.

"Let's do it!" Will stated.

As they opened the door slowly, they saw that the television was on. The room was dimly lit, with the window blinds slightly ajar. Alex and Will walked in and saw Ruth looking out the window. She turned in their direction.

"Hello, Mrs. Putnam," Alex said.

"Afternoon, Mrs. Putnam," Will followed.

"Dr. Anderson said it would be all right to speak with you," Alex explained. "Are we interrupting?"

"No," Ruth said in a soft voice. "The television's on for company only. I'm actually bored and wish . . ." Ruth's voice fell off into a silent nothingness of sound.

"You look pretty good, if I may say so myself," Alex continued.

A small smile crossed Ruth's face. She had a bandage on her head that she was sure she did not need. Her face was slightly bruised. There were also two bandages on her left arm, one on her wrist and the other on her elbow.

"I actually thought things might be worse," Will admitted. "I'm glad to see that you're better."

"I'm not sure if I remember either of you. I apologize," Ruth said. "Do I know you?"

"No! No, you don't," Alex assured her. "However, we're here to try and put some of the pieces of the puzzle together."

"My name is William Barrish, Mrs. Putnam. This is Alex Miller," Will said, pointing to Alex. "It was my car that you almost hit on the freeway. I'm so sorry for the accident."

"Actually, Mr. Barrish," Ruth said as she looked away from him and then turned back. "It is I who should be apologizing to you. I don't know where that came from. I can't recall how I got to the car. I do remember feeling very hot and perspiring a bit. I never do that!"

"At least you're safe," Will said. "That's what's really important."

Ruth turned off the television. The room became silent as she stared at the window. A small tear traveled down her cheek, and she brushed it aside.

"I'm having trouble with life right now," Ruth informed them. "I don't do that. I value life too much to purposely take it away."

"I don't believe it was entirely your fault, Mrs. Putnam," Will said.

"Please call me Ruth. Mrs. Putnam hasn't been a part of my life for quite some time," Ruth replied. "Actually, I was hoping it would have been something else by now."

That confirmed one of Alex and Will's questions. Her feelings about Dan Adams could be the denouement of their story.

"Would you mind discussing what happened?" Alex asked.

"I'm not sure I really know what happened, Mr. Miller," Ruth admitted. "I was at the front of the house when all of a sudden I was struck in the face and head by two rocks. I saw the first travel from the back of the house. After, I became terribly dizzy and vomited, and then the second rock came and knocked me out. When I woke up, Dan was gone."

"Do you know what he was working on?" Will asked.

"Actually, I do," Ruth said. "It had something to do with a new form of energy. Something to benefit all mankind and decrease global warming."

"What did he call the apparatus he built in the backyard?" Alex asked.

"It's a geothermal energy plant," Ruth said.

"Ruth," Alex continued, "geothermal energy has been around for a long time. What could Dr. Adams possibly do with it to enhance mankind?"

"Dr. Adams felt he could find a way to power vehicles using geothermal energy," Ruth explained. "He called it AGE. The A stood for 'alternative,' and Dan knew it would work. In fact, he knew that when it did work, it would provide endless energy with no harmful exhaust fumes."

"How would it move a vehicle?" Will asked.

"That was the key," Ruth said. "Dan was testing the final push in his puzzle." Ruth started to tear up. "That's when I lost him."

Alex and Will watched closely as Ruth explained the entire incident. They saw anguish and hurt in her eyes and noticed her entire body twitch as she recalled the events. When they informed Ruth about the hole in the ceiling of the lab, it made total sense to her even though she was unable to explain how and why it occurred.

For Will, the situation was a bit uncomfortable. Even though he had been a professional reporter for more than a few years now, this event was too close because Ruth had caused the accident that could have killed him.

Alex was just listening with professional ears. He had taken a small notepad and pencil from his pants pocket and was writing down key words. Alex knew they would be needed later in order to write the story.

"Why did you leave the hospital, Ruth?" Alex asked.

"I don't know," Ruth answered. "I felt something was calling to me. I saw a vision of Dan falling. He called out and I needed to get back to the house."

"Back to what?" Will asked. "You knew he was gone. Was he supposed to be there when you returned?"

"I must have been delirious," Ruth admitted. "When I heard what I did to that poor man, I wished it had been me. He didn't deserve that. All he was doing was giving me a lift."

"Who told you about the accident, Ruth?" Alex asked.

"Dr. Anderson," Ruth replied. "She's been a friend ever since my husband was killed in a different car accident when we first arrived in Arione. She has been there every day since. As was Dan Adams. I fell in love with him about a year after the accident. I just never spoke to him about it."

"Why was that?" Alex asked.

"I didn't want him to think his love could be bought. He made me a very rich woman, but never asked for anything in return."

"Isn't he a very wealthy man himself?" Will asked.

"Yes, he is," Ruth admitted. "Dan Adams was wealthy in more than money. He was rich in kindness, consideration, respect, admiration, friendship . . . all the kind adjectives in the dictionary are the only way to describe Dr. Daniel Adams."

"He sounds too good to be true!" Alex exclaimed.

"He really is too good to be true, Mr. Miller," Ruth added. "He's one in a billion. And yet, Dan Adams is a friend to anyone who needs a helping hand."

The Death Maze

The conversation subsided for a moment as Ruth looked into thin air and then smiled. She saw an image of Dan in her mind. Alex and Will watched her face go from troubled to happy. Then her face changed again.

"What's wrong, Ruth?" Will asked.

"When the car rolled over . . ."

"You remember that?" Will asked.

"Dr. Anderson told me. Don't you remember me saying that?" Ruth looked at Will as if he wasn't listening and continued without waiting for an answer. "I thought I would never wake up. I relive that nightmare each time I close my eyes. It brings me back to my late husband's death and then fast-forwards to me being responsible for another life. Maybe I should be locked up."

"You didn't know what you were doing, Ruth. You were heavily sedated," Will told her.

"Ruth," Alex uttered, "you're the only link to Dr. Adams."

Ruth looked at Alex. She knew there was something on his mind and wanted him to expand on his thoughts without her having to ask.

"Okay. I'll say it!" Alex continued. "Do you think you could help the scientists find him? If he's still alive, I mean."

"Oh, he's alive, Mr. Miller," Ruth said. "I'm sure of it!"

"How can you be so certain?" Will asked.

Ruth waited a few seconds before answering. Alex had an idea of what she was going to say.

"There have been too many unexplained dreams," Ruth said. "It's as if I've been taken to another world to see him." Alex and Will looked at her. "Call it women's intuition."

"Well, what would you think if we tried to get you out of here and back to the house?" Alex asked.

357

"I would love to get out of here," Ruth said. "I'm going nuts doing nothing."

"Any ideas of how we do this?" Will asked.

"I think the nurse at the desk would be willing to assist," Alex answered. "Why don't I just speak with her and distract her? I wouldn't want to get her in trouble."

"Why not just call Dr. Anderson?" Ruth asked.

Alex and Will looked at each other. "I'm not sure Dr. Anderson is in a position that would allow her to receive that call," Alex informed her.

It was then that Alex and Will explained what was going on back at the house. Ruth couldn't believe they had to booby trap the house in order to avoid getting arrested by Chief Dressler and Bone. She thought such things only occurred in the movies.

Chief Dressler was a good friend of Dan's. He would want all the help he could get to find him. Why was he being so pigheaded? Ruth knew that all they needed was to tell Chief Dressler that they had the best of intentions and would write the story responsibly. The outcome had to be positive in the long run.

They decided that they would just walk out of the hospital one by one and drive to Arione. Alex would leave the room first to speak with Nurse Emily. Will would follow and just leave. Ruth would then leave the room and say she needed to walk. She would not take no for an answer if stopped.

Alex handed the car keys to Will and then opened the door. He walked to the nurses' station while Ruth went into the bathroom to change. When she emerged from the bathroom, Will was at the door and ready to leave.

"I'm dressed and ready," she told Will as he exited the hospital room.

The Death Maze

Ruth went to the window and looked outside. Her view was of the parking lot. A few minutes passed until she saw Will arrive at the car. Will looked up at the window, gave the thumbs-up, and opened the car door.

Alex was speaking with Nurse Emily. They were having a pleasant conversation about Shirley Anderson, and he assured her that he wanted to take her out.

Trying not to be conspicuous, Alex turned to look at Ruth's room. He saw Ruth open the door, ready to leave. Alex turned back to Nurse Emily.

"So do you think her schedule is clear for tomorrow evening?" Alex asked.

"She is always on call, Alex," Emily said. "However, I'm sure she'll be pleased."

"Great! I'll call her when I get back to the motel."

"Why not call her now?" Emily suggested. "She's just at the Adams house helping out. Do you have her cell phone number?"

"Actually, I do," Alex responded.

Just then an alarm went off at the station. Emily picked up the phone, pressed a couple buttons, and waited for the intercom to engage. A second later, she called for assistance for another room down the hall and then hung up the phone.

"I have an emergency, Alex," Emily said, walking rapidly away from the station. She quickly turned back. "Call her now and let me know what she says." Emily turned the corner and disappeared.

"I'll do it now," Alex called out.

Ruth popped out of the room and walked in the opposite direction of the emergency. Without looking at Ruth, Alex followed. One minute later, they were in the car with Will at the wheel.

"Fasten your seat belts," Will said as he pulled the car out of the parking spot.

Just as they left the parking lot, a police car pulled in. Alex turned his head and watched an officer get out of the car and walk into the hospital. He figured they would have at least a five-minute head start. Emily had vowed to assist. He was sure no one would go into Ruth's hospital room for a while. She wouldn't be missed until someone checked up on her.

Arione was just a few minutes' drive away. Many questions would be asked once they arrived at the house. Alex thought that maybe a few fists would fly as well. The three needed to stick together to make sure there would be no unusual overtures or outbreaks. They could and would explain everything if given the chance.

"So we have a plan. Right?" Will asked.

"Let me talk to Chief Dressler," Ruth said. "He'll listen to me."

"And if he comes on like a madman and wants to arrest us?" Will jumped in.

"I'll make him listen to me, Mr. Barrish," Ruth stated. "I can be pretty demanding when I need to be."

"Okay," Alex agreed. "Will and I promise not to make this into a huge, over-the-top deal. We'll write the story without any sensationalizing."

"I just want to know where Dr. Adams disappeared to," Will added. "The story can begin with a disappearance followed by a car crash that involved me. We can intimate that the authorities are looking into the whereabouts of one Dr. Daniel Adams and refrain from any conclusions due to this being an ongoing investigation."

"We'll even agree to an exclusive, and . . ." Alex began before Ruth interrupted him.

"I just want peace." Ruth lowered her head. "I want to be happy and I want a future." She lifted her head and looked at Alex. "That's not too much to ask. Is it?"

Alex just stared at her. Will's eyes left the road and briefly turned to Ruth.

"No," Will said somberly. "It's not too much. It's never too much when all it is . . . is simple happiness and a normal standard of life."

Peace! That was a word Ruth had thought a great deal about during the last few years of her life. She had had a great deal of peace and happiness while growing up in Miami. And marrying Ed had been the right thing to do. They had nothing but the normal goals of a young couple wishing to build their lives anew in surroundings not truly explored.

The terror and pain she had lived with from the moment she arrived in Arione had left her empty and unfulfilled. Dan Adams had opened her heart again. He allowed her to become the beautiful and giving woman she had been prior to her new life in Arione.

Now all she wanted was the balance of her life to be peaceful. Ruth wanted the serenity she and Ed had craved. It was not too much to ask for. Having Dan Adams back in her life was all she wanted.

Ruth was tired of turning the other cheek only to have the other slapped. There had to be a better place to run if she truly wanted. This place had to allow her to rest and feel safe for the balance of her life. She not only wanted it, she needed it.

Ruth tried to resign herself to the outcome of this nightmare. God was telling her something, only she was unable to figure it out. Was He telling her she'd have to live life without the companionship of the man she wanted?

Arione was the quiet town she and Ed had sought and longed for. Circumstances had made it unbearable at times but also quite remarkable. In any case, she figured her three malevolent happenings had already occurred. Wasn't that how many each person was to experience in their lifetime? The first was the car accident killing Ed. The second was Dan's disappearance. The third was the most recent car accident involving William Barrish and a stranger who was just trying to be the Good Samaritan. Ruth's time for peace was now. This was what she would explain to Chief Dressler.

Will turned the car in the direction of the Arione exit. He drove down the two-lane road until he came to the road leading to Dan's house. He then turned north and stopped in front of the house.

Unbeknownst to Will, the officer dispatched to the hospital had followed them. He kept a safe distance after discovering Ruth was not in her room. His instincts were correct; they were on their way to the house. He decided not to contact his boss, Chief Dressler, as he wanted his due rewards when he brought the reporters into the hands of the waiting crowd.

The officer's name was Miguel Arvada. He had been on Dressler's team before Bone showed up. Officer Arvada should have been Chief Dressler's right-hand man. He knew everyone in both Arione and Vera. He was well liked and trusted.

Officer Miguel Arvada had one drawback. He was three years older than Chief Dressler and would probably retire before his boss. Age had not been kind to this devoted officer of the law, and all he wanted was some respect. His bones were rattling and his reflexes were slow. Dressler wanted a younger man.

Chief Dressler had told Officer Arvada many times that Vera could be his territory. However, he would never be able to run it on his own and would always have a chain of command above him. He would not be the chief. Miguel Arvada would always have to report to Dressler. Those were the simple facts of life.

Will, Alex, and Ruth slowly got out of the car and walked up the porch steps to the front door. They were going over their stories when they heard a noise behind them.

Officer Arvada's car screeched into the driveway, and he got out as quickly as his old bones would allow. He pulled his gun from the holster and ordered Alex, Will, and Ruth to stop.

Bone heard the car door close. He went to the front window. "I don't believe it," Bone yelled out. "Chief, come here. Quick!" Bone rushed to the front door.

Alex, Will, and Ruth turned to see who was yelling behind them when the front door opened.

Officer Arvada heard the noise from the front door and thought they would rush into the house. He took aim and fired.

At the same time, Chief Dressler saw Officer Arvada from the front window and rushed to the door screaming, "No! Don't shoot!"

Alex saw the gun before the shot was fired. He pushed Ruth to the floor and, like a hurricane, rushed to push Will away from the door.

Ruth screamed and Will called out. Alex fell to the floor of the porch.

As the front door slowly opened, Dressler ordered Officer Arvada to lower his gun. He did as he was ordered. Officer Arvada slowly walked to the base of the porch steps.

Bone rushed to Ruth and picked her up off the floor.

Will slowly got up and saw Chief Dressler at the door.

Alex didn't move.

Shirley had heard the gunshot. She ran to the door and saw Alex on the porch. She lowered herself to Alex and saw blood seep from his head. "ALEX," she screamed.

"What?" Will asked. "Alex?" he yelled as he squeezed next to Shirley and saw the blood.

Dressler couldn't believe it. He ordered Officer Arvada to holster his weapon and move away from the scene. He had totally forgotten to undo the orders he had given after the town council meeting. This was his fault.

In his entire tenure as chief of police of Arione and Vera, not one person had ever been shot. It was an achievement he had always been proud to hang on his shoulders. There was a message hanging in a frame on a wall behind his desk. It read: "To live totally by the gun means you must use the gun. It's a man of higher calling who understands the power of the word. —Author unknown."

Bone took Ruth into the house. She needed to rest.

Chief Dressler picked up Alex's body and carried it into one of the bedrooms.

Will was crying, as his only source of comfort and wisdom was gone. Shirley helped him off the porch and into one of the chairs in the living room.

Officer Arvada retreated to his vehicle and sat. He wouldn't move until Chief Dressler gave him orders.

After Dressler laid Alex's body on one of the beds; he covered it with a blanket. He came out of the bedroom and closed the door. He then walked to the laboratory and saw Dr. Allyson Rayburn and Samuel Ryan staring at him.

Dressler felt alone. He walked away from the lab. His feet dragged him into the kitchen, where he sat down at the table. He lowered his head into his hands.

Bone walked into the kitchen and stared at his boss. He was confused. Everything had happened so fast. The man he admired was all but a shell of what he had been just a few minutes ago. Bone wanted to say something but was at a loss for words.

Shirley left Will in the chair in the living room. She walked into the bedroom where Dressler had laid Alex. Staring at the body of the man she had wanted to get to know, Shirley started to cry. She cried for the lost hope and lost possibilities. Her tears dripped down her face as her thoughts went wild in every imaginable direction.

Uncovering his hand, she took it in hers and brought it to her breast. Shirley held on tight. She wanted Alex to return the touch. She wanted the coldness of his hand to bring heat into her body.

After a few moments, Shirley lowered his hand and placed it next to his body. She covered it with the blanket. When she was finished, Dr. Shirley Anderson walked out of the room. There were other people who needed her attention.

Living people.

Chapter 41

There were no signs of a quake. There was no hint of a tremble. The ground under his body did not move, and the walls did not cave in and crush him. The lights illuminating both switches suddenly turned off, making his enclosure pitch-dark. Dan wished he could smile, but being in the dark suddenly turned his stomach.

Then he heard it. It was faint for a moment but grew in loudness. His conclusions were wrong and he knew his end was near. Dan rested his head against the wall where the switches were and wanted to scream. He wanted to argue, rant, and rave. He felt betrayed and tricked. He had lost.

The Elders also watched. They now knew that Apep was not ready. He possibly would never be ready. It was time to eliminate his gift and retire his soul to a different depth. Apep needed more than the kindness of a clean soul and new incarnation. He needed to know what it would feel like to be left totally alone for his soul to question and reason within itself without any gifts or powers.

Apep was that unique of a monster. Even more time would pass before he would finally dissolve into nothingness due to his failures or a full resolution of his id would be restored. It was totally up to him. He would need to learn and, when the time was right, ask to move forward to restore his damaged soul.

The Death Maze

However, the Elders first needed to allow Apep to finish what he planned to do with this gifted and wonderful human being. They would again be ready to intervene as they had the other two times. It was just a matter of precise timing.

Stanley Moser was the kind soul with a special, unfulfilled gift. Mr. Chou was the gentle keeper who watched over the massive wall. And Dan Adams was a brilliant mind who only wanted to enhance the lives of the world. They would all need to meet.

Dan waited as his body rested. Then, to his surprise, the floor opened and he fell. It wasn't far, and for some strange reason he felt a smile cross his face. He thought he would immediately be crushed by his enclosure. Instead he fell only a short distance to a lower room. It felt as if he had fallen longer, as the fall, like before, was controlled.

When his body stopped moving, Dan sensed something different about this new room. Bright lights suddenly revealed a huge square room. It was totally unexpected. It was much bigger than even the first room he had experienced in the sixth dimension.

Dan felt like he was the center of attention in a circus. Four beams of light lit the room from four different directions, and four even larger spotlights surrounded Dan and lit his body. One centered itself on his lower legs. The second cradled his waist to his knees. The third hugged him from his chest to his waist. The fourth concentrated on his head and neck. Dan felt as if each light was holding him snugly in place. He wanted to stand up for what would have been the first time in many hours. However, when he tried to move, the four spotlights sensed the motion and lifted Dan to his feet.

The lights moved in tandem and allowed almost total motion. Dan tried stretching his neck. The light concentrating on this section of his body slowly moved as well. Dan heard the cracking of his neck muscles and then straightened his head once more.

When his mind told him he should look up, the light sensed this thought also. It moved slightly behind him, allowing for his head to move back and his eyes to look up. Dan saw that the ceiling height was about twelve feet before returning to his original position and staring ahead again.

"I can move my body myself," Dan said loudly.

There was no response. Dan hoped Apep would say something.

"Apep," Dan said in a louder tone. "Release me so I can move freely. Where the hell could I run even if I wanted to?"

All four lights immediately turned off, releasing the bond that held him. The room was still lit brightly. Dan started to thank Apep but knew better. He kept quiet for the moment. This was not a thank-you moment, as Dan knew Apep was toying with him before the final breath would leave his body. But what was Apep doing?

Dan slowly walked around the empty room. He couldn't figure out where the lights had been or where the illumination had originated. He saw only pure, clean, white walls. There were no chairs to sit on. There were no doors to open and walk through. There were no windows to look through or break.

He looked up and thought he could see the sky. Dan was sure the color was blue. The vision appeared real, and he followed what looked like a cloud rolling from one side of the room to the other. It was surreal.

"Apep," Dan suddenly said. "Stop it! Get on with what you're going to do. Stop playing games. Damn you!"

Again, no response from Apep. Dan didn't know what he was thinking or where he had gone. The Elders had no response either. The lead wanted to whisper into Dan's mind, but he did not want Apep to realize that he was being watched. The Elders needed to be prepared for the worst. They needed to move quickly.

"What are you waiting for?" Dan now yelled. "Apep! You miserable coward! What could possibly keep you from voicing your words now? Cat got your tongue?" Dan laughed, knowing jokes and sarcasm wouldn't make a difference.

Just then a loud hiss and cat meow filled the room from one end to the other. The noise was hideous. He saw an image of a large cat carried by an even larger hand. It continued crossing from one side of the room to the other.

Then the cat squealed horrendously and flew in front of Dan. The hand choked the cat as a second hand grabbed the cat's jaw and opened its mouth. A third hand pulled at the cat's tongue.

Dan wanted to turn his eyes away. One of the spotlights appeared, directing him to look only at the cat. Dan couldn't turn his head from the inhumane treatment of this poor cat. Dan could only dream what was next.

With one hand holding the cat's throat, a second holding its jaw, and a third tugging at its tongue, a fourth hand appeared with a large, thin knife and immediately sliced. The cat screamed; it sounded like a human screaming in pain. The cat writhed as it was thrown into the far wall. It disappeared into nothingness.

Dan wanted to puke but didn't have any saliva, much less food, in his mouth.

"It is I who has the cat's tongue," Apep roared with delight. "Your joke is beautiful, Dr. Adams. Are there any more?"

"You sick bastard!" Dan screamed in disgust. "You actually have no soul. Only a poor, demented, sick individual would do such a miserable, godforsaken act."

"Actually, Dr. Adams, you are finally correct!"

Dan waited for a few moments. He needed time to recover from what he had just witnessed, even though it had been an image played out only for his benefit. Apep hadn't really done anything that Dan couldn't conjure up in his own mind.

And yet Dan's breathing was hard. His eyes were red and sore. His mind was terribly tired. He wanted to pray for a quick end. He knew, however, that Apep had no quick end in mind and would only relish seeing him squirm.

"Tell me," Dan finally said softly, resigned to his fate. "Did I succeed or fail in completing the maze? Because if I succeeded, I want to get the hell out of here. Just tell me where the doors are and I'll walk away from your world and leave you alone."

Even though Dan couldn't see Apep, he knew he was smiling as wide a grin as anyone could give. Apep was that gruesome and disgusting. And Apep enjoyed every morsel of hideousness that he could dish out. *It is truly wonderful,* Apep thought, *that Dan Adams finally realized the depth of my evilness.*

The Elders hadn't realized it, though. They honestly thought that after so much time in the sixth dimension, Apep's soul would wake up and finally ask for forgiveness. All he needed to do was release Dan Adams and then move away into a neutral zone in order to reincarnate.

The Death Maze

A few more minutes passed before a large, cylindrically shaped object appeared. There was some writing on it, but Dan couldn't read it from where he was standing. At first, he didn't know if he should move toward it. His curiosity got the better of him, though, and he began inching toward it.

What Dan really wanted was to hear Apep's voice before moving toward what he realized could be his fate. He wanted to hear Apep instruct him. He wanted to listen to the salivating in this sick mind's voice. However, he didn't know why he wanted to hear it. When he reached the object and turned toward the writing, he read ENTER THE TUBE!

"It's a trick," Dan yelled out, full of fight once again. "If I enter the tube, you'll kill me."

Dan stepped back, thinking Apep would devise a strange wind to blow him closer to the tube and force him into it. He pressed his feet harder to the floor, trying to secure his position even though he knew this was a ludicrous feat. *Pardon the pun*, he thought again.

It was then that he realized something. This thought should answer any and all questions concerning the maze.

"Apep," Dan said, turning in all directions and trying to figure out which way to address his captor. "If I made the final mistake, why didn't the maze shrink and crush me? There was a tremor and quake. Wasn't there?" Dan waited for a response. "Come on, damn you. You go back on your word? Are you afraid to admit that you were defeated by a mere mortal from another world? You feel inferior?"

Dan waited for a response. Still there was nothing. He couldn't understand why Apep was suddenly so silent.

The Elders thought this might be a perfect time to intermingle with Dan's mind and let him know he was in safe hands. He should not worry. It was then that Dan spoke again.

"Apep! Does your dimension go back on its word? Did you lie? I wouldn't be ashamed to admit I had lost. Why should you?"

Dan suddenly thought of a question that should really hit Apep squarely in his gut. "Was this world, at one time, filled with humans instead of voices and minds? Were you at one time part of that world?"

Nothing!

"WHAT'S THE MATTER WITH YOU? DID I HIT UPON A TENDER NERVE AND YOU'RE AFRAID TO ANSWER?"

There was all of a sudden a loud crack of lightning followed by a huge roar of thunder. The room began to shiver from an unusual tremor. Then, as quickly as it had begun, it stopped. Everything became deathly silent.

The Elders had seen that phenomenon twice before. Only twice! However, that was after Stanley Moser and Mr. Chou had been saved. The Elders knew that the Superior One was not pleased. They knew Apep would be done.

"Enter the tube, Dr. Adams!" Apep suddenly said.

"Why should I?" Dan countered.

"It will take you to your destination," Apep said smoothly.

"How do I know it's not a trick?"

"Was there a tremor?" Apep asked.

"Yes," Dan said defiantly.

"Was there a decrease in the maze?" Apep then offered.

"No, but . . ."

"But what, Dr. Adams? You're now in a room that is larger than the one you were in when you first arrived," Apep reminded him. "You are able to stand and move freely. What would you conclude by this? Obviously, you chose correctly."

"That's what I already pointed out. What took you so long to speak?" Dan asked.

"Those are questions that I do not have to answer," Apep said in an even voice. "After all, you invaded my world. You were experimenting with something you did not even know was too close to a portal linking our worlds."

"A portal brought me here?" Dan asked, not realizing Apep held him because of a mistake. "It wasn't because of my experiments?"

"You're not listening, Dr. Adams." Apep's pitch grew slightly. "You built the geothermal energy plant too close to the portal opening. Its vibrations grew too violent without you even knowing it and caused a rupture within the two dimensions."

Dan couldn't believe it. He was in this miserable place because of a stupid accident, and now Apep was explaining why he should be eliminated because of it. At least he thought he would be eliminated. Apep hadn't actually finalized it.

"You've never made a mistake?" Dan asked.

"Let me ask you a question, Dr. Adams. If you were robbed in your own home, wouldn't you want to be able to protect your home at any cost?"

"If I caught the robber and knew nothing had been taken and knew that I was safe, I would ask him why," Dan informed him. "There are reasons for every action. If it was for the benefit of feeding this person's family, I might even give him money or food. If it was because this person was just a crook, then I would call the authorities and let them deal with the robber."

"I see. You appear to be a compassionate man," Apep said.

"I believe I—"

"I'm not," Apep interrupted. "I caught you in my world. I dealt with you as I saw fit. Now I will take you to your destination."

Dan needed to think. He did not believe Apep. He was saying one thing and meaning another. His final destination was Arione, California, and his home. Maybe Apep meant that his final destination was his death. Dan couldn't tell from the manner of his voice. He needed more time to decide what to do. And yet Apep was ready to move now.

Dan was sure there was some catch to the tube. He knew if he entered it, his life would either cease to exist or he would suffer more at the twisted mind of his captor. Something was not making sense.

And yet, Dan did reach his final destination. But did he secure his passage home? Or did he make his fifth mistake, ensuring that his death was imminent? After all, if he did choose correctly, Apep could make him choose countless times until the last mistake was obtained.

It appeared to Dan that for each positive thought there was a negative one waiting on the opposite side of the spectrum. It was yin or yang. It was taking one step forward to only realize you're two steps behind.

Dan looked around the room again. It was huge. There didn't appear to be any buttons, switches, doors, odd entrances, or windows. This was his last enclosure in this dimension. He was at the end and alive. And that was the key. He was alive.

He realized his face was dripping with sweat. The room was a bit hotter than a few minutes before. Dan's clothing was damp. With all the crawling he had done, it was not surprising.

The Death Maze

However, something just didn't meld. Dan felt his life was holding on by a string and couldn't come to a conclusion on what to do.

"I'll ask again, Dr. Adams," Apep suddenly said. "Will you enter the tube?"

"I don't know," Dan answered.

"You have no choice," Apep reminded him.

"The hell I don't," Dan retorted.

The Elders were trying to figure out where Apep was going with this. All of them were ready to intervene once they projected the final outcome. They already knew it would be in the tube.

But Dan Adams was a fighter. He was extrapolating information without Apep even knowing it. Apep didn't have to inform him about the portal, but he did. Apep didn't need to explain the vibrational phenomenon behind his experiment and the portal, but he did. Dan didn't need to be informed that all of it had been caused by a mistake. However, Apep had told him, and the Elders had made sure that Dan received the information he needed. However, they were unsure what it all meant or where it was going.

Dan knew. If he played Apep long enough, perhaps it would lead to his home. His only doubt was that it may leave him in his home in a state of consciousness or unconsciousness, dead or alive.

Dan waited for some response to his abrupt remark. He knew Apep was getting ready to do something. He just didn't know what, as this nightmare had a twist or turn at every junction.

All of a sudden, he felt it. It was gradual at first, but definitely noticeable. Dan's sweat ceased to fall. His clothing lost its dampness and grew colder. A quick shiver led him to move about the room and check each wall for some sort of thermostat. There had to be something to tell him what the temperature in the room was.

Then he realized he didn't need it. He saw his breath. It was not unlike Apep to reach this decision. Dan knew this was Apep's finale. Apep was tired of playing with him in the maze and wanted a permanent fixture in the sixth dimension.

The Elders now knew it also. This would eventually drive Dan into the tube. This would be Apep's denouement. The final act was beginning, and Apep was sure he would not lose.

The Elders also realized that the lightning and thunder would no longer come again. It was their sign that they should be ready. Dan Adams needed to live, and Apep needed to end.

Chapter 42

Dan was amazed to feel how fast the temperature decreased. Since there was no shelter to speak of except the tube, which he did not want to enter, Dan clutched his arms around his chest and tried warming himself. He knew this wasn't enough. The temperature kept falling, and fast.

Dan then felt his hair. He sensed there was something on it he hadn't felt in a long time. Reaching up to grab a section of hair, he felt a small icicle forming. The sweat on his face also began solidifying into ice. His clothing was another sign that he could soon freeze to death if he didn't think of something.

The only object in the room was the only one he wanted to avoid. Dan knew that if he entered the tube his life would end. Otherwise Apep wouldn't be so adamant about getting him into it. The tube represented Apep's finale, and Dan needed to do everything to avoid that trap.

The Elders could only watch and prepare. The end could arrive at any moment, and they needed to be ready. One wrong move by Apep, and they would lose the chance to save Dan Adams. This outcome was totally different from that of the other two. Apep's previous victims had been easy to save.

"Having a chilling effect! Don't you think, Dan Adams?" Apep said. "I'm sure the Elders will also be surprised by this event."

The Elders were stunned by this remark. They had stayed in the upper realm far from Apep. How did he know of them? What could they possibly do to save Dan Adams if their identities were revealed?

"What are you talking about?" Dan asked, his jaw starting to stiffen from the cold. Dan tried not to shiver or chatter when talking. He knew he needed to keep Apep involved so the cold could subside. He didn't know if that was possible.

"The Elders are the ancient minds of the sixth dimension, Dr. Adams," Apep explained. "I'm sure they contacted you at least once. Don't you remember?"

"No one contacted me except you," Dan tried to explain.

"Come now, Dr. Adams," Apep spoke condescendingly. "The Elders were the ones who informed you to be prepared. I know you thought it was me. I know they thought I would not notice. Guess what? I did!" Apep laughed.

"What are you talking about, Apep?" Dan asked, tired of what he thought was stupidity spilling from Apep's mouth. "You were the one trying to trick me."

The Elders were shocked by this revelation. They had always thought that they were in control of the sixth dimension. They always knew who would move about where and when. It was their decision how and why things traversed in the sixth dimension. The knowledge of their being was always kept from any and all mortals who entered the sixth dimension. This included Apep when he entered twenty-five centuries ago.

Apep had to learn. Apep needed to understand. Apep was obliged to comprehend and master all avenues of humanity, good and bad, and discover the trueness and oneness of the soul. This would be the only path to reincarnate and turn around a life that had once been so evil and vicious. His soul depended upon it. A person's soul required it.

"Do you recall the lightning and thunder?" Apep asked.

"Of course I do. It was your way of trying to scare me and somehow trick me," Dan said.

"Not true, Dan Adams," Apep admitted. "That was the Elders trying to scare you. They think they're in command when in fact it is I who have mastered what they wanted me to learn and utilize."

This was not a true statement. The Elders immediately understood Apep's still twisted mind. They knew he had not mastered the ultimate realization of the id. This was good news and a relief to the Elders. Even though Apep was aware of them, he was unaware of the Superior One. It was a privilege to even comprehend the upper entity and controller of all. The Elders still had the upper hand.

Dan didn't know what to think except that it was getting colder. He figured that if he started jumping up and down maybe he would generate some heat. He looked at the tube. It remained the centerpiece of the room as he moved around.

The jumping and constant movement seemed to be working. Dan felt his body gradually warm up and sweat begin to drip from his head. His face, body, and clothing were now damp.

It was no wonder. Dan stopped jumping and realized the temperature in the room had started to reverse itself. He couldn't believe how fast the change was occurring. Within seconds, the room was stifling hot. The air grew pungent as Dan's clothing began to stink and grow stale.

Dan's hair was matted down with perspiration. He was dripping all over and wanted to take off both his outer and under shirt. It was good he decided not to remove both, because Apep was sure to change the temperature back at the first sight of Dan's mistake. He decided to remove only his outer, buttoned shirt.

Dan used it to wipe the sweat from his face. When he dropped it to the floor, Apep worked quickly. A beam of light shot at the shirt, causing it to incinerate into ashes. Dan barely had time to stand up before his shirt was in another form. He knew not to remove any other article of clothing.

"Will you enter the tube, Dr. Adams?" Apep asked again.

"Tell me, Apep." Dan stood up quickly. "What kind of a human monster were you when you lived?"

"I was a genius," Apep announced proudly.

"You must have been a maniacal genius, old buddy," Dan said mockingly. "You must have been worshipped by few and far between. It must have been totally frustrating not to be liked or loved by anyone."

"Enter the tube, Dan Adams," Apep ordered.

"How did it feel not to have anyone to hold or caress, Apep, dear friend? Did you walk around your world feeling superior? Were the masses so afraid that they parted when you walked? COME ON, DAMN IT! BE A MAN!"

A huge gust of wind blew in Dan's direction, knocking him to the other side of the room. Before he had a chance to get up, a second gust picked him up and tossed him past the tube and into the opposite corner.

Dan felt, for the first time, the pain of hitting the wall. His falls had always been controlled, and he had known that the sixth dimension, or Apep, would fully protect him. Not now. He had riled Apep to the point where he was not sure that he would return to Arione, even if he did choose correctly. Dan slowly picked himself up. He was hurting.

The Elders were now ready to interfere, even though Apep knew who they were. A summons had gone out asking all Elders to be on call. The entire population of Elders was now swarming around the room, ready to pounce to protect Dan Adams once given the order from the Superior One. They all knew he was watching.

It was up to Apep. They were amazed Apep could not feel they were there right now. This they did not understand. However, they did know that Apep was not as powerful as he thought he was. And why the final order had not come was a mystery to them. They remained patient. They stayed ready to react.

The temperature of the room then rose quickly. Dan felt a wave of heat fly across his face. It was blistering. He looked at the hairs on his arms and noticed they were parched and beginning to singe. He guessed the heat was a stifling 120 degrees.

Taking another look at his arms, he saw sweat pour down. Before the drops were able to fall, they stopped and burned into his skin. Not one droplet hit the floor.

Dan also realized that his face was probably just as bad, even though he had not felt one drop on it. He touched his right cheek and felt the tenderness of a blister. A piece of skin rubbed away on his finger.

How long will the room remain like this? Dan thought as he tried to figure out what to say next to Apep.

Before he could finish his thought, the temperature changed again. It was suddenly a comfortable sixty-five degrees with a cool breeze. The wind felt good against his battered face and arms.

It was fast, though. Apep was causing it to change so rapidly that Dan was sure he would become sick. He felt a small tickle in the back of his throat and let out a small cough.

"One more time, Dan Adams," Apep warned. "Enter the tube or suffer the consequences."

"Do I have your word it will take me home?" Dan asked.

"You're willing to let me say yes or no, not having trusted me since you arrived?" Apep asked. "Now that is a laugh, as you would say in your world." Apep guffawed hideously.

"Screw you, you Neanderthal piece of crap!" Dan didn't know where that had come from. But it felt good, even though he was sure he would be the recipient of something worse.

Dan also knew there were no more questions to be asked. If Apep was playing games, game time was over. He sensed that the final change was coming. Whatever it was, Apep would make certain Dan landed in the tube.

Dan didn't have any idea what would happen next until he heard it. It came from behind him in the corner of the room and away from the opening of the tube. He turned his head and saw it. The loudness grew as the wall opened up to reveal a two-foot hole.

Then the water came. It flew across the room, almost hitting the tube.

Dan's eyes opened wide as he rushed to the water. He stuck his hand against the hole, thinking he could block the water from gushing out. He felt pain pour into his hands. The water was ice cold, and Dan barely felt the coolness soothe the blisters on his hands.

Another loud noise, this one from the opposite side of the room, caused Dan to look behind him. A second hole had opened and more water began to gush out.

Dan looked down at his feet and saw that they were covered in ice water. Then he noticed the temperature drop once again. He wanted to move closer to the tube but still didn't trust it.

The Elders all watched with great interest, as fear was not a part of their overall being. They had now figured out what would occur and began to assemble all their minds as one. It would only be a matter of minutes at the most. But they were ready. The final act was forming.

Dan slowly moved to the tube. It was all he could do, as the water was beginning to solidify at his feet. Then he realized he couldn't move fast enough. The tube was still a good four feet from where he stood.

He heard a third loud noise to his left. A third hole opened up in the wall. A third spout spewed cold water into the room.

The water was now up to his knees and beginning to freeze. The air in the room would soon be at thirty-two degrees Fahrenheit. And Dan was unable to move any closer to the tube. His feet were frozen in the ice, and he began to shiver violently.

"Dear Lord," Dan began to say in a low voice. "H . . . hel . . . help me," he said, his teeth chattering.

Dan didn't know what else he could do. He needed to reach down deep in his soul to find the trust required to get him to the tube. How was he going to get out of this mess? He was sure Apep would not intervene, and didn't really care if he was in the tube or frozen solid outside the tube. Apep would finally win.

Dan's entire life started to flash before him while he stood frozen in place. He remembered his father, the workaholic who wanted him to take over the business. There was his mother, who nourished his intelligence, fed him as many books as he wanted, and consoled him each time he received a lecture from his father.

His sister never got the recognition she deserved. She was the most business-savvy member of the family. She would eventually take over and expand the fortunes of the family, much to their father's amazement and his eventual undying love and gratitude. She said she wished Dan would join her because it was so much fun building the "empire."

Allyson Rayburn flashed by next. Her smile the first time they bumped into each other. Their daily routine of breakfast, lunch, and dinner. The long, wonderful lovemaking sessions in their dorm rooms. The trips to the many bed-and-breakfasts in the area. Even the weekend romps to the Bahamas that they kept to themselves.

Ruth soon flashed before his eyes. Kind and considerate Ruth Putnam. She brought him back from the brink of total solitude. His work became more of a reason to succeed because of her reaching out and wanting to be a part of his life. He wished he had reached out to her and consummated their love. That was supposed to have occurred before he disappeared into this hellhole.

"What a waste." He spoke so low he could barely hear himself.

With death imminent, Dan had ceased to struggle. The ice was now frozen to his knees. He could barely feel his toes anymore and knew they would be frostbitten within minutes, if not seconds.

He was still able to turn his neck to look at all three spouts. The water was still pouring in without a sign of abatement.

Dan didn't even want to think anymore. All he wanted to do was lower his head and drop into a terminal metaphysical state. He had never done this standing up, much less while frozen in water. However, it was all that was left.

He closed his eyes and concentrated, letting his hands drop to his sides. He thought about heaven.

The Elders watched, knowing there were only a few more seconds before they needed to take over. Apep had secured his fate, and they knew this was good. There wasn't anything they could do anymore to remove the terrible, vile hate from his soul. Apep would be lost forever.

Out of nowhere came a beam of light that shot through the water and into the ice. A second beam focused a few feet from the first. A third. A fourth. A fifth.

Dan awakened from his state and noticed his feet were moving. He was gliding toward the tube. A sixth beam of light shot out in front of him and he glided farther. A seventh came and brought him next to the tube.

Dan reached out and grabbed the door of his future enclosure. The water was now up to his waist. An eighth beam shot out and freed him further, allowing him to enter the tube along with a few feet of water. He closed the door.

It wasn't more than fifteen seconds before the water was eliminated from the tube. Another fifteen seconds passed before Dan's clothing was totally dry and free from any of the grime or dust he had picked up while crawling. It looked as if he could even see the pleats on his trousers.

Dan wanted to know how this had all occurred. He needed to know why, and what he could possibly glean from his release from the ice. Did Apep do this? Was it the Elders?

Dan looked down at the bottom of the tube. He lifted his left foot and noticed a large green dot. Then he raised his right foot a saw a large blue dot. He remembered the beginning of his ordeal and Apep saying the green dot on the screen was the beginning. The blue dot was the end. All Dan wanted to know was if he won and beat the maze? Or lost and was now to die!

"It is good that you saw fit to enter the tube," Apep said, voicing approval. "I thought that maybe you would have rather frozen to death."

Dan was tired and withdrawn. He didn't know what to say anymore. He wanted out of life. "Just get it over with, Apep."

"Cat now have your tongue?" Apep said mockingly. "Such a shame that you needed to experience this awful event. All I wanted was for you to enter the tube."

"May God bury your soul in the deepest pit of hell," Dan said under his breath.

"Even though I did hear that, I understand your feelings. Good-bye, Dan Adams. You were the best of the three."

Dan thought he heard correctly. Three!

He looked outside the tube at the room. The water was now above the tube and had frozen halfway. It really was beautiful to see. Icicles hung from the ceiling, making the room look like a cross between a barren Arctic glacier and a cave. It was a stunning sight.

The Elders knew. It had been a sign, and Apep was taking credit for it. It was because Apep couldn't explain it anymore and needed to feel superior to this man. But the Elders knew better. No matter what happened now, they were ready.

Dan was alive, and they had him by the invisible cord that would stretch as far as the universe existed. Wherever Apep was taking him or whatever he had in his decrepit mind, Dan Adams was tied to the Elders.

The Death Maze

The tube then twisted and turned. Dan fell backward before one strap magically wrapped around his waist and secured him from falling. A second strap appeared and secured his left leg. Dan was still able to move, but knew the ride was going to be rough.

The tube lifted from the floor, where the ice and water had miraculously disappeared. The beautiful glacier and cave were gone, and the four white walls had returned.

It was over, as far as Dan was concerned. Whatever happened now was just icing on the cake in the mind of one so pathetic and evil. Dan was now a slave to Apep, and there wasn't a thing he could do about it.

The tube then began to spin. It was five feet off the floor and beginning to turn. He knew from experience that Apep would make this thing spin like a centrifuge before deciding to eliminate him from the sixth dimension.

Spinning faster, Dan tried to focus on the floor of the room. This became useless as the tube lifted farther from the floor. He thought he was at least ten feet in the air when the spinning increased to the point where he couldn't discern if he would dry heave or see his guts roll out of his mouth. It was too much.

Then a beam of light hit him in the eyes, and Dan was able to focus upward. He saw the room disappear. He stopped spinning, yet the tube continued turning as if he were in some sort of spaceship.

The tube still rose higher. The room was gone. The darkness increased.

Dan couldn't tell where he was. The beam of light was now gone. Was he in the sixth dimension? Would he hear Apep's voice? Was he on his way to heaven?

Or hell?

Chapter 43

William Barrish was now seated, albeit very quietly, with Ruth and Shirley in the living room. No one had said a word for quite some time, and no one could do anything but think about what had happened. It was so traumatic that they just stared in various directions.

Chief Dressler was in the kitchen with Bone. They were trying to understand and recall all the incidences that had led up to the horrible event that took the life of Alex Miller. Dressler was consumed with the guilt of having forgotten to rescind his order. But he couldn't unwind the tape from the past hour and insert a different ending.

"I need you to go outside and tell Officer Arvada to return to the Vera substation," Dressler explained to Bone. "Inform him that nothing will transpire against him for the accidental death of Alex Miller and let him know I want a full report, beginning to end, on my desk in Arione by tomorrow morning."

"Right, Chief," Bone responded. "I have one other suggestion for you, if you don't mind my saying."

"And that is?"

"How about I call the office and rescind the order?"

"How about you do just that. And afterward, get a hold of the coroner and have him come out to take the body away. It doesn't need to stay here," Dressler explained. "By the way, no one is to fire their weapon for the rest of the day. We've had too much killing for the year."

"Got it, Chief," Bone said, leaving to go out to Officer Arvada's police vehicle. Bone used the kitchen door instead of going through the house. He knew everything was very tense at the moment.

Ruth couldn't believe she was sitting in her home in the living room with no Dan to speak with. Instead she had just witnessed another stupid mistake that had developed into another accident that had caused another life to be lost. What more could possibly go wrong?

Shirley looked at Will Barrish and knew he needed help. She also knew there really wasn't anything that could be done to bring back the life of the man he considered a hero and she considered a future relationship. Even though she was hurting as a woman, her professional life needed to be kept separate due to the fact that there were two patients with her in the living room.

Will had his head in his hands and did nothing but look at the carpet. He didn't care about the wires holding his jaw together. He had just lost one of his heroes. It had been a senseless shooting. The incident that was a huge loss for him would be a monumental void for the newspaper. Alex was the most popular reporter at the paper.

He wanted to call his boss but didn't have the stomach to do it just now. How could he possibly inform Robert Graves that his star reporter had been killed, and by accident? Something like this wouldn't seem like an accident to Robert Graves. He'd have additional reporters and lawyers out in Arione before tomorrow morning. This was going to get too big for even him.

Will knew that Alex's body had to be brought back to the medical center and then transferred to Los Angeles.

He slowly rose from his chair and started for the kitchen. He quickly took one look out the front window and saw Bone walking to the officer still waiting in his patrol car. Will saw them exchange words calmly. The officer started his car and drove off. Bone then walked back to the house.

As the front door opened, Will confronted Bone.

"What's going on?" Will asked.

"Chief Dressler had me talk to the officer. He's returning to the Vera office."

Bone looked at Will. Will waited for more information before Bone continued.

"The chief wants me to call the medical center to get an ambulance out here and take the body back to the hospital."

"How soon?" Will asked.

"Now," Bone said, looking at Will. He moved toward the kitchen.

Will just stood and watched Bone walk away. He looked at Shirley, then Ruth, and then sat down once again. They would now need to wait.

Dr. Samuel Ryan and Dr. Allyson Rayburn were in the lab. Since the shooting, they had ceased all experimentation as they were unable, or unwilling, to continue for the moment. There was nothing they could do. They had looked at the few notes so many times that doing so became futile. They had both agreed there was more to the disappearance than just the geothermal energy plant out back. Everything had been constructed properly and to the precise measurements.

Allyson knew in her heart that Dan's experiments had nothing to do with his disappearance. She knew it had to be the alternate theory. Allyson figured another dimension was the only logical explanation.

The Death Maze

Then there was Ruth. She seemed like a lovely individual. She knew Ruth was probably as wonderful as everyone would eventually tell her. But Allyson didn't want to think about her. Allyson wanted to think only about her love lost. The years she had studied and built to regain the only man she had ever loved. The only man she had dreamed of for so many years. She was so close and now so very far. She needed to concentrate and figure out what had caused Dan to disappear. Then she needed to find a way to bring him back. If it took the rest of her life, she would dedicate it to Dan Adams.

Ruth slowly stood up from the couch and took her time getting to the lab. Since she had been informed that the notes were only partially complete, she felt that the least she could do for Alex was to read them. She understood why Alex and Will had brought her back. Now Ruth needed to understand what might be missing and what could bring Dan back.

Walking into the lab, Ruth first nodded to Dr. Samuel Ryan and then turned to look at Dr. Allyson Rayburn. She just stared at Allyson; she didn't know why. She just felt she needed to.

Allyson returned the stare. She had a feeling Ruth was trying to figure her out. There was something Ruth couldn't put together. Then Ruth dropped her eyes and looked at the pages on the table.

Both were attractive women. Both had a mystique that aroused one special man who was a part of both of their lives. Allyson knew. Ruth lifted her eyes from the pages and back to Allyson.

Ruth was able to put the pieces together. The rust-red hair. The green eyes. No wonder Dan had fallen in love with her. She was everything he had told her. Allyson had all the equipment and the brains to make the perfect package.

But now he was hers. If he ever returned, Ruth wouldn't have to fight to keep Dan. She had never left Dan. She had been by his side ever since she came to Arione. Ruth had never disappointed him or turned her heart away. Allyson may be a brilliant scientist, but she was only a guest in the home that Ruth shared with Dan.

Allyson understood the thoughts going through Ruth's mind. They were valid, and solid, impressions. Allyson looked away briefly and then brought her eyes right back to Ruth. She couldn't deny that Ruth was right. She had left Dan a long time ago. She had not called or kept in touch. She had not given a reason for Dan to still love her.

Allyson then saw the hurt, the anguish, and the love that plagued Ruth's body. Dan had grown very special to this woman, who had gone through so much. Dan was the reason this woman stayed. They were making a life together. Ruth was the type of woman who would never leave her love and walk away hoping to regain him years later.

But Allyson still loved Dan. She still yearned for him and remembered the way they held each other back in college. The tether had never been severed as far as she was concerned.

Ruth turned and started to walk out of the room. The pages she needed to read would have to wait. She wanted to read them by herself without Allyson in the lab. Ruth made a mental note to ask Allyson to give her some privacy with the notes at a later date.

All of a sudden, Ruth quickly did an about-face. An impulse inside of her called at her to turn back.

"Doctor?" Ruth asked with an unearthly thought in her mind. "Do you . . . do you see anything unusual?"

The Death Maze

"No," Dr. Ryan quickly said.

"I . . . I feel . . . I feel something is changing," Ruth stuttered.

"I'm not sure I understand what you mean," Dr. Ryan continued. "What is changing? What are you talking about?"

Then Ruth began to see it: an image materializing into the room. Dr. Ryan soon opened his mouth in awe, and Allyson felt like her feet were locked in cement.

"Shirley! Mr. Barrish! Come in here. Quickly!" Ruth yelled.

Shirley ran to the door of the lab, followed by Will. Dressler and Bone heard the screams and ran out of the kitchen. They all stood inside the lab as the image became more defined. No one said a word.

The image came into full view. A cylinder was spinning like a twister turning inside the house.

The turning began to subside as all seven surrounded the object and stood in astonishment. What they saw was the miracle they had been searching for. The image and then body was that of Dr. Daniel Adams.

Ruth couldn't believe her eyes. She started to cry. Then she reached out to the tube.

"Don't touch it!" Dan cried out.

Allyson also wanted to reach out, but painfully refrained from doing so. This was Ruth's moment.

"What are you talking about?" Ruth asked, startled by the remark.

"I don't know if it's real," Dan tried to explain, not believing his eyes. He didn't understand that what he saw was real. He was back home, but somehow knew he couldn't get out of the tube. His mind told him he had beaten the sixth dimension and Apep. However, he was hearing something else.

"Glad to be back home?" Apep said, knowing only Dan could hear.

"Let me out of here, Apep," Dan ordered.

"Dan, what are you talking about?" Ruth asked. She couldn't understand that Apep was only talking to Dan. No one could.

"Open the door, Apep!" Dan ordered.

"My orders do not come from you, Dan Adams," Apep reminded him.

"Then why did you bring me back home?"

"To have you look one more time," Apep explained.

"Dan?" Dressler yelled. "Who are you talking to?"

"He's not letting me out of here," Dan tried to explain.

Then he saw Allyson. It was quick and startling and wonderful. He saw her mouth the words *I love you*. But all he could think was, *How did she know I was here? What is she doing in the lab. And why the fuck can't I get the hell out of this tube?*

"Damn you, Apep. Let me out, you miserable piece of crap!"

"Who are you talking to?" Ruth yelled again.

"I'm speaking to Apep," Dan explained. "He's the one holding me in the sixth dimension and now this tube. Do you see the opening of the door?"

"Dan, there's no opening," Ruth insisted. "What can we do?"

Dressler took out his gun and aimed it high at the top of the tube. The bullet ricocheted off and lodged itself in the far wall of the lab. He felt like he should shoot again, but then stopped. Dressler didn't want to take the risk of a bullet hitting one of the people in the lab.

The Death Maze

"Dan," Ruth screamed. "What can we do to help? Who's Apep? What's the sixth dimension? I don't understand," she continued as she began to cry uncontrollably.

Ruth then hit the tube with her hand. She felt immediate heat, and her fist turned red and then melted away. Ruth screamed and then watched as her hand became whole again.

It was an uncanny and impossible feat. Everyone recoiled and then stood in amazement.

Allyson began to understand. What everyone was seeing was real and fake at the same time. The tube was the object holding Dan prisoner. The man she loved was actually standing in front of them. And yet he was also some sort of projection from another world.

Dan was actually in two different places at the same time. In real time! It was like television, with him in a studio and his image projected in front of an audience. However, he was actually real in two different worlds at the same moment.

Whatever was holding Dan, this Apep of the sixth dimension, was powerful. He was angry that Dan was in his world. And unfortunately for Dan and everyone standing in his lab, Apep was not going to let him go. He wanted Dan to remain his slave.

Allyson didn't know what she could do right at this moment except watch and be hurt by this terrible thing that was happening in front of them. She knew Dr. Ryan had no idea how to help. But suddenly, she did. She just needed to know one thing.

"Dan?" Allyson asked. "Where's the entrance?"

Dan suddenly realized that Allyson knew or had an idea about what could be done. "Be careful," he instructed. "It's somewhere between the geothermal plant and the side of the house. Don't disrupt the parallel fields or you'll end up in the sixth dimension."

"What's he talking about?" Bone asked. "There are no fields on the side of the house."

"Let him explain further," Dressler said. "Dan, which side of the house do you mean?"

Dan was getting frustrated but knew they would eventually get it. "Do some research about someone who was here some time ago. It would be before any of Arione was even built. That has to be the key!"

"Tell everyone good-bye, Dan Adams," Apep said mockingly. "Tell them you'll see them in another world, another time, or another place. Isn't that how you explain it?"

"Apep, you bastard! One day you'll regret this. One day you'll pay for your evil."

"Not today, Dan Adams," Apep replied. "Not today."

Dan began to gradually disappear. After about sixty seconds Dan was gone. Where, when, why, how, and what had caused all this were all questions needing answers. But they were drenched with fatigue. They all needed to rest.

Ruth was beginning to get hysterical. She was the first to walk away. She squeezed past Shirley, Will, and Bone and went into the living room. Even though she was physically and mentally wiped out from what had just transpired, she knew she needed to be well. Being totally fit and aware would be the only thing that would help her get Dan back. She would not believe he was dead. She tried to stop crying.

William Barrish left next, trying to recall everything he had just seen. He wouldn't even need written notes to write the story. First he wanted facts, and only Dr. Allyson Rayburn had them right now. He would have to wait to speak with her.

Chief Dressler and Bone were next to leave. Dressler reminded Bone to keep everything he had seen under the table until he could summarize all the events he had witnessed. The town would not be happy knowing there was a parallel field crossing this property. Hell, he didn't even understand what that meant. He only knew that he and Bone needed to talk and make a plan.

Dr. Shirley Anderson left after Dressler and Bone. She needed to get back to Ruth and Will and help make arrangements for Alex to be sent back to Los Angeles. She also wanted to speak with Will and let him decide how to write what he had just witnessed. She wanted to speak with Dressler and get the reports from the coroner and Officer Arvada.

"Dr. Rayburn," Dr. Samuel Ryan said. "I'm going to go back to my hotel room and let you decide what to do next."

"I'm not sure I understand, Sam," Allyson admitted.

"I cannot continue here anymore. You understand more than I want to know and more than we have just seen. I'm returning to the office tomorrow morning. Just keep me up to date."

"How did you know?" Allyson asked.

"I've known for a long time, Allyson. Just please be careful. What we have just seen is not of this world."

Allyson only shook her head. She knew where to look and what to research. She also knew what her obstacles would be in Arione and the sixth dimension. One of them she could handle without any problems. The other was totally unknown for the moment.

Dr. Ryan left the room, leaving Allyson alone. She pondered everything for a while and then picked up the toy car. It was something she could understand and physically hold.

She walked to the window and stared at the geothermal plant. Holding the toy car up to the window, she imagined the car filled with the energy Dan had made. She lowered it to the floor and pushed it away from her.

Allyson felt a tear fall from her eye. She didn't even bother to wipe it away. Feeling the tear fall down her face and drop to the floor was therapy to her. She was crying for three things and knew she needed to rediscover them. Her lost love, her missed past, and her possible future were all hanging in the balance. Allyson needed to hold them all together.

Allyson was about to leave the lab when she felt the change again. She turned away from the window and saw Dan appear once more. This time he was by himself without the tube holding him in. He was pushing against an invisible object. Dan saw Allyson and then disappeared.

***

Ruth laid in her bed in the Vera Medical Center that night. Her tears had subsided long ago. All she could do was to think.

Ruth knew Dan was still alive. She knew this because when Allyson saw the image of Dan appear in the lab, it had also appeared to her in the living room, where only she had seen it. It was a sign.

Ruth spent the rest of the week and the following week resting in bed and exercising. She was determined to regain her strength. She was eager to become the strong woman she had been when she moved to Arione. Ruth wanted to be a healthy woman in full control so she could find this parallel field and get her man back.

Ruth also knew that Allyson would be staying in Arione.

Chapter 44

"We have him!" the Elders said.

CPSIA information can be obtained
at www.ICGtesting.com
Printed in the USA
FSOW01n0817220914
3139FS